Some 'Opes

of Brody Street, E.1.

By

Doris Farran

The descriptive illustrations on the cover, depict a calendar of events and images of life as it was before and during the horrifying days of war.

Scenes like these, were to disappear forever, as the deadly Blitz of London took it's toll.

This story is dedicated to my wonderful family, who have journeyed with me through a hitherto long and fruitful life.

All artwork done by my son David Allison, with thanks from me for a thoroughly good job, as well as his patience with me, a real pain in the neck at times!

First published in Great Britain in 2003

Printed in Great Britain by
S.M.D. Print Centre
218 Broadway
Bexleyheath, Kent
DA6 7AU

ISBN 0 9534925 3 2

Some 'Opes

of Brody Street, E.1.

This absorbing story tells of the Hope family. Struggling along with other folk of Brody Street and beyond, in the East End Docks Area of Wapping.

Set in the depressive, down on your luck days after the First Great War, and on up to the next grim ordeal of the Second World War.

This true to life, realistic tale, is of Mag and Bert Hope, and their three kids, Robin, Jess and Jim. The 'Opes, – and others of the same identity in their hard battle to survive.

Always with the same waggish, breezy, and the put on a good face fortitude of the East End Cockney. Even in the horrifying dark days of War.

It is hoped, you will Laugh and Cry, with the 'Opes of Brody Street E.1.

Doris Farran, now 83, was born in Greenwich, a very close neighbour to the East End and has good knowledge of how it was, living during those hard times. Of it's deprivations, but mostly of the pure grit and guts shown, in between the two Great Wars and after.

Other books by the Same Author:

PICTURES FROM A LIFE
. . . ain't it a game eh!
An Autobiography of Nobody in Particular

AN UNFINISHED SYMPHONY
A True life Love Story

TRANQUIL THOUGHTS
Pleasing Poems

The Good old Days!

We own a wealth of memories,
Have seen a lot of change.
In the many years we've lived through,
To some, would now seem strange.

Growing up was a challenge, then,
It was not all milk and honey.
Mum pawned clothes, and things for food,
Becos', we had no money.

Days when newspaper was our cloth,
On the table, when we fed.
If we didn't do as we were told,
It was, 'Right you, – up to bed!'

Dad stood knocking back the pints,
At the bar of his local pub.
While Mum stood sweating at the sink,
Giving his shirts a scrub.

The wash went through the mangle,
Which stood out in the yard.
Tho' drying clothes in Winter,
Was always ruddy hard!

Hours we'd spend out in the street,
Running, jumping, skipping.
Mum would call, 'Come get your tea,'
But it's only bread and dripping.'

Learning the five times table,
Grappling with Sums and Spelling.
But it was great, out playing in the street,
Kids screaming, and kids yelling.

When in Spring, – Hot Cross Buns,
Summer, – the ice cream van.
Come Autumn, it was chestnut time,
Winter, the Muffin Man.

Christmas, nice, if we had toys,
Shops were pretty, lights so bright.
Pressing nose onto window panes,
We'd stare – we'd hope – we might!

There was no Telly in them days,
Radio – just a dream.
The cinema, – a Xmas treat,
Chaplin was a scream.

Mum would take us for a walk,
Trundling behind the pram.
Hungry, – how our feet would ache,
Why couldn't we go by Tram?

Forever Mum, weighed down with care,
Would wonder, – how to cope.
Though life, if not much fun those days,
You always lived on hope.

Hoping it would improve one day,
And be no more provoking.
But saying that now, as we look around,
Cor' Blimey – You must be joking!

Doris Farran.

Chapter: One

My! But it was foggy out there on the old River tonight! Wreaths of damp, swirling mist wrapped around the river craft, rocking fitfully to and fro' and from side to side, in the murky smelly waters of the Dock basin, there by the wayward, restless old Thames, – that imperturbable, and indifferent old River.

Not a sound was to be heard abroad, except for the occasional muffled blare of a distant foghorn downstream, breaking the deep silence.

Maggie, cold, wet and tired, shivered and pulled her coat collar tighter up around her neck.

Not a night for even a cat to be out, – let alone any human, she felt sure, as she made her way cautiously through the dark dimly lit and deserted alleyways, back home after a long tiring evening's work down at the 'Crown and Anchor,' a pub, classed among the dock workers, as their favourite, and they were a choosy lot!

Maggie did not much like her job there as a barmaid, or the lewd remarks she got, and definitely not the low wage she received, but it helped towards the rent and rent days came around much too quick, for her liking!

"Goodnight Missus!" a voice came eerily out of the fog.

Startled for a minute, Maggie stopped, –

"Oh! Er, – G'night Bill," she called out in answer to the voice of the half hidden night watchman, as he stood by the Dock gates, slapping his cold hands together and stamping his feet.

1

"Blimey! What a job!" she muttered to herself.

"'E mus' be 'arf frozen, – poor sod!"

She hurried along, wanting to get away from this scary scene. It made her flesh creep! The gaudy funnels and tall masts of sea-going vessels laying captive in their allotted anchorage's, – swayed ghostly in the encircling fog.

Big ships, little ships, some weather-beaten, some illustrious, coming from India, – Russia, – from South America, and other far flung countries all over the world.

They would leave faraway safe harbours to make for the Pool of London, which surely must be a most dreary prospect to the incoming ships. Black walled decrepit looking warehouses, Gasometers, Candle and Soap factories and cranes. – Cranes and even more cranes.

Once a ship dropped anchor, these cranes would begin their dipping and swinging, for the waiting stevedores and Dockers straining to unload the rich cargoes of exotic fruits from the East, – gaudy silks from the Orient, – barrels of wine for the London Vaults.

Vast armies of workmen, striving to make a living from the needs of indigenous humanity.

They laboured by day and lived by night these Dockers, – a hardy race, – applying their life to the full. – The Salt of the Earth!

Maggie had good opportunity to view how these men spent their relaxation, putting behind them for a few hours, the sweat and the toil of a hard day there on the docksides of this never idle Thames river.

The 'Crown and Anchor' was just one of the many retreats for these workers, as there was no shortage of public houses along the water fronts and alleys by the Docks, and Maggie was hard put, trying to keep up with the demands of these ever thirsty watermen. She was run off her feet attending to the wants of the cheerful, yet sometimes rowdy customers, letting off steam, –

"Come, come, let us 'ave a drink or two!" But this time it was not "The Old Bull and Bush!"

Maggie quickened her pace.

"Lets git in art a this lot an' in ter the warm!" She shivered again.

"E'd better 'ave got the kettle on fer me cocoa," she thought, – he, meaning her husband.

Bert, her old man was one of the best, but, –

"Poor bugger! – 'E 'ad really been frew the 'oop, when 'E'd gawn and copped it, back in the Great War!"

Shell-shocked, and almost losing the use of his left arm. Bert Hope was not the man she'd married all those years ago. "'Ow long ago was it nah? Twelve or thereabouts?"

Even so! – He always had a ready smile and a cheery word for everyone. "A lovely little job he had got, down at the 'Shades', the busy noisy street market, just off the Commercial Road."

"Fifty bob, – 'Ere, me ol' China. Whad'yer fink a these suits then? – Straight from Saville Row!"

"Ello luv!" Bert greeted Maggie, as he opened the front door to her. He had been listening for the sound of her key in the lock.

"Come on in, – yer must be frozen stiff! I've got the kettle on, – bin busy 'ave yer?" he wanted to know.

"Give us yer coat gal!"

Taking Maggie's coat, Bert hung it up on a nail on the back door.

"Sit darn there an' git warm!"

3

"Alright then, – where's me slippers?" said Mag.

Breathing on her cold hands and rubbing them together, she bent forward and held them in front of the blazing coals in the kitchen range and soon felt the warmth returning to her body.

"Kids in bed?" she asked and cocked an ear, but she couldn't make out any sound at all from upstairs, – not even a whisper!

"Blimey! That's a change, but don' speak *too* soon!" she mused. There was usually an uproar, when Bert tried to get the kids in, washed and off up to bed.

Maggie and Bert, they'd had three kids and that was going to be the lot, – lovely as they were, but three was quite enough, – thank you!

Robbie, he was the eldest, and had just gone eleven. Then came the other two, – Jessie was nine and Jim almost seven, – a right nice trio!

"Nah!" she sighed with relief, – "Fank Gawd they're asleep, I kin 'ave me cocoa in peace." Stretching out her feet towards the fire and wriggling her toes, –

"Ah! This is a darn sight better! – Crikey, – me poor ol' plates a meat, Bert luv," she said, "They don' 'arf take a bashin', eh?"

"I'll jus' 'ave forty winks!" and she closed her eyes.

"Good Morning Mag!"

"Blimey! – She's got 'er washin' art already! – Must a bin up all night."

"Never stops workin' that one, – always polishin' an' dustin', – even the poor bluddy cat gets dusted!" Maggie thought and giggled to herself as she answered Kate her neighbour from next door and leaning from the kitchen window, she called, "G'mornin' Kate" and popped her head back inside, thinking to herself, –

"Snooty bitch, all she seems ter fink abart is 'ousework an' cleanin' 'er bloomin' winders!"

Maggie sniffed, she didn't have much room for the woman. All spit an' polish, she was!

"Er, an' 'er posh talk, – why can't she talk like everybody else does up our street?"

Kate called back to her, –

"So glad the fog's gone, I don't like it. It tends to make my nets grubby!"

Kate had lost her husband in the last war, she was another one of the many war widows.

"I bet she gits a nice little pension, though!" mumbled Mag and shut the window with a bang.

"I got better fings ter do, than stand 'ere gassin' to 'er!"

"Come on nah, eat yer toast you two and stop messin' abart – yer'll be late again fer school! – And nah what's the matter wiv you Jess?"

"Oh! Go on then, be quick, – dip yer crusts in yer tea, and no Jimmy that's not for playin' wiv neiver, leave it alone," Mag said, taking the bread knife away from him.

Jim pulled a face behind her back, but luckily she didn't see or she would have clipped him one.

"Oh Dear! – More washin'!"

Bert had filled the copper with water for her bits and pieces. There seemed to be always washing. But what with three kids, – yer never stop!

She found the matches and set light to the rubbish up the copper hole. As she fished out the scrubbing board from under the sink, Mag had a thought.

"I've 'ad this ol' board a few years nah," as she tied it to the handle of the tin bath.

"It gits yer cloves clean, but it don' 'arf do yer ruddy knuckles in!"

"That's it, all done," she wiped the floor over, picked up her overloaded washing basket, opened the back door and climbed up the two steps to the line post.

As she unfastened and let down the pulley, she screwed up her face, –

"Blimey Bert," she moaned, – "This fing don' 'arf wanna drop of oil on it. 'Ark at it! It does me 'ead in, it really dus!"

"I say this every time, yet nuffin ever gits done abart this everlastin' squeakin'."

Bert's answer to all this, was inaudible. He was used to Maggie's niggling, but then he exploded with a real loud voice, you could have heard him up the top of the street.

"That bluddy cat from next door, it's dug up the last a me crocus bulbs I put in!"

"I swear I'll kill it. – I will! – So 'elp me."

"Oh! Stop yer wingin' Bert," and Maggie went back indoors and dumping the empty wash basket down on the floor by the sink, she put the kettle on.

"Cuppa Bert?" she called out, –

"It's bad enuf tryin' ter do everyfin' wiv a gammy arm, let alone 'avin' ter clean up after some blasted moggy, – the ginger sod!" he said, as he came in the door.

"Well, I'm orf nah Mag, – wan' anyfin' darn the Market?" Bert called. He was off to work. Mag reached for her purse off the dresser and took out half-a-crown.

"Yers, Yer can git some more a those King Edward spuds, yer brought me back last week orf that bloke, – an' tell 'im, I don't fink much a the fruit 'e sells there though, those Worcesters of 'is were 'arf rotten!"

Bert tutted and went, shutting the gate behind him with a mighty bang.

Now Maggie reckoned she could have a sit down now, have a bit of peace and quiet, and browse through the smart clothing catalogue her friend Mavis across the road, had fetched over for her to have a look at.

Pouring herself out another cup of tea, she began to turn the glossy pages, gazing pensively at the latest lines in black underwear.

Yes, all very nice, Mag thought, but she couldn't see herself in that, for a start! That scanty black silk chemise and the slinky nightdress. –

"It don't leave nuffin' ter the imagination!" she gasped, – "Nah, this is different, more like it." Studying the picture of a skinny model wearing a real lovely looking warm topcoat, in dark red.

"Nah *that*, – I really *do* need!"

"Just me colour too, – but Crikey, – look at the price!"

"Well, – that's that then," and she slammed the book shut, for what was the good of looking, – She'd never have been able to pay for any of it."

There came a tap at the back door.

It opened at Maggie's, – "Come in," and there Mavis stood, her blonde head completely swathed in a large gaudy pink scarf, covering her hair curlers. Maggie realised, she had hardly ever seen her friend without them! On those few occasions Mag had sighted Mav completely scarf and curlerless, was when she went to visit her son George and his wife in Kensal Rise and that wasn't often.

Mavis did not get on very well with her daughter-in-law, Sybil. She was by Mag's way of thinking, just a stuck up bitch! A bit too big for her boots! And she knew, if Sybil had her way, George wouldn't be seen anywhere near Wapping ever again! Her precious George was a cut above the kind of people who came from the East End.

"Who the 'ell does she fink she is?"

"I don' rightly know wot 'e ever saw in 'er!"

"'E should a stuck ter 'is own kind."

"What's the chances a gettin' our washin' dry Mag? – I've put mine out. There's a bit of a wind tho', we might be lucky, eh?"

"Found anyfin' yer like in there yet?" Mavis asked, pointing to the Catalogue on the table.

"Oh! Yeh!" answered Maggie. "There's plenty in there I like, but I 'aven't a 'ope in 'ell a gettin' it!" Maggie was sure of that, – "Nah tell me, 'ow I can?"

"Fancy a drink a somefin'?" she asked.

"No!" came the reply, –

"Look I can't stop 'ere long. I only come over ter see if yer want ter come ter the pictures wiv me this afternoon. – There's a nice film on at the Tivoli with Greta Garbo in it. Its called 'Anna Christie'. Dunno who's in it wiv 'er though. We could go directly the kids 'ave gorn back ter school after dinner and be back 'ome by the time they come art at four, – what say?"

Mag had gone all quiet, she was thinking.

"Well alright, I guess I can find a bob from somewhere," she said.

"O.K Mav! – What time?"

Mav departed and the clothing catalogue went with her.

Looking around the kitchen, she frowned, –

"High time I done a bit a clearin' up rarnd 'ere," said Mag, and ripping up the coconut mats, got the broom and shovel out. Now she had to think what she was going to give the kids for their dinner!

"I know, – I'll nip darn 'Alf's' and get a couple a pies and some mash, that'll do, I'll 'ave ter put it on the slate though! But 'e won't mind."

What would she do without Alf? What would anyone up the street do without Alf, the corner 'Eel and Pie' shop owner. How he made a living, she could not begin to fathom out! Most of his customers just put it on the Slate!

"An' if only poor trustin' Alf knew it, 'arf of 'em were as slippery as 'is eels!"

"Picture was good eh?" Mavis was saying, –

"Cor, must be nice ter be a film star Mag? Fink of all the nice clothes yer could 'ave, an' live in a luvverly 'ouse, up there in 'Ollywood!"

But Mag had other things on her mind. The kids would be out of school by now. They would have to hurry. So they would cut through the footpath, back of the Gasworks, as she didn't like to leave them too long on their own.

Still they could always get in and only had to put their hand through the letter box flap and pull the key out from inside. This would be hanging on a bit of string behind the door knocker.

She had left them out a plate of bread and jam as well, as they usually came home hungry, – but she hoped Jimmy wouldn't be playing up. He always seemed to start something and the other two would lay into him. It would often end up in tears. Jim being the youngest, was the odd

9

one out, but he was ever Maggie's baby and woe betide the others, if they went too far.

Many's the time Jess and Rob had gone to bed with a clip round the earole!

Bert, he'd had a really rough day down at the Market. He just couldn't put his mind to what he was supposed to be doing at all!

The Guvnor's words had kept on ringing through his brain all the afternoon, tho' really, it was ever since he had been told right out of the blue that same morning, –

"I am afraid Bert, I will 'ave ter lay yer off after this week. I am right sorry, but yer must 'ave seen it fer yerself, we ain't done nuffin' near like we should 'ave, at this time a the year."

"There just ain't no money abart!"

But although Bert had been knocked for six, he couldn't help feeling some sympathy for his Boss's impossible situation. It couldn't have been easy to suddenly drop a bombshell on someone like that.

"We've 'ardly sold a fing this past month but there it is, – and if it goes on like this fer much longer, I shall 'ave ter shut the stall darn altergevver! – then we'll all be arter work. I'm sorry mate!"

Poor Maggie, how was he going to break the news to her? She was finding it damned hard enough now, to make ends meet. Even with the measly handout she got from her job at the Pub, it was a struggle.

Bert had never taken lightly to Maggie being a Barmaid. There were too many shady characters who hung about there outside the Pub. Many's the time he'd had to hurry along there after the Pub shut, to walk her home, and get her away from the brawls, specially when things had turned real nasty, with the Bobby's turning up, to cart the culprits off to the Cop-Shop.

So what would they do now? – him with no job, and who'd want him with a gammy arm! It had been a stroke of luck when the gaffer at the Shades had taken him on, but there were not many blokes around like him!

There was barely enough to put on the table now and the kids wanted shoes.

Jim was already wearing a pair of Robs left-offs, – two sizes too big for his little feet.

Poor Mag, what could he say to her? But whatever it was, it did not lighten the fact that now they would really be down on their beam-ends.

He really wasn't looking forward to telling her, and took his time walking back home.

Maggie heard the catch go up on the door and only had to take one look at Bert's expression to see something was well and truly up.

He came in the door and without a word, he'd sat down and slowly untied his bootlaces, as if to delay telling her the bad news of him getting the push.

Mag waited, fearing the worst.

"Well old girl, – I've got the sack, – lost me job, so I ave! Joe poor devil, 'e's ad it bad darn there lately, 'e's 'ardly taken a fing!"

"There' no money abart Mag! Who's got money these days to buy new clobber?"

He shrugged his shoulders then, and tried hard to conjure up a bit of a smile.

"It's bad, – still it could be worse, – eh gal?"

All this was a blow for Maggie and as it was, she wasn't feeling too bright at the moment, – in fact she was bloody well fed up, having to scrub out the privy in the back yard.

"If people want to keep cats, why don't they blasted well look after them proper, and keep them in their own back yards!"

It appeared, the tom-cat from next door, had been in Mag's lavvy and left his trademark. It stunk to high Heaven out there!

But now Maggie seeing the defeated look on Bert's face, as he sat staring into the fire, couldn't but help feeling pity for him.

"Oh! Come on nah Bert, – it ain't the end a the world yet yer know! We'll manage, uvvers 'ave ter, and there are many that's far worse orf than us!"

She picked the kettle up off the Hob and walked out into the scullery to fill it.

"Let's ave a nice cuppa, eh? Luv?"

"A cure for all ills is a nice cuppa tea, so cheer up mate, eh?"

But Mag wasn't going to let on, how much this news had affected her, – she felt a little sick! It would be harder than ever now, though Mag was a born fighter.

Pulling herself together, but with an effort, she suddenly remembered. They needed a cleaner down at the Pub. They had taken on one woman, some weeks ago, but she hadn't turned up for work for a few days. "That was her lot." The Landlord had said.

"Wiv a bit a luck, I may stand a chance an' git the job, that's if no one 'as beaten me to it." Maggie hoped not.

"It won' kill me ter 'ave ter scrub a few extra floors!"

*   *   *

12

The terraced house that Maggie and Bert lived in was small, – a two up, two down. Front door opening onto the pavement in a street of identical dwellings. Brody Street also had a most imposing view of the town's Gas works, and from where on most days when the wind was in the wrong direction, there would erupt the most vilest of smells. This invaded the whole darned house! – And it would be then, – "Fer Gawd's sake shut that blasted back door Rob, – before we all choke ter def!"

The small back yards of the houses were hemmed in by high brick walls on which the kids, don't matter how much you told them, – "Don't do it!" – climbed up and over.

"'Ow many times 'ave I got ter warn yer? Keep orf that bluddy wall, yer'll break yer bluddy necks, do yer 'ear me? I'm not tellin' yer again!" But the walls were smashing to kick a football against the kids found.

Just outside the back door stood her tired old mangle, on which the wooden rollers had become so rotten and splintered, with wear and the elements, – never being covered over, – that Maggie spent more time picking pieces of wood out of Bert's underpants and the kids vests, than she actually did ironing them!

Maggie looked up at the alarm clock on the dresser.

"Is that the bloomin' time? – Crikey! The kids will be wantin' their tea, – better git a move on."

Bert had cheered up a bit, by now. Mag always had the knack of making things look only half as bad as they really were. She was good at that.

"A right good lass is my Maggie," – Bert knew she was one in a million. If only he could make life easier for her, she deserved so much better, – 'His Duchess,' – she was, – 'Even if she did moan a lot!'

13

Maggie sat lost in thought, trying not to get too irritated by the noise the kids were making, playing Shove ha-penny on the kitchen table. "It's my turn, no it ain't, it's mine!"

Why do children have to make so much noise? Still they wouldn't be kids if they didn't. She was darning some of their socks, already thick with previous patching, and trying to make some sort of plan, – how to make ends meet.

There was a howl, – "Mum, 'e 'it me!" It was Rob. Jim was having a go at him.

"E was cheatin' mum, I saw 'im, 'e fort I wasn't lookin," Mag put down her darning, – "Oh dear!!" The time was knocking on now, anyway they ought to be in bed.

"Come on all of yer, put that away and git yerselves washed, – and I do mean washed, Rob! Don't fergit ter do be'ind yer ears, – do yer 'ear me?"

The culprit pulled a face and went out into the scullery. He never liked washing at any time, the water was always cold, but he could never escape Maggie's eagle eye!

"Caught yer! Nah go an' do it agin, – go on, – art!"

The other two weren't so bad, though young Jim would often need a helping hand.

Mag was tired and it had been a long day.

'Bin on the go all the bloomin' time, she 'ad!'

Upstairs in the bedroom, it was like an Ice-well!

"Mum, I'm cold!" Jim moaned. Mag sighed, and pulled the worn blankets up around his neck tucking him in.

How could she possibly manage to get some more bedclothes from somewhere and get rid of the old coats they were compelled to use?

Maggie bent and placed a kiss on Jimmy's forehead, and whispered, –

"Go ter sleep nah son, yer'll soon git warm, shut yer eyes. G'night all a yer" and she went downstairs to Bert. He was sitting by the kitchen range, listening in to his Wireless set, he had got off a mate down the market. A studio audience was laughing, – at a Rob Wilton Show.

"It was the day War broke out!" Rob Wilton's classic line destined to get a lot of laughs, – He always got them going with that sketch!

"'E's a silly blighter Mag." said Bert, chuckling away, then he had a thought!

"Oh! An' by the way, we want anuvver accumulator, this one's runnin' darn. Send Rob art tomorrer darn ter Williams's."

"But it's 'eavy," said Mag. "He carn' carry that, besides 'e'll upset the acid in it!"

"Oh! It ain't that 'eavy," said Bert, "Then 'e can git anuvver, this one 'ere needs toppin' up."

This was to be another of Rob's many errands carrying the heavy accumulator in both arms down to Eddy William's shop, where it was put on a charger.

Eddy's shop was a mess. He sold bykes, tyres, tools, paint, oil – you name it, – He had it.

So the kids were in bed, – Were they asleep? – She couldn't hear anything.

And so they sat, Maggie and her Bert, listening to their new Wireless set and enjoying the last of the dying fire.

At least they still had that, – *and* each other.

Chapter: Two

Maggie woke. Turning her head, she looked at Bert. He was laying there flat on his back snoring, his mouth wide open, catching flies. Poor old Bert.

She shivered as she quickly got out of bed.

"Blimey! Is that the time?" She had a fit!

Then suddenly Mag realised, "It's Saturday! The kids didn't 'ave ter go ter school terday!"

"Thank Gawd fer that!"

Throwing a cardigan around her shoulders, she went quietly down the stairs, – she didn't want to wake them all up yet, she needed five minutes to herself.

One of Mag's pleasures was to sit and have her first cup of tea in peace and quiet and by Crikey! – She didn't get much of that, for soon the rumpus would start. – First with Rob, – griping, –

"Why can't I 'ave football boots like me mates 'ave! – Joe, 'e's got some!" he'd whine.

Then Jess, she would pipe up, –

"If 'e's gonna 'ave football boots, then I kin 'ave that Fairy Doll, that's in 'Price's winder!"

Poor Jim! – He didn't get a chance to put his order in, – he'd started to open his mouth to speak, – but nothing came out of it, as Maggie, slamming the plate of bread down with a bang on to the kitchen table, shouted, –

"Oh! – Fer Gawd's sake! – Shut up, you lot!"

"You keep on, an' yer won't git nuffin' at all fer Christmas. Be'ave, – why can't yer?"

"Poor little buggers!" Mag thought, as she did the washing up after they had all gone out to play. –

"Why am I getting so bloomin' crochety! – It's not their fault. – I shouldn't take it art on them!"

"I'm just a miserable old crow!"

Though now, Mag was getting really worried. Christmas was only a few weeks away, it was nigh on impossible for her to even think about it! Bert with no job, – What were they going to do?

But this won't help, she had to be down at the Pub, ten minutes from now. At least she had been lucky after all, in getting that cleaning job, and she was now on her second week there. It was pretty tough going she found, having to see to the kids every morning before she went off to the Pub, then rushing back in time to get them something to eat, dinner time.

Luckily she had the afternoons to do a bit of cleaning up indoors. Get some washing done and out on the line. Take a trip to the shops to find something to knock up for the next day's dinner, and maybe get a bit of scrag-end for a stew, with a piece of suet thrown in for dumplings, they were a treat. Pieces of bacon ends for a bacon and onion pudding, some days, and if she had a few pennies left over, Mag could buy a bag of broken biscuits cheap for the kids. Jim was always the first to dig down deep and find a few cream ones among them.

One of the nicest things too, was to come home to a plate of sprats, bought from old Fishy's stall in the market. It was a high tea for them all, – but first there would be a fight between them, Rob, Jess and Jim, who was going to help roll the sprats in flour both sides, ready for frying, that was after Mag had washed them.

The smell though of frying fish! It would hang around the house for hours afterwards.

But they were surviving the best way they could, just like everyone else in this rough and tough area of East London, and it was no good griping about it, they were all in the same boat, – even if sometimes, one would find themselves up the creek without a paddle!

She, – Mag, was determined her lot, wasn't going to go short, even if she was, at the end of her long hard day, so blessed tired, – she would fall into bed exhausted, almost before she could get undressed.

But Bert was getting more and more down in the dumps every day. It wasn't doing much for his self-respect, knowing that Mag was taking over his role as the breadwinner for them all!

Early each morning at five o'clock sharp, Bert willed himself to walk down to the Dock gates, hoping upon hope, that the powers that be there would have a job for him. But they only had to set eyes on his gammy arm, raise their eyebrows and that was it!

This was happening every day now and he was getting sick to death of it!

It was a cold crisp and clear evening, and the 'Crown and Anchor' was doing a pretty fair trade, in those weeks running up to Christmas.

Mag had been run off her feet all the evening in the 'Bottle and Jug' when she suddenly remembered, – it was Pay out day at the Slate Club down at the 'Working Men's' Institute.

The Saloon and Public bars had been busy too, with the doors, swinging back and forth the whole time, and fat

Annie from down in 'Sadler's Row', had been in a couple of times already with her jug, cap and shawl.

"Pint a Porter Mag, in me jug 'ere, and 'arf ounce a Digger Shag fer me old Man!"

She slammed the jug down on the counter, wheezing as she did so.

"Got a right bad froat, 'e 'as. Nah its gorn darn on 'is chest. Does nuffin' but corf! corf! corf!"

"'E 'as ter 'ave 'is pint, to ease 'is corfin!" Mag smiled, – It wasn't her old man's throat that was worrying Annie, – It was Annie's own, by the sound of it!

Then the bar door was swung back, noisily this time, and it was Mavis' head that appeared round it. She spoke, – her voice, it sounded agitated.

"Mag, yer gotta come quick! It's your Jess, – She's bin taken real bad!"

Mavis took a deep breath, –

"I've got 'er over at my 'ouse. Bert is wiv 'er nah. She just collapsed all of a sudden like!"

"Yer'll 'ave ter git a Doctor Mag!" Then she paused for a second or two.

"Don' know what's the matter wiv 'er. Poor kid, she's shiverin' and shakin', jus' like a Jelly. Yer'd better 'urry Mag, – Come on!"

Maggie, stunned, tried to pull herself together and then with no more hesitation, she lifted the flap of the counter, shouted something to the Landlord. – What it was, he made a guess but it was plain to see, all was not well!

The Doctor, – he did not mince his words! –

"I am sorry, Mrs Hope? – I am afraid your Daughter is very ill! – She has pneumonia. Her temperature has now reached 103 degrees. – You'll have to hurry!"

19

"We must get her to a Hospital, and as quickly as possible! – Have you a phone near?"

Then, leaving orders for Frank to phone an Ambulance and instructions on how to make a steam kettle to aid Jess's breathing, which was dreadfully laboured, – he left.

The next few hours were a nightmare for Maggie and Bert. He had been up twice to the Police Box at the top of the road, to get the copper there to phone the Hospital for an Ambulance to, – "Get here as quick as possible!"

"Why? Oh why doesn't it come?" All they got was promises and excuses. Maggie was sick to her stomach, she had never before felt such desperation.

That evening was proving to be one, they would never ever forget!

The Ambulance eventually arrived. It had seemed like hours they had waited. – Now Jess was unconscious, – plainly very ill!

Maggie, stricken with fear, choked back a sob, as the men carried her Jess out on the Stretcher to the waiting Ambulance. Mag climbed in behind and sat gripping her little girl's hand tight, as they journeyed the two miles to the Hospital.

Would Jess be alright? She must get better. – She must!

None of her kids had ever been ill before. Mumps, Measles, – Whooping cough, – they'd had the lot! But not like this. – This was different!

On their arrival at the Hospital, the Matron said she was sorry, but Jess would have to be put in the Women's Ward, as there was no room in the Children's. That was not a problem, all Mag wanted, was for the nurses to make her Jess better.

Then it was going to be three long trying days, anxious hours, before they knew Jess was out of danger.

"It has been touch and go." said the Matron, and even this tough die hard, had melted a little at their ordeal, seeing the dejection on Mag and Bert's faces as they'd waited hour upon hour outside in the cold corridors.

When at last they saw Jess sitting propped up with pillows, giving them a wan smile, as they entered the ward, evidently so pleased to see her parents, Maggie fought hard to stem the tears that threatened to flow, and a feeling of utter relief swept over her.

Though never before had she'd any reason to thank her God, – she did so now, as she sat quietly by Jess' bedside, holding her little hand tight in hers.

For her Jess, – her baby, was going to be alright, nothing else mattered. She made up her mind at that moment, by fair means or foul, Jess *would* have that Fairy doll, from out of 'Price's Winder!!'

A keen north-easterly wind was blowing the last of the dead leaves along the street.

Maggie pulled herself up from her kneeling pad and straightened her back.

Pushing the loose strands of her hair back from her eyes, she picked up her bucket and went indoors.

"Blimey! But it ain' 'arf nippy art there!" She shivered and gave the fire a poke.

She'd been up early and whitened the step out the front, for no matter what, come rain, come shine, and even if they were down on their luck, her front doorstep would be as clean, and whiter even more, than any of the other neighbours doorsteps up the street.

Even Kate, that snooty stuck up woman next door with all her high and mightiness, her posh talk and that, and her everlasting dustin' and polishin'. She could not outshine Maggie's snowy white step. 'It didn't matter whether you *were* hard up, you could still be clean and tidy!' Maggie's mother had always told her. Even when some idiot the worse for drink had come out of the Pub the night before, and walked all over *her* step, she would be out like lightening the next morning with her hearthstone cloth.

Maggie stood motionless for a few moments, looking at the piece of paper in her hand. It was a bill of some sort! She looked again, –

"We are requesting payment of two shillings and sixpence for services rendered by Dr Swift plus the sum of five shillings for the ambulance call out."

Now Mag had known the Doctor had to charge a fee, but the Ambulance! It had never occurred to her!

How was she going to pay it? She had a sick feeling in her stomach. Maggie was a proud woman, and had never been the one to hurry off to the Relieving Offices to beg for money. By hook or by crook, she would rather go without than resort to that, but she could not see her kids go hungry. She would find a way.

But Maggie forever after, would say they had a Guardian Angel, looking out for them.

She had spent a few fearful days and nights with a heavy heart and was on the point of seeing Bert sinking his pride and going to get some kind of help, down the Relief. She knew at least, they would be given vouchers for tea sugar, milk and bread, – and that was not proper milk either! Also Maggie had heard say, of a man coming from the Relieving office, to see if you had furniture or something, which was not a necessity, and tell you to sell it, – before they gave you any more vouchers.

"Please, don' let things get ter this state," she prayed that night. If only Bert could get a job, or if there was any other way of getting some money.

She could take in washing! But how could she find the time to do that, she was run off her feet as it was!

She heard a step outside the door, and putting her bucket and mop down, Maggie turned to see Bert standing in the doorway, and was it just her fancy or had his mood changed? When he had said goodbye to her that morning, going off down the Docks, with a bit of hope that he might be lucky for once, his step was flagging and Mag had felt so sorry for him, poor luv! She remembered how full of bounce he once was. Bert, he never laughed much these days either. Now, there was certainly a difference in his whole manner. He came towards her, grabbing her by the arm and he was smiling broadly as he said, –

"Mag, what d'yer know! I've been and gone and done it. I've got a job! – Yer a job, so I 'ave! – And what d'yer fink a that then?"

"Oh! Bert, 'ave yer? – That's good! – Tell me where? – When d'yer start?"

She was so eager to hear his marvellous news.

"Yer know that Pawnbroker at the end a Rupert Street, Percy's, that's the name. 'E wants an odd job man, packing parcels away, clearin' up, and so on."

"Money ain't a lot, but it's somefin' eh, Mag! An' I do 'ates goin' darn the 'Labour' every week – It ain't good fer a bloke! – Gor' blimey it ain't!"

Bert, he had his pride, he knew he could do a good day's work, as well as any man, – gammy arm or not!

23

Of course Maggie knew 'Percy's' the Pawnbrokers! Funny thing was, it had crossed her mind lots of times, that at a last resort when things got really desperate, she would have to do as most others around here did, and that was to pawn something or other, so she could get over Christmas without disappointing the kids.

That promise she had made to herself, come what may, – She was determined to get that doll for her Jess, whatever happened!

The small pale faced invalid had been home from Hospital for some days now, convalescing on the couch in the front parlour.

She could see the kids out playing in the road from the window, and with a wistful look on her face, wishing that she too could be out there with them all, skipping and playing hopscotch.

"You must hurry up and get better!" Everyone who chanced to see her, had that bit of advice to give her.

But she was still quite weak and would be for a while yet, although Maggie was dosing her up well with "Parrish's Food' tonic, and cups of 'Bovril', but how she hated that daily dose of 'Cod Liver Oil and Malt'! Ugh! It was so horrible! But Jess lapped up all the attention she was getting, – it was so nice to be spoiled!

And what was Jim and Rob's reaction to all the comings and goings, and the attention that Jess had been getting of late. It seemed they had taken a back seat while everybody's thoughts were on Jess. They had purposely been very good and kept out of mischief, knowing Mag was otherwise occupied with poor Jess, 'Who was very ill,' their Mum said and, 'You must be good boys!' They'd talked in whispers, and even went to bed early, with no arguments!

Maggie too, felt things had taken a turn for the better. Jessie was almost her own self, getting stronger every day, "Fank Gawd!"

Her Bert, had regained his self respect. His step as he went off to work, if not jaunty, was more confident and assertive.

He liked it down at Percy's the Pawnbroker and had many a tale to relate to Maggie at the tea table, mostly of the queer and bizarre assortment of articles pledged. Some just outlandish! and of the hopeful sometimes pleading looks Angus Percy perceived on the embarrassed faces as the parcels were pushed over the counter.

So Mag was counting her blessings, as it seemed everything was looking up! Even the Doctor had been paid and the Hospital and Ambulance bill settled.

So she, just for a while could breathe a few sighs of relief, and put her mind to other things.

"Better shut that bluddy winder up, its like a perishin' ice 'ouse in 'ere!"

Annie shuffling about in her scuffed and mutilated slippers, and a pair of 'Arry's old socks, crossed the cold draughty scullery mumbling away to herself.

"It's nah almost eleven a'clock in the mornin' and the old bugger ain' up yet!"

"The lazy sod leaves me ter do it all. 'Im and that blasted Corf of 'is! Keeps me awake 'arf the night! Don't git no wink a sleep, I don't, – Corf, Corf, Corf. – Gits on yer bleedin' nerves, it dus!"

Annie bent down with some difficulty and put a match to the old newspapers and bits of rubbish, she'd poked up the copper hole and pushed the metal door shut fast.

She was still mumbling as she sorted out all her bits she had to wash, – mostly 'Arrys. "Wiv 'im corfin' so much, it resulted in 'im 'avin' a few accidents 'ere 'nd there, – 'as ter be forever changin' 'is pants, 'e does!"

Reaching for her wooden scrubbing board, again having to bend, to hook it out from behind the long tin bath hanging on the wall, – she winced.

"Oh! Me pore ol' back!" she groaned, wheezing away, as she tried to straighten up.

"It's no joke bein' so blasted fat!" she said out loud, but there was no one around to listen. "'Arry was still in bed, snorin' 'is bluddy 'ead off!"

Annie and 'Arry had lived down in Sadler's Row, ever since they could remember.

Their modest domain was one of half a dozen old dwellings, poked away in a Cul-de-sac off Wharf Street. Goodness knows how long they had been built, but it was heard tell, – the woodwork was so old that it was a literal hot-bed for the bugs and vermin. It had only been a matter of a few years that taps were installed into these hovels for clean water!

There were many tales the folk hereabouts could tell, of the seamy side of living in this part of London and they were the East Enders themselves

When a bloke called Jack the Ripper terrorised and frightened the daylights out of folk, that they were too scared to put their noses outside of their own front doors!

Gory stories and tales of him cutting up the bodies of his victims after he had murdered them, in and around Whitechapel's dark alleyways, and stories of the impoverished families and the many poor children, who lined up to receive a bundle of donated clothing for the sum of one farthing. Annie herself was too old to have benefited at the time this service first came into being. But she remembered many folk who did so much good work for the needy. Doctor Barnardo was one of these.

Any poor ragamuffin who had become one of Dr Barnardo's boys himself, had only praise for this man and others of the same ilk. So it was because of their good work, the most poorest of children were able to have food and shelter, and the right to live.

If you were lucky, you could get Annie talking about her childhood and the hardships she'd faced, if you plied her especially, with a jug or two of Porter!

And our Annie too, was noted for the much sought after toffee apples she made. These prompted a small queue of the local kids, who jostled one another in order to get to the front of the queue first. But there was one miss, namely Mabel Sims, although diminutive, made up for her size with her fists and her mouth!

"Git back there you, I was 'ere 'afore you, Joey Biggs. – You git back or I'll wallop yer." And she would too! Big as he was!

"It don't look as if I'm 'goin ter git me washin' art agin today!" thought Annie and plonked herself down in her shabby old armchair by the open grate, where she picked up the poker to stir the fickle embers, before she threw another few knobs of coal onto it.

"Oh! 'Ere 'e comes, an' abart bloomin' time too!" Annie had heard 'Arry stomping down the stairs. He had to duck his head as he came through the low doorway, just missing it by a whisper.

'Arry in complete contrast to his wife was all of six foot three in height, and as thin as a rake!

Alas! poor Annie was the opposite, – short, dumpy and a real roly-poly!

When they were out together, the difference between them stirred up many a ribald remark. But, if Annie was ever in earshot, she didn't beat about the bush, – stopping to give them such a lashing with her tongue, that the recipients made a mental note to steer clear of "That little ol' woman, with the big marf!"

"If yer don' shud yer gob, I'll come over there, an' I'll bluddy-well shud it for yer!"

It didn't seem quite so hard getting up in the mornings now, especially as it seemed to Maggie that things were slowly improving. Bert was in work, and doing quite well it seemed, even with his gammy arm, he could still work hard and pull his weight.

He was fitting in a treat down at Percy's, – named aptly 'Everybody's friend.' Sorting out bundles of pledges and storing them, and there was never any shortages of these parcels the locals brought in, hoping to receive a few shillings for the rent and a bit of grub.

They relied on 'Uncles', – who noticeably seemed to be doing a good trade about now, only a couple of weeks before Christmas. How else could money be found, to buy a few toys and sweets for the kids stockings?

Bert was surprised and sometimes amazed at what some customers brought in to pawn, – it might be the old man's overcoat, (although it was the middle of Winter!). There'd be ornaments, grandfather clocks, gold rings, and watches.

"A Rembrandt??"

"Yers, it really is, Mister!"

"Belonged ter me Granddad it did!"

But one memorable morning, Bert was titillated at the sight of an old gent grappling with a set of bag-pipes!

Mr Angus Percy the owner of this gold mine of a shop, was as amiable a man as you would wish to meet. A self satisfied master of all he surveyed. He had made his money in a round-about way, by helping others who had none.

He would appear at intervals from the back of his darkened living quarters, and would walk into the shop, wearing a broad smile and a gold watch and chain draped across his ample proportions!

His smile was one of complacency and satisfaction at the way things were going for him, how each transaction was adding even more to his already overflowing coffers!

There he would stand, rocking back and forth on his heels with his fingers tucked in his braces and a congenial look on his face.

His customers really liked Angus Percy and looked upon him as their benefactor, – their Fairy God Father and Saviour from many a scrape.

But although he was blessed with being called by these names, he was not the only Guardian Angel of the needy.

There was one other who provided a light at the end of the tunnel for those poor in possessions, but rich in so many other features, – Humanitarianism, fellow-feeling and the love of life kind, in a neighbourhood where everybody was somebody's friend!

Ted Price patted his silver grey hair flat to his head, – It had a nasty habit of sticking up at the back. He then smoothed down his large spotlessly white apron, and went out through the door leading from the living quarters and into the shop.

He was greeted at his appearance, by several voices of his young customers, waiting to buy their sweets. It was now only 8.30am. Then the pushing and shoving began.

"Allo! Ted, – Penn'orth a these please," said one of the boys, pointing to a large glass jar on the counter, filled to the brim with bullseyes.

"Penn'orth a Fleas! Did you say son?" This was a favourite game Ted had with the eager youngsters, who were lucky enough to have a penny to spend. How they would giggle and laugh at Ted's banter, then take with them, pockets bulging with all kinds of treasure that would keep them happy, – gob stoppers, tiger nuts, black jacks, liquorice sticks, sherbet dabs, – over the road to the school opposite.

Ted's shop to the kids, was an Aladdin's Cave! Apart from the sweet counter, the rest of his shop was given over to being a storehouse for everybody's needs.

Filled with everything from a ball of string to a clothesline. He had brooms, firewood by the bundle, paraffin for lamps, gas mantles, fire lighters, headache powders, Zam-buk for your back, syrup of figs for whatever, and so the list went on.

Anything everyone needed and if the folk living anywhere near Popular Street, ran short of something, Ted was sure to burrow deep in his treasure trove, and he'd find it!

Well-loved, Ted was kindly, stupidly over generous, he should never have been a shopkeeper.

He had found, through years of experience, how hard up and sometimes desperate the folk were from around large areas nearby, never knowing from one day to the next, where their next meal was coming from!

Ted had a large-leaved book, ever open upon his counter and he wore a permanently placed pencil behind his ear, for jotting down, – "So much for Mrs So-and-So, and I must remind her she hasn't paid anything this week for last week's! – Old Nanny Shaw – the sum of three shillings and sixpence." – He'd get it sometime! – Maybe! – Maybe not!

Nine out of ten of his customers seldom possessed any cash to pay for their few purchases, – so it just went on Tick in the book!

But Ted did not appear ever, – to be worried whether he got his money or not. – He'd get it one day! – But then, – Pigs might Fly!

He too had been badly wounded in the war receiving severe head injuries, resulting in him having an operation to have a silver plate inserted in his skull.

On most days, he suffered frequent headaches but these he would brush aside with a shrug and an embarrassed quip. Ted's motto was, – "Take each moment as it comes!" For him every day was a bonus "You never know," he would say, – "Keep smiling!" – was his policy, one which lots of pessimists, could follow.

Maggie, she went tripping along the road, humming to herself, and opening the door into Ted's shop, stumbled over several sacks of potatoes there blocking the doorway.

But no matter, she was feeling pretty perky this morning, for in her purse she had money. Money to spend!

First thing she had to do, was to secure that Fairy Doll for Jess, – then something nice for the boys.

Ted came round the counter beaming and wearing his usual welcoming smile, and turned to Maggie with a cheery greeting, which he gave to all his customers.

"Good morning Ma'am!" Then he paused, frowning, – Had he seen this woman somewhere before?

"Yes, of course! – She worked in the 'Crown and Anchor', the pub down Brick Street."

Not that Ted was in the habit of visiting public houses. It was only when Betty wanted a drop of rum for her cough. Betty was his wife, a shadowy figure his customers hardly ever saw. She seemed to prefer staying in the background.

Betty was not happy living here, miles from her family in Tottenham. There they were not so liable to fly off the handle. Less hot headed and demonstrative were the people living over in North London.

"That Doll, – the one yer 'ad in the winder there Ted, the one wiv the Fairy dress on, an' the silver wings. – 'Ave yer sold it?"

Mag hadn't noticed the Doll as she entered the shop, she was sure it wasn't in the window.

Ted scratched his head and thought for a minute, then! –

"Oh! I know the one you mean. To tell you the truth, I did put it away for a young lady a few weeks ago, but she hasn't been in for it yet!"

Maggie's face dropped, it looked as if Jess wasn't going to get her Fairy Doll after all.

But Ted, as always, he had an answer.

"Look, I can get you one like it. – Don't worry, come in again next Wednesday!"

She could have hugged Ted, right there and then!

"My Jess will be so pleased, she'd set 'er 'art on 'avin that doll, she did Ted!"

Ted had heard of the girl's serious illness, and now he would make sure she did get her Fairy Doll.

So it was a very satisfied Maggie, who walked back home on Wednesday evening, with a shopping bag containing, – one blonde haired, – blue eyed, – Fairy Doll, plus a box of Tin Soldiers for Jim. Rob, he'd got his request for a football, and Ted had slipped in a box of bon-bons too. Now Mag could face Christmas better. The other bits and bobs could be attended to, later.

Chapter: Three

It was a bitter cold morning, an icy wind battled with the unfortunate individuals who were unlucky enough to be out on such a day as this.

Maggie was one of those. The thin material of her coat, was no protection from the biting wind that chilled her to the bone. With teeth chattering and her fingers ready to drop off, she hurried along by the river on her way to work, and even as cold as she felt now, in no way could she be as frozen as the poor bugger who stood there at the Docks entrance! He was blue with the cold, poor devil, and had not the inclination or desire to call out his usual greeting of 'Mornin' Missus!

Mag thought, as she struggled along, about the letter she'd found on her mat that morning, from her mother over there in Hackney.

She wanted to visit Maggie and Bert, "See her grand children," she said.

"I haven't seen you lately! Isn't it time you asked me over?" But it was no use her whining, it was her own fault.

Mag was not at all happy at the prospect of having her Ma, to come and stay. Mag couldn't help saying, she had to admit it, that she just didn't get on with the old gal. Ever since she could remember, she had been nothing but a troublemaker, a right pain in the neck!

Bert and the kids couldn't stand her. – Well! their lives weren't worth living when she was around, and everything had been so nice lately.

Christmas had come and gone. After all her worrying, it had been lovely, thought Mag. She and Bert striving to make it a good 'un for the kids.

She had got them to make a few decorations with strips of coloured paper, glued together and with a bit of holly here and there, it looked like it had a real touch of Fairyland. – Pity they had no fairylights!

She cherished the look of joy on their faces on Christmas morning, when they each spotted their sacks of goodies at the foot of their beds and as they emptied the socks they'd hung up, with an orange, nuts and sweets tucked in the toes.

Jessie's face was a picture when she clapped her eyes on the Doll! Her Fairy Princess, she called her, – and the boys! They were over the moon! Santa had been specially good to them this time.

"Look Mum! – Look Dad, what Farver Christmas 'as brought me!"

It was worth all the sleepless nights. Sadly it had not been a white Christmas, only the usual drifting dirty grey fog off the river, that enveloped everything and everyone!

But it was really cosy and warm all together around the crackling fire and, – they were even lucky enough to have a few chestnuts to roast!

Now Mag wondered, "Would they 'ave some snow? It was cold enough. Better 'urry up nah an' get crackin', she 'ad ter scrub the pub floors terday, a job she 'ated, specially when it was cold like nah. Er' 'ands an' elbows would be chapped, always 'avin 'em in water, which got cold quick, though it 'ad not been all that 'ot in the first place!"

"Still, she would pop over Mavis's an' borrer some of 'er 'Melrose' an' cream, when she got 'ome!"

Mavis, come to think of it, seemed to have a remedy for most things! She wasn't short of a shilling, her old man was a trader of some sort. Mag had an idea he was in the rag trade in one of them there places along the Commercial Road, – she'd heard they called them sweat shops! It was bloody hard work, and the pay was peanuts! She knew that she for one, wouldn't like to work there, she'd heard too many horrible stories about them places. Mag liked old Mavis, she got on alright with her. But what Maggie didn't like, was knowing her friend was a little too fond of anything in trousers!

With her bleached blonde hair, and curvy figure, she attracted quite a few stray looks, especially from the Lascars! – Sailors off the boats from the East, not forgetting the Horse and Van drivers coming up from the Docks with their loads off these boats. Though Mag was sure, that Mav, – even if she was pretty pleased by the effect she made in her short skirt, she would only just flirt, and make eyes at the men, but never would go off the rails. Sid, – her old man would see to that!

Sid Lewis, he managed her alright, he'd had enough practice, – wasn't he one of the snouts down at the sweat shop, seeing that he got a fair days work out of weary toil worn low paid girls and men, labouring over their benches?

Mag was more than pleased to reach the back door of the pub and get in, away from that blasted wind and the piercing cold. Elsie looked up from her newspaper as Mag walked into the kitchen.

"Crumbs Mag, you look perished. – Come over here by the fire and get yourself warmed up! Here, – There's a cup of tea in the pot!"

This to Mag at that moment, was manna from heaven!

Elsie, with Frank her husband ran the 'Crown and Anchor' A nice couple and had two kids, originally they had come from over the River from Kent. They had always wanted to be in the Brewery trade and somehow or other they'd ended up over here in Wapping! And they wouldn't want to be anywhere else.

They fitted in here. They loved the East End, the smell of it. The river, the ships, the good-humoured watermen's voices in the bar, their ribaldry, vagaries, and their raucous laughter, and most of all, the community spirit. Everybody wanted to help one another, and everybody was somebody's best friend!

Despite the greyness, the poverty, the overcrowded slum-ridden narrow alleyways and workhouses, you could never take away the camaraderie, cordiality and benevolence of these folk, whose roots were embedded here in, what some would presume, – This God-forsaken quarter of London.

Maggie sat fidgeting with the handle of her cup, every now and again taking a sip from the warming tea. Elsie seeing the frown on Mag's face rumbled something was on Mag's mind.

"My God! What's up, you look like a wet week in a thunderstorm. Something troubling you?"

Should she tell Elsie, would she really be interested in my troubles? Mag wondered.

"Oh! It's me Ma, – I 'ad a letter from 'er, she wants to come down and see us, but Bert, 'e 'ates the sight of 'er. Calls 'er, a meddlin' old perisher! – What shall I do?"

She sat and told Elsie, over a second cup of tea, all the ins and outs of 'ow the old woman 'ad nearly caused a bust up between 'er and Bert, a few years back. – "That's why we left 'ackney, Else."

"It nearly got ter blows once, Bert swore he would 'ave ter 'it 'er one day.

"Ow Gawd Else! – What shall I do?"

"Not much you can do! You have either got to let her come, or tell her straight! Either you keep a still tongue in your head or stay away. One way or another, she's got to know! If she wants to see her grandchildren, she's gotta keep Mum! That sounds kind of funny doesn't it Mag?"

Maggie couldn't help smiling at the joke.

"Ow well! Fanks fer listenin' I'd better git on wiv me scrubbin' Else. – Standin' 'ere gassin' ain't gonna pay the rent as they say!"

She screwed up the sheet of notepaper, – that was the third page she'd tried to write to her Mother.

Bert had submitted to her pleas, now he was resigned to the fact that now his mother-in-law, could be coming for Easter. At least that was still a few weeks away from now, "Fank Gawd!" Then, as Rob put his head round the door, –

"'Ere Robbie! Run darn the post box wiv this letter, and make sure yer post it!"

"Ow! An' while yer at it, yer can git me somfin' from the corner shop. Get me 'arf a Marg. I've run art. An' 'urry up back wiv it, or it'll melt in yer 'ot 'ands! – Be careful a the road," Mag called out, as an afterthought.

That's that, she sighed, that was off her mind.

"Mum! Kin I 'av 'n ice cream? Quick the 'Wallsy' man is goin'!" – That was young Jess!

"Ow! 'Ere 'yar, 'ere's some money, better git the uvvers one as well!" Mag opened her purse and took out a tanner.

38

That was about all she did have. Never mind, – Bert gets paid tomorrow and then she would be feeling rich again.

It was a clear moonlight night with the sky dotted with a million stars and the old 'Crown and Anchor' was packed tonight, as there had been a couple of big boats in down in one of the Docks nearby. That caused a look of satisfaction and a big smile on Frank's face. The till was working overtime, with Elsie run off her feet, pulling pints alongside Mag, who had never known the old pub to be so busy.

Reggie Miller sat with his wife in the corner of the smoky bar. Reggie and Peg enjoyed a pint or two, and were regular customers there, engaging in the gossip and yarns from the seamen off the boats.

Their jovial banter and crude tales they came up with were way past raising eyebrows from the listening customers. Everyone was used to it.

Someone started singing over by the old joanna and it wasn't long before everyone joined in 'You made me love you,' and 'Show me the way ter go 'ome', – but not yet, some of them would shout out! And a laugh would go up.

Everyone there seemed to be in an animated mood on this cold February evening, but the atmosphere in the bar was far from chilly. Things were going a treat, ,and the beer was flowing. The air was filled with the humming of voices and loud laughter, when suddenly from a group standing by the bar, rose a yell, and then shouts of recrimination.

Maggie turned sharply to see the figure of a man laying in the sawdust on the floor trying to shield his face with his hands, while a couple of hefty bully boys were kicking and beating the daylights out of him, mercilessly attempting to half murder the poor blighter.

The unfortunate bloke didn't stand a chance with a bunch of bullyboys attacking him, two more of them had joined in. Then from around the back of the bar, quick as a light Frank appeared. He burst through the open counter flap and waded in.

Now Frank was no light-weight himself, he'd been a good sparring partner in the boxing ring, so he knew his stuff! With arms flailing, he threw a few swift punches, which found their mark. Frank was shouting, – "Yer don't fight in my pub, do yer 'ear!" and laid a real wallop on one bullies chin, but everything was not to be on Frank's side tonight. He never saw the coward who hit him over the head hard with the bar stool!

He went down like a ton of bricks. All this time, Elsie had been yelling, "Stop it! Stop it!" at Frank. She gasped and put her hand to her mouth to stem another scream as she saw her husband laying there on the sawdust floor, with blood spurting from a deep gash behind his ear.

She ran round the counter, crying "Frank! Oh! Frank!" The bullyboys had disappeared.

Elsie knelt and cradled Frank's head in her arms sobbing, – "Get the Police," someone shouted. The whole place was in just one big uproar. Some just looking at poor Elsie with Frank lying there motionless, his face bloodless. It seemed ages before the Coppers came, followed by the Ambulance.

Everyone watched as Frank was put on a stretcher and then taken out to the Ambulance, with Elsie wringing her hands and crying.

Maggie all this time had been dumbstruck! From a pleasant evening with all there, enjoying a pint and a sing-song, it had, in a few minutes been turned into a nightmare!

Everyone was quiet now, some had drifted off home. There was to be no more jollifications that evening! She could see that it was useless hanging around there in the bar, and wondered if Molly and Joe, – Elsie's son and daughter would soon be in.

They had gone to the pictures with their friends. She'd better hang on a bit till they came in. Mag hoped Bert wasn't worrying. Wasn't it really time she was off home?

Luck was on her side, with the appearance of both Molly and Joe, who not surprisingly were shocked, wanting to know what they could do?

"Where have they taken them? Which Hospital?" She couldn't tell them. She knew about as much as they did, but she must get back home now. They would be OK, and were not kids anymore, both getting on for adults.

Maggie lay awake half the night tossing and turning, thinking of all the events of the evening. She still could not believe it had ever happened!

"How was Frank? Was he hurt bad? And Elsie! Poor Elsie, she had been in such a state, where was she now? At home or still at the Hospital?"

Bert had tried to calm Mag down, he'd wanted to hear all that had happened when she got back from the Pub and it was late before she eventually dropped off to sleep.

Some bad news greeted her on her arrival at the Pub next morning. She saw, as she turned the corner into Brick Street, a group of people standing around speaking in hushed tones. They were joined at intervals by more neighbours, as the word got around of last night's shindig.

Mag noticed Peg Miller on the edge of the crowd. As she reached the door of the Pub, she was not surprised to find it locked and bolted.

Peg came across to Mag when she saw her, eager to give her the news.

"Oh! Mag, it's 'orrible, – Frank, – 'e's dead!"

"'E died last night in 'ospital, 'e never regained consciousness! Poor Elsie, – She's in such a bad way!"

Mag was stunned, – "Frank dead! 'He couldn't be! – It wasn't possible! Only a matter of a few hours ago, he was joking and laughing with everyone at the bar!"

What would happen now? – She couldn't think, – Should she go back home?

Mag was at a loss, what a terrible tragedy! As she walked slowly back along the quietly emptying street, the crowd was splitting up and drifting homewards.

But Mag felt she didn't want to go home just yet.

Her steps turned towards the River. She wanted to walk, – to think. Nearing one of the jetties, she stopped and gazed across the river, which was an oily grey.

It wasn't a bad day, – calm, quiet, with no sign of fog. Mag's thoughts were racing as she walked along.

She tried to imagine what might happen now?

"Would Elsie continue to run the pub on her own, or would she give it up and where did that leave her? Mag, – she would be out of a job!" All kinds of thoughts were running through her head.

Then Mag realised, she was only thinking of herself, –

"What of Elsie? – How must she be feeling?" She put herself in her place.

"What if it had been Bert?"

Maggie turned and made her way back, – at least she still had *her* husband and her kids. "Poor Elsie!"

She reached through the letterbox and pulled out the string with the key on it, and opened the front door.

Strange to think that it was only a short while since she had left to go to work! But she hadn't been indoors ten minutes, when there was a knock at the door! Opening it, she saw a Policeman standing there. "Oh Gawd, nah what?"

With his notebook at the ready and licking the point of his pencil, he said, – "If yer don't mind Ma'am. I would like to ask yer a few questions." He wanted to know some details of last night's violence at the Pub.

As Maggie related to him all she knew about the whole sorry mess, she was saying to herself, – "This is all just a bad dream," and as quick as a flash she would wake up and realise it had never happened. –

"But no such luck! It had happened and poor Frank was gone. He who never did anyone any harm!"

It was a sombre grey morning, the sky leaden with gathering clouds, which foretold rain. A bitter wind from the East, whistled through the bare boughs of the trees in the old churchyard, bringing even more provocation and discomfort to all those gathered around the graveside.

It was a sad scene, the black clad mourners grouping closer together as if to defy the pitiless gusts that threatened to disarrange the array of floral tributes that lay in profusion around the graveside. – There were so many of them!

Maggie was touched by the kindred spirit of the people who had known and liked Frank. She looked around and couldn't help feeling heavy hearted and sad at Elsie's efforts to keep control of her intense grief, and a wave of anger and rage overtook her.

"What kind of creature could do this to a fellow man and cause such suffering and pain to ordinary decent, hard working folk." – It was just awful.

It was a sad day. Frank had been laid to rest, and now his attacker was waiting to be sentenced, Maggie hoped he had repented for what he had done.

Elsie had to face life now without Frank but she was made of sterner stuff, keeping the Pub going with the help of a trainee Landlord.

Mag still had her jobs as a Barmaid and cleaner, to her intense relief and gratification.

Life had to go on, even if at times it seemed to be, – such stuff as only dreams are made of!

"Nah listen 'ere all of yer, yer Gran is comin' this weekend! She will be stayin' fer Easter, so I want yer ter all be on yer best be'aviour, – Remember!"

There was a short silence, then Jess she was the first, –

"Ow Mu'um! Why is Gran comin'? She's always gittin' on ter us!" – Then Rob, –

"Why does *She* 'ave ter come?"

"Because *She* is yer Gran, – That's why!"

Jim just shrugged and looked down his nose! Maggie could see it was going to be a marvellous Easter!!

"Ello Robbie. – My! An' who's gettin' a big boy then?"

He went crimson! – He was eleven now and not a boy any more. Jess giggled and nudged her brother. She was enjoying this, until then it became her turn, –

"Time she went inter long stockin's Mag, – showin' all 'er legs orf like that, tain't proper!"

Jim made up his mind, he wasn't chancing a ribbin'! Trying to make himself half the size he was, he stood behind his mother. But it was too late! Mag turned to him and said, – "Jimmy, Say 'ello ter yer Gran!"

So Easter and Gran had come, luckily without too much hassle. The kids were on their best 'be'aviour,' except for Jim blottin' 'is copybook, with Gran catching him wearing her lovely imitation Fox fur neck-piece, complete with head and beady eyes, around *his* neck, pretending to be Gran.

It took quite a while before she got over that, but later she relented and busied herself, thinking of ways how to spend the Easter Sunday, –

"Get 'em out in the fresh air Mag, – take 'em over ter Victoria Park!" – 'Ave they ever bin?"

"Only once," Mag answered, –

"That was wiv' the Chapel Sunday-School artin'."

"But don't say nothin' yet though, in case it's rainin' cats an' dogs on Sunday! 'Ain't yer ever noticed 'ow it always rains on Bank 'olidays?"

They were lucky, the Sun did come out, and so had a few of their neighbours! – Mag noticed them as they came out of the front door. Sitting on wooden chairs, on the pavement, arms folded across their pinnys, chatting away, talking about everything and nothing.

"Luverly ter see the Sun, ain't it Mag?"

"Strewf! We can do wiv it!" one called out and, –

"Oi, Sidney! Stop tormentin' that dog, 'e'll bite yer!"

"Ain't got no sense, some a these kids!"

They caught a Bus to Victoria Park. – Gran's treat this was. – She didn't believe in chocolate Easter Eggs, –

"Bad fer yer teef!"

That hadn't gone down well with Jimmy, but now was all-agog with excitement and fidgeting about on his seat.

"Sit still, – young Jim!" Gran said, –

"We won't get there no quicker, you bouncin' up and darn on that seat! What's the matter wiv yer, – got worms?"

45

She may as well have saved her breath, it was like talkin' to a bloody brick wall!

Jim was first off the bus, and anxious to get in there on the swings, dashed off through the gates of the park, where they all made their way, along to the Bandstand. There, a lot of activity was going on, the bandsmen setting up music stands ready to play.

"This is nice," Mag decided and looked at Gran. For once her face had lost its sour look, and Bert, who'd never cared two hoots for Brass Bands, found himself whistling to the sound of 'Colonel Bogey'. And what were they playing now? 'Roses are blooming in Picardy' – No, that was too sad fer 'im.

"Let's go an' find the Parrot 'Ouse," said Bert, taking Jim's hand, – "Jess! Rob!" he called, leaving Mag and her Ma to jaw their heads off!

What is it that women find to talk about when they get together? – It was a mystery to him.

"Coo! Look Dad, I ain't never seen a red white an' blue bird afore, – looks like a flag, don' 'e?" Jim was quite taken up by the exotic colourful Parrots and Parakeets there.

After they'd eaten the last of their bloater paste sandwiches, and before traipsing back to the bus stop, they all heartily agreed, –

"Thanks Gran, – It's been a luverly day art!"

"What a pity!" Mag thought after. Why did her mother have to be a bit of an old harridan? Why couldn't she be like her Bert's Mother Dolly? A sweet kind lady who had died long before her time, with an incurable disease.

But it was more like hard work, and worry that had killed *her*! How Bert had missed her, his lovely Mum with the laughing eyes and a heart of gold.

Chapter: Four

Annie shuffled along the road, her hand gripping her jug, – it was only a few minutes walk to the Pub.

She was feeling thirsty and crochety! It had been a stinking hot day, and Annie, – "Don't like this 'ot wever, it makes me sweat cobs!" she said.

As she pushed the Bottle and Jug bar door open, – Mag at that moment looked up.

"'Ello, Annie, what's the matter, too 'ot fer yer?"

"Yers Mag, I don't like the Summer, – roll on the Winter! Even if yer feels the cold, yer kin always git yerself warm, – put somefin' extra on!"

"But this 'ere 'eat, it knocks all the stuffin art a yer!"

Then Annie suddenly remembered something, –

"Ow's that gal a yourn, – Jess, – ain' it?"

"I keeps meaning' ter arst yer."

"Oh! Fine, Ann. – Comin' on a treat, she is. Bit thin though! It really did pull 'er darn. Like a rake she is! Still, she'll soon put it back on agin."

Annie jerked her head towards the closed door and whispered quietly, –

"Ow's Elsie? Poor gal, ain't people wicked? – Never arst fer that, did 'e? – Nice bloke 'e was, ol' Frank!"

She carried on, Annie was in a talkative mood and a nosy one. "Ere! And 'ow's your Bert doin' darn at Percy's? – I wondered abart 'im?"

"Wot's 'e like ter work for, – Percy, I mean. –'E's ever ser rich ain' 'e? – So they say!"

Picking up some glasses from the counter, Mag rinsed them in the sink underneath.

Poor old Annie, – once she got goin, there was no stoppin' 'er. Talk a donkeys 'ind leg orf she could!

"Pint of old and mild, Mag." – "OK, comin' Charlie."

She made her escape just in time, but no, – Annie, though she was on the point of leaving, had a thought. Turning back to Mag, saying in muffled tones, –

"Yer know, – I wondered, – Will Elsie still be 'avin' the artin' ter Sarfend? – Yer know, – Frank, – D'yer fink?" Annie was struggling for words.

Maggie helped her out.

"Elsie is not the sort ter, disappoint 'er customers, so it should be in July, – That's soon, why? – Are yer finkin' a goin' Annie?" she asked.

"Me? – No, I'm too long in the toof. Leave all a that ter the younguns!"

Mag could not help smiling at the mental picture she got then of Annie, holding her skirts up high, showing all her bloomers, doing the Can-Can!! down the middle of the Charabanc.

"No" Annie carried on, – "I'd sooner 'ave me tipple at 'ome wiv me 'Arry, – D'yer know, – 'E don' keep corfin' arf ser much nah!"

Mavis stood doing some ironing at her kitchen table feeling really fed up to the teeth.

"What's the bluddy use! – I'm standin 'ere ironin, – 'is shirts, 'is trowsers, mendin' 'is soddin' socks, week after week. It gits on yer bluddy wick it does!"

She put the heavy iron, she was holding, back on the kitchen range, and picked up the other one, spitting on it, watching it sizzle. "Yers it was 'ot enough," she decided, then got out another shirt from the heap in the wash basket.

"Lucky 'e kin afford ser many shirts, uvver blokes around 'ere can't!"

"Never takes me out nowhere, dunno' why I stay 'ere, – Really I don't!"

Sid was out from early in the morning till late in the evening, so Mav hardly ever saw him anyway!

His job in the shirt factory kept him busy. So what time did he ever get to take her out? "'E's always too bluddy tired when 'e does git 'ome," she thought, – "What a life!"

"Good job she 'ad Mag across the road, ter go over an' 'ave a chin-wag to!"

She put down the iron, she wasn't going to do no more. "Sod it!" and off she went, over to Mag, curlers and all!

"Yer must 'ave read me mind Mav! I was jus' goin' ter call yer over. – Wanna cuppa?"

Maggie put the kettle on the hob.

"Won't take long, – Bin 'ot ain' it terday?"

"Wot yer bin doin' Mav?"

"Don' arst me, Mag, – I'm that bored. – Stuck around the 'ouse all day. He don't like it, if I say I'll go and find a job, anyfin' rarver than die a boredom!"

Mag went quiet for a minute, "Blimey, I wish I was in your shoes, sometimes. Yer got it cushy mate!" she thought, then realised her friends dead end situation.

"Not very nice, I wouldn' 'ave it!" Mag didn't like Sid much, not that she saw him a lot.

"Come on luv! 'ere's yer tea, drink it! It'll cheer yer up!" hoping for the best.

Just at that moment, Rob appeared in the doorway, straight from school.

"Mu'um! Can I go over Stan's 'ouse, an' see 'is Fagcards?" – Then it was Jess, alongside her friend Maisie.

"Mu'um! Wan' 'anyfin' darn the corner shop? Maisie wants me ter go wiv 'er, – fer 'er Mum!"

"Two down, one ter go." Mag thinks, "Any minute nah it will be our Jim. – I wonder what 'e'll come up wiv?"

"Yer 'ad ter larf tho', – Who'd be a mum?"

But Mag wouldn't change her lot for the world. Not for all the tea in Lipton's!

"Couldn't be a better day eh? Mag? I said ter meself as I got up an' see the Sun. It was scorchin' me eyeballs art! An' I said, Fank Gawd! – Won't need no brollys terday."

All this, Mavis called out to Maggie who had just arrived with Bert and the kids, to join the gathering of eager trippers all set for their day out at "Sarfend!"

The over excited youngsters were clutching their buckets and spades, salvaged from previous outings, and were having difficulty in staying in one place.

"Gor Blimey! Where's 'e gorn nah! 'Ere Ned! Stay 'ere by me, Yer'll get lorst. It a be yer own fault if yer gets left be'ind, – I shan't care!"

"Allo! Mrs Ryan, 'Ow are yer? Ain't seen yer fer ages. And glad ter see *you* George. You alright, eh? – Good!"

Mag thought how nice it was to see so many well-known faces, everyone gathered together going off for a few hours to forget about work and unpaid bills. The landlord, the cat next door and the bloody dog who does nothing but bark all day and all night, over the back!

The Charabanc arrived, with squeals from the excited young mites. It was a scramble who was getting on first, to get the front seat, so they could see everything!

"Full up, – Everybody 'appy? – We're off!" – More squeals. Chock full, was the Charabanc, everyone in an animated, jubilant mood, chatting, joking, but when the sea came in sight, there were no holds barred. Well! They were lucky, they *did* actually behold the sea, – The tide *was* in!!

What a day they had too, the Cockle and Whelk stands, were hard put to see to the many little hands holding ready their pennies for a plate of cockles, –

"Plenty a vinegar mister, please!"

Ice cream cornets and what was that stuff?

"It looks like pink cotton wool on a stick Mum!"

The Kursaal was the highlight of their day out. Trouble was, how to decide what were the best rides they could have for their precious pennies!

One of the nippers got away from his mother's sight and there was one hell of a shemozzle! Everyone going which way, till they found him, fascinated by the Bearded Lady!

They had a go on the bumper cars with Bert and then it was the haunted house.

Jim, he ups and says, "Yor not gittin' me in there! I'd rarver go an' look at the Elephant Man!" After that they had a walk back down to the beach.

"Kin we go fer a paddle Mum?"

Jimmy was that excited, – he couldn't remember ever seeing the sea.

"Don't go art too far nah, – Watch 'im Jess!" But Rob now, he was more interested in the pier. It was such a long one and a train on it too! – "It mus' go right art ter sea, or p'raps, even right art ter France!" – So his Dad said.

"Rob! When 'e grew up, 'e was goin' rarn' the weld. 'E would be a sailor, like Francis Drake, or was it Captin 'ook? – One or the uvver!"

Mag was taking a look in her purse, wondering if she had enough left for Fish an' Chips. – Would it stretch to some for the kids? – Looking at their sunburned faces, yes, they were really enjoying themselves! It seemed to them as if it was Christmas and Birthdays all rolled into one! Mav, she'd sloped off earlier with Lily, who'd come on her own.

Bert, he was having a nap on the pebbles. He'd just turned over, he did, – pulled his cap down over his eyes, folded his good arm across his chest, and he was off!

Mag looked down at him, laying there and sighed, –

"Dear old Bert, he was a good un!" She couldn't have done any better!

She called over to them all, "Come on, dry yer feet, let's go and get some Fish an' Chips" – "Cor! Yeah!" an excited yell went up! They didn't have to be asked twice! But then there was another cry, –

"Mu-um look at Jim, he's splashin' water all over me knickers!" Jess had tucked her dress in them for a paddle.

"Oh! Fer Gawd's sake, – Come on!" cried Mag.

It wasn't hard to locate a Fish Shop. Why? –

"Every uvver Caff along the front was one and yer could smell 'em a mile off!"

"Rob! Go an' git five separate penn'orf's a fish, wiv five 'a'porf's a chips, 'Ere!" – Mag gave him some money.

"Wait! – She shouted after him, "Don't fergit ter put the salt an' vinegar on 'em!"

Traipsing back to the Charabanc, she found a few odd coppers, to get them each a Hokey-Pokey ice cream, off the Moakses' man with the van, doing a good trade nearby.

That rounded off the day a treat. A good few tired, but happy souls, journeyed back home that hot evening, so, –

"G'bye Sarfend! – See yer agin soon!" – Maybe!

The Summer rolled on with its good days and bad days, as it does in dear old England.

Raining like blazes one day and then scorching your eyeballs out the next!

Mag was niggly, – the kids were on their usual Summer holidays from school, and always under her feet, more so when it rained.

"Fer Gawd's sake! – Why don'cher go art an' play."

"Surely there's somefin' yer kin find ter do."

"Look, – all yer mates are art there!"

The heat was getting her down, her work was proving too much for her, continually back and forth to the Pub. Even Elsie had noticed how harassed and tired Mag looked.

She needed a break, but how could she afford it? There seemed to be no answer.

But! There could be one, and old Annie came up with it! She had just come in the bar with her jug.

"Mag, 'ere! – The 'op pickin' season is startin', over in Kent. Marfa Dow is takin' 'er family ter 'Adlow, or it sounded somewhere like that."

"'Er ol' man 'as got someone wiv a lorry who's takin' 'is lot over there. They go every year!"

"Why don'cher take the kids Mag, they say it's not 'ard work an' yer gits paid an' all!"

Annie had been and done the same thing regularly, not so many years back, and would do it again.

"But I'm too old fer that lark nah Mag. So why don't yer go an' try it?"

"Ow kin I Ann! – I 'ave me job at the pub, 'ere, an' what's Elsie gonna do if I ain' 'ere?"

Annie again had the answer, –.

"Leave it ter me, gal!"

Mag had only just stepped inside the door of the old 'Crown' a couple of days after that, when Elsie popped her head around the door.

"Ello! – Mag, – I want you a minute!"

"What's up Elsie?" – Mag, she thought, – "Nah what's 'appened." 'Ad she done something wrong?

Elsie noticed Mag's frown and hastened to put her right.

"It's like this Mag, – I think you ought to have a break, you deserve one."

"Look, – my niece is comin' to stay for a few weeks, and she's willing to take over your job, while you're away. She can serve behind the bar.

Mag, she's done it before!"

"Don't worry!" Seeing Mag's crestfallen look.

"It's only for a few weeks. I'll see you will be alright for your wages."

She couldn't believe it! – Here was Elsie giving her a chance to get away, and have a break with the kids.

"She could take 'em 'oppin'!"

"'Old on! 'Ad old Annie got somethin' ter do wiv this?" She remembered their conversation, the other day.

"I bet she 'as, the crafty old devil!"

It was like a bolt out of the blue, but what was Bert going to do?

It's no good, she couldn't manage it.

"What, – Take the kids 'oppin'! – And how were they supposed ter get there?"

"Forget it!" – She must! – It was just too much to think about, though it seemed Fate was conspiring to have a hand in all this and Bert to her surprise, – was all for it!

"I might be able to come down at weekends," he said and that to Maggie, settled it.

So, maybe it wasn't going to be so difficult after all. Mag even started to like the idea!

They left the smoke and soot of old London Town and had their first glimpse of the Kent countryside from the back of Bill Davis's old lorry that rattled and shook so much that Jim just put his hands over his ears and curled himself up in a ball, and remained silent until they reached the farm.

There it was all so different from what they had expected. To have to sleep on filled mattresses of straw and on the floor of a hut! And with only hurricane lamps for lighting, – otherwise it would have been pitch dark!

Rob treated it as a big adventure, but Jess, – she wasn't too sure. It was the earwigs, and the dark! She stayed close to him most of the time, and Jim, he wouldn't leave his mother's side, if *he* could help it.

The first night there was the worst.

"Don't like the dark Mum, – I want ter go 'ome!"

"Oh! It's not like this all the time son, wait an' see what its like tomorrer."

Mag tried to reassure Jim, but this would be a whole new experience for all four of them.

"When yer get up yer'll feel different abart it. Go ter sleep nah, all a yer!"

But Mag, had misgivings and as she lay awake in the dark on the hard straw bed, she thought of her bedroom back in No.27, Brody Street.

Although it lacked a lot of things, such as warmth and some of the little necessities, such as a bed which didn't sag in the middle like a hammock, – a few warm blankets and maybe a decent dressing table, that wasn't pitted with

55

woodworm, – It was a damned sight better than having to sleep on straw!

But it was surprising how they came to get used to it, and being so tired after pulling down the hop bines over a bin, and picking off the hops all day which took ages at first, – they fell asleep, as soon as they 'hit the hay!'

Everyone was paid so much a gallon for the hops they picked, weighed after, by a Measurer.

It was a back aching job, but they soon mastered it. Then found it fun in the evenings with the other families, sitting around the big fires singing old songs, and Mag discovered it a novelty cooking a stew, or eggs and bacon over a fire. A man from the shop in the village, came round the fields selling meat and eggs everyday.

Bert came down a couple of weekends, taking Mag over to the Pub with a chirpy crowd of the hop-pickers, and had a rip-roaring Sing-Song round the piano in the Bar.

'Pack up yer troubles', 'The Drunken Sailor' and especially. 'Old McDonald had a Farm!' – Quite apt!

One of the merry revellers, keeled over drunk and had to be pushed home in a wheelbarrow, singing at the top of his voice, the whole time! – But, 'Blimey wasn't he happy!'

Chapter: Five

It was Rob's big day!

He was up with the lark this bright late February morning, and was starting his first ever job as Butcher's errand boy.

Full of enthusiasm, – as now, – after a few weeks of looking for work, since he'd left school at Christmas, having reached the ripe old age of 14, – he had struck gold!

His pleas of "D'yer wanna erran' boy mister," had fallen on a sympathetic ear, in the shape of the owner of a small factory half hidden from the road, down Cable Street.

"Yers, I kin ride a byke, even as big as that one mister," he'd said, eyeing this sturdy, large framed, heavy two wheeler, leaning up against a wall.

Attached to its handlebars was a big square wicker basket, with a steel plate on its side and the words, – 'Wapping Meat Products' emblazoned on it, advertising their famous meat pies, saveloys and potted meats. "They make your mouth water!"

But this wasn't exactly the job he had been hoping for. He had been thinking more along the lines of a cinema technician, or a newspaper reporter, or even a Chauffeur to a famous politician! – Maybe one day, – you never know, – a politician himself!

Rob knew though, that what he might earn, which wasn't going to be much, would anyway be a little bit of help towards his upkeep and he would feel proud when he handed over his first week's pay to his Mother. It must be jolly hard for her to fend for them all, and most of the time, they went to bed hungry!

Maggie felt a twinge of sadness, and a little tear in her eye, as she saw her Rob, her first born, go off that morning to his first job. She thought of it too, as the first step into a New World and what it could mean to him.

What lay in store for him out there?

During the past three years, she had seen a lot of changes in people's lives in her street and in the streets around her

Mag could not believe so much had happened in that short time.

Bert, he was now really settled in his job at Percy's, and she still had hers in the 'Crown and Anchor.' Though now there were new owners.

Nice too they were, Les and Maureen, good to work for, she got on OK with them.

Now Mavis! – Mag felt a pang of regret, and was saddened when she thought of Mav, how she missed her and the Curlers.

It had been a bad state of affairs, but she had seen this all coming!

Mavis' old man had done the dirty on her and cleared off with one of the women in the workshop.

'The Blighter!' Mag thought, and although she knew that her friend Mavis, had never been the one to dress up, or to even make the best of herself and show Sid she could look as attractive as any of them down there in the factory. – 'She did not deserve what he had done to her.' – What Mag would like to do to him was nobody's business!

Mav had needed for a while, Mag's shoulder to cry on, but she had now pulled herself together, put her fingers up to her nose at Sid and gone over to live near her son George in Kensal Rise. 'That had pleased dear Sybil no end, I bet!'

She couldn't help giggling at the thought.

And there was poor Ted, he'd had to give up his shop at last and moved away, much to the great disappointment of the kids from school. – 'No more humbugs, black jacks or sherbet dabs.' – Ted's shop was now a Barbers!

But our Annie, 'Gawd bless 'er, she kept on goin'! She was like an ol' war 'orse, she'd live ter be one 'undred and they'd 'ave ter shoot 'er, in the end!'

Jess was doing very well at school and very dertermined to get on, – bringing with her lots of home-work, though she had got more and more disgruntled at Jim's teasing and interference.

"Oh! Will yer go away Jim, fer Gawd's Sake. I can't fink, wiv yer keep on, takin' me mind off me rifmatic!"

Poor Jim would then slink away after pulling faces *and* Jess's hair.

There were a few newcomers in their street and things seemed to be changing all around them, but not at the Docks. It was always touch and go whether a hopeful chap was taken on or turned away.

There were more men than jobs, with many being passed over again and again, and having to go back home to their missus' with the same words, –

"Sorry luv, – no luck agin terday!"

Rob looked sceptically at his image in the pock marked mirror that hung on a nail on the back door in the scullery, and frowned, – "Why did that quiff ov 'air 'ave ter always stick up in the front. – It makes me look a bit like that Stan Laurel at the Saturday mornin' picher show at the Roxy!"

Wetting his fingers with his spittle, he had a go at trying to smooth the quiff down onto his forehead, but after a few frantic goes, he gave up.

"Ave yer got yer Sandwiches Robbie?" Mag called from the yard, where she was hanging out some washing.

"Yes Ma! – They're in me pocket, I'm orf nah," he shouted, trying to appear mindless of the fact, that this was not just like starting school again. – This was the day he was making his mark in the world as yet unknown to him.

His heart was really thumping, and taking a deep breath, he thought, 'This is no use, I must be on me way!'

"Bye, Mum! I'm goin'!" Mag came in from the yard.

"Yer sure yer'll be OK Son? – Don' yer wan' me ter come darn wiv yer nah?"

"Cause not Mu'um, – I'm not a kid any more!" and off he went, walking the few streets towards the small factory shop that was to be the start of Rob's initiation into the big bad world!

Mr Cyril Snelling sat behind a desk in his small office, surrounded by papers, ledgers, books and phones, and not feeling one hundred per cent. It was one of those days!

Rob's knees were shaking as he stood outside the office looking at the plate glass window, on which plainly indicated the words, – MR. C. SNELLING MANAGER. (Please knock before entering!), and this was the man he was looking for!

In answer to his timid tap, a voice sounding very bad tempered called out, – "COME IN!"

Looking up from the desk the voice beheld a white faced bewildered boy of about fourteen to fifteen, standing there wishing he was somewhere else.

"Yes," very short and curt, the voice wanted to know, "You wish to see me?" Looking Rob up and down.

"Please Sir, I 'ave ter start work 'ere terday! – I'm the new erran' boy!"

"Oh! Are you now?" the owner of this voice boomed, making Rob's face turn even paler.

"Then what the blazes are you doing here! Go and find the Foreman, – he's the one you ought to be talking to, – get off with you boy, – I'm busy!"

Rob, he didn't need to be told twice, he was out of that office door as quick as a bloody light, and dashed straight into the Foreman's arms!

"Hold on Son, – where yer goin'?" he said and seeing the scared look on the boy's face, he forced back a smile, with great difficulty.

"What's yer name son? Yer know yer supposed ter come ter me first! – But OK, never mind!"

"So you are the new lad, – right foller me."

Rob felt calmer now, this bloke seemed a lot nicer than the BOSS! Handing him over to a chargehand who began to show him the ropes, Rob then went off with a warning, –

"Mind 'ow yer go wiv that byke lad. It's a bit too 'eavy fer yer, I reckon!"

"No, it ain't mister! – It ain' 'eavy, 'onest!"

"Call me Ben lad, – there's no misters 'ere!"

Giving Rob his orders and the addresses of a whole list of customers, Bob sent him off on the right road that was in the radius of a few square miles around.

A bit later, after a few entanglements with the byke, – the "No, Mister!" he had said, and "It ain' 'eavy 'onest!" he hadn't counted for the old cobbled streets that weren't exactly easy on the chassis, – Not the byke's, – Rob's!

Though he was not what some would class a strapping lad, he was quite strong. But measuring only five feet in his socks, he could not be considered the ideal build to handle the heavy roundsman's byke, for all he had maintained, –

"Yers, Mister, – I kin ride it!"

It had been more like wishful thinking on his part. This cumbersome machine was really intended for someone, – 'bigger 'n 'im!'

It was to Rob a thorn in the flesh. Yes, – in his rear end!

So he finished up having to push the darn thing around, having come off it a few times, much to his downfall and also down with some of the provisions meant for Mr Cyril Snelling's waiting customers!

When he eventually arrived back home late. If anyone then had made the mistake of asking him how he had got on, he would have told them in no uncertain terms!

He had the appearance of an old cowpoke, who'd been performing on a manic steer at a Rodeo Show, as he limped in the back door.

There was something about his walk, and on his face was the most dejected look Bert had seen in a long time!

"What's up, boy?" trying hard not to let Rob see the look of amusement that threatened to add to his son's misery, – he said, –

"How did yer git on! D'yer like yer job?" But Bert had to wait a while for an answer to his questions, while Rob tried hard to control the tears, almost ready to flow.

Taking a big gulp, he answered his Father, looking dejectedly down his nose.

"I s'pose it would 'ave bin alright Dad, but I didn' know there was so many 'umps an' bumps in the streets ov Wappin' an' Whitechapel!"

"What! – D'yer mean ter tell me yer bin all that way over there? What's this bloke finkin' abart, – 'E's a blasted slavedriver!"

"I'll soon be seein' abart this, – look at yer!"

"No Dad, – don't say nuffin', – please!"

Mag then came into the kitchen and seeing the state her lad was in, she didn't mince her words either.

"That's it, – yer ain't goin' no more. Mr Bloomin' Snellin' can stick 'is job, an' I'll tell 'im where, to 'is face!"

"That's 'is lot!"

The door then suddenly burst open and young Jim came rushing in, –

"Mu-um! The Muffin man is comin' darn the road. Can we 'ave some fer tea?"

"Ow! Go away Jim boy, can't yer see I'm busy talkin'!" Then noticing Jim's downcast look, she thought again, –

"Alright! I s'pose so, – Ere y'are then," giving him some loose coppers out of her purse.

He chased off after the man with the tray of Muffins balancing on his head, while ringing his hand bell, and shouting out at the top of his voice, –

"Muffin man, 'ere's the Muffin Man! Then Jim, he almost collided with the local Bobby, – who stopped him in his tracks, –

"Where's the fire lad?" he asked. "In a 'urry ain't yer?" smiling broadly at the boy.

So, – It was inevitable, that there was to be inserted in the local rag the following week, an advertisement, –

'Wanted urgently, 'Wapping Meat Products', – needs able bodied lad, preferably school leaver, to deliver meat, poultry and provisions, capable of handling a heavy trade byke. 'Not for the faint hearted!'

"Rob! Can't yer find anyfin' ter do?"

"Ere, 'elp me art in the back yard wiv this 'ere mat."

"Look. – You take that end, and we'll frow it over the line, and yer can beat it fer me."

Mag handed him a gadget, which to him looked like a long handled tennis racket and then showed him how to whack the mat with it, knocking the dust out.

All this was in order to give him something to do, she didn't like seeing him mooning about with nothing to occupy his mind.

But he started to take it into his head to wander every day down to the Dockside, watching the activity there, and even walking as far as St. Katherine's Dock, near the Tower, watching the boats discharging their cargoes.

With each visit there, he found all these river scenes captured his imagination more and more. He watched the cranes, that dipped and swung, the Dockers toiling and sweating, unloading the valuable merchandise.

Rob, loved the smell of the River, albeit at times, the stench from some of the waste refuse dumped there, and piled up by the water's edge, caused him to puke. But that did not daunt him or stop him from dreaming, as he lay on his side of the bed at night, – Jim, he'd be fast asleep!

One day, – he vowed, – he'd go sailing away on one of these noble stately ships to find the mysterious lands and empires, whose names he had never yet heard of, but he knew there would be many moons go by before then, and what was he going to do while he waited?

"I know!" Then he had a brainwave. His mate's father had been a sailor back in the war. He'd get Pete to ask him "What's it like bein' on one a them there big boats?"

*   *   *

These people of the East End, – these indomitable, deep rooted inhabitants that lived and worked on the banks of this timeless old Thames River, who'd withstood the ravages of time, setbacks, uphill struggles, somehow, just to survive, – what tales could they tell?

What scenes had they witnessed in the decades in which this old River had rolled along, – down to the mighty sea!

They had endured all kinds of weather. Balmy Springs, baking hot Summers, mellow Autumns and now another Winter was almost over. There had been long weeks of icy freezing fog that had gone on and on.

Sad, grey faces that matched the fog, which never seemed to lift.

Maggie, sick to death of getting up each cold morning, trying to light a fire in the kitchen grate, with it refusing to raise a spark, even with the odd sheet of newspaper she held patiently in front of it.

"Why oh why, does everyfin' 'ave ter be ser bleedin' 'ard, – fer cryin' art loud!" Mag moaned to herself.

"Yer need ter 'ave the bleedin' patience ov a Saint ter be an 'ousewife!"

But noticing then, the miserable look on the face of Rob as he came down the stairs. Mag abandoned the job of trying to get the fire to light, and went over to him, putting her arm around his shoulders and saying, –

"Don't look ser down lad! Somefin' will turn up. It won't always be like this. It can only git better, – one day"

"It'll soon be Spring! Yeah, I know it's 'ard ter believe it nah, but we will be gittin' nice warm days an' we'll all be able ter git art a bit more then, won't we?"

"Look!" she said, "Let's 'ave a nice cuppa tea, eh? Nah I know yer won't be turning' yer nose up at that!"

"Gis a smile, – There, – an' Ow Gor' blimey, the fire's suddenly decided ter catch light!"

"See! – That's a good sign nah ain' it eh? Ol' Son."

Now, our Rob had heard a lot about a Naval College and the Observatory over the water in Greenwich. Although he'd known there was another land across the Thames, it seemed out of reach, and almost in another country!

But, he had darn well made up his mind, that by hook or by crook, he was going to get there, someday, somehow. When and how though, – was to be in the lap of the Gods!

He wanted to see the Naval Museum, and learn a bit more about Nelson and Drake and all the famous battles, that had made History his favourite subject at school.

He would say nothing, but when he found his chance, he would do all these things.

"I 'ave ter be patient," he thought with all the assurance and optimism of a fourteen-year-old!

Jess came down the stairs, yawning and scratching her head. Pushing a chair nearer to the fire, she sat down, and looked at Rob who was sitting staring into space.

"Why's it ser cold in 'ere?" she said, and, "Is there any tea goin' spare?"

"Wish I didn' 'ave ter go ter school. You don't, do yer?"

"Oh! Stop whinin' Jess! – I'm goin orf art!" said Rob, getting up from his chair, departed, slamming the door hard.

Half way down the road, he bumped into Pete.

"Watcher! Where yer goin'?" he asked Pete, – who answered Rob's question with, –

"Well, me Dad told me once, there was a Tunnel yer kin walk frew under the Thames, an' it comes art in Greenwich on the uvver side!"

"Yer gits a Bus. See! – An' it takes yer ter this Tunnel, an' we kin go when this fog lifts. We can't go while the wevver' is like this, eh?"

Pete, like his mate, always kept his eyes wide open for jobs, but it seemed there were too many Mr Cyril Snellings about, wanting to screw the very last ounce out of you, for next to nothing!

"Oh! There yer are Robbie luv. – 'Ere pop darn the corner shop will yer! – I've run art a spuds an' milk. Git me a tin a condensed milk 'Goat Brand' it is. – An' while yer at it, yer kin git 'arf a parnd a Cornbeef, it'll do fer our teas, wiv some chips."

Mag had her arms in the sink full of water, up to her elbows, scrubbing the collars of Bert's shirts.

"Blimey! 'Ow 'e manages ter git his fings ser dirty, darn at Percy's, it's a bloomin' mystery ter me!" She was mumbling away to herself, every now and again, pushing that bit of hair back out of her eyes, – It had a way of forever doing that. Long thick and shining, – her hair was her crowning glory.

Mag was not particularly pretty but with her dark brown hair and eyes to match, she had stirred Bert's interest from the first time he ever saw her, and he knew without a doubt then, she was the girl for him, and told her so.

He had never regretted that evening, it was only a short time after they'd met, when he'd asked her to be his wife!

Their's had been a whirlwind courtship, Bert had been on leave at the time, and on his very next furlough from France, they had tied the knot, and from then on, had not looked back.

He was a good old stick, her Bert.

Did she ever have any doubts about being his wife? –
"No! – Not on yer Nelly!"

Their marriage had borne fruit, – Look what it had produced! Three lovely kids! So whatever was pre-ordained for them, – Come what may they all belonged to each other, and, no one could say them nay.

Mag scrubbed away at the stubborn stains on Bert's shirt, her mind now on Rob.

Her first born had all of Bert's attributes, and some of his characteristics, – 'A chip off the ol' block.' Rob he wouldn't go far wrong, if he continued to take a leaf or two out of his Dad's book.

But she wished a little job would turn up for him, to give him something to occupy his mind. It did no good at all for him to have idle hands, too long. There were too many rough characters, who lounged around the street corners near to home!

So Maggie prayed that her big son could always stay the way he was now!

Chapter: Six

It was Spring at last and a brilliant April morning, with a radiant Sun climbing ever higher in a clear blue sky. The warmth of it brought out from the houses and on to the pavements in Brody Street, the chairs and the smiling faces of Maggie's neighbours, who were taking this opportunity, after so many long months of bitter cold weather, and enveloping fogs, to sit and chinwag to their heart's content.

"Ello Mabel! – Glad ter see yer back on yer feet again, after breakin' yer leg like that."

"How come yer did such a daft fing?"

Gladys shouted this across the street to Mabel, who was sitting, resting one leg up on a stool, outside her front door.

"Need yer arst!" said Mabel dryly. "I kept tellin' that old man a mine, not ter put polish on the lino in me passage. I said ter 'im, – One day some soppy sod's gonna slide up on that an' go arse over 'ead! An' that soppy sod, turned art ter be me, didn't it?"

Maggie couldn't help laughing as she continued on her way to work. A picture had shot through her mind of poor unsuspecting Mabel flying up her passage, – all 15 stone of 'er. – It must have been the fastest she'd ever moved.

She was a lazy old sow!

Mag carried on down the road. She was feeling quite perky this morning, as things seemed to be, – at least for the moment, – on the up and up! The warm sunshine, giving a spring to her step, as she walked along by the river. It was lovely, feeling the balmy breezes on her face.

Even Bill, the gatekeeper at the Docks seemed to be welcoming the sudden change in the climate. He was all smiles, as he caught sight of Mag, as she turned the corner.

"Morning' Missus! This old Sun's a sight fer sore eyes ain' it, eh?" Blimey! ain' I glad ter see the back a Winter. It's been a bad 'un, – an' yer kin say that agin!"

Giving Bill a smile and a wave Mag left him to his irksome job, "'E must get bored stiff standin' there all day. Blow that fer a lark!"

Yes, things seemed to be a lot better all round. Bert was well entrenched in his job at the Pawnshop. He got on fine with Percy, – A good man to work for.

The kids were OK too. Jim still the unruly one, was always in and out of mischief, bless 'im! There wasn't a day go by, when he didn't come home without a bruise, or a chunk out of his knees, tho' young Jim, he was a real love, you couldn't really get mad with him.

Jessie now thirteen, couldn't wait to leave school. A real dreamer Jess, she had many visions of becoming a ballet dancer. Just like the girl in that film she'd seen at the Roxy! The Poxy Roxy, as some of the local lads called it, when there was a duff film on. She had that head of hers in the clouds these days, that Jess.

But at long last, Rob had found himself a nice little job, and was in his glory now, working in a small factory making cardboard boxes. Although it was tedious work folding the boxes up and tying them into bundles, ready to be loaded on to the lorries, – it was good company that he was in now, working with lads of his own age. Mag thought how nice it was to see him smiling again!

Maureen looked up as Mag walked into the Public Bar. "Morning' Mag, – you're early! Is it the Sun that's brought

70

you out?" Putting down some clean glasses she'd just dried, on to a shelf by the counter, she said, –

"It won't be long now 'till Easter, we must think of something to brighten up this place Mag!"

"It's got a bit flat of an evening here lately. I thought we'd get rid of that old piano and get a new one in."

"We'll hire a resident pianist who knows his stuff! Someone who will liven all of them up!"

"Could get some new Curtains and have a bit of a Spring clean. – Yes, I'm looking forward to getting started now how about you Mag?"

The 'Bottle and Jug' bar door then opened, and in shuffled old Annie complete with her shawl and jug.

"Mornin' Mag, – usual please."

It did not go unnoticed that Annie was not her regular cheery self and when Mag inquired, – "What's up Annie?"

"'Ow! It's 'Arry!" she said. "E's not ser good yer know! 'E 'ad a bad turn in the night, an' I says, – Arry, I ought ter call the doctor! But 'e's that obstinate! – I'm alright gal, 'e says. – Just git me, me pint a beer, an' I'll be fine!"

She stood talking to Mag a little longer, then, –

"I'll be orf nah then" and she went, leaving Mag to clear the tables of glasses.

Moving around the bar, she received the usual cheeky but harmless backchat from the male customers, especially the hardy seamen, standing knocking back the pints. They sometimes went a bit too far with their hands. – Couldn't keep them to themselves. But they got back what they deserved with the length of her tongue!

There was the time, when one of these Cheeky Charlies was told, what to do with the sprat to catch a mackerel he tried to give her, hoping to get something back in return.

It was a gift of a real silk scarf from one of his ports of call, but Mag saw his ulterior motive, – it stuck out a mile!

"No fanks!" She did not bandy her words, – "Yer know wot yer kin do wiv that nah! Yer kin stick it right where the monkey sticks 'is nuts!" Needless to say no other would be 'Lothario,' ever tried it on in future.

Mag looked up from drawing off a pint, – she'd heard Annie's name mentioned. It had only been about half an hour since she'd gone back off home with her jug of beer. This voice was saying, –

"Yers! She'd been gorn abart 10 minutes a so, that's all! But when she got back she farnd 'im layin' on the floor! 'E must 'ave 'ad a stroke or somefin'. They've taken 'im away. Annie's gorn wiv 'im. – I 'ope 'e's gonna be alright!"

Mag listened to this account of poor Annie's shocking discovery, with disbelief!

"'Ow is it that some fing so awful can 'appen as quickly as this! Poor Annie must be 'arf out of 'er mind wiv worry. – 'Er 'Arry is all she's got! – She may 'ave stood 'ere in this bar calling 'im all the bleedin' names under the sun, and complainin' of 'is corf, corf, corfin' all night! – But *that* is just anuvver way of showin', ow real close they are to each uvver. – Sounds daft, but its true!"

Something had been niggling at Mag for quite a long time. She'd felt uneasy at times and had quietly called herself, a few not very nice names. It was about Kate! Mag hardly ever saw her, but knew she was at home, as her milk bottle was taken in every morning. Kate never came outside and sat with them all, and entered into conversations with them and had a laugh. – It was sad, but on the other hand she shouldn't behave as if she was better than *them*.

She'd have to do something about this, and take the matter into her own hands.

Mag knocked at Kate's front door. – No, she wasn't being nosy or anything like that. – Maybe the poor woman can't help being like she is!

The door opened and Kate stood there, somewhat surprised to see Mag at first. Mag herself, was lost for words, and began to stammer, then blurting out, –

"Kate, are yer alright? We 'aven't seen yer abart fer a while. I 'ope yer don't mind me knockin', but I just fort yer may need somefin,' p'raps?"

Poor Mag, started to feel like a carraway seed cut in half, and wished she was somewhere else at that moment, and turned to go, – but Kate suddenly recovered her speech, and touched Mag's arm.

"No! – Don't go, – please come in!" and closed the front door after Mag had stepped inside.

"Come into the parlour," and showing her in, said, "Mag, please sit down," shifting the cat off the settee.

Mag didn't know where to start or where to look. But it took only a few minutes for her to take stock of Kate's immaculate parlour.

"Blimey, ain' it posh!" she thought.

"Would you like a cup of tea?" Kate asked. "I'll put the kettle on," and she went out into the kitchen.

"What am I doin' 'ere?" Mag thought, gingerly rubbing her hands across the plush velvet of the settee and the satin cushions. Looking at the pictures on the walls and the umpteen photos of who could only be Kate's dead husband.

A good-looking man in naval uniform. "Sad!" thought Mag and felt a little ashamed. She'd had Bert for all these years, and her three Herbs. It must be awful to be alone!

Kate came back in with a tray of tea and biscuits and set it down by Mag on a little cane table and starting to pour the tea, she said, – "Now how do you like your tea Mag? – Do you take sugar? – and – Help yourself to a biscuit!"

Mag fidgeted and had a tidy old job to stop from spilling the tea into her saucer. "Why had she thought of this hair brained idea," she said to herself. "What could they talk about?" that's what was worrying her now! Kate was sitting opposite Mag, sipping her tea. It looked like it was her best China tea service being used as well. Mag liked the pattern, all sorts of blue pictures, of Chinese pagodas or something or other and Willow trees.

"Must 'a cost 'er a bomb!" thought Mag.

"How is Bert and the children?" asked Kate. "I have seen them outside playing, – do you know I really envy you Maggie, I would have loved so much to have had children. One or two maybe, but it was not to be, so sad to say!"

Mag thought, "Strewth, she envies me? – Kate wiv all she's got 'ere! 'Ow can she?"

Kate got up from her chair, saying, "Would you mind if I showed you some photos of my Philip, – that was his name, he *was* a dear man!" She took down an Album from the bookshelf and proceeded to turn over the leaves.

"Here, come and sit beside me, you will see them better." Mag crossed over to sit with Kate feeling not quite so awkward now.

As Kate turned each page, showing with enormous pride, a photo of her husband in different poses. In uniform, in a dress suit, and an informal one of Philip with Kate, together. This one Kate sat holding some minutes longer than the previous ones. She was quiet now, she'd stopped speaking, and as she continued to gaze at the photo, Mag didn't like to look at Kate, she felt conscious of an awkward prolonged silence.

Suddenly, Kate burst into tears and felt for her handkerchief. – Poor Mag, she was really at a loss for words, – when Kate apologetically said, –

"Oh Mag! I am so sorry, I cannot help it! I do miss him so! Why do these horrible things, have to happen?"

"We were only married for a few weeks and we'd hardly had any time to be with each other!"

"Why did they take him away from me? Sometimes I feel I cannot stand it anymore, – Mag, I really can't!"

Maggie put her arms around Kate. It seemed strange and yet so easy now! And how sorry and ashamed of herself she felt, that for all these years, she'd been such a selfish bitch!

Poor Kate was living just next door, crying out for someone to understand what it was like to be left entirely alone. Mag had been self-righteous and oblivious to the fact that Kate really had a heart, with feelings, sad longings and beautiful memories that hurt. That was why she had got stuck into her everlasting dreary housework, shutting herself away from everyone else, feeling she would let herself down. – This now had to change!

"Come on nah Kate, let's go art and wash up these few tea fings. Show me yer nice kitchen. I bet it's much nicer than mine is eh? And yer must come in ter me next time fer a cuppa tea. – Did I 'ere yer say yes?

Kate looked up and gave a shy smile, and said, –

"I'd love to Maggie! Very much! Very much Indeed!"

It was a very happy and contented Mag, who sat that evening with Bert thinking over the happenings of that day.

She had lost Mavis, but had now gained Kate!

*   *   *

That was another one gone!

First it was 'Elsie's Frank,' and now 'Annie's 'Arry!'

It had been a needless waste of a young life when Frank copped it, but it was different with 'Arry,' – he had been ailing for a long while.

He never recovered from his stroke. Annie had sat by his bedside hoping and praying he would suddenly open his eyes and see her there. But no, –

"'Er 'Arry, 'e was nah at peace! So what could she do nah? – Life would be empty wivart 'im."

Never to hear him again plonking down the stairs and ducking his head, just missing the top of the doorframe! "An' 'is Corfin'?" – No more would she be able to moan her head off about, "'is Corf!"

Yes, Annie would 'miss 'er 'Arry,' a whole lot.

Someone said this in the pub that evening, –

"What shall we do towards 'elpin' Annie? I don' suppose she's got a lot a money ter pay fer the funeral."

"Let's get a collection up!" One of the blokes standing by the bar suggested.

"Too right," said another, "We've all known both of 'em, donkeys years, Annie an 'Arry. Come on, I vouch we start right nah!"

Although the bright sunshine, on this delightful Spring morning, belied the magnitude of the sadness showing on the faces of the mourners, behind the funeral cortegé, as it wended slowly along the little streets and byways on it's journey, to what was to be old 'Arry's last resting place.

Old Annie, Bless her heart, had no reason now to doubt the depth of sincerity and good neighbourliness that was being shown here, at her dear old 'Arry's final journey.

Maureen had been a mite shocked at the amount of money collected in the large glass bottle she'd had on her bar counter. In no time it had been practically half filled with donations and everyone had been more than generous. It was being shown now, by the floral tributes, and wreaths, on the coffin in the hearse that was now making its way from Annie's house.

It was being drawn by two raven black horses with black plumes and was a magnificent sight, – slow, majestic and quiet. The road had been strewn with straw, to muffle the sound of the horses' hooves on the cobbled stones.

Royalty could not have had a better send off. Many blinds were drawn in a show of respect, and men doffed their caps and stood silent until the hearse had passed.

And so Annie said goodbye to her 'Arry, but though she had lost her old man, Annie still had many, many friends.

Bert stumbled and knocked his shin against a stack of old books in the back of the Pawnshop. He cursed under his breath. "Ow the 'ell did they git there, – they wasn't there this mornin'!" This was the second time today he had walked into something stuck out where it shouldn't be, and was it all because he was in a hurry to get done early?

He expressly wanted to get the last of the bundles of pledges, brought in earlier that day, away and up on the shelves at the back of Percy's shop. It never ceased to amaze him, – the assortment of articles that the poorest residents around this area brought in, – just to get a few shillings. Enough to buy the barest necessities to put on their dinner table.

As well as clothes, suits, overcoats and footwear. There were clocks watches and Jewellery too. Bert stacked also, such items as sheets still damp, taken from the bed and washed and not quite dry, wrapped in newspaper and brought in to pawn. All kinds of musical instruments, bugles, mouth organs, accordions and he wouldn't have been surprised if some aspiring soul hadn't dragged along their old joanna down to pop it!

Today happened to be Mag's birthday and Bert was taking her to the pictures so he had to get a spurt on. A special treat was in store for her. Her favourites, Fred Astaire and Ginger Rogers in the film, 'Top Hat.' It amused Bert to witness Mag's starry-eyed fascination for their dancing. But even Bert had to admit, –

"They were good!"

It was lovely! – Mag was lost to the world for over two hours, sitting in her one-shilling and ninepenny seat, her eyes fixed on the screen, and for that space of time, it was *She* not Ginger, being twirled around in the arms of Fred Astaire and, – Oh what a perfect partner he was!

Coming out of the Cinema, Bert looked at Mag's face, – he squeezed her hand and smiled at the obvious pleasure that she showed.

"Did yer like it gal? No, don't tell me, I can see yer did. Come on, let's go an' git some Fish 'n Chips, the kids will still be up. Yers! We'll 'ave a slap up supper, – all of us."

Bert had guessed right, they were all awake, and full of beans. No way were they going to bed without being practically chased up there, and the argument that had been in full swing, as Bert and Mag walked in, was stopped dead in it's tracks.

"Carn' you lot be left alone fer five minutes, wivout startin' up a rah? Come on! Git some plates art, I got somefin' fer yer suppers!"

Chapter: Seven

It had been an unusually fine and warm Easter, and the populace around and about Brick Street had found good cause to drop in to the 'Crown' to wet *their own* whistles, sitting in and outside the pub. There, not just to chinwag and discuss the weather, but also to talk about another important topic of conversational interest.

The newspapers and radio of late, had been making much of the forth coming Silver Jubilee of King George V, and it had captured the imagination of the Winter weary, and in many cases, the dejected residents around, not only living in the surrounding district, but for much of the vast Docklands area.

The whole country would be celebrating in one way or another, so why not them? It had started to take hold, one evening in the Pub, someone with an eye to the future, leaning up against the bar, had lifted his glass and proposed a toast, in his thick slurring tipsy, boozy voice, –

"'Ershs ter the King, blesh 'is old cotton shocks, may yer be wiv ush fer a long time yet, yer maseshty!" and he meant it! That got Maureen thinking, she needed to talk to Mag, who was busy as usual attending to the needs of some burly seamen just off one of the boats. She waited till Mag was free, then broached the subject.

"That bloke just now, saying that about the old King's Jubilee, – It's set me thinking. It's time we thought about getting up a street party or something. What do you reckon Mag? Got any bright ideas?" ... And that's how it all got started. They had only a few weeks until May, so they would have to get cracking!

Mag let herself in the front door, and taking off her jacket hung it over the back of a chair. Putting the kettle on, she then started to peel some potatoes. She'd have to get a move on, – Jim and Jess would be in for their dinners soon. It would have to be egg and chips, that would be quickest.

She was all behind after a conflab she had with them, – 'The Committee' as they called themselves at the pub.

Discussing plans for the street party, had made her forget the time. It was really quite exciting, they were all taken up with it, and wanted to get started on the planning.

Jim was first to put his head round the back door,

"Lo' Mum!" Wot's fer dinner?"

"Ow no! Not eggs agin, I'll be sproutin' fevvers soon!"

"Yer'll eat wot I gives yer, sonny Jim! – Fink yerself lucky, yer got anyfing at all! There's lots round 'ere, who won't even git that!"

Jim sat down at the table just as Jess came in, and Mag could see by taking one look at her face, that something was on her mind.

"Nah, what's up gal? Yer look as if yer've got all the bloomin' trouble in the world!"

Jess didn't speak right away, but sat looking down onto her plate and making no attempt to eat. Mag had noticed, that for quite a while now, Jess had suddenly changed from a wild tearaway tomboy, all arms and legs and never still for five minutes, – to a now quieter, more calm and less excitable, young lady, Mag supposed!

She was growing up, well wasn't she?

"Mum!" Jess suddenly spoke, and looked up at her Mother, – "When kin I 'ave a new frock? A nice one, so 'as

I kin go ter Enid Smiff's party. All the uvver gels 'ave got nice new frocks. – Me Sund'y best's got ever ser old, an' it's too short fer me nah!"

Mag listened, and sighed, "Where?" she thought, could she rustle up enough money to get Jess another dress. Trouble is, the girl was growing so quickly now, and getting more clothes conscious. Jess couldn't any more, get away with somebody else's hand-me-downs.

It was nice seeing the kids growing up, but it was costing more and more to feed and clothe them!

"Don' worry gal, – I'll see wot I kin do. Nah eat yer dinner. – If yer don' eat, yer'll git ser fin, we *won't find* any frocks ter fit yer!"

Then Mag remembered that though up till now, she had shied away from such things as 'Provident Clubs' or 'Tally men' calling at her front door, the do or die way of life, that so many other poor devils, who lived in these streets had known. – Now it was finally a necessity.

And so it was, that Mag knocked at the door of Number Seven, Friendly Street, and right away it was opened by a woman, only Buxom would not be the right word to describe her, – She *was* more like the back of a bus!

"Yes, I am Mrs Broadbent." Mag was tickled. She certainly was something. Her name should have been Mrs Broadbeam! So this was the Provident Club Lady!

It was a quick transaction. Mag parted with half-a-crown and received vouchers, enough to buy the goods she needed. A frock for Jess and some trousers for Jim. There was no room left in the ones he had now, for any more patches, and there was a new pair of long socks for him, with red stripes round the tops. Now this was nice! Mag found she had enough left over to buy herself a sixpence three farthings pair of silk stockings. It had been a long while since she had managed that, – it was always Lisle stockings fer her!

Bert was asleep, dead to the world in his armchair by the open window, his face covered with the front and back pages of the News of the World, and as he breathed in, the paper went too!

It was Sunday afternoon, and Bert was sleeping off the couple of pints he'd had with his dinner. He felt he'd earned this nap he was having. It was all go down at the Pawnshop. No easy task humping parcels and boxes, plus outlandish articles, some of which, caused more than the raising of an eyebrow. Where Mr Percy found the room for all this conglomeration of impedimenta was nothing short of a minor miracle!

Mag was in her usual position at the sink washing up the Sunday dinner things. In more of a hurry this afternoon, as she wanted to get the place looking nice and tidy before Kate came in.

Mag had taken the bull by the horns and had invited Kate in to have tea with them.

Bert had brought in some winkles and shrimps off the bloke outside the 'Crown', (his regular pitch every Sunday) and although Mag was looking forward to it, she couldn't help feeling jittery.

Kate had been in once to have a cuppa with Mag, and it had gone down well.

"You have a nice house Mag, it's really cosy. I feel at home here," This had pleased Mag no end, but today the kids would be here,

"Blimey! I do 'ope they be'ave!"

"I believe Robin you are interested in joining the Navy, when you're old enough. Is that right?"

Rob, who had been sitting quietly reading his latest Biggle's yarn, looked up at Kate. Surprised it seemed, to having been spoken to by this neighbour whom he'd hardly ever noticed before.

"My husband was in the Navy you know. Like you, he found he was attracted to the Sea when he was your age."

Rob changed his opinion very quickly now, about this woman sitting opposite him. He had not been the least bit interested when his mother had said, Mrs Howard from next door was coming to tea. – To him, she could have been a fly on the wall!

"You will have to come and see some photos of the ship he was on, and of the places he has been to, in many parts of the world."

Kate had broken the ice. Then suddenly too, it seemed Jess took notice of Kate, – she liked the way she spoke, and had heard people speak like this in the pictures she saw at the Roxy on Saturday mornings.

Mag was very proud of the way her kids behaved. She never had any need to be worried, they had really surpassed themselves.

The afternoon passed favourably with a tea of winkles and shrimps, and slices of bread and *real* butter in honour of Kate's visit and she *had* caught the muffin man in time.

Jim amused himself and Kate too, in his usual arranging of the winkle hats, – all round the rim of his teaplate.

Mag sitting back in her chair, feeling a glow of satisfaction, and looking around at them all, asked herself again the question that had bugged her, ever since she had known Kate. Somehow she didn't seem to fit into this area of London at all! How did she ever come to live here in the first place?

Though Mag had never met Philip Howard, she was to learn later from Kate that his family had lived and worked in the Dockside area for many, many years. His parents had raised four sons in this part of the East end, enduring hardship and poverty, that ever seemed to be their lot!

Two of the boys had fallen foul of an epidemic of a severe tropical disease, brought back off the boats and had come to an untimely end, before they were sixteen.

That had not deterred Philip, who at his first opportunity had run away to sea at fourteen, and braving all odds had succeeded in reaching the rank of a Petty Officer.

In the first few months of the 1914-18 war he was assigned to a battleship and was sent to the Eastern Mediterranean.

He had only two spells of leave and during his first, at a gathering in London, at the house of another officer, he met Kate a young nurse. They immediately fell in love, and as it was in wartime, the couple made the most of their short time together. They were then married on his next leave.

Kate and Philip spent an idyllic four days, in a small farmhouse tucked away in the rolling countryside of Dorset, but then they had to part. Kate went back to her nursing in the Military Hospital on the South Coast, and her husband was recalled to his ship.

This was the last time they would see each other ever again, his ship was sunk in the Dardanelles, during the battle of Gallipoli in 1915. But Philip's roots had always been here, in the East End.

So Kate decided to go back to live in Wapping after the war as Philip would have wished. But mainly it was her own wish too, feeling she would be ever near to him, in the very house where he was born, which he loved, and the one she would come to love as well.

"Anuvver cuppa tea Kate?" asked Mag. "And 'ave yer 'ad enuf ter eat? – Go on 'ave anuvver muffin!"

Kate smiling, shook her head and said, –

"No thankyou Maggie, I have had quite sufficient," and looked across the table at Jim, who had been squirming about in his chair dying to get away from all this palaver.

He wasn't used to it, – "'avin' ter wash 'is 'ands, and makin' sure they was clean before he could sit at the table, and feelin' 'is muvver's eagle eye on 'im."

He was, – "'itchin' ter git art in that yard an' play wiv 'is five stones, or 'ave a go at makin' a cat-a-pult. – All the uvver kids 'ad one, – t'aint fair!"

"If yer've finished Jim, yer kin git darn nah," he was getting on Mag's nerves, screwing about there on his chair.

"Let's go in ter the front room Kate, shall we?" leaving poor Bert to do all the washing up.

Mag began to wind up the gramophone that had belonged to Bert's Mum, then put the record on of, – 'In a Monastery Garden,'– Funny, for all of a sudden the kids made themselves scarce! They would much rather be out there in their own garden!

"Do you know Maggie, it has been a very long while since I have enjoyed such a nice afternoon, like this one!"

Mag, suddenly felt so sad. Kate must have spent many a lonely day or dreary Sunday, stuck there in that house next door. Never mind tho', she thought, – not any more, – She'd see about that!

*　　*　　*

85

Bert was calling up the stairs, – "Time ter git up Mag! Yer said yer wanted me ter call yer!"

"Gor,' blimey Bert, – What time is it?" Jumping out of bed, Mag hurriedly put on an old woollen jacket over her nightgown, and went down into the kitchen.

There was a lot to do today, a lot for everybody to do! Wasn't it the day of the street party, everyone had planned and argued about for the past 3 weeks? Where it would be, and in which street?

They all wanted to do their bit, – I'll do this, – you can do that! There'd been a few who'd had to bite their tongue, – or bite the dust!

But it seemed it had all squared off and it was full steam ahead. It was to be outside the Pub in Brick Street.

Bunting had been put up a couple of days before, hoping there wouldn't be a tornado or something, to rip it all down again, – but no, it was still intact!

Maureen and Les had been offered some forms and tables from the Church Hall. So there was a job for some willing party to collect and assemble.

Mrs Miles from number 10, had made no bones about allowing her Piano to be dragged out, not without difficulty, into the road, and standing by it, an eagle-eyed sentry was put on guard, dispelling all thoughts of any unruly kids trying to knock hell out of it, when everybody's back was turned. Woe betide them!

All the groundwork had been done and now all that remained was the important part, – the food and drink. That lay in the capable hands of the ladies of the Committee.

While all this donkeywork was taking place, Mag prayed, – "Please, don't let it rain!" – It would be such a bitter disappointment for all, not just the kids but for the grown ups too. There was never much to brighten up their lives in this much maligned area of East London with the presence always of insufficiency and hopelessness.

Whatever little each of the families could spare out of their never flowing with milk and honey larders, – they pooled, plus some very acceptable goodies from down the road in Davis's corner shop.

Maureen came out from behind the saloon bar looking for Mag. "Oh there you are! I think we are almost done, don't you Mag? How are your poor feet? Mine are just about killing me! – You know, we've been on the go ever since after the Pub shut at two!"

"I'll 'ave ter pop back 'ome and see what the kids are up to an' then tart meself up. See yer later Maureen!" said Mag, and left her talking to some of the other locals and went off home.

If the old King George himself, could have been a spectator in Brick Street, outside the old 'Crown' that afternoon, he would have had no cause to be disappointed at the jocundity and the measure of rejoicing that was on show there, he would have joined in, no doubt!

Mrs Miles 'joanna', was bearing up well, with the trouncing it was receiving, with bountiful doses of 'Lily of Laguna,' 'Daisy, Daisy,' and no party would be complete, would it? – Without a good old, 'knees up Mother Brown!'

"Enjoyin' yerself luv,? – Ain't yer tired yet?"

Bert was having a hard time trying to keep track of Mag, who darted in and out among the merrymakers, helping Les, who had brought out and set up a barrel of beer, and drinks for the kids.

"Whatyer say Bert? – Can't 'ear yer!" she shouted back If Mag's feet ached, she was doing a good job ignoring the fact. It wasn't often something like this happened, – So enjoy it, she'd say. But, – "That was a day to remember that was, Bert love!" she did say, as he unlocked their front door. "Nah Jim, Jess, Up ter bed nah!" but they didn't need any prompting. Jim couldn't keep his eyes open. Rob was not long hitting the hay, he would not argue now, that he was grown up, all he wanted, – was his bed!

Now Rob knew the time had come, to make that journey across the river, to see what had become to him a shrine. – To Nelson, to Drake and to all those others he considered to be his heroes.

There was no work today, it was the Whitsun Bank Holiday Break. He called at Pete's, – he was at home kicking his heels, bored stiff.

"Yer doin' anyfing terday Pete? Fancy that trip over the river ter Greenwich. – I'm all for it! – Comin' wiv me?"

They set out for the Bus stop at which plainly stated the number of the Bus they needed, to reach their destination. – The entrance to the foot tunnel on the Isle of Dogs, which would take them to their goal, – Greenwich!

Rob, from the moment he'd set out that morning, he'd had great difficulty in keeping a tight rein on his extreme excitement, his eagerness to be sure, and to note every detail of what he might see when he got there.

It was one of those balmy late May days, with just a whispering breeze, as they jumped off the Bus and viewed with eager eyes, the lazy old River Thames, now showing a brighter countenance with the Sun shining upon it.

They couldn't wait to get to the entrance of the Tunnel, and began to step it out, feeling just a little sceptical, as it was hard to believe they were actually walking under the

River Thames! All that water that was up there! – tons and tons of it! – They gulped and started to walk quicker.

"I 'ope it don't spring a leak Pete! I wonder 'ow long this tunnel is?" Secretly Rob was wishing they were almost to the end of it.

They emerged into the bright sunshine once again, and took stock of their surroundings.

"It don't look much different to the uvver side, does it Pete?" as they started to walk towards what looked like a massive park, with large buildings. Palaces of some sort, they thought.

It was a grand sight! – That one there, it might be the Royal Naval College! Rob and Pete were overawed. They stood awhile looking through the railings, wondering what to do next, – when a voice, – it said,

"That's a fine building son, don't you think? They turned around to see a middle aged man, smiling down at them. "All these buildings you see here, have a story to tell. Museums of Naval History and tradition."

At first they both felt a little uncertain of this chap, – who was he?" They had been told not to talk to any strangers, though he seemed a nice enough old codger!

But they were not going to get into any dodgy situations and started to make their way towards a road leading to the commencement of a very steep hill, winding its way up to what they found must be the famous Royal Observatory!

"Yes it is Pete, we are 'ere, – Cor! der yer know, it's more 'n 260 years old? Built around the year 1675!"

Rob couldn't believe it. He was really here! He felt he was treading on hallowed ground, and what a view they had from this vantage point, – across the vast green expanse of grass and trees of Greenwich Park. From here, high up on this hill, they could see all the fine buildings that lay there below, gleaming white in the bright sunshine. The Naval College, the Museum, – thinking to himself, there must be lots about Nelson there, and the Seamens' Hospital. These buildings must have been Royal Palaces, centuries before.

"There's the river, Rob. An' yeah, – Look! I bet yer can see our 'ouses, across it there somewhere, among all those streets, – Cor! What a view. Ain't yer glad yer come?"

They suddenly realised they were hungry, and so sitting there on top of this high hill, looking over for miles around, they felt like Kings of the Castle, as they ate their fish paste sandwiches, and, – there was also an apple each!

Rob knew during these moments, what his future foretold, and that what he was feeling now, must have been how Nelson had felt, all those many years ago!

Both boys then lay back on the grass in the warm sunshine, each with their own thoughts. There would be no prizes for guessing what Rob's were, as he looked down the hill and across to where he knew Nelson's statue would be standing, and that was at the entrance to the Painted Hall, so he'd been told. He would give anything to be able to see it! But wishing was of no use! He sighed, –

"It's time we went 'ome Pete. – Come on, – I'll race yer down the 'ill!"

A bright sun pierced the worn net curtains at the bedroom window, and shone its rays across a bed in which a young girl lay sleeping. They seemed to be saying, –

"Come, – arise, – today is not one to be disregarded, – this day is *special!*"

Jess's eyelids flickered and then slowly opened. Blinking at the strong sunlight, she sat up and rubbed her eyes and wondered whether Rob and Jim were still fast asleep, it seemed nothing or nobody could wake them.

She suddenly had a feeling, – what was it? Something was different, – Then . . . . .

"Me Birfday, – it's me Birfday!"

"Yes. Today I am fourteen, I am grownup!" She jumped out of bed and hurried downstairs.

Mag was in the kitchen and as she heard Jess's footsteps, she turned and looked up. She grabbed a towel and wiping her hands, she cried: "Nah look who's 'ere! It's the birfday gal 'erself!"

"'Appy Birfday Jess luv!" After Maggie had given her a big hug and a special kiss, she took down from the dresser shelf a little package and gave it to Jess.

"'Tain't much gal, it's only a little present, but I 'ope yer like it. It's bin in my drawer for years."

Jess opened the box, which contained a small Cameo Brooch, which was decorated with pink rosebuds and wrapped in a silky handkerchief.

"That brooch belonged to your great-grandmother Jess. I fought yer would like it, – it's very old, – Yer'll look after it won't yer?"

"Ow! – Mum! – Course I will, it's luvverly!"

She was ever so pleased, and hugged her Mother tight and sat with it in her hand just looking at it.

"Nah yer fourteen, yer'll soon be leavin' school eh?" said Mag, looking wistfully at Jess. She couldn't help thinking, – it didn't seem very long ago, since she had held the small hand of a four-year-old Jessie, taking her along the highway to start school. A new phase and a new road to whatever may be in store for her! –

Mag sighed. "Pity kids 'ave ter grow up ser quick!"

"This won't do gal! – 'Ere I've made yer some porridge, git that darn yer. – Nah, 'ere comes the uvver two! No peace fer the wicked! – Yer'd better pull yer socks up Rob or yer'll be late fer work! – Ow! Stop wrigglin' Jim!"

"Gawd 'elp us Rob. What yer got on there? Is that the best shirt yer kin find? I fort I'd chucked that one away!"

"It was always like this every blessed mornin'!"

Mag sometimes wondered how her life would have been. – Say, if she hadn't met Bert or if she had been born into a rich family and had become the wife of a Lord or something, or maybe a film star! Now she was beginning to sound like Jess. She was always mooning about pretending to be can you believe it! A Ballet dancer trying to stand on her toes, pulling faces 'cos it hurt her ter do it.

"'Course it would, – Silly gal!"

"Still, Jess was no worse than her," Mag thought, –

She would like to be a lady and have servants to fetch and carry for her. "Oh! Well!" Mag sighed, and then picked up the bucket and went out and scrubbed the privy floor!

Jess might have had her dreams, of maybe becoming a Ballet Dancer, but deep down she knew really, –

"What bloomin' chance did she 'ave?" Her destiny lay more in standing behind a counter in a Woolworth's 'Everything for 6d. Store!' – or in one of them Department Stores, – If she was lucky!

Then she could find out the secret of those contraptions, where you puts your money in a pot thing and you pull the handle and it whizzes off, –

"Gawd knows where to, an' then it comes back agin, wiv the change! Bloomin' marvellous!"

She'd seen these and other fascinating gadgets when she'd gone to Whitechapel with her Mum for something or other. That was an idea! She'd liked the look of Whitechapel! There were more shops and it seemed there was plenty going on with a lot more life to be found than around her locality. Just streets and streets of houses and dark alleyways.

Maybe she'd try and find herself a job over there!

Jess, wanted to see even more of the world and what lay beyond the boundaries of Whitechapel and one day she vowed, she would go and see all the things she had only read about. *'St. Paul's Cathedral,' 'Buckingham Palace,'* and would even go in the *'Bloody Tower,'* which she could see if she looked up river from the Docks. But still keeping in her mind, all that she had built up. Her idealism and romanticism. It came as a shock, to discover it was no easy task to have it all fall into her lap, just like that!

Jess with her schoolmates, were going out into the real world working hard for a living. There would be no ready made cushy job at the snap of a finger. She was going to have to learn the hard way, as other young school leavers had found. To give Jess her due, she did not let the grass grow under her feet, but would have to take a few knocks before she eventually found, after much searching in shops and laundries, and then this factory making Army uniforms.

So keeping her fingers crossed, it was, "Start Monday lass," the gaffer had said. Jess was in. Her very first job!

Chapter: Eight

It had been one of those heavy, sultry, late Summer days with not a breath of air and the Pub had filled to capacity, on this hot Saturday evening.

Mag was finding it more and more difficult, to keep up with the demands of these thirsty Seamen, who stood clamouring for service around the bar, shouting their orders in loud, sometimes, even *rude* voices.

"Alright, alright," Mag shouted back, –

"Can't yer see I've only got one pair a 'ands? Yer'll all 'git served, so keep yer' air on!" she hollered over the din.

"Blimey Les, it's 'ot! I don't like this 'eat der you? She tried to make him hear, – but it was very difficult. He was doing his best, – like her, pulling pints as fast as he could.

"I reckon we're in fer a storm, don' you Les, I guess this 'eat's got ter this lot by the way they're goin' on!"

"Too true Mag, it sounds like a bloody bear garden in here. I don't know where they get their energy!"

At that moment Maureen came over from the Bottle and Jug, looking a bit harassed. She called across the bar, –

"Mag! Can you come here a minute, Annie wants to speak to you. Go on, I'll take over here."

"Wonder what she wants?" Mag thought, as she pushed past Maureen, and went to find Annie, – Dear faithful old Annie, She had been in and out of that Bottle and Jug bar, more times than she could count!

Mag couldn't think of one day that Annie's face hadn't appeared around that door, without her jug in her hand, saying, "Allo' Mag Luv, A Pint of Old and Mild fer me 'Arry!" Annie was waiting for Mag, standing there with her jug. She had still continued to come to the pub, but now for only half a pint! Ever since 'Arry died.

"'Ello Ann! – Yer wanted ter see me, – are yer alright, nothin' wrong I 'ope?" "No gal, I ain' alright. I've come ter tell yer, I'm leavin' Wappin' I can't cope no more! I'm goin' over ter live wiv me sister in 'Ornchurch."

Now she had never told Mag about any sister, as far as she knew, – Mag was puzzled!

"Yer didn't know abart ' er did yer?"

"We didn't git along, me an' 'er. Gert was too much of a flirt. – That's right, we called her that, Gert-the flirt!"

"Used ter row like mad, we did," said Annie,

"It all started when she tried ter git round my 'Arry, fought she could take 'im away from me."

"But she fought wrong didn't she?"

"I 'ad a bluddy great row wiv 'er, didn't I? So we moved away, an' came over 'ere ter Wappin' ter live."

Mag had said nothing, only listened, but wondered why now Annie had suddenly decided to return to Hornchurch!

Annie looked down her nose, guessing what Mag was thinking, she tried to explain, –

"Well Mag, I ain't what yer calls a young chicken no more, and nor's she! We bowf need, what we can give each uvver. That's, some 'elp, ter 'do what 'as ter be done aroun' the 'ouse, an' a bit a company as well."

"So's, we've called a truce, Mag."

Now all the while Annie had been talking, Mag had been hard put trying not to crack her face. – She really was a character that Annie! If all she had just told her came to pass, Mag would miss the old girl a great deal,

Why? – She was part of the Pub. Part of the furniture. She belonged here!

Everyone, not just Mag, would miss dear old Annie. Mag went back to the bar to Les, who seemed somehow to have dealt with the avalanche of customers that had descended on the 'Crown', for it had quietened down a lot. It stayed that way, "Fank Gawd!" – for a while.

She told Les about Annie's decision.

"I have not known her as long as you Mag, but every Pub seems to have one character who leaves their mark upon others, which never fades, and that could be your Annie, Mag!"

It was still as hot as blazes and Maggie couldn't wait for chucking out time.

She would go home and soak her poor 'plates a meat in some cold water,' she told herself, as she cleared away the glasses and folded the cloths over the pumps.

"Get off home Mag, we'll finish off here," said Maureen, – "You look all in."

"G'night then!" – Mag called out, as she went, shutting the door behind her. – "See yer termorrer." – Wasn't she glad to be on her way home at last!

It was uncommonly dark, she thought as she made her way up the road. The gas lamps flickered, giving scarcely enough light along these, it seemed more than usual darkened streets.

She couldn't ever remember feeling afraid to make her way back home alone, as she had done night after night for many years now. Bert had never been happy about it, and he had said so, more than once. "I don't like it Mag!"

She hurried along, quickening her steps. All she wanted to do now, was to get indoors.

"Don't be a fool!" – she told herself, after she had looked behind her a few times.

"G'night Missus!" Oh, wasn't she pleased to hear the sound of Bill's voice, – she felt better now, and knew she didn't have much farther to go.

She turned into the alley leading to her street, –

"Nearly home," she thought. – But then, – Mag was never to know what happened after that. She had screamed but no sound had come out! There was a tightness around her throat, and as she struggled to free herself from the fierce grip, kicking and rolling now upon the ground, an awful fear that she'd never experienced ever before, was upon her. Still she tried to scream, and again kicked out as hard as she could, but she felt herself being dragged along.

"I'm going to die," she thought. This was it! Her strength was going, then everything went pitch black. There was a gurgling sound and a moan and she knew no more.

Mag was aware of voices, sometimes fading, then returning. – There was a light, – it moved, – another voice. It was saying something, – her name, – Was it *her* name? – From afar it came, –

"Maggie!" then it faded away.

She heard it again, – "Maggie gal! Can yer 'ear me?" – It sounded like it was a voice she knew.

How tired she felt, she wanted to go back to where she had been. – Now there was that voice once more, –

"Maggie," It's me, – Bert, – Can yer 'ear me?"

"Oh! please Maggie, say somfin', darlin' Mag!"

She tried to swallow, but she couldn't, her throat hurt.

Opening her eyes slowly, she blinked at the light and little by little she could make out faint objects.

Then a face, it slowly took shape, – It was Bert, bending over her. He took her hand in his and gave her a smile.

Maggie tried to speak, but heard another voice, this time a woman's, – low and gentle, –

"Please leave us for a while Mr Hope. Your wife should be alright now. Yes, I'm sure she will. You may come back and sit with her later."

Bert went out again into the corridor and sat with his head in his hands, saying a quiet prayer of thanks. What an ordeal! Bert was not the type to cry, but oh, how he wanted to, sitting there alone, in that empty passage way.

His Maggie, was laying in that room, in pain!

All through some evil bastard, who had drunk himself out of his mind and had followed Mag home. If it had not been for Bill, the Dock's gatekeeper, who had sensed something was fishy, things could have been much worse!

He'd risked leaving his post, so sure was he that Mag was in some sort of danger from this undesirable unkempt looking individual, who had been seen hanging around here, for a few nights, definitely up to no good!

"The bugger was locked up nah, 'e'll get 'is just deserts, an' it serves 'im bluddy well right, – I 'ope they keeps 'im in there till 'e rots!

When Bert put his head around the door of the ward, his heart gave a leap, for he saw Mag looking a little brighter than when he had left her half an hour ago.

She managed a smile when she saw him coming towards her. "No, don' talk back luv. I'll do all the talkin', – That'll be a change nah, won't it?" – He saw a smile again.

"I can only stay a few minutes, the Matron says, – anyway, I got ter git off 'ome ter the kids, – they will be wonderin' – Don't worry, I'll be back soon luv!"

He patted Mag's hand, then bent and kissed her forehead. "I'm goin' nah, but I'll be 'ere termorrer luv, yer git a good night's sleep! Yer will won't yer nah? Yer gonna be alright, yer wait an' see!"

"G-night, me ol' darlin' I'll be orf nah!"

Bert hurried out of the ward, he did not want Maggie to see the tears that had welled up in his eyes. He took his handkerchief out of his pocket and blew his nose hard!

"Just you wait till I get hold a yer! – Yer bastard! – You, what done this ter my Maggie!

Bert was choked, but as he walked back into the house, he was composed, he couldn't let the kids see him any other way. – He told them, "I bin ter see yer Mum!"

"She's goin' ter be fine, so yer can go ter bed nah and yer not ter worry. Yer Mum sends yer all 'er love, and so go ter sleep nah, all a yer!"

They seemed satisfied, but Jess cried herself to sleep, so was not aware of Rob's and Jim's hidden tears!

Jess was putting the finishing touches to the table. She moved the cake dish and straightened a knife and then, – "That's better." she was satisfied at last!

She ran to the door, somebody was coming. "Rob, Jim, quick she's 'ere! – Mum's 'ere, – don't let 'er see us yet!"

It was a fragile, pale faced Maggie who walked into her front parlour that Sunday afternoon and looked around with surprise at what she saw.

A table laid with a white linen cloth, teacups and saucers on a tray. – "They are not mine!" She recognised them, – "They are Kate's!"

There were little cakes, and dainty sandwiches, *and* a vase of pink flowers too.

"Welcome 'ome Mum," and it was from then it seemed, an avalanche of arms, kisses, hugs, – Rob, Jess and Jim. – And who was this, now?

Kate herself, smiling and holding out her hand! –

"It's so nice to see you home again Mag. – We have all missed you. – Haven't we children?"

There was a chorus of, "Yers, Mum?" Then Jim's voice, "Nah kin I 'ave a cake?" It brought them all back, once again to reality.

Maggie was *more* than a little overwhelmed and could find no words to express her feelings, for more than a few minutes, – to see the show of affection and the care they had all put into this, her homecoming, and "Oh! how good it was to be home."

The memory of that awful night, she hoped would go away eventually, but it would be a long while before she lost the images, that had penetrated right into her mind. The face of that fiend, a beast in human form, leering at her, while he had his hands around her throat. Those cold piercing eyes! – She shuddered, – But she was safe now.

Her kids here, depended on her returning to full health and strength, and be their *'ol' Mum* once again. Mag knew she would never be able to repay Bill, the man who had saved her from an unknown fate. And she would be forever in debt to him, for life. – Yes, in more ways than one!

Her body may have been scarred and bruised, but Mag was not beaten. – Not by a long chalk, – She was made of sterner stuff than that!

It was a lovely afternoon they spent there all together. Bert gave her a smile every now and then, plainly showing how glad he was to have her back with them all, her brood and with Kate too. That was an extra special bonus!

Mag had been very touched to find Kate by her bedside, after one of those traumatic bouts of panic she'd experienced when she thought she was back there in that dark alleyway, and had woke up in a cold sweat. Feeling the touch of Kate's cool hand on her brow, and the soft words she had spoken to her.

"Maggie, it's alright, – you are quite safe now!" and Kate had sat with her, the whole afternoon. – "Why had she wasted so many years being so darned stupid, not understanding one little bit about Kate!"

"How's the Missus, Bert?" Mr Percy had come into the shop, as Bert was putting the last of the parcels up on the racks. Getting down from the steps he looked at his boss who was standing there with a concerned look and saying to him, "Yes Bert, it was a nasty business. The wife she agrees with me! – There are too many queer looking types around here nowadays. Don't know where they come from. But I'm dead sure we don't need 'em!"

Bert had been battling with his conscience all afternoon. It wasn't right that Maggie, after all that had happened, and the terrifying experience she'd been through, still seemed quite adamant that she was *not* packing up her job at the friendly old 'Crown!'

"No Bert, I can't! – I won't let Maureen and Les down. I'm not givin' up somefin' I like doin', and even more important. – It's the money, – We need it! – Just because of some drunken blighter, I'm OK nah! – So stop worryin,' will yer!"

"Alright! – If you want, yer can come and meet me as yer said yer would, after the pub shuts." So it looked as if Mag was going to have *her* way. She was a real hard nut, his Mag. Still he would most certainly see that nothing like it would ever happen again. He was sure of that!

"I'll swing fer the bastards first!"

Things returned to normal, as Christmas approached. The chill Autumn winds had seen off the last of the dead, once golden and bronzed leaves. But now, the indomitable pea-soupers had returned, and again was heard the sound of the familiar boom of the foghorn on the reaches of the old River out there.

Winter was on its way, not a nice thought, reflected Maggie as she put the last of the washing through the mangle, "No 'ope a gettin' it dry terday, she said to herself, "More wet clothes 'angin' around the fire guard!" and went back into the kitchen,

"Oh! Gawd Jess! Yer'll turn the milk sour with that look on yer face, try an' cheer up a bit!" Mag opened the larder door and looked in. "Not much there ter be 'appy abart," she thought, "Looks like bluddy Muvver Ubberd's!"

"Come on Jess, let's go up the Market, it'll do yer good, – sitting round 'ere nah, wiv a face as long as a fiddle!"

"There might be a job goin' up there fer yer!"

Jess pulled herself up out of the chair and put down the copy of the 'Picturegoer' she had been reading. At least she could lose herself for a while like this, imagining she was Carole Lombard or one of those uvver film stars, and she could fall in luv wiv Clark Gable. – Cor! 'E was nice! – (But most likely she'd finish up more like Zazu Pitts.)

"Ow alright Mum I'm comin!" – Yeh, maybe she'd strike lucky this time, wiv a job! That uvver one she'd 'ad 'adn't bin much cop. That miserable ol' harpy of a forewoman, 'ad 'ad it in fer 'er, ever since she'd caught 'er 'angin' out the time in the privvy! – Still, she'd never liked the job in the first place, sittin' there sewin' on, it must 'a bin, farsends a buttons on men's trowsis! Cor! wasn' she glad when she got the push. They'd 'ad ter find anuvver silly sod ter do it!

"Oh! Better not let me Mum know I swore, or me Dad'll knock me block off!"

Christmas had come around again and went by with Mag wondering where the years all go to? It was hard to keep track of the months. Though the excitement was still there, the opening of presents, after breakfast had all been cleared away. Still Mag felt something was changing, and not for the better.

Rob now, you could not expect him to believe in Father Christmas any more. All those tales of a bloke wiv a snowy white beard and scarlet cloak, shinning down a filthy chimney! – How come he never got a mark on him?

Still, it was nice to hang on to the old traditions, but Jim, he did and he didn't, – believe all that, one way or another, but he'd 'ang on a bit an' see!

'E was in no 'urry ter grow up, – 'E still liked ter git artside there in the streets and play till after dark wiv 'is mates, – plenty a time ter 'ave ter start gittin' up early an' go out ter work. – Blow that fer a lark!

Now Jess, – she was completely the opposite! She'd got into a nice little number down in the cutting room of a factory, which made ladies stylish underwear, along the Commercial Road.

Happy at last, especially as she had taken the eye of one of the lads in the factory, who had not been long in noticing this pert, pretty lass with the jaunty walk. He soon got to chatting her up and she'd learned his name was Steve.

So Mag, determined she would get her own way, was soon back at work in the Pub, knuckling down to it as if nothing had ever happened! She wanted to forget it, and told Maureen and Les so, too. "It's not going ter beat me," she said and wanted to hear no more of it. Bert, he bided his time, he didn't like it! But regular as clockwork, he was there on the dot, waiting at chucking out times, – Rain, blow, hail or snow, for his Maggie, his dear ol' Dutch! Stubborn as a mule, she may be!

Chapter: Nine

"Gawd, strike a bloomin light! Ain' it cold?" With teeth chattering and still half-asleep, Mag got out of bed and went downstairs. It was a bitter cold January morning, and the snow lay thick out there in the streets. The milkman was having a lot of trouble with his horse and cart and he was looking half frozen, poor bugger.

Mag turned on the wireless, as she filled the kettle for the tea. She always listened to the news, it was nice to know what went on beyond the fringes of Brody Street.

She caught the sound of mournful music, the announcer was speaking in low muffled tones, and Mag heard then the sad news that came over the air, – "The King is Dead." "Long live King Edward VIII." What a shame, only last year they had all been celebrating the Silver Jubilee, and now they had a new King!

"How very sad!" But she had to get the kids up out of bed, as the time was getting on. But Rob, he was already dressed and ready for work. Gobbling down a slice of toast she'd had done for him, and saying, "Bye Mum I'm orf!" – he gave her a kiss and went out, where he bumped into Pete, who too, was on his way to work. Skylarking about for a few moments with snowballs, they reached the corner where they then parted company.

"S'long Rob, – see yer in Church!" called Pete. Rob, as he continued on in the direction of Cable Street, realised how much he enjoyed his job at the box factory, but he'd overheard some of the lads there talking, and it had set him thinking, "Yer best ter keeps yer eyes open. I've 'erd tell, that once yer start askin' fer a rise, they gives yer the push, an' takes on anuvver school leaver. You take a look ararnd, – Yer don't see many lads 'ere, what gets much past 15. There's a lotta factories rarn' 'ere, what does this! Yer better watch art!"

This did not sound very comforting to Rob, who himself had thought of asking for a raise in pay. He had been there at this job, for almost a year now. To all appearances, and if what he'd heard was true, any day now he could be in for the chop!

It hadn't taken Mag long to settle back in to her job after her long vacation, as she called it. She missed Annie and the laughs, she'd quickly realised that, but it wasn't long before she found someone to take Annie's place.

A quiet Monday morning and Mag had just begun to clean out the four-ale bar, when the bar door burst open and it was some minutes after, Mag heard such a clatter, she thought it sounded as if someone had dropped the whole percussion section of an Orchestra in there. Startled, she looked up from her kneeling position on the floor ready to give it a good old scrub, when she saw the most peculiar and strikingly funny sight she'd see for a long time after.

A man, well! – She could just about make it out to be a man's form, when they had extricated him from the mass of musical instruments entangled around his prone figure.

The bloke, who turned out to be a one man band, complete from top to toe with a fiddle, mouth organ, piano accordion, drum, and cymbals tied between his elbows and knees, with bells on the heels of his shoes, that Mag thought, "Somewhere, – there must be a joanna!"

Feeling the need to wet his whistle, he'd literally, – dropped in to the pub. The soppy sod had tripped over the Welcome Mat! He was a sorry sight, and also one to make everyone there and even a ruddy rice pudden, laugh!

It needed something like this to liven up a miserable gloomy Monday morning, and when they'd all had a go at straightening him out, he received a well earned pint of the best beer on the house.

So Tommy Larkin made his debut into the lives of the folk around about these streets near the 'Crown and Anchor,' and became a famed character, – 'Well, he had arrived with a bang! Hadn't he?' and was destined to cause many more laughs. Mag, she couldn't stop giggling at the thought of it, for days after. She swore it was all done for her benefit, it helped to shake off the last of the cloud that had hung over her, and the memory of that fateful night.

That perisher was now locked away in prison and was, – "Good riddance ter bad rubbish!" said Mag!

"Mag, are you there?"

Looking up from the tiresome jobs of sorting out the whites from the coloureds, dirty clothes to put into the copper to boil, Mag heard Kate's voice from the other side of the garden wall calling to her.

"Yer, I'm 'ere Kate, whad'yer want me for?" she answered, and picking up her washing basket she went out into the backyard.

"Now Mag," said Kate, "I'd like to know if you would care to come over to the West End one day next week with me. I have some business there to attend to."

"You don't have to give me an answer right away, but I would like your company, very much."

"Blimey!" Mag's mouth had fallen open with surprise, and she nearly dropped the basket of washing. She wasn't expecting this.

"Well," she answered, "It's a case ov wever I kin git the time orf, yer see. I'll arst Maureen, but I carn' give yer 'n answer nah.

"I'll tell yer tomorrer Kate!"

"The West End, that's like bein' arst ter go ter the Norf Pole! Wasn't that near where the Queen lived?" It was around that way she was sure, she'd seen pictures of it!

It wasn't near Billingsgate, she knew, 'cos' that was the farthest she had ever been away from Wapping. Her old dad had been a fish Porter there in the Market, years ago. 'E'd wore a funny 'at, 'n 'e always smelled a fish. Still that was better 'n smellin' a beer, like a lotta 'er mates dads did.'

Now this had set off a new lot of problems for Mag, –

'What abart the kids, 'n what the 'ell could she wear? She'd really let 'erself in fer somefin' nah!'

Bert too, was in a meditative frame of mind, as he traipsed back home from the shop, along the cold alleyways. He shivered in his thin jacket, and pushed his good hand, which was like a dab of ice, down deeper into his trousers pocket.

Would it always be like this? Every day the same as the last, working like a Trojan to get enough to survive, and Mag too, who was slaving all the hours that God made.

Backwards and forwards to the Pub day in, day out, never a break. Stretching out the bits she got down the market, to cook and make a dinner for them, as well as making do, with clothes that came mostly from second hand stalls, – always someone else's left-offs!

They had been doing this same thing for years.

Why could he never afford to take his Mag out for a treat, – a break, – right away for a while?

He could have got a decent job, if it hadn't been for his gammy arm. And that was because he had got in the way of that Jerry shell, out there in the trenches, during the Battle of the Somme.

'There mus' be somefin' almighty wrong wiv their way a finkin,' – All those up there at the top. If it was left ter 'im, an' people like 'im rarnd 'ere, there'd be no need fer no more blasted wars!'

'Why? Yer didn' 'ave ter look far, ter see all a those poor devils standin' there in the bleedin' cold, tryin' ter sell boxes a matches, – an' beggin' even, – ter learn just what chuckin' shells an' fings at each uvver, 'ad done ter 'undreds a losers like them, an' 'im.'

'Wars! – Who starts these Wars? – If it wasn't fer the ord'nary likes ov 'im, an' farsends a poor sods, who were made ter go an' fight, against some uvver poor sods, – who never wanted no wars eiver!'

'It was a bluddy funny world!'

Then for a couple of years or so now, there had been rumblings of another sort. An effort to stir up more trouble, by a rabble-rouser named Oswald Mosley! It wasn't nice to read some of the things written in the papers either, about another upstart in a brown uniform, with scrubby hair slicked down on his forehead, and a dirty black patch under his nose, – name of Hitler!

'Where der they find 'em, – eh?'

There was the rattle of a key turning in the door.

"I'm 'ome Mag, – Gawd it ain' 'arf cold mate!"

"'Ere let's git in an' near the fire, gal!"

"What's fer tea? Bert flopped himself down in the armchair near the stove. Taking off his boots, he began rubbing the soles of his feet, chafing them back to life.

"Kids in?" he asked.

"Jim's upstairs, I give 'im a job ter do! I said, – Nah git up there *an'* clear *that* bedroom up! It's all *your* stuff there layin' abart! 'E's got the sulks nah, but 'e ain't comin' darn fer no tea, till 'e *does* clear it up!"

Bert smiled, he liked to watch Mag's face when she was in one of her Barney's. Ah! But she was a comely lass, his Mag, with her cheeks flushed with aggravation at Jim's show of opposition to her demands. And, as well, as it happened, she'd been standing all afternoon ironing, trying to break the back of the pile of clothes stacked high on a chair nearby. But it was more than likely, she had succeeded almost in breaking her own back instead!

Putting down the iron again on the hot stove and straightening herself up, Mag looked across at Bert, she waited a couple of seconds before suddenly blurting out, –

"Kate's arst me if I'd like ter go wiv 'er ter Regent Street. Well I fink that's where she said it was!"

"When's that then luv?" asked Bert.

"Next week, she says. – Well, what shall I tell 'er?"

Bert took a look up at Mag's expectant and hopeful expression, she was waiting eagerly for the answer to her difficult question.

"Well, – tell 'er yer'll go. That's what gal. You go, be a nice change fer yer!"

"Yer don' mind then Bert, but what abart the kids?"

"Oh! Gawd Blimey Mag! They can take care of themselves fer a coupla 'ours, – I'm sure. It ain' as if yer goin' ter the Norf Pole!"

Mag couldn't be off smiling at that remark. Funny, Bert should say the same as she did.

"The Norf Pole, – Daft weren't it?"

"Nah that deserves a nice cuppa eh? Bert Luv? An' nah, I got yer a luverly pair a Kippers fer yer tea, – so sit yerself darn there."

"Thanks luv, – Gis a kiss!" she said.

Mag was ready, – well almost. She took a final look at herself in the mirror, and "Hmm" she mused. Her one and only warm coat had been given a good brush, but it was a pity her hat didn't exactly match the coat. Gloves? She didn't possess any, so that was not a worry, but would Kate notice how down at heel her shoes were?

"Oh! They'll 'ave ter do," she decided and shutting her back gate as she went out, she went round and gave a nervous tap at Kate's half open door.

"Oh! Mag, do come in. I'm almost there. It seems we might be in luck with the weather. It's now stopped raining, – that's good!"

Kate observed with great interest, the expression changes on Mag's face. The wonder and amazement as the bus passed each well-known building on the journey through the City. The Monument, St Paul's Cathedral and on towards the Strand and Trafalgar Square.

Nearing Piccadilly Circus, Kate said, –

"This is where we will soon have to be getting off, and mind how you cross these roads. Now let's look at some of the lovely shops along here."

They had reached Regent Street, where Kate told Mag,

"Here is where most of the rich people buy all their nice clothes. Though we would never be able to pay, even for the bags they put them in!"

111

To Mag all this was just like being in a Wonderland, – she was bedazzled!

They halted a while and gazed in the immaculately dressed windows, showing off beautiful dresses, fur coats, jewellery. Priceless pearls and diamond rings. The amount of cash for each article there, just staggered Mag. To buy one even, would cost the earth.

Then Kate had to attend to her business, the reason in the first place for their visit, but after, she said,

"I know where I'll take you Mag."

They turned off Regent Street into an even busier road.

"So this is the famous Oxford Street!" and walking along the wide pavements, passing so many well-known shops, towards Marble Arch with Kate, it all seemed a wonderful dream!

"Here we are Mag. Shall we go in!"

Kate looked at the sign, "Maison Lyons," and her eyes boggled as they entered this striking establishment.

They were ushered to a table by a trimly dressed female in a black and white uniform dress. A crisp white starched apron and a white lace, black ribboned cap shaped like a coronet, on her head. – She looked just about perfect, and as Kate informed her, she was called a 'Nippy!'

Mag took a look around at the décor and gasped at glittering chandeliers, mirrors, rubber plants and slender palms, in the whole splendid interior of the huge rooms of 'Lyons Corner House.'

They were seated at a table, laid out with matching china and cutlery. There too, a little vase, in it a rose.

The Nippy brought them coffee, 'Real' coffee, not something that had come out of a bottle with the name 'CAMP' on it!

Cucumber sandwiches, and dainty pastries and jam, little fingers of toast with butter too, made a very tasteful and enjoyable choice.

Mag took an attentive look at some of the occupiers at other tables. They all looked reasonably dressed, some quite elegant! They made her feel all of a sudden, – dowdy! If she was that, Kate wasn't aware of it. She'd thought Mag looked very nice when she had knocked at her door first thing that morning.

Ever since Maggie had made the kind gesture, of calling on her, Kate's thoughts were much the same. How time had been wasted, and now Kate meant to make up for it.

Leaving the bustling activity of the restaurant, the rattle of cups and plates and the buzz of a multitude of voices, they went out once again into the crowds and turned towards the Hyde Park end of Oxford Street, passing the Regal Cinema near Marble Arch. The big film of the day then, as displayed on a giant billboard outside was, – "The Great Zeigfield," a spectacular film. "One day Mag, we will both come up and see a film in there." Kate told her.

Walking along Park Lane and looking across at Hyde Park and at the green trees and lovely landscape, she felt a little dampening of the spirits. All this and much more there was to see in this London of theirs, and yet not once had she and Bert, been able to find the money to bring their kids up here to see it all. And to think it was only a few short miles away from where they lived! It was sad.

So Bert was in for a real good earbashing with her account of her West End visit. Telling him of all she had experienced on her wonderful day out, and he smiling at every breathless description of all she had seen.

*   *   *

Bert, he was in a sprightly mood! He looked over at Mag, she as usual at the sink, wading through a daffy of washing up, (Where the heck does it all come from?).

He tip-toed across the kitchen and sidling up behind Mag, pulled the strings of her apron undone and put his arms around her waist! Running his lips then across the back of her neck, he nuzzled her ear.

Mag turned and gave him a shove, "Nah, 'ere! Yer kin stop that, the kids will see us!" she said, laughing at him.

"Kids! – What kids? – I can't see any, they've gone art."

"Well, they might come in!" and Mag wriggled free of his grasp.

"I don't know! We never really get a few minutes alone to ourselves," moaned Bert, and he cleared off out in to the back yard.

"Poor Bert," thought Mag, – "Avin' kids was lovely, but from there on, all time fer romance goes right art the winder. – But yer can't have both it seems."

She melted a little and drying her hands on her apron, she went out into the back yard. Bert was bending down and straightening up some plants that had been displaced and strewn all over the plot.

"Ow! That damned cat!" he moaned.

"Come on in Bert and stop wingin. Yer dinner's nearly ready. I've made a Toad in the 'ole, an' bring that mat in orf the fence, as yer come. I don't wanna find it arf way up the street with this 'ere bloomin' wind!"

"Sit yerself darn there luv," and putting her arms around him, she gave Bert a hefty kiss. His eyes brightened immediately and he made a grab for her, as she walked by.

"Oh! No's yer don't, – Gives yer 'n inch, 'n yer takes a bloomin' yard." Then with a laugh at his sudden glum look, she said, "Just you be patient me lad," and turning to look at him, – she gave him a huge wink.

"Yer know what you are, don't yer? – Yor a tormentin' 'ussy. I don' know why I married yer!" – Then a more sober look came over Bert's face.

"But I wouldn't 'ave anyone else, yer know that, – not fer all the tea in yor Lyons, Me ol' China!"

Jess opened the back door and called out "Anyone in?" as she took off her coat. She couldn't hear a sound, – Mum must be out somewhere, but couldn't be far, as there was a lovely fire in the kitchen range where the kettle was singing away merrily. It was a nice homely scene.

She looked up at the clock on the mantelpiece, the hands stood at a quarter past four.

Jess had come out early from the factory, – it usually kept going until five, but they'd all been let off home for some unknown reason. But she was not going to quibble about that!

There were hardly any occasions when she found the house empty, and Jess liked her own company, and valued some time on her own. Now she had a chance to listen to some nice music. So putting on the wireless, she sat back on a chair, with her feet up on another and listened to a Johann Strauss waltz tune.

Jess was off, – she imagined she was in one of them fine ballrooms, being whirled around in the arms of a dashing young officer, amidst many pairs of other beautifully dressed women and their handsome partners.

The orchestra was playing the 'Blue Danube' waltz, up there on the raised dais, among the potted palms, and under the soft, dimmed lights of the Chandeliers.

Jess and her beau, were lost in an enchanted fairyland of dreaming and dancing to the strains of this beautiful music.

Ahh! – She wished life could always, be like this.

"Jess! Turn that blasted rah down, yer can 'ear it 'arfway up the street, Gor Blimey! – Dunno what the bluddy neighbours must fink!"

Mag came into the kitchen, and put her shopping bag down on the table with a big sigh of relief.

"Put that kettle on, let's have a cuppa tea, I'm fit ter drop. I dunno! – Eiver I'm gittin old or somefin', but everyfin' seems ter git 'arder these days!"

"So that was that," thought Jess, her flight of fancy had been short and sweet, but it had been nice to get away, for even a short while to a dream world where there were no relief queues, no sickly children, no squalor or disease. Where you had a decent meal on your table, and when you could hold your head up with dignity, even if you had nothing but a hole in your pocket.

That day will come maybe. – Someday. ......

"Where yer bin Mum?" Jess asked.

"Nah yer know where I bin. – Darn the shops, gittin' sumink fer yer dinners!"

"Urry up wiv that tea gal, – I'm that dry, – I couldn' spit sixpence!"

"Look what I got yer though fer yer teas. Some 'errins. They got 'ard and soft roes, yer kin 'elp me flour 'em."

Jess was pleased, but she made sure that she turned her head away when Mag without any compunction whatsoever brought the sharp knife down, severing the head and tail of each herring from its body, with the skill of a lass whose father had worked in the fish trade most of his life. Then she gutted the fish without even batting an eyelid!

Jess shuddered.

Jim came bursting in the door, –

"Cor Mum, are they fer tea? Kin I 'ave the 'ard roes, Rob always gits 'em, taint fair!"

"Go an' wash yer 'ands Jim, an' stop whinin', yer'll git what I give yer."

Then the back door opened again and in came Rob, his face as long as a fiddle! Mag looked up from cutting up the bread for tea. She had bought a nice crusty cottage loaf from down the market. There again, was a fight as to who was going to have the biggest crusts.

"What's wrong wiv *you nah* Rob?" But she guessed what he was going to say.

"I dunno!" he let out a big sigh.

"As I expected Mum, they've given me the push. I knew it! Me mates told me, they don't keep yer on after a certain time. They couldn't care less Mum. Nah I gotta find anuvver job from somewhere."

Mag bit her lip, "Poor Rob!"

"'Ere sit darn lad. I got yer favourite! 'Errin's! Yer like the 'ard roes, don't yer?" – giving Jim a don't you dare say anything look.

"It never ends," Mag said, "Just one damn fing after anuvver, always somefin' ter worry abart."

The days began to get a little warmer. Spring was almost here. Mag, as she made her way through the streets to the Pub, thought to herself, "Why was it that Spring made yer feel ser much better?" It seemed to quicken the heart's pace and made all things feel a little bit easier.

But something must happen soon to cheer them up. All they got on the news was doom and gloom!

Unemployment was rife, especially in the North of England, – Shipyards were closing, the Jarrow march had achieved nothing, and now after George V's death, there were rumours surrounding the new King Edward!

But it was these advertisements that splashed out their new invention of labour saving, 'For the little woman.' The washing machine and the Vacuum cleaner.

This gave Mag the hump. Why didn't the bright designers of all these new contraptions, ever put themselves out to come down here, to the slum ridden East End, or a locality like it, to see what bloody hope there was for any poor hard-working and frustrated woman, who just had to carry on, and do what they had been doing for years.

"Git darn on yer knees and scrub the floors, wearin' art already callused 'ands an' knuckles, wiv only a ruddy scrubbin' brush, Sunlight Soap an' sum elbow grease!"

"Alright fer some," Mag thought, "These bright idiots should come 'ere and see the bug ridden flea pits we are livin' in. *We* 'ave ter use our blasted 'ands and almost break our backs. – It makes yer laugh, it does!"

"We ain't got no money for no soddin' machine, that does it all for yer!"

Rob still held on to the belief, that he *would* step on board one of those big ships, such as he saw every day of his life, living so close to the docks, and sail away down that wide river. When on days out with Pete, they'd sit by the waterfront, talking and conjuring up tales of far off lands that lay beyond their reach.

He noticed more and more, how the numbers of the many different races of people around here grew and grew. Foreign gentlemen in strange clothes, some with their hair in pigtails. They, he was told, were originally from China and lived over in Pennyfields. Limehouse, it was called. Some, they were Lascars, from the East, and there were Jews too, who had made their homes here in the East End and set up their different trades.

But now Rob, he wondered, would he ever make those journeys, across seas and oceans which were up till now unattainable to him.

He would though, and took an oath on it! But he still had to find a job here first, and soon! Mag, feeling concerned for Rob, spoke to Kate of it, telling her how he had his mind set on becoming a Sailor one day. But Kate had already gathered that, when Rob responded to all she told him about Philip, her husband.

She'd noticed his keenness, his curiosity over all things to do with Navy life. Kate wished she could help!

Pete, he had an idea! They were sitting by the river, throwing stones into the water, watching the ripples.

"Rob, we could git a bus ter North Woolwich one day. It's not far! Then we kin git on the Ferry and cross the river over ter the uvver side."

"Whacher talkin' abart! What we gonna use fer money, shirt buttons?" Rob had an idea this was another one of Pete's dopey brainwaves, but his mate persisted.

"Old on a minute stupid! Don'cher know, or 'aven't yer 'eard? It's free! Yer don' 'ave ter pay! Only the bus fare ter the pier an' that ain' a lot."

"Ow! Go on!" said Rob. "Yer talkin' art the back a yer neck!" But giving Pete the benefit of the doubt, –

"OK, I'll come wiv yer, an' we'll soon see if it's anuvver one a yer cock 'n bull stories or not!"

119

"Kin I come too?" asked Jim, peevishly when one day he overheard them making plans for their trip.

"No! Yer can't, – See! Yer ain't old enuf!"

That was always the answer, – poor Jim!

"Why do they 'ave ter treat me like a baby, I'm goin' on furteen nah, – it ain't fair!"

Pulling a face at them he cleared off, and shinning up the wall in the yard, he jumped over and down the other side, straight into the arms of Bob the Policeman!

"Whoa nah! Me young cock sparrer, – where d'yer fink yer orf ter? – Bob was tickled pink at the scared look on Jim's face.

"And I'd like ter know what yer bin doin'?"

"Please mister, I ain't done nuffin, 'onest! I was jus' goin' ter find me mate Dan."

"Go on then, git orf wiv yer, an' you mind old son, you'll break yer flippin' neck, jumpin' over that wall, one of these days." Jim then belted off up the street to find Dan, who, – with a face as long as his arm, was sitting on the kerbside, idly dropping stones down the drainhole. He looked up, and seeing Jim, his expression changed to one of sheer joy!

"Cor! Ain' I glad ter see you!" he said,

"Blimey! At least somebody needed his company!"

"Where shall we go Dan? Come on let's go over the Sandpits an' see what we kin find? Yer never knows. Cor, there could be a dead body buried in there!" he said, with all the vivid imagination of a twelve-year-old."

Mag hurried along the street, she was in a bit of a rush to get to work and turning the corner, she bumped into Mabel from across the road, – now, no longer limping, as she noticed.

"Ello! Mabel, – ain't seen yer ararnd fer a bit. 'Ow's the leg? Took a long time to mend it, didn' it? – Nasty eh?"

Mabel snorted, (well that was putting it mildly)

"Yer kin say that agin Mag! – Could a done wivart that 'appenin'! All 'cos a that soppy sod ov an' 'usband a mine. Daft as a box a dates, 'e is!" Then Mabel, she quietened her voice down a bit.

"Still, – I gotta say this, 'e's made up fer it yer know! I 'ain' 'ad ter do no 'owswork at all, the 'ole time I bin laid up in me bed!"

Maggie squeezed back the beginnings of a good laugh, with much difficulty, for as long as she'd had dealings with her neighbour, she'd known that housework and Mabel had absolutely nothing in common! Poor Will, her old man had done it all. Coming from a hard working, straight-forward family life style, his old Ma had told him many times, –

"She's just a lazy trollop! And, we warned yer lad, she'd be no good ter yer!"

"But yer didn't take no notice, did yer? Not at nobody, and look at where it got yer."

"Yer made yer bed, – Nah yer gotta lay on it!"

That was all the consolation he got from them. Poor William, but that wasn't to say he didn't get it from somewhere else!

Will, he had a little bit on the side, didn't he? By the name of Dolly, (he kept that well under his hat!).

She helped run a fried fish and chip shop over in Friendly Street, off the Highway, and Will was very partial, 'To a bit a fish 'n chips!'

Well, – 'Where there's a Will, there's always a way!'

But Mag couldn't waste any more time standing talking to Mabel she had to get off to the Pub.

Arriving a couple of minutes late, she met a very red nosed and sniffling Maureen, her cheeks very flushed, and with a rotten cold. – She did look in a bad way!

"Blimey, Maur, yer look like death warmed up!"

"Yes, I've been waiting for you Mag. Now I am going to have a lie down for a while. Can you and Les manage without me?"

"Yers, – Go on, luv. An' take a coupl'a Aspros an' git inter bed gal, we'll be OK! – I'll only give the floor a quick lick an' a promise terday."

And Mag, hoping the morning would be reasonably quiet, she was unfortunately in for a big disappointment. A couple of large freighters were in dock and the more than usual thirsty dockers and lightermen, appeared through the entrances of the 'Crown and Anchor,' as if just in from the Gobi desert! Gasping for their pint of brown, or in most cases, a tot of the old rum!

Mag didn't know, after the doors had shut at closing time, – 'Wever 'er 'ead, 'ad bin punched or bored!'

She had been like a cat on hot bricks! And to top it all. Who was it that had turned up there? – Tommy Larkin!

Alexander's Ragtime Band, all in one piece! It was just like a mad house! –

"'Ope Maureen had managed ter git some shuteye wiv that noisy lot,' – Some 'Opes!"

Chapter: Ten

The rumblings were getting louder. You couldn't pick up a newspaper, without the name Mosley and *Fascist* hitting you in the eye. Those who were intent on causing hatred and mayhem, along with Pacifists ignoring all the warning signs. Scraps of news still leaked through about King Edward VIII and a divorced woman called Mrs Simpson, so there was certainly plenty to keep the tongues wagging.

But life went on as usual in the streets around Mag and Bert's humble domicile and it was hard to believe that such things as the turmoil and unrest implemented by the rabble rousers was going on all around them. When all that the ordinary people only really cared about, was that the sun was shining, – 'It was Summer!' – A really and truly baking hot one too!

With the kids off school for their long, end of term Summer break, it was difficult to keep tempers from fraying, with them under your feet all day, – every day for nigh on six weeks.

Luckily, or unluckily, whichever way you chose to look at it, the sun brought the kids out in the roads and their shoes brought back into the houses, – melted Tar! That was unless the street was cobble stoned. Then there was hell to pay from Mum, with Tar everywhere you looked. Such were the glories of Summer!

Jess was on her way home from work, feeling both hot and clammy with perspiration. It had been like an oven there in the overcrowded and airless factory, and all she looked forward to now, was that maybe everyone would be out, so she could have a good soak in the long tin bath, that always hung on a nail outside on the lavatory door. But it would be too good to be true, to find she might get her wish. They would all be at home!

When they were young, Robin, Jim and Jess would have to put up with sharing the same bath water on bath nights, one after the other, that was until a few years back. Unfortunately the last one in, would find the water murky and almost cold! But now it was different, Jess was a young lady, and a very genteel young miss at that!

"Mum, I wish we 'ad a room, which we could barf in, like in some 'ouses I've seen in books. Must be nice Mum! A girl at work 'ad one, – a book I mean! – It showed a lot a new 'ouses that's bin built. It was not rarnd 'ere though. They all 'ad barfrooms in 'em. P'raps one day eh Mum, we can have a 'ouse like that?"

Mag listened to her speaking, with a lump in her throat, her Jess was no longer a girl, but on the way to becoming an attractive young lady, and now she had a boy friend too!

Steve and Jess made a good pair and seemed to have much in common.

"Don't worry luv, I'll see yer get yer barf later on, after they 'ave all gone up ter bed." That entailed the long tin bungalow bath being dragged in, and set in front of the kitchen range, naturally not in use now, and the bath being filled with jugs of hot water from the copper, and it was there, Jess laid and soaked herself to her hearts content!

A letter came. It was from Annie! – "Dear Mag, I'm thinking of coming over to see you and some of my old mates, I shall be staying at Bessie's a couple of days. You know old Bessie, she used to live next door to me, when I was back there."

Annie went on to say how she was well and "I look forward to seeing you Mag, I missed you gal. It ain't the same here in Hornchurch as dear old Wapping', – Not by a long chalk!"

So Annie was fine, and was coming back over soon, to see everyone! Mag felt a little guilty, that she had not kept in touch with her as she'd promised. The back door then opened and in came Bert. He looked kind of agitated, frowning as he spoke.

"I don't like it Mag, there's somefin' brewin'. Yer kin see it goin' on all around yer. I just bin talkin' ter Fred Ryan, an' 'e says there's trouble comin', you mark my words!"

"It's that feller Mosley! 'E's bin causin' unrest a lot ararnd different areas all over lately, but so far nobody's takin' a lotta notice of 'im an' 'is big talk!"

Mag could see Bert was quite concerned. Usually, he wasn't the one to listen to a lot of backchat as such.

"Ow! Come orf it nah, Bert 'Ope! It's just a lot a barmy ol' rumours. Yer shouldn' worry yerself abart it, maybe it's just only gossip."

"Alright lass, let's talk a somefin' else. Yeh! Somefin' like, "When 'm I gonna get a cuppa tea then?" giving Mag a kiss on the cheek. But Mag found she had a bone to pick with Bert, and handing him his tea, she sat down in a chair opposite him, and giving a very wry smile, she said,

"Tell me if I'm wrong Bert luv, but I seem ter remember askin' someone ter fetch me back some odds an' ends from the grocers shop."

"So! – Where are they then?"

Mag was tickled pink at the comical look of surprise and guilt on Bert's face. He looked exactly like a young Jim, who had been caught out for some misdemeanour.

But Bert, he was saved by the bell! When Rob came in the back door looking for something he, had forgotten! – Mag pounced on him instead. –

"Ah! – Just the one I wantid ter see!"

"Robbie! Come 'ere! – Nip darn the grocer's shop, an' git me these! 'Ere's a list a what I need. – It's not a lot!"

"Rob an' 'ere! – Don' let 'em palm yer orf agin wiv stale bread this time!" she said with a frown.

How that poor victim of circumstance, in other words Rob, wished he had not gone back indoors at that very moment, to look for something he could have managed without anyway!

But it was done, and scowling as he took the slip of paper with Mag's list of needs on it, he went off out through the back door.

"Sorry Pete!" he said to his chum outside, "I've got roped in ter goin' darn the flippin' shops on a' errand fer me Mum, – Shan't be long!"

So whatever it was they'd had up their sleeves, –

"It just 'ad ter wait awhile, – didn' it?"

"Les!" Maureen called from a crowded four ale Bar. "We need some help down here!"

It had turned out to be an unusually hot weekend, and the Pub was packed with many thirsty throats to quench.

"Alright!" Les shouted back from the other bar, "But I can't do much about it now, – I haven't got arms like an Octopus! Do your best love!" was the reply and he continued pulling pints as fast as he could.

The place was chock-a-block with Seamen off the colliers and cargo boats. In the spit and sawdust bar, it was shoulder to shoulder with many thirsty watermen.

Today was Sunday and to any person being 'proverbially let off the hook', there in the old 'Crown', – they found the bars full, of 'Wills Woodbine', and 'Capstan' cigarette smoke, – plus plenty of hot air!

From the other side of the bar, came some raucous singing of, 'If you were the only girl in the World', mingled with another rival bunch, singing, 'My Old Dutch'. You could hear them a mile off!

There would have been no need, if you as a complete stranger, had happened to be in that vicinity and was to ask a soppy question like, – "Are yer enjoyin' yer noggins, me ol' Cock Sparrers?" – You would have had an equally soppy answer!

Maggie pushed some damp strands of hair out of her eyes, and handed across the counter already swilling with beer, a brimming glass to a bleary eyed drunk, who was using the bar as a prop!

"Fanks gal" he said, "'As anyone ever told yer, what a sight fer sore eyes yer are?" – He hiccuped, then belched, and in a befuddled sozzled voice, he leaned over and caterwauled out at Mag, –

"If yooou were the ownly gal in the wowld. – Whoops, sorry darlin'! – An' Ieeee was the ownly. – Oh! Gaw' Blimey!" The drunk then hit the deck. – In other words he bit the sawdust floor. – The silly old sod went out like a light. He was gone for a Burton! Maggie raised her eyes up to the ceiling and let out a heavy sigh! She asked herself, –

"What is it wiv men, that makes 'em want ter see 'ow much beer they can drink all in a couple a 'ours, and then every ten minutes stagger out to the privvy an' make room for another belly full, – It beats me!"

"Ello Maggie!"

Mag shot round quickly, almost dropping the glass of beer she was holding.

That voice, she would know that familiar sound anywhere, and there with a big smile on her face stood Annie, her dear ol' Annie, standing in the doorway, – but *without* her jug!

"Ow are yer gal?" said Annie holding out her hand to Mag, who took hold of it and squeezed so hard, she felt Annie wince!

"It's good ter see yer Ann, when did yer git 'ere? But where is Bessie then?" she asked, looking around the bar.

"Ow, – She wouldn't come, she's cookin' a nice dinner. We got a bit a brisket down the Shades. I like a bit a rolled brisket. Don' you Mag?"

"Go down a treat that will gal!"

Mag thought Annie looked well.

"'Ow a fings? What's 'appenin' over in 'Ornchurch then Ann?" she asked, but it was noticeable the change that had came over Annie's face.

"Nah yer askin' Mag! Worst days work I ever done, goin' over there. I should a known better! We do nuffin' but git on one anuvver's nerves, – always fightin'."

"Nah I'm finkin' a comin' back 'ere again. Bessie says she'll 'ave me. I kin go an' stop over wiv 'er, she says, – be glad a me company." Mag beamed at this news.

"Nice Ann! – I'm ever ser glad. – We missed yer!"

"When are yer comin' back? – Soon I 'ope!"

Maggie had been taking stock of Annie as she spoke, noticing the old girl didn't seem to be as rumbustious as they had known her, but then the old warrior must be getting on, and could now be pushing eighty!

"Nah Mag, yer can give me, me usual, but I ain't got me ol' Jug! – It'll 'ave ter be a glass this time eh?"

It had been a real tonic to see Annie, Mag thought as she made her way home after closing time. Though she had never ever experienced such a hectic few hours. The noise and the heat had been unbearable and she now had a splitting headache!

But Mag found it much cooler and quite pleasant walking along by the river. The old Thames came to life, with the sun shining across the little waves being churned up by the few river craft there. A police boat went chugging by, and was it her imagination, or did she get a wave? The new watchman at the Dock gates called out a greeting, for it was now no longer Bill who stood there. He had been gone some time now, and his place taken by a newcomer, by the name of George.

I wonder if he knows what he has let himself in for, she thought, remembering poor Bill's bloody near frozen stiff effigy's in the many winters he had stood out there! And the number of times too, that she had said to herself, "Sooner 'im than me!"

Kate had popped round for a cup of tea, and as they sat in the kitchen, it again struck Mag, –

"It's a funny old life, ain' it?"

Here they were the two of them, jawing away, the best of friends, when it seemed only a little while back, they hadn't had two words to say to each other!

After they had spoken about the usual topics of conversation between two friends and neighbours, the weather, – the price of the daily loaf, – aches and pains and so forth, they were now on their second pot of tea.

"Mag!" Kate said, "What do you think of all the paper talk recently, or is it all propaganda?"

Maggie frowned and thinking to herself, "That's a new one on me, – proper, what?" but Kate went on, –

"All the talk about things happening out there in Germany with that war-mongering individual Hitler! And now this Oswald Mosley! Is there going to be another war? We have not yet got over the last one!"

But this was beyond Mag's way of thinking, she'd rather brush it aside, and preferred to talk of happier things.

"Wan' anuvver cuppa tea Kate?"

Mag's neighbour saw the warning signs, suddenly realising the implication. Rob was coming up to manhood and that must be going through Maggie's mind!"

"Did you hear George Formby on the Wireless last night Mag.? He is a fool, but you can't help laughing at him, can you?" Then she remembered, Mag had little chance of listening to such entertainment on the wireless as she was always working in the evenings.

There was all of a sudden the sound of the back door being flung open and young Jim came limping through from the yard.

"Mu'um! I fell over! – Me knees bleedin'!"

"Yer bin climbin' on that wall again?" Mag cried out.

"I dunno! It beats me! 'Ow many times 'ave I got ter say it? – Keep orf the bluddy fing! – I shan't tell yer *no* more!"

Kate smiled at all this malarkey, but thought, –

"This must be all part and parcel of having Children!"

Chapter Eleven

The months simply flew by, the Autumn passing with early snows and hard frosts, plus the usual crop of coughs and colds. Bert had brought home the Flu' bug from somewhere, which went through the house like a dose of salts, with the sound of snuffling and coughing, eased only at intervals with the tablespoonful or two of 'Galloways' cough syrup and packets of soothing 'Zubes'.

Poor Mag! It was always left to Mum as usual to render service whenever possible, irrespective of how she was doing her very best, to hold her own head up.

Still, they survived, you just had to get on with it, so they said! But there had been *some* breaks in the clouds.

Rob had found a job, as near to being on his beloved ships as he could get. A factory making ship sails!

No matter, – he could maybe conjure up some pictures in his mind, that one of those great canvas sails would be blowing *him* in a mighty schooner across the high seas. Maybe going far away to some Eastern land. All a dream! – But a very nice one.

Jess, she dreamed too, but not any more of being a ballet dancer. That was much too far-fetched and not for the likes of her. 'It was just like prayin' fer the moon!'

No, Jess was settled nicely in her job in the clothing factory. In amongst rows of womens' delicate and fancy undies, satin petticoats, silky nighties, ready on hangers for the wardrobes and chests of drawers belonging to the elegant looking ladies she saw in the glossy magazines.

But these were not for the likes of Jess. She could only hope it could be, – one day!

She wouldn't say no to a raise in her wages though, they were a little too tight on the pay there at the factory. Then she could give Mum a bit more.

Jess and Steve had been together a fair old while now, and as they would have it, were only friends, they said.

But recently, while walking and looking in department store windows, up the Whitechapel Road at such tastefully set out furniture and homeware, meant to catch the eye of any prospective bride to be, it did make Jess think!

'Idiot! I'm just bein' stupid, that's a long way off!'

She blushed a little at her thoughts. But it stayed with her all day, the thrill of sometime becoming a married lady!

Mag was having a quiet half-hour, sitting on her own in the kitchen, a half-empty tea cup in her hand. She was staring up at a photograph on the mantelpiece. It was of Bert, dressed as a soldier, in khaki uniform with a peaked cap, puttees and a big smile.

The picture had been taken while on leave from France in 1916 before he'd been wounded.

A good-looking man Bert. Mag had been proud to be seen with him, parading him before her workmates from the matchbox factory.

She'd been just about the happiest girl in Wapping when he had popped the question!

It hadn't been easy, seeing him off on the troop train, on a cold bleak grey morning, with so many other sad faced wives and sweethearts, saying goodbye, full of wondering and dreading the inevitable.

Maybe it might be their turn next!

But, – "Please God, – No!"

Then the awful day she had received the dreaded news of his terrible wounds, and later his discharge.

But no matter what, Mag knew she now had her dear Bert home once again, and hoped, she could help to blot out the memory of the trenches. The mud and the stench. The hideous smell of Death that hung around everywhere.

She believed and felt sure, that having the three babies when they had come along, as they did, one after the other, that most if not all of Bert's nightmare had been eradicated.

Robin, Jess and Jim, thank God had been gifts sent from Heaven, Bless them.

Then, – "Mu-um", –

It was Jim, he'd just come in from afternoon school.

"Oh! dear, – Nah what?" –

Mag's reverie had been sadly terminated.

"Mum!" Jim tried again, "Kin I 'ave some long trowsis?"

"These make me look silly! They're too short fer me, 'an me knees get cold an' all!"

" What's the matter wiv yer lad, – d'yer wanna grow up more quick than yer are already?" Mag sighed.

Once more, Jim tried, – "All the uvver boys in our class 'as got long trowsis," he moaned.

"I dunno!" Though Mag *did* know! Jim was right. She had to admit he was growin' up and so quick too, it was no use her ignoring *that* fact any longer. Her Jim, was definitely not her baby anymore. It showed too, – for as she put her hand out, to give him a pat on the head, Jim this time, he avoided the gesture, – (She must remember, – not to do *that* any more!)

"Alright then, we won't worry abart that, just nah, Jim, will we?"

"We will see if we can go up the Whitechapel Market on Saturday. Maybe we can sort somefink out, eh?"

On the other hand, she could go round and see Mrs Broadbeam! – She smiled to herself, –

('If I was 'er, I'd change me bloomin' name!')

"Maybe I kin git a Provident cheque orf 'er!" –

Mag then looked at Jim's glum expression, and softened a bit. Digging in her purse, she said.

"Ow! 'ere, – go an' git some sweets, 'ere's a penny, – 'an don't spend it all at once!"

Jim was out of that back door like a shot out of a gun, –

It didn't take much to make him happy!

"Ow! Well! No peace fer the wicked!" her quiet half-hour had gone up the spout! Now it was time she found something for their teas.

Then the thought flashed through her mind, –

"Whoever invented eatin'?" It was always, –

"What we gonna 'ave for dinner or tea?"

Wouldn't it be nice if she could just press a button, and a trim parlour maid would appear saying, –

"Dinner is served in the dining-room, – My Lady!" and she, Mag, would sail across the hall, like Lady Muck and sit down on her chair at the head of the long banqueting table, and look around at her guests who were waiting for her to say Grace.

Then Mag, on giving the butler a nod, –

'The big nosh up would begin!'

First, – Soup and Fish, then, –

Pheasant, followed by Peach Melba, – finishing with, – Cheese and Biscuits, –

"Coffee? – White or Black madam?"

"Blimey! – Where am I? Soppy ha'porth!"

For Mag had been suddenly plummeted back to earth with Bert's voice calling out, –

"I'm 'ome, Maggie luv, – I'm 'ungry!

What yer got fer me tea?"

'Dear ol' Bert, 'ow could yer ever git peeved wiv 'im? 'E was a real luv, 'er ol' mate.'

"Comin' luv, – 'Ow's yer day bin? Sit darn there, an' I'll make yer a nice cuppa."

She gave him a peck on the cheek as she passed him by, but she wasn't quick enough to escape Bert grabbing hold of her, and pulling her down on to his knee.

This time there were no kids around, so for a while the thought of what they wanted to have for tea went right out of the window!

"D'yer know somethin' Mag, – yer still the bonny lass I married, all those years ago."

"Hey! – Nark it!" said Maggie,

"Watchit nah! It ain't bin that long, – though it may seem like it sometimes."

"We got a lot ter look forward to, you an' me, me ol' luv. It's gonna be a mighty sight better nah there's a bit more money comin' in, what wiv the kids startin' work."

Then Mag remembered something.

"Ow! While I fink ov it, young Jim wants some long trowsis. – 'E says 'is knees git cold!"

Bert laughed, –

"Jim! – 'Im in long 'uns, – I can't believe it!"

"Ah! Well! It looks as if before we know it, you 'n me we'll be a right ol' Darby 'n Joan, eh? Mate?"

Mag rubbed her cheek against Bert's now stubbly chin.

"Do yer know what Bert, me ol' darlin,' that sounds pretty nice, – don't yer fink?"

He replied by giving her a long lengthy kiss, which for just a few moments, almost made Maggie forget all about anything to do with eating!

But it was too good to last it seemed. There was the sound of footsteps, someone running. The garden gate opened and was shut with a bang, and Jim came flying up the path in the yard and nearly fell in the back door.

"Dad, – dad" he was shouting," 'ere there's ever such a fight goin' on somewhere, me mates say, – It's over in Cable Street an' – but Jim didn't finish what he was saying as Bert got hold of him by the scruff of his neck and yanked him in the door.

"They are what?" he shouted, –

"What yer doin' over there?"

"No 'onest Dad, I ain't bin there, it's jus' everyone's talkin' abart it. There's P'licemen an' all an' some of 'em are on 'orses! – People are shoutin' an' frowin' all sorts a fings at the P'lice."

Bert gripped hold of Jim's arm and pushed him through into the kitchen and slammed the door.

"Nah listen ter me you. – Keep away from goin' anywhere near that place, I'm tellin' yer nah, or yer'll git a bluddy good 'idin', – Der yer 'ear me?"

But Jim, he heard, he didn't need telling twice. He'd got the message alright!

Though he had been hoping to see a bit of the fun along with his mate Dan, but now he thought better of it!

"'E didn't want no 'idin', – a good one, or a bad!

Bert, he sat himself down and picked up the newspaper. But it seemed that everywhere you looked now, it was the same news splashed all over the front pages.

"What's the world comin' to?"

There was this upstart Mosley, causing all that rumpus, "An' nah 'e's darn 'ere in the East End, tryin' ter git support fer 'is gang ov anarchists, – The perisher!"

It did not sound too inspiring on the whole and, –

What now? – Everyone said when the news broke of King Edward's surprisingly short reign coming to an abrupt end. The papers had a *ball* about his abdicating in order to marry his Mrs Simpson, – A Divorcee!!

It caused an uproar. And so, – Was it to be now a new King and Queen maybe?

Then it was Christmas and once again as Mag reminded Kate, –

"Time flies ser fast, yer can't keep up wiv it, can yer?"

But as nice as it was, it would have been made much more enjoyable, if there'd been a few extra pennies to spare. For Maggie had hardly ever been in the position to buy something really nice for Bert, and vice-versa. Things like this only happened in a Hollywood movie. Though it had never really worried Mag, – No, not one little bit! And after all, this time it turned out to be especially pleasing as Kate had also spent it with them.

Kate brought in a chicken to roast, and also a plum pudding and Mag could safely say when it was all over, – That this was the best Christmas dinner they had ever had!

Jim, – he wore a paper hat he'd found in a cracker, and Hey-ho! There was a tin whistle too!

"'Ow, fer Gawd's sake Jim, I fink yer bin blowin' that fing long enough. –

"I'm askin' yer. – Nah pack it up! – Will yer?"

But Bert should have saved his breath. – It was like water, running off a duck's back!

So, 'A Christmas to remember', they all agreed, but they couldn't help wondering, What had 1937 in store for them?

Jim swaggered up to meet Dan, full of the joys of Spring, in his new long trousers. – One of his most wanted Christmas presents! It was their first day back at school after the long break. Jim felt like a King!

"I shan't say anyfin', I'll see if 'e notices," as Dan, he was lucky, he'd had his first pair of long trousers for his birthday last October! Dan's family seemed to be a bit better off than his, "But I bet 'e ain' got a pair a Boxin' gloves like me!" he said to himself.

He had Kate to thank for these, he hadn't recovered yet from finding this prize in his stocking.

Since Jim had discovered the identity of the donor of the gloves, his mood towards Kate had changed from one of apathy, to nigh-on reverence!

So now, – "When I grows up, I'm gonna be a boxer, jus' like Jackie 'Kid' Berg." I'm damn sure a that Dan!"

"D'yer know 'e was a pro' when he was only 15! They called 'im 'The Whitechapel Whirlwind! I bet yer didn' know that, did yer? He fought in America too!"

"Yer must be mad, – I wouldn't want *my* 'ead bashed in! I'm gonna be 'n engine driver, an' drive a train, like I went ter Margit in last year. Cor! Yer should a sin the size a that engin', I fink it was the Flyin' Scotchman Jim, yer!"

Dan was full of scorn at Jim's choice, but his new long trousers did in the end meet with Dan's approval, much to Jim's satisfaction.

"'Ere d'yer want this Fag card a Jack 'Obbs the cricketer, Dan?"

* * *

Now It didn't seem five minutes, since the old King George's Silver Jubilee celebrations, and here it was, exactly two years later, that there again was much excitement and planning going on, for yet another great Royal occasion. The Coronation!

It had been the general topic in the Bars of the 'Crown and Anchor' for weeks ahead. The jollification and enjoyment of the Silver Jubilee Party was still fresh in the minds of the residents in and around Brick Street and everyone agreed it was nonsensical to change the site of the Coronation Street Party. It would take place outside the Pub, to the great delight of all concerned.

"Mag" called Kate, from out in her garden one morning,

"I want you for a moment. You can say no if you have other plans for the big day, I have a suggestion to make to you, I know Jess and Rob may have their day cut and dried, but it's Jim. Would he like to go and see the procession with me, – if that is, – we can get near enough!"

As Mag listened, she couldn't help being a little surprised at Kate's handsome offer, it was very big hearted of her. Kate went on, –

"I too, would so much like to see it, but I'd hardly enjoy standing there watching it on my own."

Kate understood Mag could not be with them, she was needed at the Pub, – which was such a pity!

"Maybe Jim would like to bring along one of his young friends," Kate offered, –

If anything, all these preparations for the Coronation festivities would temporarily take peoples minds off the thoughts of war, which seemed now certain and Mag for one, was finding it very distressing and worrying, but determined as ever to keep her mind on her job and her home and not think of something that, – "Please God, would never happen!"

It was too awful to contemplate.

"Jim, ain't yer nearly ready yet? Come on don't keep 'em waitin'! – Dan's 'ere!"

"Ow Kate!" – Mag said, as her friend came in the back door. "Sit down a minit."

"That Jim, I dunno what 'e's doin' upstairs, but 'e's worse than a bloomin' girl, getting' 'imself all tarted up!"

Then there was such a noise as Jim then came clumping down the stairs. There was silence for a minute or two, while Mag just blinked, then gulped!

Running her eyes over the sheepish looking lad standing in the doorway, she smiled, yet trying not to bring attention to the fact, she could see Jim must have been at Robbie's Brylcreem! So thick was his Barnet Fair, now slicked down flat with greasy pomade all over, that to Maggie a picture came to her mind, of an undersized short arse member of the Al Capone gang!

Jim just stood there shifting from one foot to the other, until Kate came to his rescue. "Well, I must say you look very nice Jim, I think we had better be getting along, though, don't you? Ready Dan, let's go, eh?"

As Mag watched them disappear around the corner, she felt a little envious, but she had a job to do, and guessed rightly there was to be a very hectic day ahead, and if any prizes were to be given away for the best dressed and decorated street, for a good way around there, it most certainly would have gone to theirs. And the party itself?

Remembering the previous celebrations of two years before, with what it was now, it could not be equalled!

For one thing, they had the added attraction of Tommy Larkin and his Jazz band. He literally provided the whole of the background music, (that's if you could hear him over the cacophony of voices), – 'My old Man said Foller the Band.' Mixed with and drowned by 'I'm forever Blowin' Bubbles' by opposing sides. Helped along by the Pearly Kings and Queens. Bless their pearly buttons!

Maureen and Jess aided gallantly by Mag and Bert, each deserved a putty medal for their verve, dash and patience, trying to dance attendance on everyone there.

"Have you ever seen anything like it?" said Les.

"Nah! an' I don't fink we ever will again. Me feet are nigh worn darn ter me ankles," said Maggie.

"But I wish it was time fer 'em all ter sing 'Show me the way ter go 'ome!'"

The house was in darkness when they did arrive there. Everyone appeared to be in bed, too tired to give his or her own colourful experiences of a very eventful day!

But that was to come! For almost at the crack of dawn, it began with Jim's account of all he had seen, – standing, by lucky chance, – with a kerbside view of the whole procession along the Mall, not far from the Palace.

"Cor! Mum, – Dad yer orter sin it!"

"We see'd this gold coach, wiv the King an' Queen in it, an' a lot a soljers in crazy 'ats. – It looked like they 'ad black cats on their 'eads!"

" 'Ow could they a seen where they was goin?"

"I know!" – Jim he said then, with his mind quite definitely and completely made up, –

"That's it!"

"I'm gonna be a soljer when I git's old enuf!"

Chapter: Twelve

Now Mag, she was taking a shine to popping up the Whitechapel Market on this sunny very warm afternoon. In her purse a few shillings, tucked away, which was never a usual occurrence on a Wednesday. But she had managed to stretch the housekeeping money out a little further this week with a bit of help from Gladys across the road. Her old man Wally had an allotment over the brickfields.

"Ow abart these coupla lettuces fer the kids tea Mag and there's a few tomaters too." She could not ignore this offer, now could she? "Every little helps," as the Donkey said, when he dribbled in the sea!

With a slice or two of Cornbeef and a bit of Pan Yan, – very nice! Thankyou very much!!

Walking past some shops in the High Road pausing every so often to gaze into a window, she found time didn't seem to matter.

She was in no rush, Jim was going round Dan's house after school and the others wouldn't be in till teatime.

"Nah that looks nice!" Mag had noticed a little oval table with spindly legs, among a whole assortment of second hand furniture and bric-a-brac on show out on the pavement, in front of this shop, – absolutely crammed with junk of all kinds.

This kind of emporium was like a carrot being dangled in front of a horse's nose. Mag absolutely loved browsing. That table there would be just right for tea and cakes in the parlour, when Kate came in. – Then she saw the price!

"Four pounds, ten shillings. Blimey! That was more than Bert got for nearly three week's work at Percys!

"Daylight robbery!" She hurried by quickly. But the money was now burning a hole in her pocket. She just had to buy something nice to take home.

She stood on the edge of the pavement waiting to cross the busy road, when a couple of people passed her by. Both were busy arguing, – going at it hammer and tongs, – evidently man and wife!

The woman, who, built like the Eiffel Tower, was nagging the man, who just about reached up to her over-sized chest. Poor bugger!

She could almost make mincemeat of him! What a contrast to the way she and Bert behaved.

"Ah! – I know!"– Her mind was made up. She would go home now, taking in some Fish and chips and maybe some hot Doughnuts from Kessels the Bakers! This *would* be a nice surprise for a Wednesday.

After getting off the bus, she decided to walk the rest of the way, back along by the river. It would be cooler there, with the fresh breezes coming up the Thames.

Feeling quite hot, Maggie took her time. Some Dockers who had just knocked off work were walking towards her. One hailed her, calling out, "'Ello darlin'!"

Mag gave them a smile, a friendly lot most of them, these dockers. Yet, there were some that did get a bit too near the knuckle as she had learned the hard way, while working there at the old Pub, but on the whole, she had nothing but admiration and respect for the bloody hard way they worked.

Mag's shopping bag was bulging with the fish and chips when she arrived back home. The bloke in the chippy must have been in a very generous mood, as she reckoned she had enough here to feed the five thousand!

"Ello me 'ol' China!" It was Bert, as he opened the front door, he'd seen her coming along the road.

"Ow Gawd Bert, – yer in! – What's the time?"

She had been out longer than she thought.

"That smells good luv!" Bert said, getting a whiff of the fish and chips.

"Better put 'em in the oven, eh? The kids ain't in yet!"

But just then Jess who was first to arrive home, came in the door like a whirlwind, and rushing past Mag, she almost flew upstairs.

"Hey! What's the matter Jess?" called Mag.

But Bert said, "Leave her alone, yer know what a watery 'ead she is, we'll soon find art."

Mag, now she couldn't do that! Up the stairs she went to find Jess, who had flung herself face down on the bed and was crying her eyes out!

"Ow Gawd Jess, nuffing is worf all that fuss."

"Tell us, – what's wrong gal!"

A few minutes went by, before Jess turned a wet, tear stained face towards her mother.

"Ow Mum, me an' Steve 'ave ad a row. 'E don' wanna go art wiv me no more!" and off she went in another flood of tears.

Mag then thought of her own teenage years, and how many times her own Mother had gone through the same thing with her and the string of boy friends she'd rowed with and chucked up before she met Bert.

Time then, seemed to be one long heartache, pining over her lost loves, but she could only laugh about it now!

"Come on nah gal, it ain't the end of the world."

"Are yer sure 'e meant it?"

"Anyway there's plenty more fish in the Sea!"

"That reminds me, come on down nah, *our* fish is gittin' cold. Dry yer eyes. 'Ere y'ar, 'ere's 'n 'anky.

Bert gave a sideways glance at Jess as she came into the kitchen, but said nothing. He had learned a long time ago that the least said, was soonest mended.

He had never understood the workings of a woman's mind, for no matter what you said, – it was always wrong!

"Wot's the matter wiv 'er?" Jim asked, spotting Jess's red rimmed and swollen eyes, but all he got was a sharp kick from under the table by Rob.

How glad Rob was, he hadn't got himself tied up with girls. – Friends! – Yes, but he wasn't gonna risk anything stopping him from getting into the Navy as soon as he 'bloomin' well could!' and it wouldn't be long now, – he was nearly eighteen!

There were other events now which were causing more discussions on the street corners, all talking in low tones wherever people gathered. The topic was always the same, with anxious looks on their faces and sidelong glances at the growing number of people in uniform.

Was this more than just a rumour. War! They had only just got over the last one!

After a few more weeks, they said Gas masks were being made ready, and air raid shelters were being made.

Maggie didn't like it, – she tried not to listen and put her mind to more cheerful things.

Rob had now reached his eighteenth birthday, a fine tall and strapping lad, all of six feet in his socks! Though he had never got around to taking the much planned trip on the ferryboat to Woolwich, and doubted it would ever come to pass, as much more disquieting things were happening elsewhere. All the plans he and Pete had made when they were otherwise occupied, tear arsing round the alleys and back streets of Wappin,' never reached materialisation as they had got past the ripe old age of fifteen.

There seemed to be more important and novel issues on their minds. In Pete's case, – Girls!

But with Rob it was different, he knew without a shadow of a doubt, that he would be on one of those ships, like he'd seen every day of his short life. Sailing down from the Pool of London, heading for the open sea, and by hook or by crook, – He would do it!

It occurred to Mag, that a very eventful couple of years were now on their way out.

So much had happened, and not for the good either. The terrible Crystal Palace fire. She had been horrified, seeing it's glow from all those miles away, it was awesome!

Then the unbelievable news coming out over the air from Germany. There was that nasty piece of work Hitler, – what was he up to? It made Mag worry when she watched the newsreels at the pictures. –

Where was it all going to lead?

At least it seemed to be OK on the home front.

Jess had got over her feeling of rejection. – It had not been the end of the world after all, Mag noticed, as she summed it all up. Jess was growing up fast, becoming more and more worldly wise and had aspirations of becoming a Land Army Girl. If or when War did come!

Then it would give her the opportunity maybe, to discover the countryside, something she had always hoped she could do.

But young Jim, – although, according to him, *not* so young, he would be entering the real world, with a job soon. He was leaving school! What would he do? She wondered. He hadn't a clue, but she had overheard Jim and Dan chewing over what they may become and had to laugh. That Neville Chamberlain would have to look to his laurels, for, if all Jim planned came to pass, he would have a rival for his job, –

An undersized rival, but a very determined one, and for a short space of time, Jim had to put on hold his becoming a boxer, or a Soljer. –

"He would be a Prime Minister! Yer, that's it!"

Now Bert, on hearing of this mind boggling piece of news, just raised his eyebrows and giving his summing up of it, in a despairing tone of voice, remarked, –

"Gawd 'elp us all!"

Maggie put down the iron, and hung the last pieces she had done, over the already full clotheshorse and put it around the fireplace.

"Thank Gawd that's done. When the kids were young there was always a pile a washin' to bung in the copper, but it was a damned sight worse now. What on earf do they do to make so much washin'" she thought.

"I know Lady Jane." meaning Jess of course, "Is forever tartin' 'erself up ter go an' meet 'er Reg. Wait till she gits kids of 'er own, she won't be so fond a changin' this, an' changin' that, when she 'as ter do 'er own washin."

Then Mag was stopped in her tracks. She had been listening to the wireless as she ironed the clothes.

"What was this the announcer was saying nah?"

"Children were to be fitted for gas masks!!"

She couldn't believe what she was hearing!

"Ow My Gawd!" and there she had been moaning about stupid things, like the washin'.

"Shut yer marf, – yer ought ter be ashamed!"

Not thinking, she picked up the iron quick. –

"Bugger it. It was still 'ot!"

"Serves yer right. Pack up moanin'!"

It was the topic that was on everyone's lips, and that evening, all you heard was War, Gas Masks! Sand bags around Buildings of importance, the War Office, – Parliament, etc.

"Had the world gone mad?"

Les came across to Mag, as she stood solemnly behind the bar pulling pints for the dozen or so customers, some with quite puckered brows, puffing away at their pipes.

"What do you think of all this Mag? – this war mongering. You'd imagine they'd have had enough of the last one. A lot of these here must have been in that other great shambles."

"I dunno Les" she answered. "I can't understand, I never will, why people want ter be at one anuvver's froats, wantin' what someone else 'as got, instead a bein' satisfied wiv wot they do 'ave. – Beats me Les, – It does really!"

"Yes Tom! – What do you want mate?" – Said Les as Tommy Larkin came over for his half time drink during the interval.

"Don't know what you think of this idea but seeing as how everyone seems to be right browned off lately, we could do something to cheer us all up."

"Such as, – Tom?" Les looked at Mag's face, she'd perked up a bit now.

"Let's have it, what do you suggest?" he said smiling.

Tommy looked a little bit abashed, perhaps his idea wasn't so bright!

He then blurted out his brainwave.

"Why don't we have a Talent Competition, I've noticed a few of the locals here have quite good voices."

Les again looked over at Mag, what did she think of this hare brained suggestion!

He had mixed feelings, but Maggie wasn't so hasty to pooh-pooh this.

"'Old on Les, – it don't sound such a bad idea!"

"What d'yer say we put it ter the committee." She said with a laugh.

"Committee! – What committee?" he asked.

"Don't worry, we'll soon find one!" said Mag, thinking of a few well-known faces around. Sal, for one, – she'd be top of the list. You could hear her voice over all the others, when there was anything to be discussed in the pub.

"She'd be good on the Jury at the Old Bailey!" Then there were the Casey twins, never to be seen without each other, and, Charlie Cook, too?

Old Charlie was a character, well known to all. He had been on the boats all his life. He could tell a few tales of the times he'd been called out to help fish out a dead body from the Thames, with the rowing boat he owned, or on other occasions when a suspicious looking object was floating in the water near one of the bridges.

So one by one, names were put forward or eliminated, as the case may be.

"Yes," – Les agreed in the end, it might be a mighty nice idea. Take everyone's minds off the blasted dreary news!

So all this prompted a big talking point for the customers and residents of a few streets around.

Les, good with his pen and paint, made first class posters, which were placed in prominent positions, one inside and one outside the Pub.

No one could possibly miss this invitation to enter and qualify for the Super Duper prize of an engraved Silver Tankard, or in the case of the ladies, – A Rose Bowl.

HAVE YOU A VOICE LIKE GRACIE FIELDS?
– Only, Ladies May Apply! –

OR CAN YOU SING LIKE BING?
– Or groan like him? –

Put your name down right now. Don't miss the Boat!
Or the Fun, and a free pint of our Best Bitter!
Seek out our Maggie for more Information.

Maggie woke up with a start, she had been dreaming, but as it is in most cases it went clean out of her head what it was all about.

But what she did know was, –

"It's Jim's first day at 'is job." He was starting work today. Her baby, the last one of the litter was now on the threshold of life. – The hard part, but if he were lucky, her Jim would find it a great adventure. There was no reason why he shouldn't!

Jim seemed to have something the other two hadn't, – staying power and he'd had a few chips knocked off his shoulders. As the odd one out, he'd learned the hard way.

Jim didn't have very far to walk to his job, so there was to be no, – Come on 'Urry up nah!" and she certainly had

150

the surprise of her life to find, as she came from her bedroom down the stairs, Jim! She didn't believe it! – He was already washed and dressed! He smiled at his Mum, waiting for her to give him a pat on the back for his show of enthusiasm.

The lucky man, Jim's new Boss, was the Baker in the next street to theirs. His name !!!

Mr Ernie Cakebread! Now that was a laugh. He couldn't have been anything else but a Baker, with a name like that. – Now could he?

It was almost as satirical as the name over the shop of the fishmonger up Friendly Street which was, C. E. Shore! Jim's job was to take round to Ernie's many customers, their bread and cakes by the means of a byke. Now that had caused a lot of controversy when Mag found out. Still in her mind was the memory of Robbie and the Wapping Meat Products saga. Though luckily there *was* a difference.

Jim's magisterial conveyance was a lot less cumbersome than Rob's had been. Likewise his appearance differed, as he came into the kitchen, beaming all over his face at the end of his first day's work. It was one of satisfaction, not just to himself, but to Mag and Bert who had been on thorns waiting for the Rover's return.

So for the rest of the evening, they were to be regaled with every blessed detail, of the first day in Jim's life as a Baker's boy!

As a foot note, – Mag reaped the benefit by many a bag of stale buns and cakes being brought home most evenings, by Jim, – via Mr. Ernie Cakebread and his kind gestures. What a contrast he was to Mr Cyril Snelling and his establishment, the scene of Rob's first mishap.

Jim! – It seemed he had struck gold!

Chapter: Thirteen

A newcomer, chancing to come upon the scenes in the bars of the 'Crown and Anchor' this particular evening, he would have found himself getting involved too in the preparations that were leading up to the big event everyone was eagerly awaiting.

The atmosphere there was thick with cigarette smoke, and the sounds of the clink of glasses, plus the many shrieks of laughter and singing.

Maybe the owners of the voices were getting in trim for their big debut in the Talent Competition which was due to start at 8.30 p.m., – in about fifteen minutes time.

Maureen, face flushed, was pouring out a gin and tonic for Mabel, who now was completely recovered from her broken leg, and had decided she'd like to show her doubting neighbours what a good voice she had.

"Good crowd we have here, Mabel, seems it could be a success, – I do hope so," said Maureen.

"Whose idea was this, do yer know?" Mabel asked.

"Don't know why nobody never fort of it, before nah!"

"Can I have everybody's attention please!"

Everything went quiet as Les announced his intention of opening the competition with a little speech, – he began, –

"I just want to say that Maureen and I thank you for proving to us, in the short time we have been here, the true meaning of being an East Ender! That is, – showing fortitude and determination, – having thought for others worse off than you. Who can always put on a bold front in the face of adversity, and in truth, to sum up, has true grit, and GUTS! But Blimey! You happen to get on the wrong side of them, – Phew! – You'd better watch out!"

"In Short Ladies and Gentlemen, – there is no other place where we would rather be!" That comment brought forth a hearty round of clapping, – they all liked Maureen and Les, a popular couple.

"And now let's get on with the Show," Les finished his speech and one by one he introduced the nervous contestants.

"First, – We have here Effie, – she has a little ditty, – (laughter all round). – Now listen," he said, – "Be fair!"

In fits and starts poor Effie manages to get through her little ditty without too much hassle from the boisterous audience, who were now getting hotted up with the aid of a drop of the old tiddly!

Then it was Paddy's turn with his spoons and Alice was next, with her impersonation of Nellie Wallace, – she was good and yet very embarrassed at the warmth of the applause. – She blushed and returned thankfully to her seat.

There was much hilarity at Mr Percy, – the Pawnbroker of all people, taking off Geôrge Rôbey, – eyebrows an' all, but the highlight of the whole evening's competition, – the star turn, – Who was it?

"Our Mabel!"

There wasn't a dry eye in the house as she ended her rendering of 'Macushla,' followed by another tear-jerker "Just a Song at Twilight." For rendering was exactly the right word for it. Her voice, – poor old Mabel's, it practically tore you apart!

Sheer torture, would not be too unkind a word to describe it from start to finish.

The tears that flowed freely after that brilliant performance, were of laughter and not of emotion, accompanied by much applause for Mabel's courage, in daring all!"

For "She Who Dares Wins!" although she didn't merit her Rose Bowl, everyone agreed that our Mabel rightly deserved a bloody medal for her nerve!

Needless to say, after much debating, – that it was to be Nellie Wallace who blushingly took the coveted trophy from Tommy Larkin, who presented Alice with the prize and a whopping great Kiss.

Though this splendid evening's entertainment did much to take their minds off the news and the continuing gloom for a few hours, it was still there hanging over everyone like a huge grey cloud.

"Fancy a trip with me over to Club Row on Sunday morning Maggie? It's not far on the Bus."

Mag looked up from her kneeling position on the bar floor, and putting down her scrubbing brush for a minute, she pulled back that obstinate strand of hair, that would persist in hanging over her eyes, –

"'S'no use, – I must git me 'air cut!" she thought.

Maureen carried on saying, –

"I have been meaning to go there and see what its like, hearing such a lot about it."

She told Mag how much she wanted another canary.

"I used to have one when I lived over in Peckham, but it died Mag, just before we came away you know."

"I did miss him!"

So come Sunday, found both Mag and Maureen gazing at the motley of caged birds lined along the pavements, all for sale, and lines of stalls, selling all kinds of bird seed and pigeon food.

Mag was taken up by the amount of livestock there, in Sclater Street, and spent time looking at some puppies among the pet stalls.

"Maureen, 'ere look at this. Jus', look at their faces!"

One puppy especially, he looked up at Mag, so appealing, almost saying, –

"Please take me home with you!"

How she would have loved to pick him up and push him down inside her coat and take him back to the kids.

No! It was hopeless, it couldn't be done.

Maureen saw the look on Mag's face, and before she could say Jack Robinson, Mag found herself holding this soft bundle of white fur, with a pair of the most velvety brown eyes that looked up at her as much as to say, Please! She had never felt so maternally tender towards such a small helpless being. Not since she had held her own newly born babies in her arms.

"Thanks Maureen,'E's luvverly, – but I can't 'ave him."

"Mag!" interrupting her hastily, Maureen said, –

"Why can't you? The kids'll love him!" She was pleased as Punch and happy to be the one to cause the look of pleasure on Mag's face as she received the puppy as a gift. Then Maureen, a little bashful, turned quickly to go back towards her birdcages. It was not long after, when they boarded the bus to return home, satisfactorily laden with, one birdcage, occupied by a beautiful yellow canary, not so happily singing for a while, as he was wondering maybe, where the hell he was off to this time. – And of course, a very subdued puppy dog being held very tight, by a contented yet a little apprehensive Maggie.

Though she didn't have long to wonder, for Mag knew what the outcome would be.

They were all at home, so when she did eventually undo the latch of the back door, and went in, it seemed she was again back in Club Row! The reception she received was a mixture of, –

"Oohs! and Ahs!" and, "Ain't he sweet, Let's 'old 'im!" – and "What's 'is name?" as they clapped eyes on the little white furry bundle.

The poor pup didn't know, – 'Wot 'ad 'it 'im!'– Jess couldn't wait to have her turn at holding him, –

"Is 'e really goin' ter be ours Mum?"

"What shall we call 'im?"

Maggie, giving out her orders then, to them all, – with the welfare of the puppy in mind, warned them, –

"Nah, its not a toy, so its up ter you, ter treat 'im proper, or back it goes. – Right?"

"So nah, let's fink ov a name to call the little luv, – eh?"

"Let's all fink!"

"Snowball? – Yeh! We'll call 'im Snowy fer short."

Hands in his pockets, Rob was strolling along by the river. He had reached Wapping Old Stairs.

Deep in thought, he sat there alone, his eyes taking in all the sights and sounds of this vast, bustling industrious area of activity.

He watched the battle of the cranes, – dipping, and swinging, – each shifting the heavy loads of cargo, the produce and lifeblood of the masses. – For the citizens of this land, – the millions, rich and poor alike.

About half a dozen red-sailed barges went by, up river towards Tower Bridge. Maybe they were empty, but it would be in no time at all before they were back heading down river, towards the open sea.

Filled perhaps with rubbish of all kinds. Waste paper, rags, muck by the ton, from peoples dustbins.

Rob watched as the rivercraft went by, always on the move, yet he was stuck here, just looking! Would he never get his foot up on the gangway, to board one of these ships he could see there?

Be it large or small, he wouldn't care, just so long as he could feel the motion and heart beat of the ship, coming from deep down in the Engine Room.

To stand in the quiet of night looking up at the stars in a velvet sky. Heading out East and maybe towards the land of the Rising Sun.

Rob sighed a big long sigh and pulled himself up, to continue walking, this time off home. They could be wondering where he was! He'd be back just in time, and ready for his Sunday dinner, now realising he was hungry.

"Wonder what we've got fer dinner," he thought, –

"Maybe it will be, I know! – Roast Beef and Yorkshire Pud. – Hmm! Some 'Opes! (Though you were in for a big surprise,) Rob boy." He realised that, when he walked up the garden path, to undo the latch of the back door. As a most appetising aroma reached his nostrils.

He walked into the kitchen and found them all ready and waiting for him to sit down. And what was this, his mother was putting in front of him?

"My Mum must be a genius. How does she do it?"

There it was, – Roast Beef and Yorkshire Pudding! Mind you, it was only a small bit of Top side, but it was still Beef.' And then Mag gave them all the explanation of how this miracle had come to pass, saying, –

"Nah! If yer a wonderin', where I got it from, all a yer, let me tell yer, I ain't robbed a bank or nuffin' like that. You 'ave Kate to fank fer this dinner."

"Let's call it a present, eh?" said Maggie, and she then went on to say, –

"Mrs Howard nah. She's what I calls a very nice lady. So no more talkin, – git on wiv yer dinners!"

"Yer know Mag, – this old Lane seems ter git more an' more busier every time I comes darn 'ere." said Flora, quickly side-stepping a veggie porter, who with a basket of cauliflowers on his head, was only interested in getting his stock of vegetables topped up on his stall.

"Sorry Lidy!" apologising as he tipped the basket of greenstuff on to the empty space.

It was a particularly busy afternoon as the holiday weekend was near and Mag, with her mother, who was down on one of her very rare visits, had taken a bus to Wentworth Street Market. Not a place Mag was able to journey to, as much as she would like, but Flora, was determined they'd go this afternoon.

Mag had never lost the guilty feeling that she was neglecting her mother, so had backtracked a little. She'd try and make this visit a nice one. Though her mother was not exactly a lonely recluse. Far from it! She had a man friend, so she told Mag, who she'd met a year ago on an outing to Southend with the Darby and Joan Club. That had let Mag off the hook quite a bit.

"So when's the old battleaxe coming then?" Bert asked wryly, when told of her impending visit, and the time had come too, to have the usual performance from the kids when they were informed their Gran was coming.

Mag waited for it. But got her spoke in first. She then looked around at them all managing to tell them before they cleared off out.

"Nah listen 'ere you lot, I want no argy-bargy see! – No pullin' faces. You're grown up nah, – So yer gotta understand. We don' pick our parents, and though we don't always agree with 'em, we do respect 'em!"

"Rob, – get yer nose out 'a that comic book, an' listen ter me fer a minit, an' you Jess, yer'll 'ave ter mind yer P's and Q's, when Gran comes!"

Mag then turned round to Jim, who looked as if butter wouldn't melt in his mouth, waiting to hear his orders.

Smiling sweetly up at his Mother, he simply enquired, –

"Is she fetchin' 'er boyfriend along wiv 'er? I bet 'e ain' arf old!"

"Mind yer mouf!" said Mag, "She ain' doin' nuffin' of the sort, an' its none of yer business, any of yer, and nah git art in the kitchen an' put that bluddy kettle on, I'm dyin' fer a cuppa tea."

But it was only fair to say, the afternoon turned out to be quite pleasant! In fact, Mag really enjoyed it, wending her way through the stalls, there in Middlesex and Wentworth Streets.

"Blimey! There wasn' arf a lot 'a 'stalls, sellin' all sorts 'a fings," she told Bert. "Yer gotta 'ave a mint 'a money ter go there."

But she did come home with a new tin kettle she'd got off one of the cheap jacks. She needed a new one. Her present kettle was blackened by the coal fire, plus pitted with pot-menders she'd got Bert to apply to umpteen holes.

In her bag, when she unpacked it on the kitchen table, was a luvverly big bunch of bananas, –

"'Ere! A bob the lot," the bloke had shouted as he chucked in with the bananas, some grapes and apples too!

"Blimey!" Mag thought, – "Must be me Burfday!"

The kettle, Mag's new one, was singing away on the hob, ready for Mag's first cup of tea of the afternoon. She had just done work. Her legs had ached all morning, – that walk she did every blessed day, backwards and forwards to the Pub, in shoes that had seen better days did nothing for her poor feet.

So out from the coal cupboard when she got in, came the small tin bath she kept especially for such things as, soaking now for instance, her sore plates of meat.

She sighed a long sigh of sheer bliss, as she slowly slid them into the water, then picking up from the table beside her, a 'Pegs Paper' and the 'Picturegoer' that Kate had popped over to her earlier that morning, she sat back and turned over the pages.

Now Mag would have soon answered, any interested body, who happened to ask her, –

"What is it you enjoy doing most?"

They would be told this, – Finding the house unoccupied when you got in, having a few hours to yourself, if only for a little while, no one around, saying, –

"Mum, where's this? Mum why that?" and doing what she was doing now. A cup of tea in one hand and a penny dreadful in the other, or losing herself in a Mills and Boon novel, about a lowly hard working housemaid to a rich family, who finishes up falling for the son of the house, and finding herself, – in the family way!! – Stupid girl!

"How is it, that most always, these short tear-jerkers ended up the same?" – But how Mag loved em!

It was a shame that these few stolen moments went so fast though, Mag took a quick look up at the clock on the Mantelpiece. Then it was, –

"Ow Gawd Blimey! I'd better git a lackus on. They'll all be in before I've done anyfin' around here.

"Times up Mag!" she said to herself.

"Yer'd better git yer skates on, an' git that broom art! Yer've 'ad yer whack! – So Matey, – it's,"

"Back ter the Scrubbin' Board!"

Jim, he was first in, well! – He only had to walk a few yards didn't he? – from Ernie Cakebread's shop!

"Mu'um! – Me an' Dan's goin' ter the pictchers ternight, – 'e's mum's treatin' us."

Mag looked up from the gas-stove, where she was warming up the stew she had made that morning.

"What's on lad? – Where yer goin'? – The Roxy?"

"Yeh! Its, 'Ow Mister Porter', – *Will 'Ay's* in it."

"Mum, – 'Es a scream, so they say."

"Go on an' wash yer 'ands then. An' after, I'll give yer yer dinner."

Jim gave Mag a quizzical look, as his Mum still persisted in seeing they took no liberties, like she said at times.

"'Ere, – don' come it! – Yer *ain't* washed yer 'ands."

"I know, – I've bin around' longer than you 'ave!"

"I've done all the same fings as you yer know. Don' forget, I was a kid once, an' I never liked washin' neiver!"

Then it was action stations, as the rest of the tribe came in, one after the other. So, looking around at them all sitting at the table, Mag experienced a feeling of tranquillity and harmony. Assurance too, that no matter what, they would always be there for each other. Hope was their name and Hope is what she had for the future, – Come what may!

161

Chapter: Fourteen

And so life went on at a steady pace, not just for Mag and Bert in Brody Street, but for every cheerful denizen of this vast dock area of Wapping and its surrounding neighbourhood.

Cheerful they were most of the time. You'd hardly ever find a Cockney, looking as if he had lost a shilling and found a sixpence! Yet, there were occasions, which were slowly mounting up, wherever a group gathered, discussing their doubts and fears that all was far from well.

When April came there was this talk of conscription being introduced for 20-21 year old men. The cinema newsreels revealed things that were going on all around, with sights no one really wanted to see but couldn't turn a blind eye to.

Bert continued to stack up the parcels in Mr Percy's emporium, hanging up various articles which caused him to wonder what 'arf of 'em were, in the small warehouse, which was really a large shed behind the shop.

"What d'yer reckon Bert?" Angus Percy said, as they struggled to carry a large cardboard box full of unredeemed parcels out to the warehouse.

"Don't look good at all!" answered Bert, gloomily.

"Its funny, but yer can feel there is something up. Something yer don' ave no control over. An' I'm certain them up there at the top, ain't neiver!"

Although there was hardly ever a time when the bar in the old 'Crown and Anchor' didn't ring with laughter or the sound of voices all talking at once, Maggie sensed there was this evening, a cloud hanging over most of the regulars who somehow found the need, even more to socialise. Seeking out good company, if only just to talk about the gloomy situation, and maybe to take heart at any piece of information that would be to the contrary. It was like clutching at straws!

Now Tommy Larkin had had enough of this wet week in a thunderstorm atmosphere. Clapping his hands together, he called out over the unusually lowered voices, –

"Come on now, my old cock sparrows, let's do something, to get rid of these doleful looks, I can see around here. – For God's sake let's all have a sing song!"

"Mabel love, now can you start us off?"

Mag, – she was amazed at the speed of which Tommy's words, had changed the scene from one of gloom and doom, to the familiar old geniality, plus hilarity at dear old Mabel's verve, – and nerve, bless 'er 'eart!

Any despondency remaining after her Gracie Field's take-off. – Well! – It went right out the window!

Maureen sidled up to Maggie and spoke quietly to her as they pulled the pints in the now, back to usual crowded and noisy bar.

"Tommy is a real gem, eh? Mag."

"That was the best thing that could have happened, when he dropped in on us like he did!"

They both laughed at the memory of how he had fallen through the bar doorway, those many months ago now. It was really funny! But it was still a mystery to them why he had never mentioned any family, he might have.

Though Maggie continued to cope with all the wise cracks and demands of her customers, she was also deep in thought. It had quite often sprung to her mind, that it was very odd Tommy never spoke about any of his affairs or his background. – Had he a family somewhere perhaps?

He was always alone! Mag had an idea he lived in lodgings. They did say, over in Cromwell Street, – not far away, really.

Didn't seem right, somehow, not 'avin nobody.

He wasn't a bad looking chap, could be in his 40s. Then it struck Mag, perhaps he just preferred being on his own!

Then she giggled, – Maybe the reason why, was because of his 'Portable Sympathy Concert Ensemble!'

She couldn't imagine any lady friend wanting to walk out with the complete 'Royal Philharmonic Orchestra!'

Mag tittered again. Did Tommy keep all that gear on, when he went to bed?

"Now stop!" – She was being very cruel. – She'd pluck up courage and talk to him one day. Mag, really felt a little sorry for Tommy Larkin.

"Why is it nuffin' ever goes right when yer in 'urry?"

Jess bent down and picked up her hairbrush that had fallen on the floor, then fumbling again, tried to get her beads done up. She seemed to be all thumbs, – and she specially wanted to look nice this evening, for her Reg. He was taking her up to Leicester Square.

She was that excited, and had only picked at her food at dinnertime and Mag had gone out of her way to prepare a nice meal. Still, Mag could remember how she'd felt, and the daft things she'd got up to when she was courtin' her first boy friend, –

"Where's 'e takin' yer to Jess?" when she'd been told, that they were actually going up the West End. "It must be

164

nice up there at night wiv all them lights on." Mag thought wistfully. She'd seen this week, pictures of the King and Queen taken at the Empire Leicester Square, being presented to the stars of "Gone With the Wind."

And then they were both going to go around Piccadilly Circus too. – "It must be really luvely!"

Perhaps Bert would take her up there, one of these days? She could wait! – Maybe when the kids had grown up and she and Bert were on their own. – Poor Bert. He didn't get as much of her company as he would have liked. – "Still yer can't 'ave it all ways. – Can yer mate?"

But here she was wasting time musing, and Jess was still getting into a right tizzy, trying to get ready. –

"If she ain't careful, – Reg'll be knockin' any minit, an' she ain't even got 'er bloomin' 'air dun yet! – Ow well!"

"We're s'posed ter be goin' ter the Palladium ter see the Crazy Gang wiv Flanagan an' Allen, 'nd a singer called Al Bowly. 'E's got such a nice voice. Ain't yer 'eard 'im on the wireless?" – And then came a knock at the front door.

"Blimey, 'e's 'ere already Mum! – Go an' talk ter 'im fer a bit, please, – An' tell 'im I won't be long."

Rob and Jim had been gone off out a while, and now Mag realised she herself, must get a move on. It was Saturday, so it would be another mad rush, there in the bars.

Saturday evenings were always the busiest, when the wives made an appearance with the old man and maybe the kids too, who'd enjoy it really, even though just sitting outside listening to the racket that was going on inside with someone at the joanna, or being entertained by Tommy.

"Don' fergit our lemonade Dad!" – the kids would call out, – "An' our Arreroot biscuit." – If they were lucky!

* * *

165

"Bluddy rain!" It was just chucking it down! Mag, stood at the window looking out into the backyard, at the most dismal of scenes. The gutters were spilling over at the sheer weight of water that gushed down the roof.

She'd have to wait a while, she couldn't go out in this lot. She did possess an old brolly, though it wasn't sense to use it, as the wind was blowing like merry hell. Gale force really. So fierce, she could, "bluddy well take off!"

"'Ang on fer a bit gal, it'll stop soon!"

It had been a miserable week, what with the news, and now the weather, you wouldn't have thought it was August!

She looked back at the past month or so and couldn't help feeling down in the dumps.

Well, so did everyone else you spoke to. It seemed there was nothing you could do or say to alter the situation.

It was grim everywhere you went, everywhere you looked, there were signs of big trouble. There were no two ways about it. All they had heard lately, was that word War!

These were not just signs though, they'd already been listening to broadcasts, which did nothing but put the wind up yer kilt!

Rob and Pete meandered slowly along Whitehall. They never spoke, but just stared at all the strange happenings, there and they were not very nice ones either.

It was most disturbing to see all the sandbags being piled up around big important buildings. There the War Office was the most prominent, and completely surrounded by them, they also noticed lots more, going on towards Horse Guards Parade, and Gawd knows how many others!

"Don't look too good does it Pete?"

"No mate, it don't! 'Ere, we'll 'ave ter go if there is a war. I dunno 'ow old yer gotta be. Still, I wouldn't mind.

166

Would you Rob? An' yer know what! I fer one would like ter give that Bluddy 'Itler what for. – Wouldn't you?"

In fact for a long while Rob had done nothing but think about all this wretched War talk. But it seemed, at last he might be nearer to getting his wish! He was sure though, – he wasn't going into any of the other services, and was quite definite about that. –

"I'm goin' in the Navy, an' that's that!"

"Yeh, – An' I'll come wiv yer too! Yer ain't goin' nowhere wivart me. – See!"

"We're mates you an' me Rob!" said Pete.

"Are yer 'ungry yet, Pete?"

"I am, let's go an' git somefin' ter eat."

"Come on, but let's see Nelson's Column first, it's only up 'ere. That copper back there told me, when I arst 'im."

"I didn' see yer talkin' ter no copper. When was that then?" Pete looked dubious at Rob, who only laughed.

"It was when yer was talkin' ter that soljer, – the one wiv that black cat stuck on 'is 'ead!"

It was now Pete's turn to laugh.

"Yeh, – It did look like it, didn' it? – Just like a petrified cat, wot's 'ad the wind up its tail!"

At a guess, that Guardsman in question, – the one who had been accosted by Pete, must have had that same funny remark made to him, at least a million times over, by the members of the public, who stood staring at that poor bloke, day after day.

Bert had just finished work for the day and was now on his way home, passing by several shops with placards always placed in vulnerable positions destined to catch the eye of the passer-by.

167

Yet Bert would have much preferred to see news of a more cheerful vein than he did now. It was again all about War! What was all this stuff he was seeing, –

'Children may have to be evacuated soon from London and surrounding towns!' – Blacked out lights everywhere and Air Raid Shelters were being distributed!!

But these were only the start of the chilling lists of precautions, necessary now and all because of that war mongering insignificant looking blackguard called Hitler, who was nothing but a jumped up paper hanger, of no cop! But surely, it would be only fools, who were influenced by such a worthless individual.

Now Bert, he knew only too well what did result from Wars. 'So much suffering and agony!' He was just one, who had seen sights, he'd never ever want to see again. The scars left on mind and body. It was soul destroying too, him being handicapped because of it all as well he knew! Never ever, being able to do a decent days work, or to take home adequate pay as such, or to keep his family fed and clothed, as he wished.

But, – he must surely put away these thoughts, as now he had reached home.

"'Ello Maggie me luv!" Bert's kiss for her, seemed to contain more warmth than usual.

This was better! The sight of the kettle singing away merrily on the hob, ready for his cup of tea, he'd long been waiting for. There too was his Mag, darting about getting the table ready for their meal.

"What we got gal, anyfin' nice?"

Maggie looked up at him straightfaced.

"'Ang on a minit, an' I'll git yer a menu!"

"Whad'yer fink we got? – This ain't the Ritz yer know!"

"Alright old gal, – I'm only jokin'!" Said Bert.

"Don't be daft, – I know yer are, – yer soppy 'aporth!" chuckled Mag, "An' mind 'ow yer sit darn there!" moving from a chair a huge pile of clothes she had been ironing.

Just at that minute, came a rustling sound from the corner of the kitchen, near the fireplace.

Snowy the dog had woken up, and hearing their voices, scrambled out of his temporary bed, – an orange box, lined with an old coat of Rob's, – and made straight for Bert.

The little dog had settled in his new home well and was spoiled to blazes, and as Mag would tell you, more so by Bert than any of 'em!

Rob was next to come in, and Bert noticed he seemed to be more than usually quiet. But after about ten minutes he spoke, and not without a tinge of anxiety in his voice.

"They are puttin' big posters up all over the place, – everywhere yer look Mum. They're tellin' us what ter do, and where ter go quick if there's an air raid."

"They seem to be pretty sure about it all, don't they!"

"One of the places is the basement of that empty ware'ouse down the next street and in the Baptist Church near 'ere."

"Makes yer shudder ter fink of it, dun' it?"

Then came a loud knock at the front door. Maggie left Rob to answer it.

"Mum, there was a bloke, 'e give me this fer yer ter read. 'E's leavin' 'em all up the street, an' says ter be sure an' bide by it, – It's very important!"

And this was not all, as Mag read it out loud.

"It says on 'ere Bert. – They may be testin' out the Air Raid Sirens at different times. Though it is only a test, so yer not ter git the wind up when yer 'ear it!"

"Blimey! Its alright fer them ter talk, saying don't git the wind up. I can't believe all this is really 'appenin'. Can you Bert? Yer know what I'll do if I 'ear it, an' that'll be shift blue lights!" said Mag.

"Come on don't let's sit 'ere makin' ourselves bluddy-well miserable, finkin' abart what might never 'appen."

"The uvver two will be in 'ere, in a jiffy."

"Put that kettle on again Robbie. On the gas this time. Ow! 'Ere they come!" she said, as Jess and Jim came in the back door. – "No peace fer the wicked!"

Mag leaving them all to chin wag across the tea table, about the grim situation, she went off to work.

When George the watchman called out his usual, "Evenin' Ma'am," as she passed the dock-gates, she fancied that even *his* usual cheerful voice, had changed to a more sober note. – "I 'ope its not goin' ter be like this all evening," she thought, – "or I'll be tappin' a few bottles of the 'ard stuff meself!"

Kate, sitting in her cosy parlour, was clearly not feeling too happy, watching the rain just pelting down the window panes. Normally she loved the rain when it fell as gentle drops from the sky, bringing refreshment to the few resolute plants she had in her yard.

Any living green thing, struggled to survive in this harsh environment, smoke-choked and grime-laden, almost as much as its stout hearted inhabitants. For Kate felt the grey clouds matched their sad faces, – the anxious faces that were to be seen everywhere you turned your head.

She took a glance up at Philip's picture over the mantelpiece. At his face smiling down at her. What was the point, she thought, of thousands going through Hell, losing their lives. Why? Only to have the self-same thing, happen all over again? – Maybe.

It only pointed to one thing, and Kate was certain of it. That mankind had not learned much since the Middle Ages!

She sighed, arose from her chair and went out, slamming the door to, behind her. Marching up Mag's garden path, she knocked at the door, – Mag would drive away her blues, with her guaranteed solution, –

"Let's 'ave a nice cuppa tea, eh?"

Chapter: Fifteen

It was not only Kate who had been feeling down in the dumps this afternoon.

Tommy Larkin lay sprawled full length on his bed, arms stretched behind his head, in the most depressing, almost bare upstairs back room in one of Wapping's equally depressing streets.

Looking up at the ceiling, from his horizontal position on the narrow bed, a bed which had so many lumps and bumps in the soiled mattress, it had made quite a big impression on him!

He noted and wondered how many times he had laid and tried to count the fly marks and the bug stains on the ceiling, interspersed with patches of damp green mould. In fact they made a damned fine pattern, really!!

Now, as he listened to the rain lashing against the broken panes in the window frame, it took him back to another such afternoon, many years ago, one which had imprinted itself on his mind ever since. It was the memory of that day, – he would never forget it. Of the agonising hours of waiting in a room adjoining the ward in which his Mary, his wife, was fighting a losing battle for her life. He couldn't grasp it. It wasn't real! His Mary was dying, in a futile struggle, attempting to bring another new life into the world. – Their baby the one they had awaited for so long.

Tommy buried his head deep in his hands.

"Oh! Why doesn't that bloody rain stop? – It was as if the Heavens were crying too, crying for him!

It was for years after, he felt his life had ended on that fateful day, indeed he'd wished it had ended! When the Nurse had walked slowly toward him, with these words, – but he knew it before she had said it, the dreaded, –

"I am so very sorry to have to tell you, there was just nothing more we could do, Mr Holt."

Words, – only words, but they had taken away all meaning of life for him.

He had lost the world, – Mary, had *been* his world!

For she had given him back his life, when way back in the dark years of the Great War, she had nursed him in Hospital, after he had been brought in only half alive, from the Belgium trenches.

They'd taken him to a South Coast Hospital, after he had missed almost being blown to pieces by a mine. Tommy had narrowly escaped death, but he had to suffer, not only severe injuries, but also the nightmares of shell shock!

Never knowing how long he remained in a Coma, he had no idea of time or place, until one morning he was to emerge from his dark world, to hear a voice, – it was such a sweet voice, saying, – "Well now Tommy, I see you have returned to us! This *is* good news." Then the voice faded away and then again – the voice, –

"I have brought the Doctor to see you."

The bright lights hurt his eyes, he remembered, and he had the urge to close them and go back to his dark world.

"Well, you have really had us on our toes Soldier, but I think we have you on the right road to recovery now, with Nurse Mary's help here!"

So that was her name, the goddess with the sweet voice, who had woken him from his never-ending journey through a world of everlasting nights.

As he grew stronger, Tommy asked his Nurse about herself. She hailed from Donegal, – A true Irish lass!

Nursing had been in her blood. Her mother, a good midwife, had brought forth more babies to the mothers of their village than the fabled STORK!

Now Mary, with the first glimpse she'd had of Tommy as he lay helpless and suffering, his handsome face screwed up in pain, had been utterly determined that this man would be made whole again. For as the months went by, and spending more and more hours with him, she knew he was now, not just her patient needing care and attention, he was the man she had made up her mind, she'd like to be with – and care for always. There were to be many more months of vigilance, patience and tolerance, but then came the day, when they knew the battle had been won.

Tommy waited, – he'd bide his time. How could he ever forget that sweet voice, which had brought him out of his black hole. He'd watch Mary, and tried to hide the way his blood pressure seemed to rise, every time she placed her cool hands on his body, to bathe or wash him. And as she put her arms around his shoulders to lift him up into a more comfortable position, against the pillows.

Surely she must hear his heart thudding in his chest! But how could he, a soldier in the ranks, think he had the right to open his heart to this person, this angel, who had not only helped him beat pain, but had also saved his sanity?

"Damn and Blast it! – Why didn't he come out with it, why didn't he take the plunge!

Stop and tell her. – Shout it out to her, – "Can't you see I love you Mary, I want you to be my wife!"

Yet as in all true love stories, there is always a rainbow to be found somewhere along the line!

It was to be on this fine sunny morning, when all nature seemed hard at work. Bees were busy, birds were singing, the caterpillars were gnawing away happily at the gardeners cabbages. Trees were in full dress, the dark green of the Conifers, contrasting with the pale green of the Willows.

"Come along Tommy, you are going for a ride!"

Mary had brought into the ward, a wheel chair, saying, –

"Get in, we're off to get some sun on your body!" and they went, out through the doors and on to the veranda. From here, Tommy had his first view, across the South Downs, and he realised they had been there the whole time he had lain in that bed hanging on to life, forgetting there was a whole world waiting out through those big doors.

As they made their way across a wide lawn in front of this huge mansion house, which as Mary had said, belonged to some Earl, but had been taken over, at the outset of the war, as a Army Hospital.

Commandeered in other words. But Tommy was sure that this Earl, whoever he was, must have been most agreeable and felt he was doing his bit!

There was quite a slope leading to a river and up to now, Mary had been doing a good job regulating this wheelchair with Tommy in it, up to the point where a slight turn in the road meant she had a struggle to push it back up on to the path again.

Fool that she was! – Why did she come this way? – One wheel was stuck fast in a rut and try as she might, it wouldn't budge!

All this time, Tommy had been helpless to do a thing. He could only sit there, feeling so much like an idiot, unable to help Mary. This dear girl, who unknown to her, he would give his very soul to take hold of her hands, which held tight to the wheelchair handles and pull her down, take her in his arms and tell her, – "I love you!"

"Can't you see how much! Are you blind?"

But, as in all Fairy tales, there is always a Good Samaritan lurking somewhere. In Mary's case it happened to be the Estates woodcutter, – cum, – poacher catcher!

If it had been a policeman, – Mary chuckled, she could visualise it all, with him saying in a jovial way, –

"Ello, Ello, Ello, an' what 'ave we 'ere then!"

Really the man was a very welcome sight, and in a thrice, he had that wheelchair out of captivity before you could say, "Well, blow me down!"

"There you are ma'am now you can be on your way." Touching his cap, the woodsman said, –

"Good day ma'am, – Good day Sir," and he was gone.

All this kerfuffle now, had taken the wind out of Mary's sails, and also she felt very hot.

Pushing Tommy into the shade of a tree she sat herself down on the grass beside the wheel chair and was thankfully relieved to feel a slight wind appear.

Lifting up her face she had the breeze fan her cheeks, and as she did so, pulled her hair back from her forehead.

Mary was quite aware that Tommy was watching her, in fact that was her intention. It was so still there in the glade. So quiet, it seemed they were the only two people around!

She was right, Tommy's eyes never left her. So intrigued was he by Mary's lack of airs and graces, yet she had plenty of reason to be pretentious. Her face, from which showed nothing but concern, warmth and care for her patients, had a beauty, which displayed all that was good in her.

It would be difficult for any man, such as Tommy, not to be affected. He'd had a lot of time to note and admire all of her attributes, but it was always to be, her voice, and her sparkling blue Irish eyes that had initially won his heart.

So there they sat, in the cool shadow of the oak tree, Mary and Tommy, both deep in their own thoughts. He was wondering what was in her mind, and likewise Mary too.

"Was Tommy thinking, the same as she?"

They did not speak Neither eager to break the silence, and yet there was so much they had to say.

"I think we ought to be getting back now," said Mary.

She got up, patting her uniform skirt straight, and putting on her Nurses Cap, leaned across Tommy to release the brake of the wheelchair. In doing so, he saw her hand was too perilously near his, for him not to take the opportunity to grab hold and pull her towards him, and as awkward as it was, he kissed her, – hard on her lips. He had just about had enough of this game of cat and mouse!

Mary startled, but only for a second, tried to regain her composure.

It was useless. She drew back a little but he kept hold of her hand, while he tried to apologise.

"I am sorry Mary, I should not have done that, but I have been wanting to for so long!"

"You see Mary, I love you! I've loved you ever since that day you woke me from my nightmare with your sweet voice." He started again to ask her forgiveness.

"Stop!" she said abruptly, – "Will you please stop saying sorry! – Couldn't you see? – I've felt the same way about you! All these months I have tended you, it became more and more important for you to recover from your ghastly experiences, and get you well, because I'd found how so much you had come to mean to me, perhaps more than you will ever know!"

Tommy as he clasped her hands tighter in his, heard her say the words he had been longing to hear.

"I love you too Tommy. – Oh, so very much!"

And so they were married. A quiet ceremony in the Hospital Chapel. It was on the day Tommy walked unaided down the aisle to a new life with Mary, his wife by his side.

How many times had he done this same thing, over and over again, reliving those wonderful days when life was full and sweet, – days of wine and roses.

When he only had to look up and see her there, no matter what she was doing, whether just sitting knitting, as she did most every evening. Knitting for the Baby that was soon to be born, and smiling to herself as she day dreamed.

What would it be, – boy or a girl? But it didn't matter, it would be a manifestation of their love for each other.

Tommy felt at times, as he did now, on this wet dreary afternoon, that although the pain was so unbearable he *could* not, and *would* not put out of his mind, all those treasured memories.

The images were indelible, like turning over the pages in a picture book, looking at each separately. Though it was like a knife piercing his heart, he needed that, – he wanted that pain, he wanted to be hurt, but he could not explain why! It was the only way he could be near his Mary. – Even if it did hurt like Hell!

But now he lay there, wondering, what would she think of him, if she could see him now, see the person he had become. So different from the man she had left behind in Donegal, the place in which she had been born, – in the little village on the cliffs by the sea, where they had made their home. It had become too much to bear, to stay there, in that small white washed cottage that held so much that reminded him of her.

He'd left, – packed his bag and gone. Thomas Holt, – became Tommy Larkin a traveller, a vagabond, a man with no roots, no family, no nothing!

Out on the open road, with no destination, never staying anywhere long at one time. That was until he had come to London, here to the East End, for as it happened, it had completely got to him!

The bustle, the activity of the Docks, the teeming restlessness, the comings and goings of countless numbers of ships on the River Thames, the smell of it, unexplainable, which could offend or captivate. The fogs, the mud larks, – boys up to their knees in the mud, scrabbling about looking for a treasure trove.

Tommy on his travels had somehow managed to amass a bevy of musical hardware that he carried around. Amusing the public on his way. He had found his wherewithal, his resources had drained away and would have to try and find a way of earning a bob or two.

Didn't he want to find a job and stay in one place? Never, – he had to keep on the move, – always on the go.

He liked it here in Wapping, making so many friends in the old Pub, The 'Crown and Anchor'. But this room? No! But it *had* to do for a while. Anywhere else, no matter where. – Could never be the same without his Mary!

Would he *never* get used to it?

What was all this Maggie was seeing? Never in all her born days would she ever believe, one could bring themselves to tie a label on a child, take them along with literally hundreds of other poor kids who tearful, some sobbing, gripping tightly, a parents hand, not wanting to let go. Being put on a train, filled already with other bewildered kids, and watch them being taken away, out of sight to God knows where? – Wondering, would they ever see them again!

But there it was before her eyes, a long procession of schoolchildren, packaged up and posted to safer places out in the country, away from the South Coast or anywhere around London. It was much too dangerous!

Mag could only pray to God that her three would be safe here in Wapping and thankful, she was not one of those tearful mothers having to stand there helpless, at the station entrance waving goodbye to their little ones, wondering would it be for the last time?

She shuddered at the thought, and hurried on towards the Pub. It was Friday, and really a beautiful day for the first of September, and Mag could not believe so many awful things were happening all around her. Here on a lovely warm day, with such a beautiful clear blue sky, marred now by Barrage Balloons dotted about, where little fleecy white clouds should be.

What next she thought, not liking it at all, witnessing these horrible events. She was afraid too. Rob was nearly 20 and almost certainly would be called up and Mag didn't want to even think about that!

A picture of Bert flashed through her mind. He would know more than she, what horrors the mere mention of War brought back to him and to think their Rob might find himself in the same ghastly circumstances!

The atmosphere in the pub was very subdued, everyone speaking in hushed tones. It was not natural Mag decided and she had to force herself, to put her two pennyworth into the conversations. This old pub, a retreat where everyone felt they could let their hair down, had definitely changed.

Old Joe Grimley was saying to one of his mates, with one arm leaning on the counter and the other fiddling with his pipe, trying to light it for the umpteenth time, that noonday.

"I says to them, – If yer fink I'm goin' ter bury meself darn under the erf, like some bluddy bleedin' mole, in one a them there contraptions, yer got anuvver fink comin'!"

"If one a Jerry's bombs 'as got me name on it, it won't matter where I am, will it? – No I'll stay in me bed, the one I slept in fer nigh on 50 years, an' I ain't gonna shift fer nobody, – least ov all that bastard 'Itler!"

Joe, he had been alluding to the daily distribution of Anderson Shelters up his street. His house had been in one of the roads, which had a back garden big enough to erect one of these corrugated steel dugouts.

But Mag and Bert's postage stamp of a backyard wasn't! They would never know if it *was* for the best or not.

No one was ever to find out, definitely not in that vulnerable hot spot of the Docks area!

Chapter: Sixteen

She was sitting gazing into the fitful flames of a dying fire by the kitchen range, feeling utterly dejected.

Mag was alone and going over the events of the past weeks of fear and apprehension, which with a bombshell, had come to a head with the words of Neville Chamberlain in his speech on Sunday, September 3rd 1939.

It would be embedded forever in the memory of everyone who heard it.

His words, – "I have to tell you, that consequently this country, is now at war with Germany."

Only words, but it was to be a death knell to millions. Likened to the end of the world. Indeed it was to be, for many a poor soul.

It took a little time to sink in, this news, to many groups of people who'd gathered to discuss just what it would mean, and ask, – "What will happen now?"

But as they'd stood grey faced and fearful. – Another blow! A noise! It had been like a wailing Banshee and struck terror to all. Surely it cannot be an Air Raid!

"It couldn't be! – So soon?"

No! – Only a false alarm. – But it was not until after many people had made straight for their allotted Air Raid Shelters. Then everyone breathed again!

The War had begun!! "What now?" Then disconsolate and grave faced, everyone made off home.

The bars of the 'Crown and Anchor' had been quiet that Sunday evening, after the news had sunk in. It seemed families wanted and needed to be together, as there was so much to chinwag about. Maggie herself hadn't liked leaving Bert sitting there looking down his nose into the empty fireplace on his own.

Rob had gone off to find Pete, they would be full of the news, not that they hadn't expected it. For a long time now, it was all they had talked of.

Jess was even more determined than ever. She was going to join the Women's Land Army. – That left only Jim, – feeling again the odd one out. – He couldn't join anything!

"Don't be in such a 'urry me boy!" said Bert. There's plenty a time ter start rushin' orf, ter do yer bit. – It ain't goin' a be no bluddy cake walk yer know!"

But Bert was far from making light of any of this. It had not been more than 20 odd years, only a short time really, since that other disastrous war had ended.

"Quiet ain't it Maur?" said Mag looking around the half empty bar. It was strange for a Saturday, especially as it was quite a mild evening.

"Can't blame 'em though." Then thinking of poor Bert, sitting at home alone again, she sighed a little.

He was a brick, never moaned at all at Mag going off to the Pub every evening. But sometimes, it had entered her head that it was about time she packed it in.

They had been a horrible few weeks for everybody for streets around, ever since that fateful broadcast, and it would take a lot more weeks before some semblance of normality returned, – If ever! How could it ever be normal? – It was now a whole new ball game!

"Gawd, stripe me pink! I damn near broke me bluddy neck art there. Yer can't see an 'and in front a yer nose!"

Maggie looked up quickly, to see Mabel come limping in the doorway, with her face as red as a beetroot, and swearing like a trooper!

"'Ow the 'ell would we 'ave fawt, we'd 'ave ter be feelin' our way arand like a lot a bleedin' bats, wiv no lamp posts alight?"

"I've only jus' got over one gammy leg, an' that was all because ov anuvver silly sod, – me ol' man!"

Poor old Mabel was going on something cruel about the blackout. "It was blasted dangerous!" Though she was right, and it would take a good bit of getting used to. She wouldn't be the only poor devil who'd come a cropper, – not by a long chalk!

"Never mind Mabel," said Mag, a little benevolently, "But can yer remember what yer came in for?"

Now Mabel wasn't what you'd call a regular, she hardly ever showed her face in the Pub.

"Yer'll larf at this Mag, when I tells yer. – I come in ter see if yer'd let me 'ave some pennies fer me Gas Meter? – Me light's gorn!"

Maureen had been upstairs, but heard all the hullabaloo going on in the bar, and came down. Mabel's voice was not what you'd call melodious or refined! – OR Quiet!

"Oh, No!" thought Maureen, "Is it going to be one of those evenings?"

But it was mainly, on the whole, after the boisterous start, a quietish evening.

"G'night!" shouted Maureen from the back of the bar, as Mag went outside into the darkened street where Bert was waiting for her. He had just arrived. Since the blackout had begun, he'd come to meet Mag every night, picking his way carefully along the pitch-black alleyways. They had been bad enough to walk through even before the blackout, now it was a downright catastrophic feat to master all the pitfalls along the way.

"'Ello Luv!" She gave him a kiss and tucked her arm through his, as they proceeded to make their way home gingerly along by the wharves.

George the watchman called out a goodnight, but they could just about make out his dark form there by the gates.

"What a job! I wouldn't 'ave 'is lot for a pension!" said Bert, "An' I don't know 'ow the blokes can work 'ere even, wivart no bluddy lights."

It was really an eerie experience, with just a glimmer of a waning moon to go by.

"Let's 'urry up an' git in, eh?" said Mag. She couldn't help feeling scared even though Bert's arm was around her.

Rob had the jitters. He didn't like all he heard coming from the B.B.C. Radio programmes.

"Here is the news, and this is Bruce Belfrage reading it." None of it was at all inspiring, although things were mainly quiet on the Home Front. It was mostly the mood of the people.

The resentment and ill humour against the rigorous Air Raid Precautions, which were getting everyone down, for instance, –

"Put that bloomin' light art!" very often called out loudly by the A.R.P. Wardens, who were hard put to stay popular with householders who forgot at times to abide by the rules and the good advice given for their own safety.

In the complete blackout that was imposed, the slightest chink of light, would show up like a flaming beacon from the air, if there ever happened to be an air raid.

But it was not so much the blackout, the grievances, and the rest of the tight restrictions that was the cause of Rob kicking his heels, feeling restless. He wanted to get into the thick of things! So far it seemed to be just a Phoney War!

The news was mainly of the shipping losses in the Atlantic. Many of our ships were being torpedoed by German U-boats that made Rob want to do his bit, – and the sooner the better.

Even just a few hours after war had been announced, the 'Athena', – an unarmed liner had been sunk by a U-boat, in the Atlantic.

Although he didn't go much on there being a war on at all and certainly didn't go much on that Hitler, but he could help things a bit by having a go at the perisher. It meant he might now get to be in the Navy a bit quicker!

That is, if he was lucky to be called up soon, – he was old enough now.

It had been a funny old Christmas. No one seemed to be in the mood for any kind of jollification. The powers that be and the shop keepers, tried their damnedest to bring a bit of relief and cheer into the apathetic populace around this usually, – ready for the chance to kick up their heels area, but apart from a few who did put on a bit of a show and said, "Oh! What the Hell!" – there was ever that air of prevailing gloom.

Most of the families around Brody Street and none more so than the Hope's, were glad when Christmas was all over.

Mag and Bert Hope were now full of doubt and trepidation as the year of 1939 drew to a close.

It had them wondering what 1940 would have in store. So the New Year began quietly with very severe icy cold weather, hard frosts that stayed for days and there were many poor souls who joined the Red Nose and Chilblain Brigade.

Jess, – She was one of them!

The factory in which she worked was a lofty pre-Crimean War building, smoke sooted, grey and dismal along the Commercial Road, every floor cold and draughty with near freezing conditions.

Along with her mates, Jess enjoyed her job, with its easy going atmosphere and with many a giggle or joke at someone's expense, – mainly the less virtuous females, all good fun really. But most of the others were not so inclined to speak openly of their indiscretions.

Lil, – Lily Watson, – a decidedly overlarge lady with a mouth to match, came from a speculative background. It was heard tell her father had been the Bearded Lady in a well-known travelling fair!!

Lil moved freely between the looms and machines in the clothing factory, keeping a cautious eye on the girls. She was classed as the forewoman, and head cook and bottlewasher, always on the lookout for time wasters, lead swingers and shoddy workmanship.

"Woe betide anyone a yer 'ere," she would say, –

"If yer work ain' in anyway near up ter scratch!"

Poor Jess on this particular morning, herself was not *up* to scratch, she was well and truly *under* the weather, with a rotten cold, and her head! It felt about as big as a Pumpkin! But was it any use moaning?

"Ere gal, – take these" Lil gave Jess a couple of Aspros.

"That'll cure yer 'eadache!" she said, and that was it!

"No duck shuvvin' allowed, no 'angin' out the time in the lavatories eiver," according to Lil!

But Jess did get to go home a bit earlier that afternoon. For all Lil's Sergeant Major exterior, she had a kind heart. – The girls somehow, – They liked her!

"Oh! hello Maggie, are you off shopping?"

Kate came out of her front door, just as Mag was shutting hers.

"Ter tell yer the truf Kate, I was just poppin' round ter Bessie's 'ouse ter see Annie, I ain't seen much ov 'er since she's been back from 'Ornchurch!

"I'll see yer later Kate!" and Mag went off down the road. She was thinking of Mavis too,

"Wonder 'ow she's gittin' on over there in Kensal Rise?"

During the time Mavis had been back living near her son George and his wife, Mag had received a couple of letters from her friend. She told how she was working in a shoe factory in Harlesden, which was now making Army Boots.

"I wonder if she still wears her head scarf?" And had that fashion caught the public eye? Was Mavis responsible for the trend now, to be wearing your scarf tied like an Indian Turban around your head, or to have your hair just piled into a net, which they called a snood?

Bessie wasn't in when Maggie knocked at her front door. She waited a couple of minutes then turning on her heels, she wandered back along the path, particularly noticing just how many windows of the houses now, had brown paper strips glued all over them in a criss cross fashion. This was to prevent the shattering of glass by the bomb blasts. – God forbid, the terrible thought!

So many precautions. All these must have been in the pipe line for a very long time. As she got nearer Alf's shop, she had a sudden thought, –

"Crumbs, it was gettin' near tea time! I ain't got much in the Muvver 'Ubberd. Better get 'em some pie 'n mash. Dunno where the times gawn terday, – blowed if I do!"

"Oi! – Mind 'ow yer go wiv that sugar there Rob, – Don't ferget it's rationed!"

"Dontcher know there's a War on?"

That particular saying was to be heard said so many times, over and over again during the many months, – and the years to come.

Mag had asked Kate only that morning, –

"Ow d'yer manage wiv yer small rations Kate?"

"What the 'ell der they fink we can do wiv these few ounces a Sugar a week?"

"Specially you. – There's only one a you!"

"Gawd 'elp us. I 'ope they bloomin' well don' 'ave ter ration our cuppa tea!"

Having settled them down to their evening meal of pie and mash, Mag started to get her coat on to go to the pub.

Jess had been the first one to come in from work, and on taking one look at her face, as she'd come in the door, Mag said with a big sigh, –

"Gor blimey! What's the matter wiv you luv? Yer look like somefin' the cat's dragged in!" – noticing Jessie's red nose and watery eyes.

She looked really awful.

"Come on sit darn there luv, 'ere's a cuppa tea."

"I'd rarver go straight up ter bed Mum, I ache all over." Jess groaned.

"Don' say yer got the Flu. Poor ol' Jess! – Go on, get up ter bed, I'll bring yer up an 'ot water bottle in a minit. Drink this first though," giving her a small tot of hot whisky and water, (medicinal) that's what Mag had been told.

"'Ow dear it's started!" she thought, as she filled the stone bottle with boiling water, while tutting to herself.

"Flu! – It'll go right frew the 'ouse nah, I bet."

Jim had been sitting with itchy feet at the table, wolfing down his pie and Mash. He wanted to hurry up and get off out with Dan. Both were anxious to meet the couple of girls who came from Bow, who they'd got talking to a few nights ago outside the Roxy picture house up the Highway.

Jim had found it very difficult to get through the day at work, thinking about Flo, his new bit ov stuff!

"Florrie, that's 'er name. – Cor, yer should see 'er! Rob. Got red 'air she 'as. – So I'd better watch out! –

"Yer mind yer do!" Rob said. He had only been half listening to Jim rattling on, as he'd heard all about Jim's conquests before.

"I know yer fink yer grown up but yer ain' got no more sense nah, than what yer was born wiv, just you be careful!"

"Why don'cha get a proper job! Stuck in a Baker's shop makin' bread. That's women's work!"

"Yer wanna try doin' somefin like I do, darn at the ship yard, 'andlin' nuts an' bolts."

Rob no longer made his sails, he had found a better use for his hands, repairing parts of barges and paddle steamers etc. At last he was a little bit nearer his dream, he'd had both his feet on a ship's deck.

Jim, he'd had enough of Rob and his bullying.

Clearing off, he went out and found Dan, all spruced up with his hair all slicked back and in his new zoot suit looking like a young James Cagney. Dan was in the money now, and had got a nice little number at one of the clothes stalls up the Whitechapel Market.

Hence the snazzy rigout he had on.

190

But that cut no ice with Jim. Dressed like Dan was now, he wouldn't have got through their back door, if his Dad had clapped eyes on him! Besides he had no room for James Cagney, he was too short. Jim fancied himself more along the lines of a Cary Grant!

"I'll be late fer work at this rate, – better get a move on lass. Mag hurried as quick as she could, through the blacked out streets and took a few short cuts to the Pub. She'd turned down Bert's offer to accompany her most of the way. – "No yer can't keep doin' that luv, I'll be OK! Will yer see Jess don' do nuffin' daft like thinkin' a goin' out. – I know 'er. – Make 'er stay in bed."

Old Joe was in his favourite place by the bar, fiddling with his pipe. She often wondered if he ever really put any tobacco in it in the first place! It never stayed alight!

The Anderson shelter had been accepted and duly erected, in Joe's back yard, – but he still insisted, –

"They're bluddy well wastin' their time. – They ain't gettin' me in that fing, I kin tell yer nah. Bombs or no bombs, it stays as it is, – I'll put me rabbits in it!"

"'Ow yer gonna git ter feed 'em, if you won't go darn in it?" said one of his mates.

"Ow?" said Joe, "Me ol' woman will, except she's built like the side ov an old brick out 'ouse!"

"She could get stuck in the openin'! 'Ere, that's an idea. I'll always know where she is then, won't I, eh?"

They all laughed at the thought.

At that moment Tommy came across to have a chat to Les, he had heard Joe talking and smiled, –

"You know, Les, I've been thinking. I feel a bit useless, I ought to try doing something towards the War effort. Everyone else seems to be."

"I can understand how you feel Tommy, but by all accounts, don't you think you done more than enough in the last lot? – Besides there's not much going on, it's a funny or more phoney kind of war now."

"Ah! But Les, – it's not going to stay like this for long, you mark my words!"

"That blighter has something up his sleeve. It may be quiet now out in France, even though the B.E.F. have been out there since last September, and so far have only been hanging around kicking their heels waiting."

But there had been one bit of news, that'd brought back a bit of cheer into folks lives, – this was, that Cinemas, after being shut down due to the start of the war, were now going to open again, as nothing seemed to be happening. Mabel was the first one to clap her hands.

"Fank Gawd fer that!" She'd missed her three pennorth of an afternoon!

Mavis was fed up, – right to the teeth! She hated it there in Kensal Rise. Why the hell did everyone think themselves better here, than anyone in the locality she had been born and bred in?

They hadn't a bloody clue! She wanted to go back, but how, – that was the question?

That snotty bitch of a Sybil, practically turning her own Son against her. George, poor sod! – He couldn't see it though. He never knew if he was coming or going! But Mavis, now, – *She* was going and would say, if asked, –

"Surely yer not finkin a movin' back, – are yer?"

"Yeh! Too true, an' yer won't see me arse fer dust!"

Chapter: Seventeen

Maggie awoke to hear Snowy yapping and Rob shouting at him. "Be quiet will yer, – pack it up! I'm tryin' ter read this!" She looked at the clock on the washstand. – It was nearly nine o'clock.

"Robbie! – What's goin' on darn there fer Gawd's sake! Was that the Postman?" she shouted.

"Yers Ma, an' d'yer know what, – I got me papers!"

"I bin called up!"

His voice was nigh on hysterical, Rob couldn't contain his excitement!

"Oh, No!" Mag's heart missed a beat. The moment had come which she had been dreading.

"I 'ave ter report ter the Depot at Portsmouth in two weeks time fer me Basic training."

"Ma, – I'm goin' ter be in the Royal Navy."

"Can yer believe it? – I can't!"

"I'm gonna go an' tell Pete. – I shan't be long!"

Rob, he was twenty, and to see the way he was behaving, it took Maggie back ten years, to when he'd joined the Scouts, but this was different. – Vastly different!

Mag was now afraid, more than she had ever been of anything in her life. She could not stop this awful feeling, which she had at this minute of something she could not fathom. – What was it?

Rob had gone flying out of the door to see Pete. He mustn't come back and find her looking as she did now, – Rob had got his wish. He had waited for it, – so long.

Mag must hide her agitation, and behave normally and pretend to be pleased. Now *how* could she?

There was one consolation. Although Rob was leaving the fold, Jim luckily was too young to be called up. The war, anyway it would be over soon. She picked up her washing basket and went out into the yard.

"This blasted clothes line, – it's still squeakin'!"

But funnily enough, today she didn't really care. There were other things on her mind far worse to worry about.

Kate came out into her yard, and called to Mag.

"Can you come over and have a cup of tea? I've also made a batch of buns!" – She had to do something to take that look off Maggie's face, knowing exactly just what she might be going through.

Rob had gone off that very morning to make his way to Portsmouth to take his place, in 'His Majesty's Royal Navy,' and to see the expression on that certain individuals face, anyone would imagine he was about to become, not just an Able Seaman, but a Rear Admiral and command the 'Ark Royal' or do whatever Rear admirals do, do!

You could have heard a pin drop, it was that quiet! No one spoke there at the meal table. Everyone's minds were on the same thing, Rob's absence. Young Jim, whose chattering during meal times, most often had given cause for Bert's patience to erupt with, – "Fer Gawd's sake, will yer stop that blasted jabberin' an' git on wiv yer dinners!" Even Jim, – he was silent!

None of them had ever been split up before. They were going to miss Rob. – A lot!

Is this how it was to be in the now uncertain future? Mag, she was troubled. She looked across at Bert. Suddenly he gave a smile, "Come on nah," he said. "I can't stand this, it's like a bloomin' Morgue in 'ere!"

"Cheer up the lot a yer. Put the wireless on Jim. Let's 'ave a laugh at 'Arfur Askey' an' 'Stinker Murdoch,' – 'Band Wagons' on!"

It may have been a trying time for everyone around and a disconcerting one, but it was still Spring!

The few daffodils were finished, but the Lilac was out, fitful and sparse as it was, giving off its delicate scent, bringing a burst of gladness to a heavy heart. At least the evil doings of some, could not succeed in taking away goodness and beauty, that was ceaseless and enduring.

This was what Maggie found on her way to work each morning. What had once been wasteland, was now tended and cultivated by some optimistic persevering person, who had planted a few flowers and shrubs here and there.

As she entered the back way to the Pub, she espied Tommy, who was taking out some empty crates, giving Les a helping hand.

"Hello!" he said, " Nice morning Maggie."

"Oh, Tommy! – 'Ere, I'm glad I bumped into yer, there's somefin' I wanna arst yer."

"What is it Mag, you want to ask me? – You don't want to borrow a hundred pounds do you? – Only I don't happen to have that much on me right now. – You will have to wait till I go over to the Bank!"

Maggie laughed, –

"No, I ain't paid yer back that uvver 'undred I 'ad orf yer yet! – Jokin' aside. I don't mean ter pry inter yer social life. Then she paused while Tommy, looked a little puzzled!

"What was Mag going to ask him?"

"It's like this. I'm not sure if yer a one for parties or such like, but seein' as our Jess is eighteen next week, Bert an' I would like ter give 'er a bit of a tea fight. Only a few people are comin'! – Tommy, would yer like ter come?"

Now Tommy wasn't to know this, but Mag had something up her sleeve! In other words, – there was a method in her madness. She was going to invite Kate! She had thought for a long while, what a shame Kate was always stuck on her own. It wasn't right. Tommy was a smashing bloke and they were both about the same age too.

"Fortyish? – That was not old!"

Mag hadn't said anything about this to Bert yet, or he would rumble her motive.

"Ow! – You're a right old matchmaker!" he would say, but maybe think it was a good ruse anyway!

The preparations for Jess's little do, meant it took Mag's mind off worrying about Rob for a bit, but she eagerly listened for the postman's knock every day. – So far he had settled in nicely at the naval base, and the rest of the conscripted lads were a good lot. He'd said that in his first letter. And apart from feeling a slight touch of home-sickness, he was happy there.

"As happy as a Sand Boy!"

Kate was very touched, and accepted the invitation to be at Jessie's little eighteenth birthday celebration, but as she said to Mag, –

"It's quite a while since I've been amongst a lot of strangers. I will feel awkward!"

"Ow! Go on nah, I'm sure yer won't Kate. Don't worry, yer'll enjoy yerself, you see!"

Mag, she was determined, and got her own way.

196

And Annie, – now she could ask her and Bessie to the party. Since the old girl had been back with Bessie, by all accounts they both got on like a house on fire! Best day's work she could have done.

It was grand being able to see again, her Annie, as large as life standing in the doorway of the four ale bar holding her jug, though this time it was not for her dear "'Arry, but both Bessie and herself. Come to think of it though, – Maggie hadn't seen Annie for more than a week.

"'Ope she's alright!" and trying not to attach too much importance to the old gal's absence, she knuckled down and began serving the regulars in the pub that opening time.

"'Ello Mag!" Glory be, it *was* Annie, standing there grinning, waiting for Mag's reaction as she clapped her eyes on her.

"Blimey Ann, where the Devil yer bin? I got worried abart you an' Bessie."

"Well!" the indomitable old Lady in question, and not in so many words, put it this way.

"Its like this 'ere. – Me an' Bessie 'ave bin up Norf, ter stay wiv 'er Son fer a bit. – In Liverpool 'e lives, by the Docks. – Dus somefin' on the big ships."

"Ow did yer like it Ann?" asked Mag. "Tell us abart it."

"All I knows Mag, is they sound like a lot a foriners up there. They talk that funny! Can't understand a word they say. Not like us darn 'ere, we all talk proper, we dus!"

She was a case that Annie! – Mag suspected them up in Liverpool too, had wondered half the time, what the hell Annie was talking about!

"Nah you are 'ere Ann, I kin tell yer, yer 'ave bin invited ter Jess's party next week. You 'n Bessie too, an' don' say yer' carn' come."

Although Mag knew she had got this good, but a little presumptuous idea of giving Jess a bit of a do, what was she going to dig up in the way of food?

Then she had another worry, she had to refrain from inviting anyone else, their house was only small. Still she could poke them in somewhere!

So on one warm bright Saturday evening in Brody Street, a small gathering of good-humoured friends and neighbours grouped together in Mag's front parlour. But as small as it was, there was ample room for them all to chin-wag, drink tea, and partake too, of a little tipple to toast Jess on her eighteenth.

The atmosphere was as it should be, on such an occasion, with Annie there causing a few wry smiles, and Mag very pleased to see Kate enjoying herself and laughing at Annie's droll humorous banter. But it was not until later on that evening, that Tommy was able to get away from the Pub and Mag had been anxious for a while wondering, –

"Wasn't he going to turn up?" But she needn't have fretted, as she discovered.

"Come in Tommy!" Showing him into the parlour, she said, "Make yerself at 'ome!" giving him a glass of beer.

There was no shortage of liquid refreshment due to the good hearted donation of a few bottles of the right stuff for a party, the provision of these made by Maureen and Les.

As for the eatables. Kate herself, by some magical means unknown had conjured up a fine display for Mag's table, with a little help too from the neighbours rations.

Mag found it very difficult in concealing how touched she was at everybody's generosity and as the evening progressed, each moment was filled with laughter and good humour, the thoughts of anything to do with war were forgotten for a while. But Mag, she made sure she never missed an opportunity in keeping Tommy and Kate talking, once she had introduced them both, having one careful eye on them, and the other on the enjoyment of the revellers for the rest of the evening.

"It was a lovely little do," as Jess said, when it was all over, – "Mum and Dad, fanks fer everyfin. It was nice!"

"I luv yer both, *very* much!"

And so, with those last few short words. – In Mag's eyes, 'It said enough!'

For some days after that, Maggie had a great feeling of accomplishment. But she mustn't count her chickens yet!

Besides there was so much else going on around, and not good either! The radio and newspapers reported of the U-boats in the Atlantic, sinking our ships with great loss of life. Ships full of supplies and food for Britain.

This news struck fear into the heart of Mag. Her first thought was always for Rob. She only knew he had been sent to Portsmouth, and as far as she did know, he was still there on basic training.

"Nah gal, it's no good yer jumpin' ter conclusions. Rob's gonna be able ter take care of 'imself, 'e's a big lad nah, so stop yer frettin'."

But Bert, he never let on how fearful *he* felt.

Kate and Mag were having a quick cup of tea in the front parlour. Kate had some errands to do up the town, and had popped round Mag's. "Did she want anything brought back," she wanted to know?

"Funny old day Kate, it don' know wever it wants ter rain or not! – Wish it would make up its mind, I've got a daffy a washin' ter put art."

199

It was two days after Jess's do, with the memory still fresh, and looking at Kate coolly sitting there. Mag was just dying to ask her a question, and was about to pluck up the courage to get the words out, when Kate oddly enough, must have read her mind!

"What a lovely evening it was Maggie, don't you think? I thoroughly enjoyed all of it, and most certainly Jess must have done so too."

"Glad yer did Kate, though it wouldn't a bin anywhere near as nice, if you hadn't 'ave 'elped, – with all that cookin' yer did fer me."

Kate remained silent for a few minutes, then she came out with just what Mag had hoped.

"What a nice man is your Tommy, I found him to be very interesting, and good to talk to. He is not a *bit* as I had imagined, after all you had told me Mag. And of how he came to make his entrance into the Pub that day!" As Maggie listened, she glowed inwardly, forcing back a complacent smile, – Wasn't this just what she had been hoping for. – "Had it done the trick?"

"Yes", she said to herself, – "Perfect!"

"Mag! You know you're a crafty ol' moo."

"It's just what the Doctor ordered."

"I've dun it!"

But now the conversation was suddenly interrupted and to Mag's least suspecting and totally unexpected surprise, – the front door, which was already half open, was pushed back with a loud bang, and Rob's voice was heard calling out to her, –

"Mu'um! – You in? – It's me, – Rob!"

Poor Mag, she almost fell over, and with no more ado, she was all arms and legs, tripping and falling over everything, until she was across the room and hugging him. It couldn't be! – It was. – Yes, Robbie her Sailor boy!

"Son, 'Ow! – Let me look at yer?" she cried, blinking back the tears of joy. Standing back, she stared at him, this man, no longer a boy. Kitted out in his Naval uniform, plus the little 'dicky' and smart sailor cap with 'H.M.S.' proudly displayed across its riband.

Was this really her baby? – 'No! Not any more.' – She choked back a little sob. "Sit darn luv. – Wanna cuppa tea?" – What else could she say?

Kate had made a quick departure. It would not be noticed, she felt sure!

When the shock of seeing Rob had cooled down a little, he then spoke of his reason for his appearance at such short notice. He was on two days compassionate leave. Rob was now to be assigned to a ship and was to report for duty.

As a fully-fledged Able Seaman, he was ready to be called upon to serve his country.

Maggie knew now she had to be prepared for anything, if need be the worst and there was nothing she could do about it. Rob had got his wish, and when duty called, he would be off on one of those ships he had dreamed about. Out on those mighty oceans and cruel seas.

A tired and worried Bert made his weary way back along the hot dusty streets to home, after the pawn shop had shut for the weekend. – Business had been nowhere as brisk as it usually was on a Saturday, when the owners of the suits, the boots, and the clobber they'd popped into pawn at the beginning of the week, were due to turn up to redeem their much needed attire. Maybe to wear for a trip to the Pub or the Park with the Kids!

Everywhere you looked, everyone you met, had the same troubled and woe-begone look. It was being caused by all the events and disastrous happenings going on. There was this awful spectacle of our boys out there on the bombed and blasted beaches of France, with their backs against the wall, in a God forsaken place called 'Dunkirk' – being threatened with annihilation by Jerry, –

"Gawd 'elp the poor blighters!"

Bert knew only too well what kind of hell they must be going through, but he could do nothing to help them. Except he could be sure of one thing, and that was the fact Rob was doing just that, and may be on one of the many ships, large or small, with others who were also risking all.

To get somehow, across that stretch of water, in anything that could float to save those lads pinned down there with only evil and certain death, on one side, and the last bastion of hope, with everything that stood for decency and sanity on the other, in a world which had suddenly gone mad!

Tommy Larkin lay on his bed in his usual position, staring thoughtfully up at the ceiling, – there were even more fly marks now, and new bug stains!

He was going over the events of that evening at Mag's, but most of all, that meeting with her neighbour Kate! Though this was not the only time she had entered his thoughts.

How odd it was to find, during the conversation he had with her, that she had been a Nurse back in the last war too, just as Mary his wife, – and in lots of ways Kate had reminded him of her.

They had spent quite a good space of time chatting, and it occurred to him how very much he enjoyed her company.

He realised with surprise, that he would very much like to see her again sometime!

Tommy was also giving some thought to becoming an Air Raid Warden, He had to pull his weight, and must do something. 'I'll see about it tomorrow,' he promised himself. 'I'm not much use at doing anything else. Besides I am too old.' – But he was not alone!

Young Jim was standing by the lampost up the street kicking his heels. He was waiting for Dan, and feeling very fed up and impatient. He wanted very much to get into this War business too, and into all what was going on, right now. Rob was away in the Navy and Jess was waiting for her entry into the Women's Land Army. And here he was doin', – 'Sweet Fanny Adams!'

"Cum on Dan! – Where yer bin, yer took yer bloomin' time, didn't yer! The big film'll be started!"

They were now off to the Poxy Roxy!

With the scraping of locks and the rattling of keys, Maureen opened the doors to the 'Crown and Anchor.'

Old Wally Fox was the first one in. Never missed, he didn't! He lived across the street from the Pub, and everyone swore blind, he sat and watched for the Pub doors to open, to beat everyone else. He had been misnamed they said, and called him now, not Wally, – but Wiley! Well, they couldn't be far orf it! Could they?

"Pint a me usual and five Woodbines Missis."

He looked around the bar, empty now, but it would soon fill up. It always did!

It was the evening of the Darts Club meeting, and the air would again be full of tobacco smoke fumes, coughing, cussing and blinding.

'Chunky' Morris the Master of Ceremonies for the evening was setting up things ready.

Tommy was over in the corner by the piano, talking to a couple of seamen who'd just arrived back, from a South Coast port.

"The state a some a those poor buggers, – yer should see' em! Well I've seen some sights in my time, I can tell yer, but nuffin' like what's goin' on darn there."

"Hundreds of 'em bein' brought back on stretchers, carried, or 'elped along by anuvver poor devil, wiv 'is arm arf torn orf, all covered in blood!"

"Yer could ov cried! Jesus Christ! They looked arf dead some of 'em. But yer know what? I noticed a couple ov the poor blokes who could still conjure up a smile!"

"Blimey, I fawt I'd seen everyfin'! Nah, I'm wrong there. I did witness somefin' terday, – an' that was sheer unmitigated guts and Bulldog courage!"

That Bluddy 'Itler! 'E ain't got a chance in 'Ell!"

"Yer, but it ain' gonna 'elp much, nah that Mussolini as chucked 'is lot in wiv the Jerry rabble! – I've 'eard it said, Italy's declaring war on us nah!" said another bloke.

"'Ere, we don't want that kind a talk ararnd 'ere mate."

"Careless talk costs lives!" growled Joe butting in.

"Yer callin' me lily-livered?" said the culprit who had started this shemozzle, as he raised his fists up to Joe's face.

"Watchit, I've 'ad enough a this!" shouted Les.

"Pack it or you're out!"

Chapter: Eighteen

DUNKIRK'S LITTLE SHIPS!

From humble barge, to fishing smack,
Under threat from hellish air attack.
Those little ships prepare to sail,
To say them nay? – Of no avail!

Sailing away, to peril untold,
God fearing men – steadfast and bold.
T'was not their policy, a duty to shirk,
Convoys of heroes, bound for Dunkirk.

In little ships, but giant of heart,
No scruples, no qualms, feared not to depart.
To a Hell on Earth on blasted beach,
Mud covered shell-shocked troops to reach.

With dignity and pride, they patiently wait,
Prepared and ready, to accept their fate.
But for these ships, desiring no glory,
Would Dunkirk's scenario, tell a different story?

We must ne'er forget these gallant men,
Who came from village, dale and glen.
Their nightmare suffering, tears and sorrow,
For our today, they dared their tomorrow!

The sights that had met Rob's gaze as the ship neared the shores of Dunkirk, were unprecedented.

He'd had some idea what the scenes must be like, by the pictures on the newsreels back home, but in no way, was he prepared to witness this Hell, and that was exactly the right word to describe it!

Everywhere his eyes rested, were vessels of every description. Ships and yet more ships. Barges, Tugs, paddle steamers, little yachts, anything and everything that could float. They were on there way, sailing towards the beaches of Dunkirk by any means they could find, to get their boys back off those bloody beaches.

But it was the plight of these mud covered weary, red-eyed soldiers, wading out from the shore with the hope someone would pluck them from out of this Hell hole, that shocked and appalled Rob, so desperate to reach the helping hands that were held out to drag them back to safety, yet were too exhausted, with their blood oozing from severed arms, so horribly injured, that they just gave up, and let themselves sink back into the blood-fringed foam, already scarred with the many lifeless bodies of their mates.

The sky above was charged with shell bursts and gunfire, from Stuka dive bombers, taking a heavy toll of many unfortunate craft as they struggled to reach the shore and the hordes of desperate men who clung to the upturned boats, or onto anything they could possibly grab hold of, to escape the mighty waves, that were being churned up by so much action all around. Rob – he felt sick! He couldn't help it and was not ashamed, as so many of his mates there also admitted feeling, when they could bring themselves to talk about it, and of what never before in their lives, had they ever experienced.

But at this moment in time, it was more important, getting these chaps out of this hellhole!

Then the deafening roar of the dive-bombers again as they put paid to a barge, full of desperate men some way away. It went up with a bang! Nothing was left of them!

Rob was struggling to haul one who'd copped it, to lay him on the deck, just as this piece of shrapnel hit him. He felt something wet trickling down his forehead, and into his eyes, but he carried on with his task, while wiping away the blood, which almost blurred his vision. This was coming from a deep gash in his forehead.

"Fanks mate!" he heard one wounded Tommy say, as he put him alongside some of the men laying in rows on the deck. Numbers of these poor blighters were in such a sad and sorry state, – many of them 'no hopers,' but at least they had been saved from a watery grave.

Rob slaved on, with no other thoughts than to do just what he was there for, while trying to shut out the noise that was going on all around him. But it was the moans and groans that came from some of the wounded, with every now and again an agonising scream coming from one poor bloke. That was what got him! – It was over the top of the perpetual tumult, the sound of weeping from this same bloke along the deck and another voice that kept on calling "Mother, Mother," – and then, – Silence!

The shell-splintered, and over burdened vessels of all shapes and sizes, with untold numbers of crippled and shell-shocked men, scarred in body and mind but *not* in spirit, limped modestly and without ceremony back into ports that they had unflinchingly left behind hours before to perform an immense and challenging task now successfully accomplished. 338,000 men had been brought home alive!

Rob hoped that in the years ahead he would be able to look back and feel proud to have been part of such a daring feat. Wouldn't he have a lot to tell his Mum about, when he got back home?

Wholly and completely unaware of what she was supposed to be doing, Mag's mind was certainly not on her job. Her thoughts were somewhere else right now.

She'd been listening to the wireless, to the announcer saying, – "How it was all hell let loose out there."

"Was Rob art there in, Dunkirk did they call it? and in all what was going on, – Maybe gettin' 'imself 'urt?"

"Gawd! She was frightened! Cold wiv fear, she was, – she'd never felt so afraid!"

This won't do, there were the others to think about! She put her washing board back in its place under the sink, and scratching her head thought, –

"What's the matter wiv me? Pull yer socks up gal."

"Ah! Was that the milkman?"

There was someone outside the door.

"Who's that nah!" She wasn't expecting anyone!

She dried her hands, almost tripped over the washing basket, still half filled with dirty clothes she had meant to wash. – "But that can wait. Better open the blasted door!"

"'Ello Ma! – It's me, – Rob."

Mag let out a shriek!

"No! It can't be true," she put out her hand and touched the sleeve of his tunic, it felt rough. Yes it *was* him. – It *was* Rob! – Large as life standing on her snowy white doorstep.

She looked him up and down, but noticed right away how he was not quite the Rob with the usual ready smile. He looked strained and in an odd kind of way, a little concussed! He was, like somebody who had experienced deep shock, and what was that dressing for on his head? She witnessed this as he took off his cap?

"Just a gash Mum." he told her, "Nuffin really!"

"Sit yerself darn there Rob lad, an' give us yer kitbag. I know what *you* need, an' that's, – A nice cuppa tea!"

She went out into the scullery to fill the old kettle, and with a deep frown on her face, Maggie wondered how to deal with this new Rob!

"'Ere yer are luv, git this darn yer!"

She waited for him to speak, but then, –

"Jus' take yer time lad," she said as she leaned across and took hold of both his hands. "Oh Mum!" He broke down there and then. At this moment Rob was no longer her big boy, but the toddler with his Mum, who was the only one who would understand and believe him, –

There *was* a bogeyman in that horrible nightmare, he'd just awoke from. – He buried his head in his hands, –

"Oh Mum, it was HELL! – Just sheer bloody slaughter, everywhere!" Maggie was so glad they were alone, and the others were not there to witness all this.

They sat there quietly for some time neither speaking, until all of a sudden Rob stood up. – He'd had enough! –

"I kin do better than sit 'ere acting this way! – Where's Snowy?" he said looking around. "I'll take 'im fer a run!" –

"'E's still 'ere 'ain' 'e Mum?"

Mag watched him, as he went off down the road, with an excited Snowy yapping at his heels. She was still shaking, for this had been quite an ordeal. – Then Mag exploded! –

"Damn an' blast this War, an all those senseless, spineless buggers responsible for all this suffering!" She was furious, and had never felt so bloody angry before, but had to calm down, for Rob had arrived back with Snowy.

And now his two days furlough was up, and it was time to go. The days had gone by in a flash. So short they had been. – But with his usual big smile, a wave and, –

"Chin up Ma, don't worry! – I'll be back soon, – It was real good ter see yer!" – and Rob was gone.

Mag sighed and pushed her hair back with her soapy hands and looked across at the clock. It was very quiet there, and for a while she was back in the past, as ghostly voices could be heard quite distinctly from the corner by the coal cupboard. – Young Jim's, with a right old whine! –

"Mum I don' wanna go ter school terday. Let me stay at 'ome. Billy Nesbit says 'e's gonner 'it me, 'cos I broke one a 'is Conkers, yesterdee!"

And there was another voice, – Jess's, –

"Can't find me uvver shoe, I'll be late fer school!"

"Ow never mind, I got it nah Mum!" and Jim again, –

"Kin I 'ave a penny fer sweets?"

Then there was a third voice, but a lot deeper this time.

"It's me Mag, – I 'ad ter come 'ome, – I feel darn right 'orrible!" In reality, it was now Bert, and he looked in a bad way, just like he said.

"What's the matter luv? 'Ere sit darn there, I'll getcher a drink!" – "Blimey, he does look rough, an all! – No two ways abart it." she thought.

"Let's git yer up ter bed," she said, getting hold of his arm. Bert didn't argue and let Mag lead him up the stairs, holding on tight to her. Once she had settled him down in bed, she went and called over the garden wall to Kate.

"Kin yer spare a minit Kate, and come over an' 'ave a look at Bert, he's real bad."

"Do yer mind? I don' know what else ter do."

"Don't worry. I'll be right over Mag!"

Kate was pretty blunt, after taking one look at Bert.

"It seems to me, it might be his appendix, I don't know, but we must get him to a hospital right away!"

"Poor Bert" Mag was in a right tizzy, thinking, –

"It never rains, but when it does. – It bluddy pours!"

But Kate she was a real gem, she saw to everything and had Bert off and into Hospital before you could say Knife!

"Strange 'ow suddenly these fings 'appen though. One minit yer sweatin' yer eyeballs art, standin' there scrubbin' their clobber, and the next minit before yer look rarnd, yer sitting in an 'orspital corridor worryin', an' bitin' yer fingernails down to yer elbows."

"Mrs Hope? I've come to tell you your husband has had a very close shave, it was a near thing you know!"

"If you had delayed calling that Ambulance, I am sure Mr Hope would no longer be with us!"

"Fank you Doctor, and Fank you Gawd," she whispered as she sat by Bert's bedside, later on.

No pub this evening for you Mag! And as she and Kate talked afterwards, of the unexpected events of that day, she argued with her conscience, – was it time for her to pack up her job at the old 'Crown and Anchor?' But Bert wouldn't hear of it, when she suggested it.

"Not on my account yer won't old gal! You like it there too much. But yer will chuck it in, if it gets more than yer can manage. I'll see ter that. So stop yer worryin', I'm O.K. and yer'll soon be seeing me jumpin' around again, jus' like a Jack Rabbit, afore yer know it!"

That was a right scare she'd had, and as she sat by the Hospital bed, holding Bert's hand tight, and looking up at his craggy face, – (Yes, he was getting *very* lined).

Mag said a quiet, – Thankyou.

"Jus' as I fort Kate, they've gorn an' done it, ain't they? They've rationed our cups a tea! 'Ow the 'ell kin we make a decent pot a tea wiv only two ounces a tea a week?"

"An' you Kate, there's only one a you. Yer tea when yer make it, will look like a lotta gnats." said Maggie, one afternoon, as steadily and little by little the tempo of the war was speeding up.

"'Ark at that Dad, – The Jerries 'ave got over as far as the Sarf coast nah!"

Jim was talking about the activity of the German Luftwaffe planes, now bombing many South coast towns.

"But they won't get any furver, not wiv our Spitfires on their tails. – Cor! Yer ought ter see the dog fights they 'ave. Wish I could see 'em! – Go on lads, give em 'ell!"

"'Old on. 'old on! I'm not 'avin' that kind a talk. Not at my dinner table! As I told yer once, – War ain't no cake walk fer no one. So mind yer marf!"

"An' I tell yer this, – No soddin' Jerry's gonna set foot on this land of ours, not if we kin 'elp it, I know!" Bert was that adamant.

"Where's Jess?"

Bert he'd then changed the subject.

"Don' see much of 'er these days. It's been a bit quiet rarnd 'ere, wiv Rob gorn back nah."

"She seems to always be chasing orf art wiv that Reg of 'ers. 'Bout time she stayed in an' 'elped yer a bit!"

"Nah Bert, yer can't say that, don' be such an ol' misery. They're only young once, an' Gor Blimey, there ain' much fer Jess ter look forward ter! – They'll be cartin' Reg orf to join the Army soon."

Bert, who had never had a very high opinion of Reg, looked up and made a wry face, saying, –

"Hmmh! The only army that boy's ever likely ter get into, is Fred Carno's!"

Jess herself, was having her mind taken up with other things, and not to do with the War either! She and Reg hadn't been hitting it off for a long time.

Silly nit pickin', that's what it was.

"Yer can't fink of nuffin else, always goin' on abart buzzin' orf in the Land Army. Yer ain't 'ad 'ardly any time fer me at all lately." – Reg would moan.

"Don't talk ser daft!" – Jess would reply.

"Are yer ready? We're s'posed ter be goin' ter the pictures. – Yer comin' or ain't yer? – Ow, please yerself!"

But now the *real* war had started! England was on her own. It wasn't a good feeling either. But did it look as if it was the end of the world?

"Not on yer Nelly" Mag thought when she'd walked past placards that seemed to be saying everywhere you looked, that France had fallen, and the Jerries were now in Paris. – So where next?

"Just let 'em try it on 'ere!" Bert said.

"I'll tell yer this much, if they ever tried ter get over 'ere, an' I came across one of 'em, – I'll take 'is bleedin' Bayonet and shove it right up where it 'urts most!"

Mag had to laugh, –

"That's a bit steep me ol' Mate. Sounds pretty painful, – if yer arst me!"

Bert had been listening intently to the wireless when he suddenly turned and said, –

"Ssh! All a yer! – Winston Churchill's made his first speech as Prime Minister, and a B.B.C. announcer is gonna read it art over the air, an' tell us what 'e says, – So be quiet young Jim!"

There was dead silence, which caused a bit of eyebrow lifting, when Jim actually heeded this warning, while the announcer was repeating Churchill's words, mustering the people of Britain to prepare themselves for a threatened invasion. Saying he had nothing to offer other than, – blood, toil, tears and sweat!

"We shall fight on the beaches, we shall fight on the landing grounds, we shall fight in the fields, *and* in the streets, we shall fight in the hills, we shall never surrender!"

What is our aim? Our aim is, I can answer in one word, – Victory! – Victory at all costs, to rid this world of Nazi tyranny, however long and hard the road may be!"

"Yer know Maggie, if anyone has been in any doubt abart this bluddy war's outcome, that speech of Winston's should 'ave made up their minds what the result *will* be."

"So although we're on our Jack Jones nah, an' that thick skulled clod over in 'is rat-ole in Berlin thinks 'e's gonna git anywhere near this little ol' Island ov ours, 'e's bluddy well barkin' up the wrong tree!"

Then Bert went off round the Air Raid Warden's Post. Gammy arm or no gammy arm, there was something he could do, in an emergency, – He joined the A.R.P!

"'Ave yer 'eard anyfin' yet Jess, abart yer visit ter the recruitment office?"

"No Mum, but I should know soon!"

Although Jess appeared to be acting normal, she was actually champing at the bit, eagerly awaiting notice of her posting as a Land Army girl to somewhere right out in the country, – to green fields and pastures new.

Away from smelly noisy factories, smoking chimneys, pollution and poverty, – from all that she'd ever known, during her short life.

214

But Mag was listening to Jess speaking, with a feeling of despair. The time was approaching, when they would be seeing Jess off too. On a journey to goodness knows where, and for how long would it be? As any mother had said and would be saying as she did now, –

"Why in 'eaven's name, didn't those creatures who started these bluddy wars, sort things art fer their selves? And not git the innocents ter go an' fight the wars fer 'em! They can't 'ave the guts!" – She feared for the future.

There was young Jim coming along now, and all he ever spoke about was how the time was getting closer, for him to be kitted out in a battledress and given a bloody gun, so he could go off and shoot someone no different from himself, who had kept their noses clean and done nobody any harm.

When you come to think of it, – really in some ways, it was a pretty unsavoury world!

"I 'ope I git sent somewhere nice Mum, like a farm in the country down in Kent or Sussex. D'ya remember when we went 'Oppin'? Jess was saying.

That was nice darn there, wern't it? I shan't fergit that first night. Mum. Wasn't it dark? I never told yer but I was really scared! – An' I know Jim was, cos' 'e told me 'e wet 'imself! 'E said as not ter say nuffin to yer. Don' let on I told yer, will yer Mum? – Or 'e'll 'ave me guts fer garters!"

Bert came in then, full of his afternoon spent round at the A.R.P. post, in Brick Street.

"Mag, – d'yer know who was rarnd there terday?"

"Tommy – 'E turned up! – 'E's an Air raid Warden nah! We 'ad a nice little chat, all abart the last War.

"Not a bad bloke, Tommy! Told me 'e used ter live over in Suffolk years ago." –

"Nice place Suffolk!"

"What yer doin' Saturday afternoon Dan? I feel like celebratin'. Yer knew I started me new job this week didn't yer? Jim was saying.

"So what yer doin' nah then, and why did yer leave 'Cakebreads'? asked Dan.

"Go on wiv yer, – wouldn't *you* 'ave done if you'd bin in my place? I got sick a lookin' at blasted cakes and makin' dough all day!" said Jim.

"Blimey Mate! – 'ow much dough *did* yer make Jim? Yer must be a millionaire by nah!" Dan chuckled.

That joke though, completely went over Jim's head, as he patiently carried on trying to get over to his friend, what he did now to earn a bob or two.

"Well, it ain't the kind a fing me Dad's very 'appy abart, – but its more of a blokes job than messin' around makin' a lot a pastry. That's only fer women!"

"This place is over in Brick Lane in a big Brewery, as a sort ov a porter. I'm 'elpin' ter load casks and barrels, on ter Drays they call 'em."

"That means I work wiv 'orsis, – And yer know 'ow I likes 'orsis Dan!"

Now Dan, he was quite impressed with all this, it sounded good to him. He wasn't too keen on where he was working, – called it a dead end job, – he worked for an Undertaker!

"I don't work this Saturday afternoon," said Jim, –

"'Ow abart us goin' over there, ter Brick Lane, an' I'll show yer where it is."

"It's quite a walk though!"

216

Chapter: Nineteen

It was one of those exceptionally hot and unpredictable Indian Summer afternoons in early September, and as it was Saturday, people kept their fingers crossed, for as the old saying goes, – 'It always rains at the weekend, – and rains on the poor workers!' They'd slogged all-week and looked forward to the only two days when they could kiss the bosses hand farewell for a breather.

A few fleecy white clouds decorated a clear blue sky, as George the gatekeeper sat in his little green hut at the docks gate, still on duty! and it seemed there was to be no peace for the wicked! He had to be there, in case some wise guy attempted to run off with one of the cranes, or even a Thames luggerboat. (He'd be lucky!

George had just made a brew up and leaned back in his chair with the newspaper.

What was happening now with the war game?

It wasn't nice reading at all.

All through the past couple of months, ever since the Jerries had marched into Paris and the whole of the Low Countries were now in their hands, people wondered, 'What has the blighter up his sleeve now?'

It was a waiting game! Apart from the dog fights over the South Coast with quite a number of German M.E.109s being brought down by the inimitable Spitfire pilots and the obstruction of Barrage Balloons. It was a nail biting time!

But the population around the East End, were going about their business as usual. Children played games.

Threw a rope over the top of a lamp post bar to make a swing, Played marbles and knock down ginger.

Busy street markets were still finding trade good for a Saturday despite the rationing of some goods, and if you kept your eyes open for the Rozzers, you could pick up a bit of extra sugar or tea on the Black Market. But you were then branded as bad as the 'What Name' who sold it to you!

But Mag on this perfect summer afternoon, listened to the raucous sounds of the stall holders, as she wended her way through the hordes of shoppers, each with their eyes open for a Bargain coming their way.

"'E'are lady! Nah yer carn't say no ter this little lot!" – The soft-soaped, honey-mouthed auctioneer was holding out a generous amount of fruit in a scale pan, to a group of likely customers.

"An' I'll frow in these as well." adding a handful of tomatoes to the pile.

"Fanks. Bless yer 'art lady!" and continued shouting, – "Anymore fer anymore?"

Mag stopped at a fish stall, looking at a big bowl full of live eels, slithering and writhing in their death throes. Although she loved the eel pies and mash that made up best part of their weekly diet, it didn't do much for her guilty conscience seeing them struggling, as they were now.

"Poor fings!"

She hurried along feeling easier when she reached the newspaper and bookstalls.

Jim would be looking for his American comic papers when she got back home. Mag had never missed, – not once, taking home a few of these comics with Laurel and Hardy's and Our Gang's antics, recreated in them. Jim would never forgive her if she forgot.

Mag felt like a drink, it was thirsty work walking along through the dusty tracks between the stalls.

"Ah! There was a refreshment stall!"

"I bet they ain't got no tea though."

But Maggie was in luck. That feels better! She'd managed to get her cuppa tea.

But it was really time she went home. Then she heard over the top of all the market traders din, a childs voice. He had let out such a howl, having received a clout round the ear'ole and was now sobbing. – "Serves yer right." his ma was saying, – "Yer arst fer that!"

"I told yer ter stay put, an' 'old on ter that pram 'andle!"

"Someone might a gorn an run orf wiv our little Willy! Nah stand 'ere, whilst I go an git me spuds and don't go away or yer'll git anuvver one."

When finally Mag decided she'd had enough, and turned to go, she heard the strains of 'Run Rabbit Run' coming from Morry Harmer's barrel organ, which was parked along by the side of the Cats meat stall.

Come rain, – Come shine, he stood at this same spot every Saturday with his organ, about as long as everyone around there could remember.

Morry, – poor devil was another bloke who had copped a packet in the last war and had not done a days work since.

Now who would go and employ a poor bugger like him, what only had one eye, and when 'arf the time he couldn't even remember his own name!

But he could bloody well play that old Barrel organ!

Then it came. – Starting at first like a cry of woe. Then got louder, rising into a great crescendo. It could only be the Air Raid Siren. – A hellish noise, but it was not as threatening as another alarming sound, which grew in volume as it got nearer. It resembled the drone of bluebottles, which was exactly what they did look like to everyone who stood transfixed, – rooted, as they stared upwards, trying to shade their eyes from the sun.

An A.R.P. Warden who had turned up, shouted at the top of his voice, –

"Bloody Hell, – they're German planes. – Hundreds of em! – They are after the Docks! – The buggers are out to smash us up!"

It was only seconds before the first flash appeared and the ground shook violently beneath them. Another shout, –

"They're bombing us!"

Jack Finney the Warden, he yelled even louder now, –

"Fer Christ's Sake, git for the shelters!"

"Belt fer yer lives. – Run like bluddy 'ell!"

It was near pandemonium! A hand suddenly came from somewhere and grabbed Mag's arm, and Tommy's voice was saying, – "Come on Maggie, run!"

Partly shoving, partly trying to calm her, he pushed her down some stone steps leading to the underground chamber of the Baptist Chapel, before he hurried off again. There were already a crowd of petrified men, women and children, squatting on the stone floors, the children were crying, Mothers, ashen faced, trying to calm them down.

"Oh! My Gawd, what's 'appenin?"

The enemy bombers were using the River as a guide to drop their lethal cargoes of death and destruction on scores of unsuspecting folk, as well as attempting to lay waste, to almost half the mighty Docks of London.

On a beautiful and serene afternoon that had begun so commonplace, with everyone going about their business, – everything now had changed. – It had become a nightmare!

In the space of an hour, nearly the whole of the Docks on both sides of the Thames River, were ablaze!

Firemen were coming from all over parts of London and faced these horrific scenes, as they raced to help.

Battling desperately with death, the high walls of blazing warehouses collapsed taking the firemen down with them. When others, grey faced and exhausted took over, they suffered the same fate.

And so it went on, that fateful Saturday afternoon, which had begun with a clear and unsullied blue sky, with only a few puffs of fleecy white cloud dotted all about. But now, blotted out with choking black smoke, which had enveloped the whole of London for miles around. People as far as Kent and Surrey, and even further afield, could see the flames, and as the hours went by they were unable to ascertain, if it was day or night, as the whole sky was afire and still blood red with angry flames!

Sparks shot up from timber burning along with the piles of cargo stacked up in the warehouses and everything that could melt, did so, in that hot and fuming, fiery furnace.

It was, as one blackened face fireman to his mate said, – "Like Hell on Earth!" as he tried to drag him to safety, but as his strength gave out, they both succumbed to the horrible heat, and perished there together.

With these murderous scenes, hundreds had experienced their first meeting with the evils of this new kind of war. Masses of innocent people fleeing for shelter, some with their clothing on fire, but still looking for their loved ones, stricken with fear. –

"Where were they?" Thinking to themselves, would they ever find them?

"Was this really the end of the World?"

Mag looked around at the others squatting on the stone floors. What thoughts were going through their minds, – Were they the same as hers?

Her heart was pounding, almost as loud as the crash of the bombs she could hear. The ground above was quaking and so was she!

Would this terrible noise never stop? It jarred every part of her body. The screech of every bomb as it fell to earth was nerve wracking, hellish. But all the while that outrage and such violence was going on up there, bringing so much terror, Mag was almost beside herself with rage. Her blood was boiling at the thought that, –

"What human being, – if they were human, had the right to do this to their fellow man?

But that evil coward back there in Berlin, who was responsible for all that he thinks he has successfully accomplished here, – would never, ever, subjugate or conquer these people who toiled here, and suffered here. Although thoroughly shaken and distressed, as well as bloody well scared, – they would *not allow it* to happen.

"Give us the chance and we'll show 'em what we'll do ter the Bastard!!"

But Mag, she must get out of this place and go and find the others, – her family.

"Sorry lady, yer can't leave, not yet!"

"Not till this bluddy lot stops." said the Warden.

George had finished his fag, and drunk the teapot dry. He stood up and stretched himself, –

"Can't keep sittin' 'ere, guzzlin tea!"

"Let's go art an' 'ave a butcher's 'ook, – an' see what's doin' out there."

Earlier on, he'd heard the Air Raid Siren but he had got used to that now.

"They must be testin it. – Cussed row!"

Shutting the door of his hut behind him, and with both hands shoved in his pockets, he stood for a while, looking out across the Dock and up towards the River.

"Not much activity goin' on there," and fumbled in his jacket pocket for a sweet his old girl said she'd popped in there. – George liked a bit of toffee to chew!

Not a bad old stick was his Lucy. Bin a good Mother to their six kids. They were all grown up now, and had litters of their own.

"Pretty good feeling, being a Grandfarver, but yer 'as ter 'ave yer 'and in yer pocket most a the time."

Little Stanley's birthday was coming up, – What was he now, – Three? Wonder what he wants! – Top brick off the Chimney I bet, – They all did these days!"

George hesitated, – "Funny! – What sort a noise is that?" – He couldn't put a name to it.

A far away drone, a bit like a bumblebee. Then it was not one, – but lots, coming up the river.

The noise seemed to get louder and louder, until it became a whirring sound, – and then he saw them. Just a black patch at first, then fanned out. He came to, – Planes!

They were aeroplanes, – "'undreds of 'em!" Then it dawned on him, – "Those are not ours!" –

"They're Jerries. – Bluddy 'ell!"

Luftwaffe Bombers flying in formation, following the gleaming strip of the winding Thames River. It bloody well hit him then, – that they were not here on a friendly visit.

"They're after the Docks, the bastards!"

"God almighty! What do we do nah?"

But there was not a thing he could do, only stare blankly at the sinister Black Armada, as the gap between them and him got shorter and shorter, poor George, well! – he never heard that bomb, – the one with his name on it!

Letting the garden gate go back with a bang, Bert walked up the path and opened the door. Somebody was already in the house.

"Is that you Jess?" he called, seeing her coat slung over the arm of the chair.

A muffled reply came from upstairs.

"Yes, its me Dad."

Jess's voice didn't sound too happy. She'd been crying.

"Ow Gawd, *not* agin! – This is *all* I need. – That gel's always bawlin'! – Better leave it till 'er muvver gits in. – She knows 'ow ter deal wiv 'er, – I'm blowed if I do. – S'pose I'd better put the kettle on, Mag'll be in soon!"

While he waited for it to boil, Bert wandered out into the yard, and took a decko around. There wasn't much growing out there, other than weeds, nothing decent would grow in such rotten soil.

There wasn't any point, it hardly ever saw the Sun! He went back indoors and found Jess had made the tea.

"'Ere ye'ar Dad," Jess looking at him with red rimmed eyes, – She'd really had a bawl!!

"Nah lass, what was all that abart, all that snivellin'?"

"Why ain't yer art wiv Reg?"

"We've finished, Reg an' me. That's why! But let's leave it at that nah, shall we, eh?"

"I don't wanna talk abart it!"

At the very minute of Jess uttering those words, the Air Raid warning started its usual Banshee wailing.

Bert and Jess they both stopped and looked at each other and then carried on drinking their tea.

"'Ow! It's only them muckin' abart, tryin' 'em art. I'm gittin' used to it nah Dad. – Ain't you?"

That was right, – It had all started off, putting the wind up everybody, – but now it was just a part of life!

But to Bert it wasn't his job to treat anything now as matter of fact. It could turn out to be, one of these days, – *The real thing!*

And so it happened that on this fine, warm and comparatively normal Saturday afternoon, it did just that, – and as Mabel moaned to her old man, –

"They're goin' on a bit ain't they? Never 'eard that siren sound like that 'afore, – Bluddy noise gits on my nerves it do. – Wish it would stop!"

But it wasn't going to. It kept up its unearthly din, for much longer it seemed, than usual.

"Blimey!" said Bert, and suddenly he became mobile. He shouted, – "Jess, – I 'ave ter go nah!" Grabbing his tin helmet and gas mask, he raced off, yelling as he did so, –

"Git round that shelter, and as quick as yer can, just in case. – I dunno where yer bruvver is though, der you?"

Jim, at that precise moment was standing outside the Roxy with Dan, arguing the toss about the film they each wanted to see!

"Blimey mate!" his voice sounded incredulous!

"Yer can't mean yer wanted ter see the one that's on 'ere, der yer? – 'The Wizard ov Oz!' – That's fer kids." – But Dan *was* adamant, about his choice.

"Well, it's a bloomin' sight better than, – Sittin' watchin' a bloke called 'eafcliff. – Nah what kind a name is 'aat? –

Chasin' 'is gel friend 'arfway across the moors in, – What's that place called? – Wuvverin' Ites?" –

"Anyway, –I've sin it!"

They were still arguing when the Siren sounded.

"Take no notice, it's only anuvver try art," said Jim.

"Come on, let's fergit the pitchers, it's cooler darn by the river, let's go there."

"We might bump inter Florrie an' 'er Mate!"

But as they were ambling slowly along, one way, up by the river, almost to Tower Bridge, with the idea of maybe catching the eyes of a couple of interesting members of the fairer sex, especially as Dan had on his knockout Zoot Suit. – They were quite unaware of the 'Sword of Damocles' hovering over them. In other words the great cloud of German Bombers flying high up above, coming up river from the South Coast.

Jim was the first to cock an ear, and his eyes upwards.

"Wassat noise, Dan?" he said, scanning the sky.

"Dunno!" Seems to be comin' from back there!" and straining his eyes, shielding them from the Sun, Dan spotted the forerunners of the waves of aircraft, as from behind one wave came more and more, until in the distance it looked like a huge black umbrella moving towards them.

Dan and Jim, – not alone, found they were surrounded by scores of incredulous looking people, all staring up, transfixed at the sight, until someone, shouted, – "Bombers, Bluddy' Ell! – They're Jerries! – It might be bluddy 'Itler 'imself! – Fer Gawd's sake, let's git art ov 'ere!"

Everyone started to run blindly in confusion and panic, some disbelieving, just stayed put. Yet there couldn't have been anyone that afternoon who had any idea what lay in store for them and their East End of London.

"Dan, come on, let's git darn 'ere!" Jim, pulling Dan towards a big red sign which said, 'Shelter', they scrambled in amongst the crowds who pushed and shoved one another in haste to get away, from what surely must be imminent danger of an Air Raid.

Dan, – Zoot Suit or no Zoot Suit, he was thankful to be sitting alongside Jim, on the cold stone floor of this dimly lit wine vault. Baffled, bewildered and afraid with God knows how many others who'd been lucky enough to reach there as the first of the bombs screamed down, violently rocking the foundation of the vaults.

They both sat looking with disbelief at each other. So much for their hopes of an evening out on the Town with a couple of Bow Belles!

The imposing Dome of St Paul's Cathedral looked out across from its lofty regal position, over the profusion of monotonous drab buildings, of warehouses Docks and Churches. – To back street hovels, bleak grimy sooted and mean, that housed the population of the London's East End. To the continuation of endless dark alleys, and passageways dimly lit and dangerous, that had been the haunts of pick pockets, thieves and vagabonds over the centuries, all of which was now in the process of being bombed to smithereens!

This too was in the minds of hundreds of tired exhausted Firemen who had raced to battle with miles of raging fires threatening to engulf the streets alongside the Docks with factories, schools, wharves and warehouses. It seemed an impossible task! As the bombs rained down Tommy and Bert, undaunting and with no fear for themselves, peered with dust filled eyes, searching for mangled bodies and

Bert, clawing with his one good hand, – at tons of rubble, they pulled out twisted pitiful remains of men women and children, totally unrecognisable.

A little tot, no more than a baby, still clutching her Teddy, both entirely covered in blood and dust. A broken twisted form of a puppy, – a man's severed arm. Tommy and Bert were badly feeling the strain, exhausted and horrified at all they saw happening around them.

Everywhere, were great gaping holes spuming out flame from gas mains, Beds and mattresses hanging precariously, out from what once had been someone's bedroom.

An upturned Bus, with people still trapped inside, lay in a huge bomb crater. The screams from many, – too terrifying even to imagine! The scenes were indescribable! Tommy and Bert too sickened, even to speak, laboured and toiled till they practically dropped, finally collapsing on to the kerbside, after staggering to a First Aid Post. They sat with their heads buried in their hands, completely and utterly done in. Then a hand gently touching Tommy on the shoulder was followed by a voice saying, – "Here Tommy, – drink this, it will make you feel better."

"No! – It couldn't be. – That voice! – Was it Mary's? – It had to be Mary!"

He looked with dazed eyes, squinting and blinking with surprise, and amazement, as there was Kate, standing over him holding out a cup of steaming hot tea, which she placed in his still shaking, blood covered hands. He took it gratefully, thanking her.

Later, – he thought, – Was it the tea or the sight of Kate's face that suddenly made him come back to life? How pleased was Tommy to find her there. But he had no doubts whatsoever as to which it really was.

Poor Bert, appalled and angry at all this Carnage, had the whole while been worried out of his mind, filled with all kind of horrible images.

"Where was Mag, and where were Jess and Jim?"

"Could they be anywhere here, in these shelters?"

"Were they safe, – and where?"

The nearest shelter Jess found, as she had raced after her Father, was the disused warehouse in Greek Street, a derelict, gaunt grey old building, not exactly the type of place to want to visit even at the best of times, but it looked as if it could be better than sitting in a hole in the ground.

"Inside one of them corrugated tin sheds? Because that's what they looked like."

As Jess neared the shelter along with a flock of others who were at first just drifting towards the entrance, for as yet no one seemed to be in the least bit anxious.

"Another one of them false alarms," – Someone said.

But they were soon to change their tune, with the sound of the distant drone of the enemy bombers as they flew menacingly and defiantly up the Thames River towards London, heading straight for the Docks, and straight for them. Then suddenly as a cry went up, –

"For Gawd's sake! Move yerselves you up front, – The Bastards are coming for us!" All at once there was pandemonium, everybody started running.

Jess found herself being pushed wildly along with others, down some steps, just as the sound of the first bomb was heard that had hit stragglers way back behind them. At one point, she had to struggle hard to avoid tipping down head first, but the mass of people there were packed tight and so saved her.

It was a horrifying experience. She reached firm ground at last, and slithered down, gasping and trembling onto the hard stone floor.

It was dark, – only a few attempts at providing some means of light proving negligible.

Jess was afraid, really afraid. Where were the rest of her family? Where was her Mother? She couldn't help it and found herself brushing away a few tears with the back of her hand, but she wasn't the only one who did that, not by a long chalk, even if they didn't want to admit it! Everyone sat quietly, only so often a child's cry, amidst the crash of bombs could be heard.

"'Ow long is this bluddy lot goin' on for? Me cat, she ain't bin fed, me washin's art, an I've left me back door wide open!" came a voice from somewhere in the middle of the congregation, who had made themselves comfortable, as far as they could on crates, boxes, some old sacks or whatever they could find, but it was very cold.

Somebody tittered at the old girl's annoyance, at the inconvenience that Bloody 'Itler was causing her. It jolted Jess out of her negative thinking, then another lively voice came echoing from the back, –

"'Ere! What we doin' sittin' 'ere like this? It's jus' what that Bastard wants, ain' it! If 'e kin knock the daylights art ov us, then' 'e's winnin', eh? Let's show 'im! – Come on! – 'Ere, sing up, the lotta yer!"

"We're gonna 'ang art our washin' on the Seigfried Line, – That's the spirit!" – "An' 'ow abart, – Maybe its becos I'm a Lun-der-ner!"

"Shshsh, quiet, stop a minit all a yer!"

"Can yer 'ere it?"

"It's the All Clear! The Sods 'ave gorn!"

Then a chink of light showed as the door at the top of the flight of steps opened and through it appeared the figure of the ARP Warden, – flashing his torch down across the gathering of relieved cave dwellers. – In other words the multitude of stiffened limbed, and bat-eyed, very tired people, as they staggered out into the daylight. But what they were all met with now, as they stared with disbelief, – was absolutely horrifying!

The sheer devastation and havoc, resulting from the violent bombing that had taken place that afternoon.

Unbelievable scenes. There were masses of tangled steel, piles of debris, great pieces of broken glass blown everywhere you looked. Beds, parts of furniture, clothing. A baby's portrait, a rusty old coal scuttle, doors and window frames blown out. An upside down smashed-up Costermonger's barrow, and so much more, as Jess picked her way through these and stacks of other articles which had been peoples' humble belongings. Now all you could see was just rubble and muck!

There were some hopefuls who were sifting through several piles of wreckage, looking for something they could retrieve from their shattered homes. Others too dazed to bother, were being led along to rest centres where they would be given tea and other hot refreshments.

For a while there was a welcome lull, and they could forget, that outside it was a hell with gigantic fires burning everywhere! Tired fireman though alert and impressive, were battling with flames, that could be seen many miles away, as far as the coast even.

Could this be the end of the London Docks, people asked? – But this was only the beginning of the end of the Docks, as they had always known them!

"Don't be too hopeful," as Joe, one of the Wardens had told the tired Jess and her companions, as they'd left the shelter, – "The Bastards'll be back!" – They did, that night to bomb again, helped by the light from the burning fires. Jess, all she wanted was to find her Mum and the others.

After having made her way through all these painful scenes, she eventually reached the corner of Brick Street. There a feeling of panic overtook her. She had witnessed the havoc that had been wrought on her way here, but what would she find when she turned the corner of her own road?

"Please Gawd, don't let it be us!"

"Jess luv! Ow Gawd! – It's you!"

"Mum! Ow Mum!"

And there, in the middle of their street, mother and daughter clasped each other tight, and wept tears of joy and relief. But as they took a look around them, eyeing the damage, it wasn't as bad as they'd feared! There was a lot of glass, bricks and plenty of slates off the roofs, but with a stiff broom and a touch of the old elbow grease, they'd soon have it ship shape. But there was bound to be a lot of swearing, while doing it, also cursing that mad swine, cringing in his rathole over there in Berlin!

They went into the house expecting to find the worst, both Mag and Jess, and it was, – as in a few short choice words, – a bloody mess!

Broken crockery blown off the dresser, laid all over the floor, a complete write-off. A picture of Bert's Dad whose mutton chop whiskers, plus a very astonished and hurt look on his face, gazed upwards at them through its shattered glass from the floor, where it had landed!

But it was mostly the thick dust and grime that covered everything that was so heart-breaking.

Sighing as she took stock of it all, Maggie said, – as Jess took off her coat, and started rolling up her sleeves, –

"Leave it, don't worry abart it nah, we ought to be goin' lookin' fer yer Dad, and where the Hell is young Jim?"

"Ow, – an' Gawd Blimey, – 'ere comes Jim!"

"You alright son? Thank Gawd yer safe! Where were yer while all this lot was goin' on?"

Hardly taking a breath, he blurted out all, how he and Dan had got separated down in those smelly wine vaults. They'd stunk, – stale, old and decayed. He'd been scared, he didn't know which was the worst, the eeriness and dreadful smell of the cellars, or the crash of the bombs!

He had got out as quickly as he could, after the 'All Clear,' and came home wondering then what he may be faced with. But there it was, he saw it. His home, still standing as if in defiance and contempt at all Jerries attempts to try and flatten it!

"Ard luck this time, mate, an' its no use 'owever yer try. Yer won't git the better of us!"

"D'yer 'ear that, yer Butcher?" Jim, put his fingers up to his nose, – He cocked a Snook! – "*That* to *you*, Adolf!" –

He felt better after that.

Bert had been on the verge of near collapse as he came in the back door covered in dust, eyes red rimmed, face blackened and bespattered with blood.

Mag, – she did no more. Shooing Jess and Jim out of the kitchen, she started to get the tin bath down from the back door. But Bert, –

"No, Maggie," he stopped her, – "Its no use yer doin' what I fink yer doin'. Cos, all I want is a cuppa tea! Don't you worry gal, those bastards'll be back ternight, yer mark my words, an' I'll 'ave to go orf art agin!"

233

"Jus' gimme me tea, an' I'll 'ave a kip fer five minits!"
It was no use arguing with him!

She went out and left Bert slumped in his armchair fast
asleep, surrounded by wreckage! – Jerries calling card, –
left by the Bombers. – But they'd be back, sure enough, –
The Blitz had only just begun!

It was all hands to the pumps as Maggie got out the
broom, and with, –

"'Ere Jim you sweep that lot up there and Jess, yer come
wiv me, an' see what the bedrooms are like, an' be careful a
the glass. – We'll soon 'ave this lot cleared up."

Jim not too keen on his allotted chore, started to protest,
– Mag shut him up, –

"Yeah, I know it'll 'appen again most likely, but I ain't
changin' my life style to suit that perisher an' 'es gangsters
– Blast 'im! – Gow on nah, clean up that mess!"

Jim could see, by the look on his Ma's face, she was in
no mood for arguing. He'd seen that look many times
before when he was a kid and paid the price, as he'd laid
crying up in bed. Sent there to sulk while all his mates were
out playing till after dark. Mag took a look around, –

"That'll 'ave ter do. – We didn't own many crocks
before, but we've got bugger all nah!"

Bert, bent on getting back to the ARP post had
swallowed a couple of mouthfuls of tea and taken a bite or
two out of a cheese sandwich and off he'd gone, no good
hanging about here he was needed elsewhere.

"I'll 'ave to run roun' an' see Maureen and Les." Mag
said later, "I can't leave 'em in the lurch." But as she went
out of the door, she called back to Jess and Jim, –

"If that blasted Siren goes, – you two git rarnd that
shelter sharpish, – der you 'ear?"

No one living around about the 'Crown and Anchor' would have been at all surprised to find the doors of the Pub shut that evening, all things being considered.

But that had not occurred to old Joe Grimley as he picked his way carefully along the streets, through the smashed slates and glass, the flotsam and jetsam, strewn about in the aftermath of the bombing, – towards his local.

For come rain, come shine, come even an earthquake! – That would not have deterred Joe. But even that old war horse couldn't help staring flabbergasted at the sight of the old Pub being given 'First Aid' treatment! The front of it was being boarded up. All the windows and doors, except one, which upon it, written in large lettering, boldly said, –

"Don't worry, It's Business as usual!" –

"We Are Open." – "WIDE OPEN!"

"Would Saturday nights in the Pub ever be the same again?" she asked herself as she stepped inside the one remaining open door. A few of the regulars, the tough old timers were there, propped up at the bar. Without a doubt, one of them was old Joe, and the conversation naturally was all about the bombing!

'Barney Bull' at that moment came in the door, adding *his* two pennorth, and he certainly had lots more to tell them all standing there open mouthed.

"Ozzie Scott, yer know 'im? – Well 'e says poor old George darn at the Docks, 'e's gorn and copped it. – Poor ol' bugger. – Never knew wot 'it 'im, 'e didn't!"

"Dunno if it's true, but they say that Sugar factory darn river, went up in flames too. Blimey! What a sight! Yer knows 'ow sugar can burn, yer kin still see it from 'ere. They'll never be able ter put *that* lot art!"

It seemed all of them there at the bar had a bit to add to the list of devastation and to talk of the pitiful scenes they had witnessed, of the chaos and disorder that the bombers had left behind in their wake.

Old Joe had just struck a match to light his pipe for the second time in a couple of minutes when it started. A faint whine at first, rising slowly to a piercing high pitched terrifying wail.

It was enough to put the fear of the Devil up yer!

"Ow, Gor' Blimey! – Out! Quick, darn in the cellar!" Les yelled. No one had to be told twice.

Barney, – he already had one foot on the top rung of the ladder, and he was down that hole quicker than a hare, with a squib up its arse!

The others followed suit, but Mag was all sixes and sevens, "Wonder if they'd 'eard it!" meaning Jess and Jim.

Should she have stayed with them?

She did no more and rushed out, running as fast as she could through the streets, not heeding the shouts of the wardens. Breathless and hot she reached the shelter where Bert should be.

Mag saw them, and breathed a sigh of relief. Jess and Jim, each carrying their gas mask boxes, were among the stream of people pushing their way into the entrance of the air raid shelter, some very impatient to get in there the quickest. Mag saw Bert doing his best to keep them in order, but mostly to prevent bad accidents, – not allowing, if he could help it, – *some* hot-headed idiots breaking their necks, and falling down the steps.

And so the long night began, with hundreds of already tired people finding what places they could to settle down. On benches, boxes, and some just sitting on the floor, cramped up together, and as the hours went by, the air became more foul and more sickening with the odour of sweating bodies.

The gunfire it was ear-splitting and deafening. So too, the crashing of falling buildings with the scream of many bombs as they fell to earth. This was like a 'Devil's Tattoo!' Each Crump and explosion burst the eardrums, shook and vibrated the very floor of the cellars, filling the closely packed assembly with the fear of God, as they tried their hardest to get some shuteye, one way or another. Others, – They just gave up trying!

Kate had been on the go ever since the first raid on this memorable Saturday afternoon. It seemed her services would now be sorely needed, as soon as it was discovered she had once been a Nurse.

A First Aid Post was set up at the infants school down in Friendly Street, and for the first time Kate had a sense of belonging, she decided it was a nice feeling, being accepted as one of the community. It also had given her the chance to speak to Tommy again, bringing as he did, some pretty bad casualties in from here and there. Kate's expert handling saved a lot of pain to many, physically and mentally, in a short space of time.

Tommy had to admit to himself, the sight of Kate's presence there at the First Aid Post, was pretty heart warming as well, as it proved to be a desire now, to get to know her more personally. To Tommy, she was now no longer Mary, but Kate, and for the first time in a long while he had a feeling of well being.

"Did he dare to call it hope?"

Chapter: Twenty

Rob's ship was laying off Portsmouth all ready to leave for an unknown destination, and that's when he heard the news from Nobby, his mate, another East Ender who hailed from Beckton, not a stone's throw from Wapping.

"'Ere Rob! – Just 'eard the news of a big raid on the East End, it came over the buzzer. Didn't sound too good eiver!" Nobby's voice sounded worried.

Rob had just come from the mess deck, and replied, –

"Wassat yer said, Nob, – Ow! An' 'ere's that coupl'a bob yer lent me, – fanks."

"Don' matter abart that nah, didn't yer 'ear wot I said? The Jerries 'ave bin bombin' all the way up the Docks and it's pretty bad, so it said on the wireless."

Now Rob sat up and took more notice of what Nobby was saying, – "Is that right?"

"Ow Gawd!" he said, – "whad'er we do nah?"

"Did they say what part, an' where abarts?"

"I dunno!" said Nobby, – "They ain' gonna tell us much nah, are they? or the Jerries would all be clappin' their 'ands. An' wiv that Lord Haw-Haw spoutin' a load a lies, – 'e's a traitor, yer know Rob! 'E's really from this country!"

"Geermany callin'! Geermany callin'! – I arst yer!"

But poor Rob, he was no longer listening to Nobby's mimicry, he had his mind on what could be happening at home. Was his family safe? – Was his Mum and Dad alright? How the Hell was he to find out? They were due to sail to Gawd knows where, at any moment!

Over in North London, Mavis too, along with everyone else who'd heard the long foreseen but still startling news of the ferocious air raids, thought of Mag and all her other old mates back in the East End, – it sounded bad. But Kensal Rise! – Now it was not so very far from Wapping! Would one feel safe anywhere?

Mavis had often considered moving back to her origins Brody Street and its familiar, free and easy surroundings. She missed the old places and *her* kind of people.

"Wish I'd bluddy well never moved!" she had been heard to say quite frequently. Now she was not entirely sure. But it was foolish to think the Jerries would stop solely at dropping their monstrous loads of death on the East End of London alone.

If she was going to be blown to Kingdom Come, she reckoned, – "I'd raver be back wiv me own sort, than wiv this toffee nosed lot up here though!"

"Maggie luv, what's the use a yer worryin' wot the place looks like, – leave it alone nah!"

Bert couldn't understand her fidgeting.

"Yer bin up all night. Let's git some rest!"

Mag looked at him, and realised he was right. She was dog-tired and so was he. Had she ever seen Bert in such a state? Black as the ace of spades, his eyes half closed and nearly keeling over with fatigue.

"Right!" she said, – "Yer know where yore goin'? – Upstairs mate, and I'm comin' wiv yer, – we're goin' ter bed, – you an' me!" Bert was even too tired to answer back, with his usual saucy quip, and a twinkle in his eye!

Jess and Jim had already hit the hay! The raiders had gone now. What was left of them. Many had been brought down with the Anti-Aircraft guns. Caught in the search lights, they'd been picked off, but not before they'd knocked hell out of the Docks area once again, and as Sunday morning dawned, many tired people slowly made their weary entrances from under the ground to find in many cases their homes were just a heap of rubble!

But Mag and Bert were not one of those unlucky people, and right now, as the Sun streamed in through their bedroom window, it shone across two kindred souls oblivious to the world, sleeping soundly, – the sleep of the just, so richly deserved, – their arms around each other.

Jim awoke and blinked at the bright sunlight, and wondered what time it was. He could remember emerging like a mole from the Air Raid Shelter, along with streams of other bleary-eyed mortals all thinking the same as he.

"What the blazes are we doin' tryin' ter sleep darn this rat infested 'ole?" They had a perfectly good bed back home! and didn't he, – Jim, – appreciate his bed, when he was able to get back to it, crawl in and curl up on the lumpy mattress, – even if it did look and feel like a furrowed field!

He wondered if Dan had got home alright. Then he speculated, – his pal must have hurried back to make sure his family was safe after they had both been separated.

"I'd better pop rarnd his 'ouse to see fer meself." Jim couldn't hear any sound coming from the others. "They must all be asleep!" Creeping downstairs to the kitchen and snatching up a piece of bread, quickly slapping a bit of dripping on it, he went out the back door and into the street. "Blimey, looks like 'No Mans' Land!" or of the pictures seen from the last World War, as he surveyed the extent of the bomb damage, as he made his way along.

Clambering over rubble, and skirting holes in the road, he went round to where Dan's house should have been, only to stand staring horrified at what he saw. There *was* no Dan's house now, just a gaping hollow shell of twisted metal, bricks and shattered glass. Fragments of torn net curtain hung from smashed window frames, pathetically fluttering in the light breeze. Contents of all the houses were blown here, there and everywhere.

Jim just gasped and looked with his mouth wide open.

"Where was everyone, and where was Dan?" All he could see were Firemen and rescue workers frantically tearing at piles of masonry looking for trapped and half buried, panic stricken souls screaming until voices became weaker and then went silent as their will gave way.

Running up to one of the firemen, pulling at him desperately by his sleeve, Jim shouted, –

"Where are they Mister? – 'Ere! – Please Mister! – Those people at number 29! – D'yer know where they are? – Are they alright?"

Jim was frantic now and gabbled away in fear and anxiety. "Maybe they were safe, they *must* have been down in the Shelters."

The fireman, poor bloke, he just looked round at Jim, and with a voice thickened by dust and smoke, answered hoarsely, – "Dunno' mate, all I know is, a lot got carted orf to 'orspital," and the man continued on with his grisly task.

One of the mud caked rescue workers, seeing the extent of Jim's agitation called over to him, –

"'Ere Son, if yer askin' abart No.29 and the few doors along there? – They've all copped it!"

"They just got back from the shelter, when the bomb went orf! – Delayed action, so someone said!"

"Poor devils! – But they couldn't 'ave known much abart it. – Best way, fank Gawd!" and the bloke carried on with his searching.

Jim stumbled back home, completely numbed, fighting to keep back the tears. Maybe Dan would not have been there, he could be safe, somewhere! All sorts of things were going through Jim's mind.

"Would he no more sit with Dan by the waterfront throwing pebbles in the river there, seeing who could throw the furthest?"

"Would there be no more of Dan's far fetched tales and fantasies, and of all the girls he maintained fancied him? Specially when dressed in his 'Zoot Suit!'

Jim almost fell in the back door when he reached home, and straight into his Mother's arms, sobbing, –

"Ow Mum! – They got Dan!" he cried.

Mag held him tight, his head cradled against her breast. She never spoke, just guessing what had happened, and let him cry as never before had she seen her Jim cry!

He would tell her in his own good time, but right now, this was her child, with a pain. Not of a sore knee, or a cut finger, – It was more a fearful dread.

This was anguish of another kind. They stayed together like that for a long while, – until, –

"I'm sorry Mum," he apologised, feeling abashed and shamefacedly he dried his eyes.

"Come on Soljer, – wanna cuppa tea?"

"Ah! – Nah 'ere's yer farver! – Gor' Blimey, 'e must a smelt the tea!" She was glad though, to see Bert.

Maggie bustled about around the kitchen table then, making as much clatter as she could. She had to break this atmosphere of wretchedness, in one way or another!

Then, – all of a sudden Jim spoke, – "Where's Snowy?" he asked, and looked around the room. Hearing the sound of his name, the pup got up from his bed in the corner, stretched, and shook himself. He had been laying there, with both his ears twitching at every sudden noise, trying his hardest to get a bit of shuteye throughout all the racket Mag was making. He ambled across to Jim, who pulled him up, on to his lap.

Mag felt there was this need for Jim to have Snowy take his mind off these tragic events for a while, but she knew he would tell her about Dan and what had happened, as soon as *he* was ready.

Along at the casualty station, Kate too was feeling exhausted. She looked desperately around at the amount of people waiting to be treated with minor injuries, mainly shrapnel wounds and gashed limbs, some caused by falling over in the blackout, which was no joke!

She was only one of the group of many willing workers down there at the First Aid Post. Many of the people brought in were shock cases. The sheer volume of noise going on was enough to shatter anyone's nerves.

Kate had been on the go for hours, hardly stopping for a rest. Tommy noticed this more and more each time he went down to the casualty station, with someone either bleeding from a nasty head wound or fainting from shock. Some with only minor cuts and often cases with a person hopelessly searching for a loved one, in a state of collapse.

And that is what Kate was almost on the point of doing. Tommy, he thought so too, seeing her when he was helping a bloke, who needed a dressing for a badly injured eye, through the doorway into a room filled with people, waiting to be attended to.

243

"Don't you think you should take a break now Kate? You look all in!" She looked up, hearing Tommy's voice and although drained, Kate smiled as she answered his appeal to quit trying to make *herself* a casualty, by overdoing it.

"Come on, let me take you home Kate. You will do more good by resting awhile!" She couldn't resist this offer and was in no fit state to argue, so she reached for her coat.

They walked the short distance to Brody Street, with Tommy holding her arm, which gave Kate quite a feeling of comfort. It was also a sensation she had not experienced for a very long time, and was she imagining it, or did her heart beat just a little bit faster there for a minute or two?

The 'All Clear' had sounded a few hours earlier, and so they walked along, passing many more gutted buildings and scores of firemen, trailing hoses, who were putting out more new fires that had been started during the last raid.

Ambulances raced by, carrying many critically injured people, to hospitals already overflowing and unable to cope with the ever growing influx.

Kate fumbled in her bag for the keys to her front door, turning to Tommy who was just on the point of retracing his steps back to the A.R.P. post.

"No, Tommy, – please don't go. Come in, at least stay and have a cup of tea with me!"

Kate, now realised with an agreeable feeling, she did not want him to leave, – Not yet!

"Go in there and sit down will you? Make yourself at home. I shan't be a moment," Kate said pointing to the parlour door as she took off her coat.

Tommy assumed, this must be the parlour, and entered what he considered to be the most pleasant of rooms he had seen for a long time. One, which matched exactly the picture he'd had of Kate, since they had first met. Cool, calm, quite unruffled, and very attractive!

He sat down on the settee (taking care not to disturb the cat) and looked around the room.

His eyes settled upon a photograph of whom could only be Kate's husband Philip, a smart looking man in naval uniform. Kate, during the conversation they'd had while at Maggie's party, mentioned a little about her husband, and he'd noticed her deep sadness, every time she had mentioned Philip's name.

"Oh! Tommy! – You should have moved Sandy, – he's getting so old, all he does now, is sleep!"

Kate had come in the room carrying a tray, which Tommy promptly got up and took from her, placing it on the little cane table. The one that Mag had admired on *her* first visit to Kate's.

"Sugar, Tommy? – You don't mind me not standing on ceremony, do you? – Help yourself to a biscuit. I'm afraid that's all I have."

Then Kate gave a nervous laugh. Tommy had not said a word, since they'd arrived at the house.

"I seem to be doing all the talking!" said she.

"Oh! Go ahead Kate, I am a good listener. It was nice of you to ask me in, anyway."

Kate was feeling mighty pleased with herself for taking the plunge and making the first move in getting to know a little more of this man, who was sitting here in her parlour. She was sure too, as she took a quick look up at Philip's picture on the wall, that he would have been in complete agreement with her intentions.

"Now Kate!" – Tommy was interrupting her thoughts.

"I have had my cup of tea, and as you know, – as much as I would like to stay a little longer, *you* must get some rest, and I have to go. I may be needed! – But it's not to say I wouldn't mind being invited again, and that *was* a lovely cup of tea!" he suddenly stopped, and looking at Kate a little abashed, he said, –

"Now, who's doing all the talking?"

They both laughed, – The ice had been broken and Tommy had good reason now, for his satisfied smile, as he walked off down the road.

Jess was riding high, though actually she was sitting in the corner of a carriage in a Southern Railway train, off now on her way to a place called Farneham, a village on the borders of Kent. – She had made it!!

Having satisfactorily come through her months training for the Land Army, she'd waited with high hopes for this posting, to where she could see open fields and green pastures, and not giant chimneys belching out smoke and grime. To where hedgerows and wild flowers grew and she could hear the sound of birds in song. Where maybe even a Cuckoo was to be heard, she hoped!

As the train left London Bridge Station, seeing all the comings and goings, the bustle of troop movements, Soldiers, Servicemen travelling to wherever, and with all that noise, the din and the racket, Jess felt it was good to settle down and breathe again.

There was, to the left of her, as she gazed out of the windows, the familiar sight of Tower Bridge. Jess felt a lump in her throat. How many times in her short life had she caught sight of that view, from anywhere you looked along the riverfront at Wapping.

Maggie, although she was pleased to see the look of expectation and joy on Jess's face, as she had handed her the letter containing details of her posting, she found it difficult to push aside a feeling of anxiety and disquiet.

Another one of her brood was leaving the nest.

She would miss Jess, Gor Blimey! – No two ways abart it. – She would an' all! – She'd even miss her grizzling, and the hours the girl spent in front of the mirror, the cracked one that still hung on the back door. Somehow it had managed to survive the bomb blasts.

Now Mag was feeling pretty miserable this morning, and had every right to be. Jess had been gone a couple of days, and Mag had received no news of Rob for weeks! Where was he? – She guessed somewhere out on the high seas and facing all kinds of danger.

The news was distressing, – Well, frightening was the better word for it. U-boats in the Atlantic were taking a heavy toll of our shipping. She was tired of it all, – It was a wonder the people's nerves stuck it.

"There's a face an' 'arf ter come 'ome to!" – a voice said from the doorway. It was Bert. – If Mag thought she was tired, what must poor Bert be feeling? They'd become as ships that passed in the night, – hardly ever seeing one another! Bert, – always with the gangs of helpers, searching or digging out people alive, and lucky enough to survive the bombing of their homes, and scrabbling about in craters half filled with mud and muck, looking for someone's valuables, they refused to be parted with.

While she, Mag, struggled to get back and forth to the Pub, – The old 'Crown and Anchor', which was bearing up well to the pounding it had received, and still able to give good service to its faithful die-hards.

"'Ello me ol' Luv!" Wasn't Mag glad to see Bert's face, even though it looked as if he belonged to a minstrel show! She forgot her weariness and took his hand, pushing him down into his armchair.

"Sit there an' – *don't* move, while I put that kettle on!"

She bent down and managed to remove his boots which were inches thick in hard-caked mud, and gasped when she saw the state his feet were in.

"You're orf ter bed an' no arguments, an' I'm comin' wiv yer! That's after yer've bathed those plates-a-meat in some nice 'ot water."

As Bert tried to put up some resistance, in a half-hearted way, the thought of lying in a bed with Mag beside him, was too much to argue about. He was completely knackered and that was that! –

"'Itler could do 'is damnedest, – 'E couldn't give a brass monkey's, – That bastard could go an' Sod 'imself, – They were goin' ter get some sleep!"

When Jim came home, after threading his way along through the chaos and upheaval out on the streets, the house was as quiet as a monastery. – He could hear no sound. – Jim picked up Snowy and went off down the road. If he was lucky, he might get some pie and chips at Alf's shop.

"That's if it was still standin'!"

Chapter: Twenty-one

It was a very tired and confused Mag, who chanced her way through the gangs of volunteers who were helping to clear a path through the debris of broken glass and rubble, blocking the carved up roads, knowing full well what a futile task it would be. It wouldn't stay that way, the bombers would be back again later on, to cause more destruction, and be another night, with hundreds spending sleepless hours in the now stinking, fetid shelters.

But Mag, she must get to her job. What ever happened, 'Itler would not stop the pub opening, or old Joe and the others going without their pint! Yet it was not for just that, did they chance their arm in poppin' in their local, – for old Joe and Barney and the stalwarts there, it was like coming home after maybe a long day spent on their Jack Jones!

As she hurried along, she thought of Annie who had been back living with Bessie for a long time now, – how were they faring! Where did they spend their nights, – In the shelters? They were no chickens, they couldn't move very fast. At the age of 80 it wouldn't be easy for them, having all this palaver, – Hope they are alright!

"Oh, here you are Maggie, bad night again eh? Listen, – leave that!" Maureen said as Mag donned her overall, –

"Don't worry about cleaning the bar today, it's a bit pointless with all this muck around!"

Mag was relieved, and felt a damned sight happier sitting back relaxing in Maureen's kitchen and drinking a nice cuppa tea, than kneeling down scrubbing bar floors.

The Blitz was now at its height, with ten terrible days and nights of non-stop bombing. The Docks had been pulverised indiscriminately, and yet still the planes came, unleashing hundreds of high explosives and incendiary bombs, causing catastrophic fires.

Down at the School Hall, Kate was kept looking anxiously at the door, as each batch of casualties were led in, – the walking wounded. She was hoping to see Tommy appear any minute through the doorway.

Earlier Connie, another auxiliary nurse there, had given Kate some disturbing news.

"I heard they gave Cromwell Street a real thrashing last night, *and* Crosby Street, that's next to it. That makes it getting on nearly everywhere around here, has had a real basin full of it!"

"Cromwell Street did you say?" Kate knew that was where Tommy was lodging. She was sure! For a few nasty moments she felt a tremor of fear. But suddenly as if in answer to her fears, the door opened and Tommy appeared, leading a practically half-crazed young woman, on the verge of collapse. She was moaning and sobbing, calling out over and over again, –

"Where is my Jamie? – I can't find my Jamie!"

Gently, Kate took hold of the woman's arm, –

"Leave her to me Tommy," giving him a relieved smile. She was so glad to see him.

"Poor woman, she'll be O.K! We have him here, a Mr Wilson, he must be her husband. They brought him in a little while ago, he's in a bad way, been crushed underneath a wall. They'll both have to go off to Hospital when the Ambulance returns." Then she looked in askance at Tommy, she was waiting for him to say something to her.

"Are you O.K. Tommy? Have you anything to tell me?"

"Don't worry Kate, I'm alright! I won't be the only one who's been bombed out. You heard about our Street then, – There's not much left of it now!"

"I am so sorry, – but what about all your clothes and belongings?"

He shrugged, –

"All gone, – every blasted single thing!"

"They must have been after my Jazz Band set. I guess they'd heard of my virtuosity!" he said with a wide grin. All the while Tommy had been speaking, Kate was doing some quick thinking, she now took the bull by the horns.

"Look Tommy, seriously, no beating about the bush. You must have somewhere to stay."

"Be it as it may, you are welcome to come and take over my spare room."

Then as he began to show some kind of restraint, –

"Listen! – No argument. – I insist do you hear?"

But still Tommy frowned.

"Will it put you out at all?"

She wouldn't answer that, but said instead, –

"So that's settled then." and as she walked away, she heard him calling after her, saying with a chuckle, –

"Well it won't take me long to pack, will it?"

Thanks Kate, a whole lot!"

The Atlantic Ocean, the 'Pond' was no place to be now. Even on a moderate calm day, there is a sharp swell. If you were a good sailor, you could ignore any signs of bad weather on the way, but as confirmed and hardened landlubbers, as poor Rob and his mate Nobby were, had no hope of at all! They were in a convoy of ships, battling heavy seas, in the grey Atlantic, protecting the merchant-men, carrying all kinds of much needed supplies of food and goods for Britain. But if you had made the mistake of mentioning food of any kind to Rob at this very minute, it would have been your lot.

He felt terrible. The thought of seasickness, had never entered his mind, and in all the many dreams he'd had of sailing the Seven Seas and braving the perils of the deep, had he believed he could ever feel like dying!

Poor Rob, he would get used to it! So the sympathetic Doc told him with a slight chuckle, which was happily lost on our Robbie.

Nobby was no help, – he was feeding the fish also, a bit further along with his head over the rail.

They had been at Sea for some days, and as yet, they had not been in any encounter with the U-boats. He hoped upon hope, they would *not* have that privilege!

Rob thought about them at home all the time. It was bad, the news that came out from Britain, – from London's East End mostly, which was really copping it. At night, Rob made certain he said his prayers, not only for the plight of his family, – "Please God, keep them safe!"

But also, – making excuses for himself, – it would not be untoward, to pop in a little prayer for Nobby and him as well. – It was no pleasure cruise they were on!!

Although the old girl, in an odd kind of way, hadn't come up to Bert's expectations as a good mother to Mag, – at least she *was her* mother, and Maggie did wonder and worry about her, but what could she do? – There was no way of getting over to Hackney which was having it as bad almost, as here in Wapping!

She was grateful now that Flora, her Ma, had her man friend. At least she was not on her own. "I must write to her!" which in itself was a stupid thing to say, Maggie told herself. She could only hope her mother would take as much care as everyone else had to, – "Keep yer fingers crossed and pray one of those bleedin' bombs had not got yer name on it!"

There was no lack of humour and goodwill among these people here. Resolute, they would stick at nothing to help others in trouble, as Kate found, learning a lot from the mixture of individuals who came through the doors there, seeking relief and a bit of comfort, from her.

Many times Kate tried to keep a straight face at some of the things she witnessed and overheard, as she sorted them all out, and trying to ease a little of their worries.

"Yers, – There 'e was, the great fat wallop! And there's me stuck fast darn a bluddy great 'ole under abart two ton a spuds an' greenstuff, orf me overturned barrer, wonderin' where the bluddy 'ell I was, wiv me eyes all bunged up wiv dirt an' a carrot stickin' art a me ear!"

"An' that soppy sods shartin' out, – 'Elp! Git me art someone! – I'm up ter me bleedin' neck 'ere in bloaters an' cod's roe. – An' nah me bluddy eels 'ave escaped!"

This very explicit description was of a bid by the Nazi planes to put paid to the market up at the Shades. The Jerries' must have at some time or other, heard of the reputation of these celebrated friendly cockney markets, and decided spitefully, to drop a spanner in the works. But, as old Annie would have said, in so many words and not pulling any punches either, –

"Those buggers kin drop as much as they like on us, – our 'ouses, our locals, our markits, – they kin chuck down a bomb as big as the Elbert 'all on us. We won' ever give in ter that Bastard! 'E kin shart an' rave till 'e is blue in the face, an' dance up 'an darn like the prize monkey 'e is!"

"I'd like ter 'ave a go at 'im meself, – I'd show 'im!"

"'E's nuffin but an idiot! An' 'e kin take it art a that!

"Let 'im put that in 'is pipe 'an smoke it!"

Dear old Annie, and she would have too, and maybe with her piece of useful advice, on behalf of everyone around her, on the receiving end of that idiot's labours in vain, the people would carry on determined to withstand all that perisher could hurl at them, by night and by day, knowing full well, he would get browned off with it long, long before they did!

"Ah, here we are!" remarked the woman driver of the car, as it turned into a road of neat terraced houses and stopped at number 116.

Saying to her two girl passengers, in a very business like, but not unfriendly way, –

"This is where you are to be billeted, for the next few months Jess and Gwen! Have I got your names right? The woman went on to say, –

"I am sure you will be well looked after here!"

As they alighted from the car, Jess took a quick glance up at the front window of the house noticing the face of a very young boy gazing at them questionably. He had seen, walking up the path towards him, two trim very well turned out young ladies in uniform. He was to learn later on, these were Land Army Girls.

The front door opened to their sharp rat-a-tat, tat, and a woman in her early twenties stood there smiling, –

"Come in please!" she said.

"Good morning Mrs Allen, you must have had my letter! I am Mrs Deakin from the Women's Land Army Recruiting Office. This is Jess and Gwen, whom you have kindly offered to have billeted with you."

"All the girls in this area are under my administration. So if you have any queries, you may contact me."

After a few minutes of giving some very helpful advice, she left, saying, – "I'll be in touch with you!"

"Come! I'll show you to your room," said Mrs Allen.

"Now I hope you don't mind having to share a double bed, but this house is quite small and I have already, another lodger here."

They looked around the small bedroom, but what it lacked in space was made up with the pleasant outlook they had on to a garden, which Jess noticed was well cultivated with all kinds of vegetables. Mrs Allen had certainly taken heed of the 'Dig for Victory' signs of advice.

But there seemed to be no evidence of any man around!

"I do all the gardening! My husband is in the Army and serving overseas. It keeps me busy you know, what with his nibs here as well," pointing to the child.

"What is your little boy's name, Mrs Allen?" Jess asked. She couldn't help but be amused at the shy looks he gave them, as he tried to hide behind his mother's skirts.

"Come on now, tell the nice lady your name!"

"Oh! Go on. You are not *always* so shy."

"You should hear him sometimes, a right chatterbox he is. His name is Benny!"

"Oh! – And please don't keep calling me Mrs Allen!"

"I'm Caroline. – All my friends call me Carrie."

"Now would you like to get settled in, while I make you some tea?"

"Come along Benny, you'll only be in the way now!"

"No he won't!" said Jess. She had already taken a liking to the little lad. But Gwen wasn't so sure, – she had seven brothers and sisters at home."

Benny hung around for a while and then toddled off back downstairs.

So the two raw recruits had made their first step into their new surroundings, but they had a lot of rough knocks to come. It wasn't going to be all honey getting up at four o'clock every morning, especially in the Winter, which was now on it's way.

Every morning during the past few days, Mag had gone to the door, hoping to find a letter on the mat, with Jess's familiar scrawl. It was a week or so since she had last written. – Jim found it first.

"Mum! – 'Ere's a letter, – It's from Jess!"

When he saw it, he felt pleased. It was real quiet here now. No Rob, No Jess, and No Dan! – A great lump came into his throat and it threatened to choke him, when ever he thought of poor Dan. – Life was not a bit like he used to know it!

Why wasn't he old enough to be called up? He had a thought there and then. Should he put his age up, and say he was eighteen? Well it wouldn't be long now, he was getting on that way anyhow!

"Hello Mum," Jess had written, – "How are you? – I hope you haven't been worrying too much about me. I have been given a nice billet and have made friends with Benny. He's the little son of my landlady. But if you was to see her, she don't look like one, she can't be more than twenty herself."

"She can't get called up for anything, as she has got Benny to look after."

"We haven't done much in the way of work as yet, but do you know what they told us? – We have to milk the cows, and crumbs, have to get up at 4 o'clock every morning to do it. I haven't seen many cows before though Mum, – Have I? There ain't none in Wapping!"

"I only hope I know which end of the cow I've got to milk! Still it's a nice farm, and the farmer and his wife seem to be very nice too."

Jess went on about the other aspects of her new venture, but it came over to Mag and Bert, that she seemed quite happy with her lot. Mag smiled, feeling a little less anxious about Jess. She gave the letter to Bert to read.

"At least we know she's found an anchor luv, let's 'ope she'll be safe darn there!"

Bert, he hoped so too, although he never let on what was on his mind. By all accounts Jess was stationed not far from the coast and right in the path of Jerry's planes on the way to bomb London, – "The Sods ain't goin' ter give up nah!"

He could only keep his fingers crossed, besides, he knew his Jess could take care of herself. – She was tough like her mother. A chip off the old block, was she!

Bert shook himself, – "I can't keep thinkin' this way. – It's gotta stop!" He looked around, –

"Where's that Jim? I gotta job fer 'im!"

"'Ere son! – Yer say yer were good at woodwork at school. – All right then, take this 'ammer an' fix that back gate fer me! – It's 'angin' orf its 'inges!"

A feeble Sun vainly tried to penetrate through the smoke and dust-filled vapour, as dawn broke. One more day with scores of bedraggled, befuddled souls, clutching bundles of their few belongings, emerging from the openings of Air

Raid Shelters, into the fresh air, to take a look around at the evidence of yet more gutted buildings, and more houses wrecked and still burning. But though these people seemed to notice all this, as they ploughed their way back to where their houses might still be left standing, it did not seem to register fully, as they were too tired and familiar with these scenes. Too many days and nights had passed with the same stench of death and decay everywhere they looked.

How much longer could they take it? "Something had to happen," Kate thought as she finished dressing an old lady's legs, which had been gashed pretty badly, as well as the side of her face. The woman was whimpering like a baby, but it was not for herself, she was upset! It was the sights she had witnessed all around her, as she lay on the ground near to others, not so fortunate to survive the bombs, that had demolished their homes. These were her neighbours. People she had *always* known, who now lay lifeless near to her. These images would forever haunt her!

Kate glanced at the clock on the wall, it showed twelve noon, though what use was time? she thought. Each hour seemed to bring more and more suffering and torment to so many! But Kate did not know then that this day would be a turning point. For her it was twofold.

September 15th, – the day the 'Battle of Britain' was won. Those damned Nazis were having the bashing of their lives! The old bulldog was showing its teeth, in the form of the battering the RAF boys were giving the Jerry Luftwaffe, as they came over the Channel.

Tommy regaled Kate with this news as he came Cock-a-hoop through the door this time. He had only one patient to bring in, and he was old Joe Grimley. He'd got a nasty crack on the head, after hearing the news of the rout of the

Jerries over the radio. He'd hurried to the 'Crown and Anchor', and in his haste he tripped outside the Pub, falling into a crater. He'd mistaken the notice 'Keep Clear!' and misread it as, – 'Free Beer!'

"You look pretty near exhausted Tommy!" Kate said, after they had recovered from the almost too difficult effort, of keeping straight faces at old Joe's highly inflammatory description of, – "That bluddy idiot who had put that hole there for some poor sod like me to fall into!"

"Oh! I'm OK," said Tommy. "I'm no more tired than you must be Kate!"

"Do you know? This is one of those times when I'd like to believe that all this is not happening. That our lives were normal again, and I could say to you, – Look! – Stop whatever you're doing and I will take you out somewhere nice, to have a good meal together."

He looked at Kate to note her reaction to his words, – "Was he being a little too presumptuous?" he thought.

"I'm sorry Kate, perhaps I am forgetting my place!" and he was about to shut up, when Kate said, –

"No, no Tommy, not at all! In fact I had it in my mind to say, would you allow me to make a dinner for you one evening? I'd like that! Of course it might be a bit out of the question, all the time these raids are going on. But maybe, – let's hope that things may soon ease up a little!"

"That's a promise Kate, I hope. I'll keep you to that, but I am going to take you out, rationing or no rationing. I'll buy you the biggest and best Steak there is!" Kate laughed, she suddenly felt a cloud lift. It was an odd sensation in a way, a kind of optimism and a hope for the future.

It seemed the circumstances that had caused Tommy's advent into Kate's life, resulting in him now occupying her very comfortable spare room, had produced good results, in a most fruitful way!

Tommy had been there now for almost two weeks, with much co-operation and good camaraderie on both sides. He had not felt so secure for a very long time, and Kate, though she would not admit it to herself, she had lost the bitterness and regression that had been her wont. It would take a fool to ask the reason why?

Maggie had noticed the change in Kate's demeanour, and gave her a few chance looks at times. Now this was one good thing that might come out of this blasted war, with all the bad news which did come from all over the place.

How was Rob? She worried so about him. She could get no news, they didn't tell you a thing on the radio, but of course they wouldn't would they? That's all that 'Itler wanted! There were *enough* ships already being sunk out in the Atlantic Ocean right now!

But where was her Rob? Her sailor boy. It was the last thing she thought about each night, as she shut her eyes, wherever she may happen to be. In an Air Raid Shelter, or in Maureen's cellar at the 'Crown'.

"Please God, keep my Rob safe, wherever he is!"

Chapter: Twenty-two

Though the Battle of Britain had been won the Jerry Luftwaffe were not going to stop at the drop of a hat. The heavy bombing continued for many weeks until they turned their attention from London to the Provincial Towns, unleashing tons of bombs on the other larger cities.

But try as they may, it would take more than those scum to kill a nation's spirit, as shown on these Islands made up of people of such calibre as Mag and Bert for instance. They continued to get to their jobs, although with difficulty, but there was more of a sense of relief having the benefit of a night's sleep, that's if they still had a house or a bed!

"Not many people could say that, – Poor devils!" thought Mag.

But 'Wailing Winnie', never stopped it's howling, as some named the 'Banshee Air Raid Siren,' which put dread and the fear of Hell into you.

Winter came with more hardships for most of those bombed out families who faced spending their Christmas in rest centres. But no one looked for a Merry Christmas this year at all, with their loved ones away. Jess was feeling the effects of Winter already, with tired aching limbs and frozen fingers trying to milk a stubborn obstinate cow who was playing hard to get, kicking over the stool at every attempt to get just a dribble of milk from her. It became easier later on when the milking machines came to the farm, but every time her fingers remained like stiff wooden dolly pegs, when trying to attach the cow to the machine!

Oh, Poor Jess! – How she hated the sound of that alarm clock waking her every morning at 4 a.m. Try as she might to bury her head in the pillow, saying to herself, – "Ignore the blasted thing, just pretend it isn't there!"

Gwen would dig her in the ribs, none too gently either, saying, – "Its no good yer know, the cows won't wait!"

"Out! Come on git out! I'm first though, to the bathroom." Now that was something Jess had not dreamed she would discover here. But this was a comparatively new Council house, one of many, built for the workers who were employed on the Estate up the hill, belonging to a squire.

When she had arrived and clapped her eyes on the bathroom, she promised herself at the first opportunity she'd be in that bath having a nice long soak, in lots of lovely hot water. – But No!

"Oh and by the way, I forgot to tell you, they told us we are only allowed to use five inches of water!"

What a let down that was! Mrs Allen informed poor old Jess of that, when she *did* pay that visit to the bathroom. Seems all you got these days were restrictions. Ration this, – ration that. The only thing that wasn't rationed appeared to be fresh air, – and they got plenty of that.

She had a little more success with Daisy the most obstinate of the cows this morning.

"There's a good girl! – See I told yer I ain't gonna 'urt yer!" Jess cooed at the doe-eyed animal who answered her with a hefty swish of the tail. –

"An' yer kin stop that an' all!" – Yes, she was going to like it here, but she wished it wasn't so blooming cold. Even with the thick dark green warm pullovers and shirts, Corduroy breeches, long woollen socks and sturdy shoes, which made up their Uniform.

Although Jess had felt sad to watch the last of the leaves of Autumn float down from the multitude of different species of trees that lined the lanes as Gwen and she walked the short way back to their lodgings and along past quiet meadows and fields. The colours of russet gold and yellow had met their eyes. She was able to see from the farmyard where they worked, across to miles of fields, now bare, but which once had been a sea of burnished golden corn.

It must have been a wonderful sight in Summer. Maybe next year she would see it all, and the orchards too, when Spring and Blossom time, came round once again. She had to pinch herself at times, to see if she was really here.

How lucky she was! This made her think of her family, and how they were.

Her Ma would have just loved all this, she had not seen much countryside apart from that short spell, when they had all been away hop picking. Remembering with a shiver how she'd hated the dark nights with only one Hurricane Lamp, – and Jim's little secret, – she smiled, – so scared he was, – he'd wet himself. – Poor Jim!

They'd reached the house, and knocked. Mrs Allen had promised to give them their own key. But now, –

"Come in dinner's ready." she said. Jess sniffed saying, –

"Mm! Smells good," and when they went off to wash their hands, Benny followed them, standing with one leg tucked behind the other, with his finger in his mouth, and wriggling, waiting for them to come out of the bathroom. There he eyed them up and down before plucking up the courage to speak. "Trousers," he said, pointing to Jess's legs and at her Corduroys, then he patted his little braced overall trousers. Jess understood, – He had never seen a woman in trousers before and must have thought it strange, but come to think of it, it wasn't a common event even before the war, Jess realised.

The dinner Mrs Allen had prepared was something out of the ordinary. At least, it was for Jess and Gwen. Rabbit pie, with peas and potatoes from the garden, Carrie had grown them herself. The rabbit, from the fields, the farmer had shot. There were plenty of them, too many in fact, who regularly ravaged the crops and they had to be kept down, Carrie told them.

Jess cringed at that news, but when she had been working in the country there for a while, – she then realised and learned a lot more about a different way of life that she had never known before.

"I like it 'ere, don't you Gwen?" she asked, as she lay sprawled across the bed on her back thinking. You would never imagine there was a war on, in these peaceful, calm pastoral surroundings, if it wasn't for the sound of those planes far above in the sky. Who's planes they were, you could not always see, except when you chanced to witness a dog fight between the RAF, and the Jerry planes, that were caught coming across the English coastline.

Things had quietened down somewhat after the deadly raids on the East End. – But for how long?

About half a mile from the farm away to the West, lay the village, with a few shops, a Post Office and a Pub, called 'The Wheatsheaf."

The two girls had discovered this 'Olde Worlde' Lilliputian village, while out on a walk, looking to post some letters home. They'd received a few odd looks from some of the locals, wondering, who were these lasses in their queer rigouts. But as time proved, they were to become part of the community, and when sometime later

Mrs Deakin, paid them a visit saying, "You will soon be working with a batch of new recruits. They are from over in South London."

"Ow, Gawd!" thought Jess, – "Are they now?"

Meanwhile, way back in Brick Street, all you could hear was the sound of a lot of hammering and banging, sweating and swearing, as some botch-up builders were doing their level best to give the poor old battered 'Crown and Anchor' a bit of a makeover. The foreman, a fat portly gent with a formidable mouth, was giving orders to a couple of lackadaisical fellahs, in trouble with the scaffolding they were attempting to rig up.

"Not there! Yer Bluddy dozy great Clod 'oppers! Who taught yer 'ow ter put up scaffoldin'? – It couldn't a bin the bloke who built the Eyeful Tower? – I bet!"

To some, it may have appeared stupid to be trying to rebuild any thing there right now. Who knows? – Jerry may be regrouping his thugs to have another go at the Docklands. But Maureen and Les, – bless their hearts, – owed it to their customers to have a comfortable retreat to enjoy their tipple. There was complete ugliness out in the streets, and it would take a lifetime to clean it all up!

That's what Mag thought, as she walked to work that evening. It was bad enough in daylight dodging great holes in the roads there, which hadn't yet been repaired, but in the blackout, – it was damn near suicidal!

She also had Jim on her mind. He had not been the same lad, since his best mate Dan had tragically been taken from his life. Maggie often observed her usually boisterous Son, who most of his time had ants in his pants, sitting looking glumly into space absorbed with his thoughts.

He missed Dan, – Why? – They'd known each other since they first started infants school and had been inseparable forever after.

Staunch friends, pals through thick and thin, sharing their joys and toys, Street games, Conker-time, Whip-taps on backs of the Coal and Milk Carts, or up to their knees in mud on the banks of the old River. They were never to find their pieces of gold now!

Saturdays for Jim were the worst. Mag had left him this morning kicking his heels out in the back yard. She hated to witness that forlorn lost look on his face.

"Jim luv! Surely yer must 'ave uvver friends' yer kin go art wiv?" Jim remained silent and just looked at her. Mag knew what was on his mind, –

" Yeh! – But they are not Dan!"

Eventually, and soon, she hoped he would snap out of his wretchedness. Of course he must miss Rob and Jess too, – A hell of a lot!

Maggie sighed and entered the Pub door, where she was met with an uncommonly loud din, such as she had not heard there for many a long day. It sounded like the good old Saturday nights they used to have! It was so good to hear, – She smiled then, and getting her coat off, she soon got stuck into easing the thirsts of the impatient waiting crowd, mostly the cry was, –

"Come on Mag, jump to it! – Where the 'ell yer bin 'idin'? – I'm dyin' a first, over 'ere!"

These and more gripes from the road menders and navvies covered with cement dust from head to foot. Mag made sure they had her best attention, for to her way of thinking, they earned every drop of liquid that passed their parched lips. She didn't envy them the huge task they had.

Clearing up the bomb damage, not knowing what they may find under the rubble and wreckage. What stomach turning sights they may witness as they unearthed a body, another poor victim of the cowardly carnage of the past few horrendous weeks.

So things started to settle down a little in the weeks coming up to Christmas, which in many folk's eyes, wouldn't mean much this year.

Apart from the fear of air raids, which were still happening, though confined at first to inland towns, sometimes with the Jerry planes managing to slip through the net, trying to get to London, determined as they were to undermine the masses of Toms, Dicks and Harrys prior to, – as they had planned, – The invasion of England.

Deplorable, the fact that churches were maliciously being bombed in the city but people made a mental note of all these atrocities, adding them to their already long list.

Mag, along with scores of others, as food rationing started to take hold, had more and more headaches as the queues got longer, waiting for maybe a few custard creams or even a couple of ounces of boiled sweets, only to be informed as they neared the counter, –

"Sorry we've run out, – No more today!"

The New Year of '41 began with bitter winds and snow, adding to the discomfort of many. A cold bleak morning and the queue was growing longer at Woolworth's Sweet Counter. A sight for sore eyes, – Real chocolates! – A whole batch of them!

The crowd behind Mag were getting edgy, – Would they be lucky, or would they sell out just before they would have their turn?

The poor sales assistant was doing her best to serve them, by weighing out 4-ounces of chocolates per person and was trying not to let her agitation show at some of the comments coming from impatient customers.

One woman just in front of Maggie was watching the poor girl adding the last chocolate to those in the scale pan, and found it weighed over the allotted 4-ounces! The girl took the chocolate from the scales, looked at it then returned it to the pan, weighed it and again took it off. She did this once more, and of course the woman had, had enough. The exasperated customer cracked and shouting, –

"Fer Gawd's sake cut the bluddy fing in 'arf!" her face getting as red as the assistants was going white. There were titters all around, but this had served to ease the fidgety queue now champing at the bit.

And this sort of thing was to happen more and more as the war years progressed, but it was only fair to say, it was going to take more than the shortage of a few sweets or custard creams to break peoples nerves. There were a lot of people who did *not* conform. A little word in one's ear in a pub or meeting place and you could become the owner of a bit of dress material or even some parachute silk to make under clothing. Maybe a choice piece of gammon ham or a welcome lump of cheese. "Sssh! Mum's the word. *All this was on the Black Market!"*

It was a queer world, and right now, a pretty nasty one, Mag thought as she walked along by the river towards the pub, this cold Monday morning and feeling saddened at the sight of so much damage that had been done to their familiar old dockside. Looking as she did for some thing, some small semblance of anything that would bring back a memory of how it used to look before it had been damn near blown to blazes by the enemy.

At some stage she could not continue her journey, blocked as it was by rubble, she gave up and found herself near the spot where she fancied she heard a ghostly voice, – George's, – the watchman at the Dock gate calling out, –

"Good mornin' Missus!" She stopped and, oh how she wanted so much to hear him answer, as she used to. –

"G'mornin' George," and choking back a sob, she hurried on. It was an idiotic thing to do, coming this way to work. Reaching the corner of Brick Street she met Mabel, shopping bag in her hand, and going off to the shops.

"'Allo' Mag, I'm orf ter git me rations nah, Wot the 'ell der they fink we can do wiv a coupla arnces a meat, or a piece a cheese, I wouldn't give to a perishin' mouse!"

"All yer git if yer say anyfin' is, – 'Doncha know there's a War on?' All right fer them. I bet they don't bluddy-well go short of a bit of, – under the counter!"

Maggie just had to smile. "Good ol' Mabel!" It would be beyond comprehension to hear the old girl say a word of praise, or commend anyone on something or other.

A right character was their ol' Mabel!

Reaching the Pub, she pulled herself together and pushed open the door.

Maureen was vigorously polishing the already sparkling glasses from the shelf above the counter. Luckily they'd had a plentiful supply stored away, after losing most of those they'd had in the bars, smashed in the bombing.

She looked over to Mag as she came in, –

"Hello love!" She called, folding the cloth she was holding and laying it to one side.

"Feel like a cuppa before you start?"

They went into the back kitchen, where Mag sat down, while Maureen put the kettle on the boil.

"How's things?" Maureen asked.

"Have you heard from Rob at all, and what about Jess?"

Mag was just about to answer, when Les came in the back door. – To Maureen's question of, – "How did he get on over at the Brewery in the old City?" he answered, –

"They were pretty bashed about as you know, but don't worry, we will still be getting our quota of beer and spirits as usual love!"

"We won't be letting any of our regulars down. It'll be a long time before Jerry succeeds in putting paid to our good old pint of beer, and in any case that will be *never*, if I have anything to do with it!"

"And now, – where's my cup of tea?" he added rubbing his hands together and warming them by the fire.

Maggie got up and putting on her overall, fished out her mop and bucket and proceeded to give the bar floors a real good old going over, even managing to hum to herself as she listened to Vera Lynn singing, 'There'll be Bluebirds over, the White Cliffs of Dover', coming from, 'Music while you work', on the Radio.

So there was still a bit of, – 'Ope left for them all!

Chapter: Twenty-three

Bert, he was so tired! He made his way slowly back from Percy's after putting the finishing touches to the clearing up and helping to get the shop back to almost its normal condition, after the near miss it had in the bombing raids, during the fierce Blitz.

It had been in a right old state, with parcels and bundles of clothes thrown about everywhere. These along with a conglomeration of musical instruments wrapped around and smashed against ornamental objects of real value in some cases. All that backbreaking work while still being on call as an Air Raid Warden was taking its toll.

"Anyone in?" he called, as he came in the back way and entered the kitchen. His voice woke Mag.

It had been so lovely and quiet there, she had grabbed at the chance of having 40 winks! She opened her eyes, blinked and looked up at Bert sheepishly.

"Ow! I must a gorn ter sleep fer a minit, Bert luv. Blimey! Yer do look tired."

"Nah sit darn there. I'll make yer a nice cuppa," pushing a footstool nearer to him saying, –

"'Ere, plonk yer feet up on that!"

"Ah, that's better, fanks luv!" as Bert sipped his tea.

"Ow, 'ere 'e comes, – 'E 'erd me voice!"

Snowy had eased himself up from his warm spot in the corner by the Kitchener and bounded over to Bert He was well past the puppy stage and had grown quite big. In fact, far too bulky for Bert to have him dive up onto his lap as he did in a most excitable fashion, almost knocking the tea cup from Bert's hand. –

"'Ere you watch it, yer clumsy brute. Mind wot yer doin', – I nearly lorst me tea then!"

Secretly though, this was just Bert's way of hiding his deep feelings for the dog, who gleefully lapped up the fuss he received from that moment on.

"Yer a real artful ol' dodger!" Bert said affectionately stroking Snowy's head. Maggie was feeling truly pleased and blessed the day she'd brought the little puppy home, – how long had they had him now? – She couldn't remember!

"Where's that Jim? I 'ardly ever sees 'im nah. 'E worries me a bit. Its time 'e bucked 'is ideas up, moonin' around the 'ouse as 'e does."

"Ah, leave 'im alone, Bert! – Stands ter reason, 'e feels like 'e does. Nah wot 'as anyone got ter be 'appy for? – Its Robbie we should be worryin' abart."

They still hadn't heard a word from Rob or couldn't make any guesses as to where he was at this moment in time. It just seemed he'd disappeared into thin air!

Jess they did know, was surviving the bitter cold weather they were having and was OK and having a bit of leave soon. But Maggie and Bert would have been amazed and quite proud of their tenacious tough young Jess, if they'd been flies on the wall of the big antiquated crumbling old barn, seeing her playing silly buggers with an obstreperous cow, determined she wasn't going to let anyone milk her, and that was that! Betsy, a young cow, a new addition to the herd, had taken it into her head to kick the bucket at every opportunity. Pail, stool and Jess too, were upended a good few times before the soothing and terribly patient voice of Jess finally won her over.

"Come along nah old girl, its no use yer giving me the evil eye! You ask yer mates 'ere! I'll be very gentle wiv yer, and I won't 'urt yer! They've all 'ad ter go frew it, same as you, yer know!"

Speaking softly, Jess rubbed her hand up and down the cow's velvety nose and then slowly, the cow becoming acquiescent, finally came to terms with her fate, which after all that, didn't seem quite so bad after all.

Thinking of her life back there in Wapping, Jess could not believe how things had changed so quickly! One minute you were working in a dark musty-smelling old factory, with only artificial lights to see by, cramped up with a dozen other assorted females, equally as despondent and apathetic as she, at the monotonous grind of helping to make uniforms for the Army.

Fancy! – Some soldier might at this very moment be wearing one of those uniforms, fastening up buttons she'd had a go at sewing on! – But what a boring job it had been!

Now here she was, out in the fresh air, – ('Mmm! Very fresh. "It was bluddy cold!" if you'd asked her?') – and pulling her thick jacket collar up tighter to her neck, as she walked along early next morning to the farm with Gwen, laughing at the two-an-eight they'd had the evening before, with one of the new girls who had been deposited at the farm to work alongside them.

Both Gwen and Jess right from the start had their doubts about having to fraternise with and work with foreigners from over the water, especially Bermondsey! Jess had heard tell these South Londoners came from the same mould almost as that of the East Ender!

Tough tenacious and obstinate. They were of the same texture, tetchy, fiery, rigid and firm, and yet deep down accommodating, genuinely kind and really warm-hearted. They found in other words, 'Their bark was far worse than their bite,' as the saying goes.

Jess had been sitting in the public bar in the 'Wheatsheaf', the pub in the village with Gwen, enjoying the hospitality there. The friendly locals and the warmth from the open log fire, which in itself had proved to be a great attraction and novelty to them both.

A log fire! They had never seen one before their introduction into rural country life! They liked looking around also, at pictures on the walls in the bar, of the cherry and apple orchards, with groups of pickers hard at work at the hop-bines, of quaint Oast Houses and sturdy farm wagons, drawn by huge magnificent Shire horses. It was a nice atmosphere Jess thought, and felt pleasantly at ease and quite contented, until suddenly the door opened and a couple of other land girls accompanied by some of the lads from the village burst in, and to say the least, in a most excitable state of mirth and hilarity.

One of the girls clumsily, or it may have been intentional, who knows? – barged Jess's table as they passed by, knocking their glasses of drink flying, spilling it into their laps. Jess and Gwen gave a shout of alarm and surprise.

"Why don'tcher watch where yer goin', yer clumsy idiot, – look what yer've done?" Jess cried.

"Callin' me an idiot are yer?" said the smallest of the two land girls. – "Yer wanna watch yer mouf, – Or I'll fill it up fer yer!"

Gwen clutched at Jess's sleeve as she made to get up and have a go at the flushed looking antagonist who herself was now being restrained by her companions.

"Come on Jess, – let's go, its time we weren't here!"

She could sense more trouble brewing, but when you really thought about it, – What a comical situation! They were all behaving like unruly kids! Now, Gwen thought it was time she should take control at this juncture.

"Come on Jess!" she said, "Let's pack it in nah eh?"

"It looks good, don' it? 'Ere we are, in uniform, supposed ter be doin' our bit, but all we're achievin', is actin' no better than 'Itler and 'is bunch a delinquents!"

Although Gwen wasn't feeling very comfortable standing there in her wet pants, trying her best to reason with them. There was only one thing they could do now, and that was, –

"Let's forget it eh? – What abart it?"

"And that means *all* of us!"

It went quiet there for a few minutes, until one of their group suddenly broke into a laugh. This came from Miss Shortarse herself, – the smallest of the Land Girls, but who it appeared owned the biggest mouth!

"Yeh, – Let's 'ave a drink eh? – An' call it quits!"

"'Ere, – my name's Nell, an' she's Florrie," she said, pointing to her mate, with a jerk of her thumb.

"Now we can't start our own private war 'ere can we? – Let's say, 'Fainits!' as we used ter say at School."

So as the two of them, Jess and Gwen continued on their journey towards the farm, to begin work at 4.30am, if you please! – On this bleak icy morning, Jess was only thinking of her nice warm bed she had reluctantly just left back there at the house, and wondered what had possessed her to want to become a Land Girl in the first place!

Was it the Uniform, or was it being out in all that fresh open air, – and by Crikey there was more than enough of that to go round!

It was eerily quiet and still pitch black. As they walked along, Jess was wondering. Whoever was it, who had ordained that all cows should have to be milked at such an unearthly hour, long before anyone with any sense would drag themselves out of a perfectly well-earned sleep and step willingly into the hard cold world outside. And on such a morning as this!

"Brrrrrrh!"

It was a near Arctic one too! Cold enough as they say to freeze the extreme components off a Brass Monkey!

"Blimey! – Me chilblains ain' arf playin' up somefink cruel this mornin'!" moaned Gwen.

They still had some way yet to get to the farm, and stepping it out, being careful how they trod along this narrow stony path of the lane, bordered either side with high hedges and meadows, when, filled in Spring with Buttercups was a joy to see. Though these fields were now covered with a sharp hard frost.

Gwen stopped suddenly and remarked, –

"It looks like their havin' it bad over there today. Poor devils!" For they knew that the coast lay only about 20 miles away from the farm. But luckily, apart from one or two lone raiders who had managed to get inland past the Ack-Ack guns, and mainly the unflagging doggedness of the Spitfire Squadrons, it had been a comparatively quiet period since Christmas.

But all that was not to continue it seemed, for becoming too complacent would be one big mistake.

It was minutes later, as they both, Gwen and Jess were nearing the farmhouse, they heard it. That sound, – the familiar drone, monotonous and then, the awesome sudden, intermittent discharges, cracks and backfiring, as of a plane's engine in trouble, and the sound was getting nearer and right ahead, – it was coming straight for them!

"Quick Jess, Blimey! Get darn 'ere!" and Gwen unceremoniously pushed and shoved Jess down into a shallow ditch at the side of the stony path, where they laid with pulses racing, and putting their hands over their ears and eyes, – they waited.

The Plane, a German bomber was limping home, hoping to reach the coast after being shot up. Its engines spluttering and failing, it was passing overhead, gradually losing height and trying to land, but not before it had released its bombs.

Then it came, – Thud! Crump! Crump! As each bomb fell across the meadows and fields, while Gwen and Jess clung desperately to each other thinking their day of reckoning had just arrived! Then a louder and more deafening noise as the plane crashed only about half a mile away from the outskirts of the village.

Everything burst into flames, the plane, hedges, and trees, disintegrated. There were screams, and it seemed that all hell had broken loose! It was horrible! The two girls just stood and stared at the awful sight, thoroughly helpless.

"What can we do Jess?" shouted Gwen awestricken, and shocked beyond all reason.

Jess herself could not control her shaking. But with difficulty she pulled herself together and took Gwen's arm and leaving the horrible scene of devastation they went on to the farm, both knowing they would not get that awful sight out of their minds.

Those poor men, though German, – they too, were some poor mothers' sons! Jess found, sometime later that the dead Pilot and his crew had been temporarily buried in a quiet corner of the local village graveyard, and it kind of pleased her to know that at intervals the villagers, put flowers on their shallow and simple graves.

"What a bizarre and odd world we all live in!!"

Annie drew her chair up closer to the fire in Bessie's kitchen which right now was as nice a place as anyone would wish to be in on such a cold night as this.

She was sitting at one side of the fire with Bessie on the other. The clicking of their knitting needles was the only sound to be heard above the crackling of the fire in the kitchen range. It threw out a real rosy heat, and Annie was thoroughly enjoying it. Bessie was a dear, hardly a bad word was to be heard said between them. Best days work she had done, leaving that cantankerous crabby old sister of hers in "'Ornchurch!"

Here they were now sitting knitting woollen Balaclavas and socks for Soldiers.

"Slip one, – knit one, – drop one! – What a game eh?"

Though knocking on 80, they both still had quite good eyesight, even if their fingers were a mite bit rickety!

"Bessie" said Annie right out of the blue, –

"What der yer fink abart that chap Tommy, yer know, he's the bloke wiv the accordion fing, and all that uvver stuff, wot 'e carries wrapped round 'is neck!"

"Yer know, 'es allus in the pub!"

"Well 'e was, but nah, 'e does 'is bit, as 'n Air Raid Warden nah an' agin."

Bessie seemed a little perplexed and then, –

"A'course yer never did go roun' the pub a lot did yer Bess?" said Annie.

"Don't say as I did Ann. Mind yer nah, I ain' got nuffin' agin anyone 'avin' their tipple!"

"Wasser matter wiv the bloke then?"

"'Ow! 'E's gawn 'n moved in wiv that woman who lives next door ter Mag. Yer knows the one?"

"Stuck up she is. Never says boo to a goose!"

"Ow! I wouldn' say that Ann, – I 'eard tell she's turned art a real good 'n, darn at the First Aid Post."

"Anyway," Bessie added, –

"Its none a our business nah is it? She's big enuf, an' ugly enuf, ter knows what she's doin!"

"Oo cares Ann anyhow. Yer never know. Wot! We might all be pushin' up the daisies sooner 'n we fink, nah wiv this poxy war on. Eh? – Live 'n let live, – that's wot I says."

Annie mumbled something under her breath and got on with her knitting.

"'Ow abart a night cap Ann? There's a drop a Johnny Walker over in me dresser drawer. I got some ov it left over from last Christmas!"

"Nah's yer talkin' Bessie luv. I'll git the whisky tots art. You jus' sit still!"

Kate and Tommy's ears should have been burning, those very moments, but their minds were on their own problems as they sat in front of the fire, there in Kate's cosy front parlour.

Earlier, Kate had been preparing some supper for herself, and searching for something she fancied in an almost depleted pantry. – Not much there!

She weighed up the situation. It would have to be bread and the small piece of cheese she had collected with her ration today.

It seemed absolutely ludicrous expecting people to subsist on 1oz. of cheese per week, quite laughable in fact, but that's how it was, like it or lump it!

As she put the kettle on to boil, she heard a key turn in the lock and when the front door opened. Tommy stood there, apologising for maybe startling her.

"I came home early this evening Kate. I didn't feel too good. Must have a cold coming or something. I'll just get off up to bed!"

"No! Wait a moment Tommy. Let me make you a hot drink. I have some aspirin. Take a couple of those!"

She made him sit down near the fire. He welcomed this a lot as he felt shivery and quite unwell.

"Here, drink this!"

Kate had come in with a tray of hot milk, some aspirins and a few biscuits.

"I'm sure it will make you feel a *lot* better after you have taken those tablets!"

Kate thought he looked done in, – he had really been overdoing it and it had now caught up with him, poor man!

Her heart went out to him. Oddly enough they were two of a kind, tragedy had struck them both in similar ways. They had lost their partners in cruel circumstances and had not been given a chance. The time allotted to each had been so short yet very sweet. The fates had not been fair to them.

She looked across at Tommy, as he sat sipping his cup of hot milk. His face was flushed, and showed signs of a temperature rise.

Kate walked across and laid her hand across his brow.

"Yes, he *really was* burning up!"

This gesture of Kate's, startled Tommy for a moment or two, her hands felt so refreshingly cool, and for a second his heart missed a beat. His mind went springing back to another time, in another life it seemed, when his Mary had touched him with hands that felt like snow flakes coming into contact with his feverish body. Why was it that Kate's hands had the same effect?

"Yes, you are running a temperature Tommy. – You *must* get to bed! – I'll prepare you a hot water bottle. – We'll sweat it out of you, – Don't worry!"

He couldn't argue. Actually he found he didn't want to, and was quite willing to have Kate take control of the situation and before he knew it he was between the cool sheets, then as he lay there hovering betwixt torpor and a sound sleep, his thoughts were only of Kate. Of her smile, her benevolence, graciousness and suddenly a feeling of utter contentment came over him.

Tommy then fell asleep with sensations he had feared he might never experience, – ever again!

Chapter: Twenty-four

There was to be no stopping the acceleration of the war, and as the months went by, saw more and more intensive bombing of cities such as Coventry and much of the Midlands. They copped it bad. For a while London was partially left alone to lick its wounds.

But the determined blighters tried it on all along the route from the South Coast towards London, 'Bomb Alley', as it came to be known, causing folk not to stray too far from the safety of their Anderson shelters, or any of the deep dugouts nearby.

Jess was obliged, along with Gwen and their mates to keep one wary eye on their herds, or when mucking out, and the other on the sky above, and an ear cocked for the sound of 'Wailing Winnie'.

But most of the Land Girls, and that included many of the villagers, did not follow the pattern of sleeping in their Anderson Shelters in the gardens. "Blow that for a lark!" as Jess wrote to her Mum, they worked too damned hard and were far too tired.

"It's me bed I need, and no scurvy tyrant over in Berlin is goin' ter keep me art of it!"

So any bombs that happened to fall nearby, or the noise of the Ack-Ack guns at the Canadian Army camp some distance away, – all failed to keep them from washing their hair, or interfered with their nightly ablutions, and certainly never succeeded in stopping them getting into bed and sleeping like tops.

"Damn and blast, that bluddy 'Itler! – Its alright fer 'im! 'E don' 'ave ter git up fer work at the bloomin' un'eard of 'our of four a' clock on a perishin' cold mornin'!"

Mag stood looking down at her front doorstep with a doleful face. No longer could she maintain the position of having the cleanest whitest doorstep in the street. It had been her pride and joy, but now it was pitted with holes from shell-shrapnel and though Bert had suggested trying to restore it to its usual glory, she had said, –

"No Bert, – leave it, – tain't werf it!"

Shrugging her shoulders, she made off towards the Pub, looking at the damage all around her. Worrying about her front doorstep was the least of their problems.

Apart from one letter she'd had from Rob, very heavily censored, – Maggie had no knowledge of where he was, or how he was. Rob chose to say he was fine, and that he missed them all very much, and not to worry!

That was ridiculous, how else could she be but worried? What with the awful battles in the Atlantic now raging. She dreaded to put the radio on, or listen to tales of how so and so, had just lost their son or husband in the fierce battles out there. How could they ever bear it and carry on as normal! Head down she started to hurry along the pavement.

"Ow! Sorry Mrs James, I didn't see yer!"

Mag apologised and helped the aforesaid lady pick up the runaway potatoes that had fallen out of the woman's shopping basket she'd knocked out of her hand when she bumped into her as she turned the corner.

She must keep her mind on what she was doing, it was just no good worrying! 'What a daft fing ter say though! She couldn't be orf it nah, – Could she?'

Now if Mag had been able to get within earshot of Rob and some of his pals in the messroom, or when off duty on their destroyer, out there in the unfeeling Atlantic, her heart would have been lightened at the repartee and the skylarking taking place.

They'd busy themselves in writing letters home and mending holes in their 'Almond rocks', or just relating some of their prize classic misdemeanours, – in many cases these could be real eye-openers, especially when it included the fairer sex!

Girls? – They were always the favourite topic of their conversation, among the youngest of the group. Most of it was just wishful thinking, but it served to take their minds off the dangerous job in hand, the main reason why they were out there in this hazardous turbulent cruel ocean, where at any time, things could become very sticky indeed.

In the few weeks since Rob's ship had been assigned to the Atlantic, they'd had brushes with the enemy U-boats, but these had been overcome by the sheer numbers of Battleships escorting the merchant ships carrying valuable food supplies. It was a cat and mouse game it appeared, – but the question was, – Who would be the winner?

And Jim, he was like a cat on hot bricks. It seemed everyone was getting into the act. – 'But no! – Not 'im! – Not Jim!'– The 'bluddy' war would be over before he'd even had a crack at it! – He was fed up to the teeth with his job, slinging casks and barrels about, this wasn't anywhere near like manning an Anti-Aircraft gun and ramming home shells with Adolf's name in big letters on them.

"'Ere's anuvver lot fer yer, yer Bastard, an' there's plenty more where these come from!"

He turned his steps towards home. Blimey, he missed Dan, and that was no mistake!

"Jim, is that you?" Mag called, as she heard someone come in the back door.

"Yers Ma it's me!"

"Alright are yer luv?" she asked, casting an eye at his solemn face.

"'Ere, guess what? – I got yer some 'errin's fer yer tea, that was a bit a luck, eh?"

"An' yer kin 'ave the 'ard roes too!" thinking that would please the lad, but she was wrong. Jim took one look at the herrings lying on the plate in front of him and then, clumsily pushing back his chair, he practically flew up the stairs towards his bedroom, where he flung himself face down on the bed.

Maggie for a moment, wondered what she had said. Then it dawned on her. She had completely overlooked the sad fact, just how much Jim must have missed Rob and Jess, all the past months they had been gone. She had done nothing but think of them, worrying about them, and hadn't given any thought to just how much Jim had been alone. He missed them too, but not only them! Dan had been killed so brutally and taken away from him. Why? Oh why, was everything so heartbreakingly cruel!

She went upstairs, Jim was quiet, he was too big to cry. Mag spoke to him, taking hold of his hand, –

"I know what we'll do, just you an' me. We are going to the pictures. An' don' git art of it by sayin' yer too big ter go ter the pictures wiv yer Ma neiver!"

"We're goin! – There's a good film on, it will make yer laugh. Charlie Chaplin is takin' orf 'Itler, it's called, – 'The Great Dictator.' – Bluddy funny it is, an' all!" –

So leaving a note, short and sweet for Bert to read when he came in from Percy's shop, she explained, –

"Your tea's in the oven love, we've gone to the pictures, Jim and me, – see you later!"

But she would have to do a bit of explaining to Maureen in the morning, though she would understand, – she was a good old stick.

As Maggie made her way to the 'Crown and Anchor' next morning, determined to make amends for letting her boss down, she couldn't help noticing there was definitely a change in the temperature. It was decidedly warmer. – Gone were the frosts and the 'brass monkey's' weather!!

That was a good sign. She was always glad to see the back of the winter but, oh how wonderful it would be to see the back of the war. Even so, Mag carried on walking with a noticeable spring in her step.

"Don't worry Mag!" were Maureen's words to her when she tried to explain the cause of last evening's absence, –

"I knew there must be a good reason, – your not the sort to intentionally let anyone down, – forget it now please!"

At that moment Tommy came in the door and it seemed to Mag there was something about his manner that was different! Maureen noticed this too, but it was Maggie's intuition, which told her the reason for it.

Here was the proof of her conniving, and this sudden change in Tommy's attitude. Mag couldn't help her self-satisfied smile, which she hoped had escaped Maureen's notice. Something had happened between Kate and Tommy to cause that look, which was almost one of complacency and gratification.

It could be likened to a cat with a dish of cream, and Maggie, who as she'd made her way to work earlier, had acquired an irritable feeling, which she found was very irksome. But this all of a sudden had been extinguished and only Mag herself knew the reason why!

Kate hummed to herself, as she went about her house work, flitting around with the duster and broom with more agitation than usual, – though anyone would be hard-put to detect any sign of dust in Kate's impeccable kitchen or living rooms at *any* time of the day.

This morning however, she'd found it hard-going just to sit idle. She was as they say, – 'Way up on cloud nine!' In other words, – 'Kate was in love!' She almost felt like a teenager and wanted to shout it out to everyone, – to the whole world! It would be wrong to argue that she couldn't have seen this coming, for some little while.

She and Tommy had from the very beginning shown many signs of being attracted to one another. So there *had* to be a spark that would ignite the touchpaper, and it happened just so, at an unguarded moment. Or could it have been planned. – We wonder?

Kate a stickler for doing things by the book had noted that this morning, as a brilliant sun was shining through the curtains in her parlour. – "Goodness!" she thought, – "They will have to come down and go through the wash!"

"No wonder, with all that dense smoke from the fires during the air raids!" She looked around for a chair to stand on, to unhook the soot-stained net curtains.

This completed, and with them all folded over her arms, she stepped clumsily off the chair and slipped, finishing up with her and the curtains in a heap on the floor, everything entangled around her neck and shoulders, just as Tommy had entered the room with a bundle of letters in his hand.

"What the blazes!" he blurted out, and rushed over to help her, while Kate didn't know whether to laugh or cry? – In falling she'd twisted her ankle, and pretty badly too!

Tommy knelt down, putting his arms gently around her, he got her onto the settee.

She was in pain, he could see that, when she bit her lip and winced as he lifted her foot to look at the ankle.

"I'll get a cold flannel," he said and was back in a flash with it. Folding the cloth around her foot he tried to make her comfortable, thinking all the while, – "What do I do now? – I can't go off and leave her like this!"

"Tommy go, I shall be alright!" she said. "Don't be foolish, you know I can't. Be quiet! – I'm going to make you some tea." – For Tommy, was now in control.

"Lay there and I will sort this all out, don't worry!" he said, giving her a smile that could shift mountains!

He turned back to her saying, – "and *don't* move!"

Kate lay back with a feeling of utter contentment, although her ankle was giving her socks, and was throbbing like a piston engine. She could hear Tommy clattering about in the kitchen with the teacups, and she was sure she could hear him whistling to himself.

He came back in with a tray of tea, and setting it beside her, he expertly poured a cup for the now enlivened invalid.

"Now take these!" he said giving her some aspirin. –

"It's my turn now, to nurse you!" remembering the pampering he'd had from Kate when he himself was laid low with a real bad cold.

"Just rest that foot and we'll soon have it better!"

He took hold of her hand and with a look in his eyes that said more than any words could, he squeezed it, tucked the rug around her, and said, – "I won't be long, I'll just pop round and tell Maureen I'm needed here. – Just don't *you* worry your head!"

He left her laying there, thinking, – "This is all a wonderful dream, and I know I am going to wake up. But Oh, I hope I don't!"

Kate, she was in a seventh Heaven. She fell asleep, awaking to find Tommy sitting across the room, watching her. Kate smiled. – No it definitely was not just a dream!

He came over and sat beside her. –

"Kate darling, he said taking hold of her hand.

"There is something I must say to you! It cannot wait any longer. It's driving me almost mad!"

"I love you so much darling, and for a long while, I have hoped you may come to love me too?"

Kate, looked up at him, –

"But Tommy you must know that I love you!" I thought you must surely have guessed it already?"

This was the moment when their lips met, in a long and tender kiss, that in all it's intensity proved, more than anything else could have done, in just those few precious moments. – At last they were as one!

"My darling Kate," said Tommy, clasping her tightly, – "I do love you so!"

What could she do now, but succumb to the strength of his arms, so secure about her. She felt no longer alone, and felt the most happiest of women in the whole wide world.

What had she done to deserve such happiness? – This question must have been asked by all lovers, everywhere since time began!

Kate just closed her eyes and gave herself up to the blessed relief and serenity of those few treasured moments.

"Now, what am I going to do about this ankle? How on earth am I going to get upstairs?"

"There is only one thing I can think of dear, and that is, – You will have to carry me!"

This last sentence Kate said with just the trace of a twinkle in her eye, then looking at Tommy, to see his reaction to that, she remarked, –

"You know, I do believe it was really worth my falling off that chair! – My good fairy has certainly been extra complimentary to me this day, darling!" she said, still with that saucy grin.

Her little speech brought forth a smile as well from Tommy, and he saw another side to Kate in that instant. She possessed a dry sense of humour, and adding this to all her other qualities, – their life together, – his and Kate's he could see, was going to be much more than most couples find in their lifetime!

Tommy, – now he knew he had at last found his niche. He too, was thinking how lucky he was. This woman Kate, every inch a lady, very attractive and full of grace, – had told him, here in this very room, with Philip's picture looking down at her, that she loved him, – he Tommy! – He gazed thoughtfully up at the face of the man whose place he was taking and saying quietly to him, –

"I am sorry I never met you, but I do want you to know that I will take care of Kate and hope to make her as happy as I know you would have done. She is a dear girl. Please, – I'd like very much for you to give us your blessing.

The dreary weeks rolled by, although the atmosphere in the old 'Crown' continued to make any stranger believe, there could not possibly be a war on!

Barney Bull and old Joe seemed to have made a pact right from the beginning, that no storm, hurricane or even an earthquake, and certainly not that Bastard 'Itler, was ever going to prevent them from occupying their usual places, of propping up the Bar in their favourite old pub.

Noticeably too, the first one on the spot at the stroke of each opening time, – was Wiley Fox no less, – at his post before any of the others had shut their front doors, and could amble along to have their topical and typical moans and groans, while supping a pint of their old and mild.

This evening was no exception in fact it was to celebrate a very special occasion, that many made their business, to get in the doors of the pub before it filled to bursting point.

It had been the most animated and stimulated of talking points that the regulars had indulged in and spoke of for some weeks, bar the raids of course!

It had started with a bit of idle chatter, and when it got around finally to Mabel's attentive ear, – everyone knew it would no longer be a well kept secret.

"Tell us if it's true, Maureen? Is Tommy and Kate really gettin' married?" Mabel was cock-a-hoop at what she had learned, mostly by her sheer craftiness.

Now the cat *had* been let out of the bag, Maureen realised. She herself had known about it only just a few days ago. Kate and Tommy had tried to keep it quiet for a wee bit longer, but to no avail. But now the secret was out, and what a buzz of conversation it made in the Bars!

Everyone was as pleased as Punch. They all liked Tommy, and had a great respect for Kate.

"This calls for a real celebration!" old Barney said puffing away at his pipe. "War or no War, we are goin' ter 'ave the *biggest* knees-up ever. – And no mistake!"

291

Now Kate and Tommy could never know what great interest was being taken on their behalf. As it happened, Kate found it hard to keep a level head, and never believed she could feel so happy.

She lived it over and over again, that wonderful moment when Tommy had thrilled her to the very core with his wonderful words of love.

"Say you will marry me Kate, let me hear you say yes!"

But she remembered too, how suddenly he had gone quiet, and never spoke for some minutes, which seemed like a lifetime.

"What's the matter Tommy dear?" she faltered.

Had he regretted his sudden decision, was he having second thoughts?

He took her hand.

"Kate, have I been too hasty? – I really have no right to ask you to be my wife."

"I have nothing to offer you. I own nothing. All I can give you is myself, and my undying love. But I will do whatever is possible to earn your love and most importantly, your respect."

"I shall work damned hard to give you all you deserve, and that is my solemn promise."

"Stop! – Please stop, darling Tommy, – there is no need for all this. What I have we will share. It is you and only you I need, and your love Sweetheart!" Putting her fingers to her lips, she placed them then on his.

"I don't want to hear any more of this, promise me you won't say another word!"

Kate's head was definitely in a whirl. It had been like it ever since she'd opened her eyes this morning, feeling a little befuddled, and asking herself, – "Is this me?"

Is all this really happening? She had looked at it hanging on the bedroom wall, – her outfit! – A dress and an edge-to-edge coat she had been able to buy at the 'Guinea Shop'.

A Twenty-one shilling, blue full-length coat, A fifteen and elevenpence flowered dress, with a white broad-brimmed straw hat to match. Her shoes, navy-blue, price twelve-shillings and elevenpence, completed the ensemble. Luckily, she had just pipped the post, 'Clothes available only with points was on its way.

She was sure Tommy would be pleased with her choice, but was being far too modest, for in that magic moment, when she entered the door of the Chapel, on the steady arm of Les, and walked down the aisle towards him, and their eyes met, Tommy experienced a feeling of deep pride and joy at the radiant picture she created.

Elegant and refined with her classic features and sleek shining brown hair, she was in Tommy's eyes, every inch a model of perfection. With his voice shaking, he found great difficulty in repeating his marriage vows. Though, so much attention paid to Tommy's sensations and impressions must not override Kate's obvious joy.

It must be said that she felt exactly the same way, and her happiness knew no bounds, as she would, in the near future, when all the solemnization and celebrations were over, be able to sit in Maggie's parlour and reveal all this, to her true confidante and friend. Every blessed impression, perception and gratification, in fact everything that she felt, which had made her glad to be alive, on this amazing day! –

Her wedding to her 'Tommy' day!

A good deal of chattering likened to the sound of swarming bees came from a small gathering of folk who had collected outside the Baptist Chapel. Heads were turning this way and that, looking at the Chapel entrance, shading their eyes from the bright Sun which had decided to shine on this distinctive occasion. The waiting crowds were getting impatient. They were there to pay their respects to their nurse, who had become quite a heroine during the heavy raids, sticking to her post through the heaviest attacks, not thinking of herself but only of her frightened helpless patients.

These folk felt they owed something to this modern day Saint, and had come to show their regard at her marriage to a man who was also a real good sport, and an entertainer in his own right! He had brought back a bit of life into the atmosphere of their favourite Pub the old 'Crown'.

Tommy Larkin was a good bloke, and he was marrying a damned fine lady, as well as a first class nurse!

"Here they come!" The voices were in unison as Tommy with Kate on his arm, appeared at the door of the Chapel, withstanding the hail of confetti, (no rice please, – there's a war on!). Wearing the broadest of smiles. they came down the steps towards the waiting car, a 'Ford Eight', no less! A brand spanking vehicle, complete with Chauffeur, kindly loaned for the occasion, on hearing of the wedding, by a Publican friend of Maureen and Les.

There were choruses of 'Good Luck,' whoops and cheers, as the happy couple drove off, but only along a few streets to another gathering waiting eagerly for the newlyweds' return, – inside the 'Crown and Anchor'.

What were Kate's and Tommy's thoughts, during the whole momentous events, from start to finish?

What were the innermost reflections of any bride and groom? – On such a day as this!

294

It was a right bright sparkling scene that met their eyes when Kate and Tommy entered the packed to overflowing bar to the sound of many voices singing, –

'Hail the Conquering Hero Comes!'

The usual chiding began, – the saucy asides, the nods and the winks, though all was taken in good part. But what about the wedding cake? – Maureen had knocked this up from somewhere, made with donated rations of sugar and fruit. A 'Utility Cake!' – Then, "Quiet, everyone!" Les's voice rang out above the raucous hubbub.

"Let's have hush!" which took a few seconds to obtain, and then Les carried on, –

"We are gathered here today, – Quiet there at the back! – No, you're not in Chapel now!"

"I am sure you will all join Maureen and me, in wishing the happy couple, long life and much happiness."

"Cheers all round, – Good ol' Les!"

Poor Les, – should he continue?

"Yes, I must say this! – It was a fortunate day for everyone around here when Tommy did us all a big favour, by dropping into the old 'Crown', that particularly eventful Monday morning!" – More cheers!

Maggie, who'd never quite got the picture out of her mind, of Tommy's impersonation of a tipsy Octopus, trying to play the fiddle while lying upside down, cheered the loudest, and Kate by this time had lost her feeling of shyness at meeting all these people and seeing so many new faces. – She who had been a comparative stranger to the Pub, yet what a grand crowd they all appeared to be!

"And so," said Les, "It only remains for me to say Kate and Tommy, as you start your life together, that everyone here wishes you both a safe journey to this very well kept secret hide out you are off to!" Then Les added, – with a wink, – "Don't do anything we wouldn't do!"

A footnote: –

The final scene was to be enacted, after managing to escape from a tumultuous send off outside the Pub, with more confetti being thrown, plus some over the mark advice coming from the back row of the crowd, and Kate and Tommy were off. Again, in the Ford Eight, to the station, – "Destination? – Unknown!"

Chapter: Twenty-five

The wedding of Kate and Tommy had taken the burden of war from the minds of the folk living in streets bordering on the 'Crown and Anchor' for a short while. Alas, it was still very evident! The queues for food grew longer, the moans and groans were heard even more, specially when they said clothes were going to be put on a points system! Then coal and coke was restricted and when soap rationing came into force with razor blades hard to find. – Well!!

It was when Mabel knew that the ladies were painting stockings with gravy browning onto their legs, because their precious points ration had run out. Although there weren't any stockings to be had anyway! –

"Blind O'Riley!" She burst out, –

"What the 'ell will they be 'avin us do next!"

"I kin see us all finishin' up soon, squattin' outside caves! That's if 'Itler keeps on knockin' darn our bleedin' 'ouses, and us looking as black as the ace a spades, and dressed only in Sheepskin loin cloths!"

"Sod that fer a lark!"

Poor Mabel, she was more than a little niggled. Still, everyone knew of Mabel's lapses in terminology and would most likely, be only pleasantly amused.

Maggie stood behind the bar polishing and carefully scrutinising each glass, as she made dead sure everyone of them was clean, but she really had her mind on other things. Life now seemed to be one long succession of doubt and suspense, and wondering, – What was Jess doing? How was Rob, and where was he right at this moment? And Kate and Tommy too! Funny how she missed Kate so much, but she had a feeling of triumph at the way things had turned out. –

"I wonder where they are now?"

She was sure that they weren't even certain, in the first place, where they were going themselves!

Things were quiet here this Monday evening. Trade hadn't been too good for a while. Ever since the bombing had started and the Docks were in a state of disruption, it had made a lot of difference in many ways to the Pub, except for the regulars of course.

Hell and high water wouldn't keep them away! Bert wasn't so busy either, with not much doing at the shop. But the road gangs and navvies had made a good job at clearing most of the roadways, which was a blessing to people who still had difficulty journeying to work. It was a hell of a task. There was not one street that hadn't been affected by the magnitude of the bombing.

Although the Jerries had turned their attention to provincial towns and left the City mostly alone for a few weeks, the bombing spree of the Luftwaffe was by no means over, for the Dockside area.

'Wailing Winnie', became a part of everyday life, "Bluddy fing, there it goes agin!" and folk just got on with what they were doing.

"Maggie, – 'Ere gal!" She looked up from rinsing a pile of glasses in the sink under the counter, and looked over at Wiley, who had called out to her, –

"Put anuvver pint in that Mag!" He said, slamming the glass down on the counter, and turning to carry on his conversation with a newcomer to the Pub. –

Mag had not seen this man in here before, – Must be one of the workmen, – But he was too tidily dressed for that!

She continued with her serving, until she heard a familiar name mentioned, which made her prick up her ears. Maggie took another look at this stranger and weighed him up a little more. – Who was he? – But what on earth did he want with Mavis?

"Yeh! I knew Mavis very well, but she's moved right away from 'ere nah!" she volunteered.

"But when I 'eard from her the last time, she was somewhere in Norf London!"

Mag waited for him to speak once more.

"Let me introduce myself," said the stranger as he walked over towards Maggie. –

"My name is Edward Hughes. Eddy to my friends! – But can I speak to you quietly somewhere?"

He nodded towards the end of the counter where they would not be disturbed.

"Mavis is my Sister, – well Stepsister. – We got split up when she left home. It's a very long story, I have to say!"

"She said she'd married this Sid Lewis. – He was a Wideboy! – Nobody liked him much!"

"There was a blasted great row and they left Stepney. Still, I don't want to bore you with too much of this. I'd just like to know where I can find her?"

Mag had been listening intently to all that Eddy was saying. He seemed to be quite above board, and his story seemed feasible. But when she came to think of it, Mavis had never mentioned anything about her family before, and never had many visitors.

She waited for a while, before she made up her mind, and saying, –

"Well I fink I kin 'elp yer, but if yer will let me contact 'er first, an' arrange fer yer bowf ter meet at my 'ouse, that is, – but it will 'ave ter be up ter Mavis a course!"

Eddy Hughes, he seemed to be satisfied with that. Mag herself, didn't want to stir up any family skeletons from inside the cupboard, she would have to write to Mavis. But Mag still had a few qualms about this arrangement and hoped she had done the right thing!

"Mum, I'm coming home for a long weekend!"

A short letter from Jess, but it was enough to let Mag know how pleased she was to be seeing her Ma, and there was no doubt about that, when Jess flung herself at Mag and almost took her breath away, as she came in the door.

"Let's look at yer gal? – My! I swear yer've grown an inch or more, since I last saw yer."

"Come on, let's 'ave a chinwag? I got the kettle on. Betcher yer ain' 'ad a good cuppa tea, all the while yer bin orf darn there in the country!"

They had a lot to talk about, and all the time Mag just couldn't get it into her head that this was her Jess sitting there, almost a fully grown woman, and a very smart and good looking one too!

The back door latch was lifted up, and in came Jim. It also struck Jess how Jim had changed, and quite a lot since she had been away. Dan's death must have done much to knock the last of the desperado factor out of him! His face wasn't at all like the one she remembered. But it brightened up when he saw Jess.

Funny how much you miss a sister or a brother when they are away, but all the while you are under each other's feet, you behave like a lot of bears with sore heads!

"Come on Jim! Let's take Snowy fer a run. I know, we'll give Dad a big surprise. – 'E don' know I'm 'ome yet!"

"'Ere Jess!" said Mag, –

"Would yer git me some potaters while yer darn that way and 'Arf a Echo Marge?"

A little puzzled, Jess looked at her Ma, then she caught on. She didn't really need them, her Mum was just remembering past times.

"Was it so long since those good old days? – Why der kids have ter grow up ser quick?"

Mag swallowed hard, – "Go on, orf yer go, and don't bring me back no scabby spuds!!" she said laughing.

She sighed as she watched them walk up the road together, with Snowy yapping and jumping up and down delightedly, lapping up this unexpected outing. It was so nice to see. Maggie waited for them all to disappear from her sight before going indoors.

She was on the point of shutting the front door, when she heard a voice calling her. She turned to see Kate standing there smiling broadly.

"Its you Kate, yer 'ome?" she said, surprised to see her.

"Yes, I'm glad I caught you Maggie. Yes, Tommy and I got back home late last night!"

"I know you haven't time to talk now, but would you like to come in later? – I have so much to tell you!"

Mag went in and closed the door, it was lovely to see them back and she was sure she would have to be blind, not to see the look of real happiness and contentment that was written all over Kate's face.

Jim had just seen Jess off on her train journey back to Kent. Sorry he was to see her go. He'd found Jess to be jolly good company. Funny, also she had recognised, that Jim had grown into an interesting young man. It would be only a few months now before he would be called up for service. – Did he still want to be a '*Soljer?*'

He must have seen the awful pictures of Dunkirk. Would he want that to happen to him?

Still she was doing the job that she had wanted, – to be a Land Army Girl, enjoying every bit of it as she was and very much so. – The hardest part was getting up early!

Coming back from the station, Jim took the long way round to home. He walked down by the river, although afterwards he couldn't think why he had done that?

Passing at Wapping Old Stairs, he stopped and stared around at the familiar site where Dan and he had sat so many times before, chin-wagging and conjuring up all their visions and fantasies, of what they would be when they grew up, and what about the *Girls*! – He sighed deeply!

"Mu-um, – You in?"

Maggie had heard the sound of Jim's voice calling the same question more times than she could remember.

She smiled, and put down the letter she was reading.

"Yeh-eh? I'm 'ere Son! Jess, did she git orf alright?" she asked. "Did she manage, ter git a seat?"

"That was quite a walk from Brody Street, all the way ter London Bridge Station. – Eh, lad?"

"'Ungry are yer Jim luv? – I'll make yer a sandwich, or d'yer want some scrambled egg?"

"Ow Mum! – Yer know I don't like that 'orrible dried egg stuff. – It tastes like a load a sawdust!"

"It's better than nuffin' lad," said Mag.

"But that's all I've got son. – Like it or lump it, – all the chickens 'ave gawn on strike!"

Now the Jerries were having another go! They just wouldn't take 'No' for an answer and had come back with more determination than ever. The raids had not been so intense for a time, Hitler had been directing his aims towards the Balkan Countries, – Yugoslavia and Greece, and now he had set his sights on Russia.

But the blighter still fully intended to invade Britain, and he might have succeeded if it had not been for the indomitable resistance of the people of this tiny Island. He had been given the thumbs down sign, and without a shadow of a doubt, – 'As ter where ter sling 'is 'ook!'

In fact, if he (God forbid) had walked into any of the bars of the 'Crown and Anchor' this particular evening, he would have received some very spicy bits of advice. It would certainly have hurt his Bat-like ears, – and a ruddy good job too! – Every adjective well-aimed at this unsavoury little Hun!

For the past few nights 'Wailing Winnie' had come into its own again, and Mabel had some more glowing additions to the already impressive list of names she had christened, – "That perishin' rotten noise! – The Bleedin' awful racket that Siren kicks up!" And more in her own words, –

"O' Gaw' Blimey! Yer don' even git a chance ter wash yer bluddy self. They're talkin' abart rationin' soap. We don't git time ter use it! We'll all 'ave ter 'ave a rub darn wiv 'n oily rag! An' nah I've run art a me 'Evenin' in Paris' scent, bought me, fer last Christmas! I kin tell yer, I'll need somefink soon, not bein' able ter git no flamin' barf!"

"And as fer that bleedin' 'Itler? – If I ever gits me 'ands on 'im. – I'll frottle the Sod!"

And Mabel would! She didn't beat about the bush, and never bothered to take a breath, all the time she was letting off steam. You could almost see it coming out of her ears! "Old on gal, yer'll boil over in a minit!" said Joe.

The regulars in the Pub were now used to seeing Mabel in the Bars. Her old man now had an excuse to get away from her a while, – he had gone and joined the band of Air Raid Wardens, and 'She wasn't goin' ter sit indoors on 'er own waitin' fer the bluddy sirens ter go!'

Peg Miller and a couple of others wanted to know, and asked Maureen, –

"When's Tommy comin' back? Is 'e 'ome yet? The place don't seem the same nah, since 'e's bin away!"

Maggie was able to tell them, –

"Yeh, I've seen 'em bowf terday. – Don' worry, 'e'll be in soon, I guess!"

She knocked timidly at Kate's door, and waited, –

"Ah! – There you are Maggie, I hoped you would come in!" Showing her into the parlour, Kate then told her, – "Tommy is around at the A.R.P post. So we can talk. How *are* you Mag?"

Now Maggie didn't have to ask *how* Kate was, – her face had lit up into a huge smile, upon seeing Mag, – In fact Kate positively glowed!

"Let me put the kettle on first." said Kate, shooing the cat off the settee.

Maggie looked around the room. Was it now her fancy, or did it have a *different* feel about it! It contained warmth somehow. A pleasing lived in atmosphere. And gone was the miserable and deflated air of emptiness it used to have.

Over in the corner of the room, near the fire, she noticed Tommy's slippers, – A homely touch.

"Here we are then Mag!"

Kate put the tray onto the cane table, and commenced pouring out the tea, while Mag watched on. How calm and confident Kate had become. It was amazing to see what a *difference* the events of the past weeks had produced.

"Yes!" Kate was saying, –

"It was an unexpected surprise to discover this quiet old market town in Suffolk, where Tommy lived for some years. I thought it a really nice place to live."

"He never came from a large family you know, but this cousin of his, made us very welcome. We did appreciate it. Yes very much indeed, and you would never have guessed at all, that there was a war on."

"Not there Maggie! – It was so beautiful and tranquil."

So now they were back home, and had to start getting used to the renewal of the Air Raids again, not really a very nice thought?

Maggie awoke suddenly, trembling and with a terrible fear, she found she was shaking like a leaf and her brow drenched with perspiration. She shot up quickly and looked round at Bert. He was sleeping, as sound as a log.

Slipping out of bed so as not to disturb him and with her heart beating umpteen to the dozen, she crept quietly downstairs to the kitchen.

"Please don't let it be true?" she kept saying over and over again. – "It can't be true?"

Mag just could not get that awful spectacle out of her mind. Rob her big boy was in danger. She could see him so plainly, – he kept calling out for her, – "Ma! – Oh! – Ma!"

Again and again he called out, his face ashen with horror. He was stretching out his hands to her.

He needed her, – his Ma!

Mag shuddered, – "I've got to stop this!" She picked up the poker and tried to stir up the dying embers of the fire in the kitchen range, then realised she could not have been asleep for very long!

"Why that dream though? Yes of course, – it was only a bad dream, – and they were never true. – Forget it!"

She made some tea and the rattling of the crocks awoke Snowy, and not only the dog, but Bert too, who appeared there in the doorway. He had missed Mag and came downstairs, and was standing there in his long white pants! How funny Mag should suddenly think of this, –

"Why do men always look their worst in long skinny, white fleecy underpants? It is so unromantic of them!" She giggled. – But should she tell Bert of her dream? – No!

"Come on, back ter bed!" she ordered, –

"We've got ter git our beauty sleep."

"Speak fer yerself woman, I don't need it! You might?"

"What!" – Maggie brushed away *that* remark, –

"'Ave yer sin yerself in the lookin' glass wiv those passion killers yer got on? – Yer look like the back-end of a Circus 'orse!"

"'Ere! – 'Nuff a that, Mrs 'Ope. – Yer'd better nip back up them there stairs, sharpish, – Or yer'll be sorry!!!"

Well, – Mag soon forgot about her bad dream!

A storm had threatened and what had been a calm smooth sea had now become choppy and the clear sky that was for one moment full of stars, was now a blanket of blackened nothingness. The sudden ferocity of the cruel Atlantic waves caused the bows of the destroyer to dip and rise continuously. Not a sensation that Rob and his mate Nobby could get used to. Things had been pretty rough, –

not just the wild angry seas, but they had met up with plenty of action from the ever-prowling U-boats.

The convoy, which stretched over a huge area as far as the naked eye could see. Of Battleships, Destroyers, Corvettes and the many Merchant ships, filled with valuable cargo they were there protecting, which had attracted these U-boats, always lurking, waiting for their prey. It seemed the whole ocean was teeming with them!

Apart from the heaving seas and the ship's bows dipping and rising, threatening to disappear at any time as the huge waves broke over the decks. It was the noise, the infernal sound of the anti-aircraft guns that deafened him. Rob felt exhausted in both body and mind, and all he craved was comfort and sleep! To sleep forever was what he yearned for, yet he still carried on reloading.

The sky was filled with shell bursts and the scene was a devilish one, with flames and smoke belching from burning ships everywhere. It was like Hades, a Hell of man's making. It hadn't occurred to Rob, that he might have no chance of ever coming out of this tumult and this pandemonium alive! – Then the worst had to happen! – A torpedo hit the Destroyer amidships. – All went quiet.

The whole ship then trembled violently, there was a roar and the vessel rocked with a colossal explosion. Nobby for a fleeting moment saw Rob slumped, – his twisted form in a heap by the gun turret with a gaping gash in the side of his head and blood spurting from it. This was the last image Nobby would have in his mind.

"Rob mate!" he cried, just as a huge shaft of steel pierced right through his body. – He had no time to scream!

* * *

"Is that the door Jim? – I 'eard a knock!"

Jim went to the door, but came back again saying, –

"It's a bloke on a bike Mum!"

"'E says 'e wants ter see yer! He's got a letter or somefin' in 'is 'and, – but 'E wants ter give it ter yer!"

Mag's heart missed a beat, she had a momentary feeling of foreboding. What was it this bloke wanted? She went to the front door, then knew her fears had not been unfounded.

Yes, it was the Telegraph boy, and in his hand he held, – this buff envelope!

"No! – No!" She couldn't take it! – she didn't want it! – Go away, she wanted to say to the waiting boy.

This was the day she had always dreaded, the one day when she'd feared she might have to face something like this. With her hand shaking, she took the envelope from the telegraph boy, mumbled her thanks, and went back into the kitchen, walking very slowly.

She put it on the table, and sat down just looking at it, her heart thumping in her chest.

"Go on. – Open it then Mum!"

Mag looked at Jim's face as he stood there. He must surely know why she was dreading to open it?

She took a deep breath, and slowly picked up the telegram. It was no good, she had to do it, and quickly she ripped open the envelope.

The words seemed to thrust themselves up at her.

"We regret to inform you that Able-Seaman Robin Hope has been reported missing, presumed. ....

The words trailed off, Maggie couldn't read any more. She just froze, and with a cry of pain, and it *was* a pain, one that she had never yet in her life experienced! – She sank into a chair, clutching the piece of paper tightly in her hand.

"Mum, what is it?" But Jim guessed, it could only be one thing. He took the telegram from her grasp and read it. He went white. –

"But Mum! You don't, You can't know. They only say, 'e is missin'. That don't mean anyfin' but what it says."

Poor Jim, he didn't know what to say, 'Gawd!' He wished his Dad was here!'

Leaving Mag, he went and put the kettle on. There was one thing he could do, though. – Kate! – Yes, he would knock for Kate. She was round there like a flash and leaving his mum in her capable hands, Jim went out. He would go round to Percy's shop and tell his Dad!

Maggie sat there riveted to the chair. Try as she may, she knew she couldn't grapple with this. Kate quietly spoke, and kneeling beside Mag she held her hands firmly in her own, saying gently yet earnestly, –

"Maggie dear, you have had nothing like this ever happen to you, that is certain! You *are* strong, you have shown that! Don't let this news break you. I am sure Rob will be alright! He may have been picked up by one of the other ships?"

"Please Maggie, think of the others, – Jess and Jim and your Bert, they will be feeling exactly the same as you!"

That made Maggie try to pull herself out of the trance-like state, which had overtaken her, replying, –

"Oh! Kate, what would I do wivart you?" and looking at her cup of tea, on the table which was now stone cold, she managed to say with a bit of an effort, –

"Let's, – Let's 'ave a nice cup a tea! – Eh, luv?"

There were heavy footsteps heard outside the back door, and Bert burst in, flinging his cap on the chair, he went straight over to Maggie's side, kneeling beside her, –

"Ow! Mag darlin'!" and putting his arms around her, he just laid his head on her breast. Kate crept out quietly and left them there alone. There was nothing she could do now.

She *would* be needed sometime, as Kate understood, only too well, what Mag and Bert might be having to endure in the coming days ahead.

Didn't she know the mental suffering, the ache and anguish, the vexation of not knowing?

Poor Mag, would she ever see her Rob again?

Chapter: Twenty-six

There was the usual combination of clatter and hubbub in the bars, characteristic of a Pub when full, as it was that evening. The chit-chat, the sound of clinking glasses, the boisterous laughter, maybe at someone else's expense. In all, it was a happy sound, and Tommy was back.

But Mag wasn't with it, – all of it went over her head. Her thoughts were elsewhere.

She had been in this state now for many days. Bert had tried to put his foot down and urged her to take some time off, but she flatly refused.

"I'll be better orf doin' somefink better than sittin' roun' mopin'!" she answered, –

"Besides, I know *my* Robbie *is* comin' back! 'E *will* you see. 'E's made a *strong* stuff, that lad!"

It had been a few weeks now since that Telegram had released the bombshell. One hell of a time for Maggie and Bert, it had been without a doubt.

Jess had hurried back to be with her family for a couple of days, by kind permission of Mrs Deakin, – and Jim was more determined than ever now, to get into the fray and, show 'em what *'e* was made of, and git 'is own back for Rob's temporary disappearance, because Jim believed he *would* be coming home. – He was sure of it, –

"Don'cher worry Ma, – 'E will!"

All through these difficult days, the Air Raids had gained momentum, there seemed no chance of them easing up. The same queues of weary, yawning, dead-tired folk, dragged themselves out of the air Raid Shelters, where they saw the same scenes of devastation. As more houses, more factories and more of the Docks, were disappearing day by day, though it would be wrong for folk to say, "We are getting used to all this," but to most it had become a way of life, or otherwise, if they happened to be unlucky!

There were many that spent but a couple of hours a day now and again in their homes. – If they still had them!

Pulling themselves out of a dugout, diving indoors for a few necessities, taking a quick look around at the thick dust covered furniture, afraid to go upstairs, just in case a lone low flying bomber got through the net of Barrage Balloons which often happened, strafing as he went.

It was a perplexing, unstable existence, grabbing food when you could, getting a wash if you were lucky, looking to see if you had any letters. – That's if the Postman hadn't taken flight!

You might manage to get a glimpse of your neighbour just before she disappeared down that hole in the ground again, after getting a short response to your enquiry, –

"'Ello, Mrs Bishop! 'Ow are yer managin'?"

"Don' ask me Mag, I'm fed up ter the teef!"

There had been several bad raids recently on the City and West End, when thousands were killed. Many shops in well-known streets and squares, and famous stores that were minus their plate glass windows, with big notices, –

'Open', 'Wide open', 'We don't close', 'We can't!!' were plastered in prominent places, creating a smile or two.

Mag picked up the letter from the mat and recognised Mavis's scrawl. "An' about bloomin' time too!" she thought. It must be three weeks since she had written to her old neighbour. It was short and very much to the point.

"I am coming to see you Mag, but I don't want you to tell that Eddy, until I see you first."

"Sounds fishy!" Mag wondered a little.

"G'mornin' luv!"

Peg Miller passed Maggie on her way to the shops.

"Nice day for a trip to the Park!" she said, ruefully.

"I keep promisin' me nephew I'll take 'im ter the swings. Poor kids, yer can' take 'em anywhere these days, blasted raids!" she said, and hurried on.

Maureen was waiting for her to come in the door, she seemed very distressed and looked very relieved when she saw it was Mag.

"What's wrong Maur?"

"Oh! I'm glad you're here. Can you take over, until Les gets back? I have to go right away. It's my mother, she's in an awful state. Their house just missed a direct hit last night. My Dad's in Hospital."

Her face puckered for a moment, and had to stop speaking. She couldn't carry on.

"Don' worry, you go orf Maur, I'm sorry abart yer Dad though. 'Ope 'e'll be alright!"

She helped Maureen throw a few things into a bag and watched her go off down the street, side-stepping as she went, piles of bricks, and smashed slates that had been blasted off roof tops and still lay scattered about.

Jim pushed his plate back and wiped his hand across his mouth saying, –

"Mu'um, that was luverly!"

"I'm glad yer liked it lad, but don' do that again, – wipin' yer 'and round yer mouf. Big as yer are, I still don't like yer doin' it!"

Jim gave a sigh. It seemed he couldn't do anything right lately where his Ma was concerned. She had really changed since they'd heard the bad news about Rob.

"I'm goin' orf art Ma. – See yer later!" He'd go down the waterside an' meet Phil.

Phil was the new hand, "Sort a nice." Reminded him of Dan a bit, except for the Zoot Suit!

Maggie cleaned away the dirty dishes, and was prepared to have a nice sit down. She'd begun to appreciate the little time she managed to get to herself. But no sooner as she'd put her feet up on the footstool, there came a knock at the front door.

"Who's that nah? – Must be Jim come back!"

She pulled herself up out of her chair and went to the door and opened it.

Well, she thought she'd been hit by a bus at first, as almost tipping over by a couple of arms being wrapped around her neck, and then this voice practically shaking her eardrums with, –

"Mag, It's me luv, Mavis! Ain' I glad ter see yer! Let's look at yer? Yer finner! What a yer bin doin ter yerself?"

When she regained her breath, poor Maggie was able to sort herself out, and got Mavis to come into the kitchen.

Well it must have been a few years since they had seen each other, but they all began to roll away as they sat there chin-wagging, just like old times.

"This is a luverly cuppa tea Mag. Yer always could make a good cuppa!"

"Nah what 'ave yer bin doin'? – Tell me!"

"'Ow did yer git on wiv all those blasted raids? – Sounded bluddy awful on the wireless. – I tell yer, I was right worried abart all a yer over 'ere."

"We got a few a the blighters tryin' ter 'ave a go back there, but not like you 'ad!" (Fer Gawd's sake, take a breaf! thought Mag.).

Then Mavis began to draw a picture of her life and goings on in her town. However, what emerged from Mavis's account of her ups and downs, since she had left the confines of Wapping, and embarked on a different way of life in Kensal Rise, which was to her regret, as she had said on leaving the old place. This seemed to have totally disappeared! Now it was exactly the opposite, leaving Maggie guessing just why it was?

Mav, told how her best mate Nellie Driver from the Boot Factory, had been the first to introduce her to a bit of the high life that lay outside the boundaries of North West London, and even still further afield.

"Ever bin to the 'Ammersmith Pally?"

Nellie had asked Mavis this, one morning in the cloakroom at work as they donned their unshapely brown overalls and proceeded to add yet another fair coating of 'Snowfire Face Powder' in 'Tahiti Rose', to the thick layer they had already loaded on to their sallow features.

"But that's miles away from 'ere, ain't it?" was Mavis's answer to Nellie's question.

"Don't take long on a bus though," replied Nell. "Yer'd like it there. Plenty of action, – If yer know what I mean!" she added with a wink.

As they talked Maggie realised just how little she'd known of her old neighbour. Yet there was a lot more she was to find out, as time went on. But it was niggling Mag! – Why did Eddy want so much to get in touch with his step sister as he called her, and why was Mav so adamant in not letting him know where she was now living?

315

"Yer never told me you ad a step bruvver? I fort yer never 'ad no family!"

"Didn't git on wiv 'em is that it? – Well, did yer go ter the Pally? – What's it like?" asked Mag.

Then Mavis gave a long detailed descriptive speech of, –

"Smashin' big dance 'all. Good bands! Only the Best ones play there. 'Enery 'All, Jack Payne, Roy Fox– Lots of 'em. – Ow, 'Arry Roy, an' Geraldo!"

"There's a big stage, an' everyfin'!" she said, But as she had been going on there describing all the grandeur and eloquence of the 'Palais de Dance' hoping that Mag would take note of it, she happened to have been barking up the wrong tree. That kind of thing had never appealed to Maggie. Still, she was no sourpuss, but listened, taking it all in with a pinch of salt.

Mag had been eyeing Mavis as she spoke, – she certainly had changed. Gone was the old Mav. (Had the curlers and the pink scarf gone too?)

There was a hardness there, maybe the brassy peroxide head of hair, the heavy make up and short skirt, all helped.

And her defiant manner. This gal knew what she wanted and she was going to get it!

There was more to Mav, than met the eye. Maggie would have liked to have the old Mavis back, – this one was a stranger. – Mavis stood up.

"Well mate, I gotta be goin', an' catch me train before the blackout starts. – As I said, if that Eddy comes snoopin' round 'ear, – say yer don' know where I 'ave moved to. Don' ferget it, – will yer?"

"Gotta luv yer an' leave yer, Mag. It was good to see yer. Don' do anyfin' I wouldn' do!" And that was that, she was gone. "Wonder if we'll ever see *her* agin?" thought Mag.

Well, she had certainly taken the wind out of Mag's sails. Sitting down and pouring out the last dregs of the tea in the pot, she went over in her mind, all that had been said during the last couple of hours.

Talk about not really knowing someone. Maggie, she had definitely underestimated Mavis.

Maureen was back from her visit to Peckham and was able to say the situation wasn't as bad as she had feared. The bomb had been a near miss she said, and thank the Lord, the house was O.K. Her Mum, an excitable fussy little woman, was always a bit neurotic. If she had a cut finger, her head was half off!

Maureen's Dad, had to spend a few quiet nights in Hospital, the shock had given him quite a turn, her mother had told her, but as Mag said to Bert, tongue in cheek.

"Most likely 'e was glad of a coupl'a days away from Mumsy, fer a rest!" Mag had seen it all differently, – thinking wryly of her own mother.

It was kind of a quietish evening there in the bars. Joe and Wiley were talking in undertones. Mag hadn't seen Annie for a couple of days. She guessed all this Kerfuffle and panic of the raids must be telling on the old girl.

It wasn't doing much for herself either! As Mavis had brought to her notice. Yes she was thinner, what did she expect? Dashing about, like a blue-arsed fly, as everyone else did now, snatching a bit of grub when you could, here and there, before that blasted siren went screaming off on a bid to stir up more exasperation, more panic. Blimey, how they were all fed up with it's wailing!

"Hello Maggie!" She looked up and the sight of Tommy standing there brought a smile to her face. He had been in a few times since they, he and Kate had come back from their honeymoon, but without his eight-piece Jazz Band outfit. That was history now! No more would he be assing about with all those contraptions. He owed it to Kate to put all that way behind him, and would be finding a job, (when and where, that was the question!)

"Ello Tommy, 'Ow's Kate?" she asked.

"You must come in one evening," Tommy offered. Don't be afraid to knock. We'd love to see you, – and Bert too!"

"Oh! I don't like to ask, but have you heard anything about Rob yet? – But you know the old saying don't you, – No news, is good news."

Tommy was feeling as he spoke, like everyone else did in a case like this. – You want to say so much, but too embarrassed to do so.

"Why was it, people felt so inadequate when perhaps their understanding and forbearance was needed more, in times of great trouble?"

Maggie wasn't sure how to answer Tommy's remark and replied with a smile, –

"Thankyou Tommy ... tell Kate we would love to come in, one of these evenings."

"Yes", Maggie thought, "I've missed Kate. It will be nice ter 'ave a get tergever, – 'Itler permittin'!"

"Alright Joe, I'm comin'! – Same agen?"

"Got no patience that bloke, I dunno!"

"What's wrong Joe, – Run art a matches, 'ave yer?"

"Perhaps yer'd better put some baccy in it!"

Someone tittered at that pass and Joe looking up said, –

"Perhaps yer'd like ter put yer 'and in yer pocket an' buy us 'arf ounce, – eh?"

* * *

318

There had been the sound of voices, but they would keep disappearing! He tried to move, but failed and felt a horrible throbbing in his head and raised his hand to try and touch it, but found it swathed in bandages.

It hurt like blazes and that's about all he knew. Rob tried to think, but it hurt even more. What had happened? – Where was he? – It was no use though. Shutting his eyes, he glided slowly back into his never-never land.

The next thing he was conscious of, was being clumsily bundled on to a stretcher and pushed into a dark place. Where? But Rob really didn't care now! All he wanted to do was sleep, and just gave up thinking.

He had a thirst, – he knew that now, he wanted a drink. – He badly needed a drink!

Then he heard the shrill whistle of a train and a feeling of being most uncomfortably jolted and bumped along, and that was doing his head no good at all. Rob gave up, he would know sooner or later what was going on.

There was the sudden sound of wheels screeching to a halt and more voices came, *lots* of them, and someone in a white coat pulled a blanket up over him, and shouted out, –

"O.K.! – This one's ready for No 2, what ever that was! Then Rob became aware of more white coats and a much lesser feeling of discomfort. A gentle hand then was laid on his feverish brow and a soft voice was saying, –

"It won't be long, we will soon have you comfortable. You're in good hands now, no more need to worry!"

Closing his eyes, Rob somehow imagined, his Mum was close at hand. – Surely, that must have been her voice!

It seemed to Rob, he had been through a long dark and never ending tunnel, the tranquillity of which was being broken by recurring noises. But it was when he began to experience more and more ungallant, abrupt, almost rough treatment, that the feeling of quietude and serenity he had had, was being very rudely disturbed, – it really irked him!

"Why didn't they leave him alone, why wouldn't they respect his need to remain in his safe and secure haven, his never-never land, the one which he'd been in for so long?

This now caused him to rebel, –

It began with jerking convulsive movements and a flailing of both arms, which was not very acceptable to the young Auxiliary nurse, who had been waiting in attendance on him, watching for signs that he was at last emerging from his long coma.

She bent over him and gripped both his hands tightly, until he stopped shaking.

"Calm down now, its alright." she whispered and there was that soft voice again.

The light hurt his eyes, and he closed them, but in those brief moments he had taken in enough to know, he must be in a Hospital ward, or something like one.

"Now lie still while I make you feel a little easier!" and the nurse began to rearrange his pillows, just as the Doctor walked into the ward.

"Alright Nurse? I see the elusive young mariner has returned to us," he said with a smile looking at Rob.

"Now let me have a look at you, – it seems you have been in the Wars eh?" Rob began to feel a little calmer.

"But where the Hell was he? – How did he get here?"

He could make out other beds in long rows, and other patients, men in various forms of disability. A chap in the next bed had one of his legs hoisted up in a pulley, not looking at all happy! Another, his eyes completely covered in bandages. Others seemed to be still in shellshock.

This place, though it didn't look like a Hospital. It was indeed, the mansion home of an Earl, who'd given it over as a hospital for the duration, while he was somewhere overseas, doing *his* bit, maybe?

But something was troubling Rob and it was not to his liking. Try as he might, he could remember nothing! Not a thing of what and how he happened to be in the condition he now found himself.

"What is your name lad?" asked the Doctor. This was a ploy by the wily Doc. – Rob only blinked and frowned.

"Why? Why couldn't he remember anything." He shook his head in despair, – "He must have a name!"

"Stop, that's enough!" said the Doctor, don't force yourself to think." He called the Nurse, –

"Make this young man comfortable, and I guess he could manage some light refreshment."

"I'll see you later lad!" he turned and continued down the long row of his other waiting patients.

"Go to sleep, just call if you need me, just press this bell here!" said the fresh faced young orderly.

"I won't be far away. – Just outside the door!"

Rob grunted and thankfully went back into his void, his empty, shadowy land.

It was one of those days when you could imagine and damn near believe the world was as it used to be. How long ago, – when you could awake to the Sun, streaming through the windows that were not covered and disfigured with miles of inch-wide strips of brown paper.

Hear the sound of the thrush singing its heart out to the sky above, and taking in the soft and sweet, rose-scented air, drifting up and in through the open window.

Instead of the overpowering stench of decay, rotting sludge and slime mixed with everlasting smoke from the still smouldering fires. Not to have to witness some poor soul searching for a loved one in the rubble, and then the poignant scenes of anguish on finding what they had feared most, – it was too painful to bear.

These scenes and many other heartbreaking experiences were commonplace now, to the folks around this East End, which was being barbarously mutilated beyond belief, and after so many months of what, could only be described as unjustifiable slaughter in the first degree, tried to reason, and questioned, – 'Where would it all end?'

Maggie was one of these sceptics right now. She had cause to feel as she did. The weeks kept going by with no word, nothing to give her any hope that Rob could still be alive, somewhere or other. Each day brought no news. Not a thing to support her belief that one day he *would* come walking up the road towards her.

But who was this now, – standing there waiting at the Pub doorway, looking all agitated?

It was Bessie who seeing Mag, came quickly forward clutching at her arm and almost crying, with a very flushed and worried look on her usually impassive face, –

"Yer gotta come quick!" she cried,

"It's Annie! – I could only think of you, Maggie."

"She's not well at all, she keeps moanin'. I can't make any sense out of 'er! – P'raps you can Mag?"

"Alright Bessie, calm yerself down nah. No need fer yer ter get all upset!"

But Mag, – yes she was more than a little worried. It was not like Annie to act just as Bessie had described. Ann was more of the old war horse type, as Mag had always known her to be. They hurried back where they found that Bessie in her haste had left the scullery door open. They went in, and heard the old lady whimpering.

"There luv, what's wrong wiv yer?" Mag said.

Taking a look at Annie's greyish pale face, she pushed back from her forehead the lovely snowy white hair, that ol' 'Arry had been so proud of, – "No one's got 'air like my ol' Dutch!" – he was often heard to say.

Hearing Maggie's voice seemed to stir the old lady, for she put out a hand, feeling for Mag's which she clung to, trying to say something.

"What is it Ann luv? – I'll get yer a Doctor, don't worry, yer'll be alright!" but she could see it was too late.

"No, gal. No!" – Annie managed to say with difficulty, as she tried without success to pull herself up. "No doctor," breathing very heavily as she spoke. Mag became aware of Annie pressing something into her hand. It was then that she realised with a pang, that her dear old friend was breathing her last and she knew it! There would be no more, 'Pint a Porter fer me ol' 'Arry.' They would have no need of it, for she was, – 'Nah, with her ol' 'Arry.'

Maggie stood silently for a moment or two looking down at Annie, and tried to stifle a sob, because it seemed wrong to cry somehow, and slowly she bent and gently kissed her, and tip-toed quietly through the door. She would go round to Kate, who would know what was to be done.

Then she suddenly remembered she was still holding the object that Annie had put into her hand. Mag slowly opened her palm and there was this little mother of pearl brooch, which she had noticed Annie had worn on her 'high days and holidays coat,' as she'd called it. – She clutched it tight and breathed quietly saying, –

"Thanks and bless you, our dear Annie, and may yer bowf rest in peace, you and yer ol' 'Arry!"

Bert came down the stairs from the bedroom where he had been digging out his only decent pair of trousers, for these were the ones Maggie requested he was to wear to dear Annie's funeral. What an unhappy day, this was going to be for everyone!

"They don' look too good do they Bert?" as she spotted a few moth holes in some very inconvenient places.

"Yer can't wear *them*!" she cried.

"Well, I ain't got nah more!" Bert created.

"Blimey, don't pull a face like that!" said Mag.

"I'll ave ter see if I kin mend 'em, but I'm sure our Ann, wouldn't care a 'oot if yer went wivout none!" Bert laughed and remarked, –

"Cor, – Be a bit draughty roun' me never regions!"

They didn't really want to show too much sadness at old Annie's passing, leaving behind her, this troubled topsy-turvy world as it was now. She their dear old Ann was at peace and 'Wiv 'er beloved ol' 'Arry at last!' Who would want to wish her back to this lot!'

So a bright sun shone down, as it should do when Annie was laid to rest. She would not be missed so much by others as Maggie would miss the old lady she felt sure, as she placed a little posy of sweet peas at her graveside and said quietly, – "Goodbye Annie, Gawd Bless yer, me ol' mate!"

Chapter: Twenty-seven

Jess felt happier now it was warm and light when she got up in the mornings. Almost harvest time, she had got her wish, seeing acres of waving golden corn, and hearing the song of the skylark as it rose up from the carpets of gold. It was a heart lifting sight, one which before coming here, she had only seen in her picture books.

Pulling the package of sandwiches from her bag, she threw herself back on to the grassy bank at the edge of the field and staring up into the intense blue of the sky, she breathed a sigh of contentment.

She'd felt the need to get away from the farm for a while, and Gwen, who at times was inclined to get on her nerves with her twittering, first about one or other of her seven brothers and sisters, who were younger than herself.

Jess didn't want to be a sourpuss, but she did like to get away quietly on her own to think and sometimes to explore the hedgerows, and hunt for bird's nests like now! It was all so new and exciting for her, even to sight newly hatched and blind baby sparrows, as they lay helpless in the nest.

"You shouldn't touch them you know!" said a voice, but not unkindly though.

Jess spun round, startled to hear this remark. – Could it have been a reprimand?

She wasn't sure if she was annoyed or not and took another look. Before her stood this nice-looking soldier, and by the badges he wore she could see he was attached to the Royal Engineers.

With a wide smile on his face, the soldier added in a friendly tone, "Don't be put out by what I said, I have been just as curious as you are. I'm from the country too!"

"It was one of my hobbies, bird watching," and so on.

Jess was thinking, should she stop and converse with the soldier in this country lane, as there was no one around! But really, she couldn't see what harm could come of it. He must be from the Army Camp the other side of the farm, about a mile or so away. Though he gave her no chance to answer, as he turned as if to go.

"Well, I guess I'd better be off now!" her intruder said.

" I have to hurry, maybe I'll see you later!" and went off down the lane. He hadn't said his name or anything.

"What a queer meeting!!" she mused.

Luckily Hitler had kept his nose clean for a brief spell of late, even for the few days prior to and since, Annie's sad passing and funeral.

But it wasn't to say it would stay like it. The momentum of War increased, – Germany had invaded Russia, and clothes' rationing had begun. There were more than a few moans about that! Mostly by the camp following hussies around the Army Camps.

'Make do and Mend' became one of the many slogans on the hoardings, which hit you in the eye, along with other words of advice on 'Keeping Mum,' – 'Dig For Victory!' and this one 'Look, Horse Meat! – No Coupons needed!' on signs in Butcher shop windows.

As these days and weeks went by, Maggie and Bert tried to be ready for the unexpected, never knowing what each day would bring. Getting more and more tired of running to shelters whenever the Siren screamed out its dreaded warning. They were heartily sick of it all, and trying to eke out the food rations. Utterly sick too of dried egg and dried milk, and found they had to eat out at Civic Restaurants at times when they were stuck for a meal. The only alternatives there, were Vienna Steaks! 'Gawd knows what was in 'em! – No one ever found out!'

Jim, after his outburst about the dreaded dried egg, was only too pleased in the end to eat it! – At least it filled him up a bit. Saying, often to his friend, –

"Ain't yer 'ungry? – I am, I could eat an 'orse!" little knowing that *he did* at times!

There was a rat-a-tat-tat at Mag's door. Bert opened it to find Gladys from over the road standing on the doorstep.

"'Ow!" said Gladys, expecting to see Mag there.

"She's at the Pub mate!" said Bert.

"'Ow don' worry." said Gladys." I only wondered if she'd seen the papers. 'Ere, I brought one over. Ain't yer sin this then? – Blimey Bert, what a turn-up fer the books, who'd a guessed it, eh?"

Gladys was another one who just loved a bit of scandal, and here it was, – 'Right up her street!'

Bert grabbed the newspaper roughly from Glad's hand.

"It's on the second page." she said. Bert turned the front page over to see splashed across the top main headline.

'Man seen running away from scene of attempted murder. Horrific scenes in flat, of woman found laying in a pool of blood, after what appeared to have been a desperate struggle. A neighbour spotted the man hurrying away from the house in a quiet cul-de-sac in Kensal Rise.'

But Bert, he was a bit flummoxed. – What was all this to do with Gladys getting so hot under the collar?

"Read on Bert!" she said, – "You will soon see!"

'Police surrounded the house, after a neighbour phoned saying she had heard terrifying screams coming from the top floor. Breaking in, the police found a woman almost bleeding to death from head-wounds, caused by blows from a heavy brass ornament discovered after, with blood and hairs on the base.'

There must have been a row and tempers had turned ugly, it proved. They learned that the woman, – A Mavis Lewis, – had left Wapping some years before to be near her son and his wife. But they had left Kensal Rise sometime after, for reasons unknown.' – Gladys said smugly, –

"Well Bert, whad'yer say ter that then?"

"Wait till Mag gets in. Blimey, what's she gonna say?"

"Yer know Bert, I allus fort there was somefin' a bit fishy abart that woman!"

"Anyway, I got ter go orf darn the shops nah!"

She hoped she'd bump into Mag on the way back, but she was unlucky.

"Mum!" Jim shouted, he had come busting in the back door, sounding very excited. It was now dinnertime and he had hurried home from work, and had something that was hot to say, by the sound of it.

"Mu-um!" he said again, – "'Ain't yer read the papers?"

"What? I ain't got no blasted time ter sit 'ere readin' newspapers all day. – Nah 'ave I?"

"'Ere sit darn, I got some nice 'ot stew fer yer. Don't let it get cold. – Go on nah, eat it!"

"No Mum listen! – It's in all the big papers, I don't know 'ow yer ain' 'eard abart it!"

"Yer know Mavis, – Well, she's bin nearly murdered!"

"What!" Mag shouted, "What yer talkin' abart fer Gawd's sake? – Where'd yer get all that from?"

But Jim couldn't get his story out quick enough, and didn't make a very good job at it, with his gabbling on.

"Yers Mum, – She's 'ad 'er 'ead bashed in!"

For a moment Mag felt she'd had a blow on the head herself. – "Wot the 'ell was Jim goin' on abart?"

Just at that minute Bert made an appearance. Looking at his expression, she knew something *had* happened. Bert just handed Mag the newspaper. She took her time reading it, looking as if she couldn't take it all in, –

"But why?" she said to Bert. – Poor Mavis, her mate. – She hadn't deserved this, who ever was behind it all?

Was it something to do with that Eddy? – Why had he been trying to find her, this sister as he'd called her?

"Blimey!" she then had a horrible thought, –

"What if I got roped in on this. – How the bluddy 'ell am I goin' ter find art nah, what really 'appened?"

The newspapers were full of it and for the next few days it wasn't nice reading at least it wasn't for Maggie.

For as she'd rightly gathered earlier, there had been a lot to Mavis that had been kept hidden and now the Police were hunting this man who was described by a neighbour and two others, who spotted him, – 'Of medium build, short cropped brown hair and quite smartly dressed.' All these could easily match Eddy. Mag realised with a feeling of panic. Though how could she say anything? She'd better keep her nose out of it. If it was Eddy, they would find him, but what a two an eight! It puzzled Mag. What was the true story behind all this gerrymandering? – And, she was still in the dark. How was she going to find out about Mavis? After all, they had been *very* close friends.

*   *   *

329

There was a rustling sound, and the curtains round his bed were pulled back. A hand reached out and touched Rob's shoulder. Rob gazed up into the face of the Doctor there, who seemed obviously pleased and was saying, –

"Well! – If I may say so young fellow, you *are* a sight for sore eyes! Can I attribute all this to our young Nurse Amy here?" The Nurse in question, quite aware of this particular Doctor's over zealous, flowery figures of speech, just smiled and looked across to see Rob's reaction to his words. – But the Doctor was right!

It was now three weeks or so, since Rob had been brought in, almost in a hopeless condition, comatose and with a great gash in his head. But he now by some miracle, had begun to recover by leaps and bounds.

Yet by no means was it easy for Rob, to re-live the ordeal of those terrible days, – the noise of the guns and shell bursts, – millions of them it seemed. The sky had been alive with them, and the nauseating smell of cordite. But worst of all were the screams of dying men! Then the searing sickening pain in his head, from the terrible wound he'd received! And after that, Nothingness! Then gradually as his strength began to return and his mind became much clearer, thoughts of his family returned. His Mum! – What would *she* say, if she could see him in this state?

Now Rob, would have no knowledge of anything, from the moment of his injuries, or how he had been picked out from a cruel sea littered with lifeless bodies, amidst tons of wreckage and scores of frightened men, clinging onto anything that could float and would stay afloat, in those cold grey angry seas, desperately hanging on for dear life.

But lucky for Rob, his guardian angel must have been knocking about there at the right time and in the right place, in the shape of another midshipman, who by struggling resolutely, managed to drag Rob with him onto an upturned piece of wreckage, and holding him there, defying the greedy ocean, until one of the Corvettes reached these two poor devils. – But, – Only just in time!

Most of the less fortunate and utterly exhausted seamen had already succumbed and had disappeared beneath the waves. Yet poor Rob, after this nightmare was over, was never to know or meet this seaman, this bloke who had saved his life! But he vowed he would never forget his heroism. And neither would Rob be aware in the days that followed his rescue, of how he had been taken aboard the Corvette and put into a sick-bay, along with many other of his shipmates, as well as survivors from other ships that had been sunk by the accursed U-boats!

Even more so, Rob would have no conception whatsoever of the crushing blow dealt to his family by the Telegram they had received, and of how they were trying to deal with the bad news. Hoping too, that there might be some other possibility, –

"'Ad some mistake been made?" and that one day right out of the blue, he would suddenly turn up, – Rob with his usual cheeky smile and a, – "'Ello Mum, – I'm 'ome!"

But, "Ow my Gawd!" How they *hoped* and prayed that, and how they *would*, – Keep on praying!

Now Jim he was getting edgy, and had been difficult to talk to. A couple of weeks or so had gone by since his birthday and still no letter, the one he'd taken to rushing down the stairs, hoping to see laying on the mat, –

"Not a sausage, – had they forgotten him? Didn't they know he was now turned eighteen?"

His mate Phil had, had his call up papers over 3-months ago, and he was now somewhere down in Dorset, – square bashing and being bawled at by a glowering red faced bad tempered sod of a Sergeant Major.

But that didn't put Jim off, he couldn't wait to get into the ranks of the fighting men, and do his bit.

"Wasser matter wiv 'em? Why don't they send fer me?"

Bert, on observing Jim's impatience, and contemplating his son's initiation and eventual admittance into the Armed Forces, had a mental picture of Jim. All 5ft 4ins of him, with all the zeal and ardour of someone who would be sent for, to stop all this messing about and hurry along this War, and get it all wrapped up and over with, – finished, – Goal attained. – In other words, 'c'en est fait; consummatum est; Finis!' or something along those lines!

But Bert, actually he was dreading that letter landing on the mat, the one with Jim's call-up papers in it. 'Wasn't he now the last one to be taken?'

Jess, – he missed her horribly, and Rob? – Well, – Rob conjured up a feeling he couldn't describe. Bert had not the confidence and hope that Mag possessed. He knew what it was like to be smack bang in the midst of battle, with no other way to go, only forward and hope for the best, and pray God was on your side!

But there was not a day go by, that he did not say a little prayer, that his big boy would be somewhere safe, and not be one of those many names that would be chiselled out on stone on a Remembrance memorial. – He shuddered, –

"Cut it art yer fool!" – No, Rob *would* be home! He must, and would keep hoping like everyone else did. There were not many homes without there being someone waiting for a loved one, hoping and praying, for God's sake!

Luckily for Jim, he wasn't to be kicking his heels for much longer. To be precise, it was just two mornings later when with such a clatter he went flying up the stairs with, –

"Its come Mum! – Dad!" he shouted as he burst into their bedroom.

"Blimey boy, yer nearly gave me 'n 'art attack!" Mag said, and Bert, he just gave a grunt, pulled back the blankets and jumped out of bed, saying as he left the room, –

"Well that's that then! – Nah the war will be over quicker than we fort!" He went downstairs, put the kettle on and let Snowy out. He had to do all this to ease the shock of Jim getting his call up papers.

"No use nah, Bert mate," he thought, –

"We gotta see it frew. Nah they've all gawn. It's goin' a be pretty quiet roun' 'ere nah!"

There was a scratching at the door, –

"Ow, come on in then!" he said, picking up Snowy.

"'S'pose yer want sumfin' ter eat," he moaned.

"And, *you* wanna go ter war too, eh?"

"'Ave yer 'eard anyfin' more abart Mavis?" Peg Miller asked Mag as she was reaching up to get a glass down from the shelf above, to put into it a measure of Gin.

"Is it Lime yer want in 'ere, Peg?"

"Yeh, please Mag! – Weren't it awful abart Mavis? – It's a queer turn art, ain' it, – I can't understand it, can you?"

"'Ave they got anyone yet?"

Poor Maggie, she felt really irritable and thought, –

"Why does everyone keep goin' on abart Mavis?"

"What der they think I am? – A News paper Reporter!"

She wanted to say, –

"'Ow the 'ell do I know?"

"Crikey! – Why am I so crabby this mornin'?"

"And Peg's such a nice woman an' all!"

Maureen then came out from the back kitchen and then said to Maggie, –

"I'll take over here for a while, go and get yourself a cup of tea and sit down for five minutes."

She had been watching Mag. She could see that the woman was nearly at the end of her tether. No wonder at it! Still no news of Rob, and now they had just seen Jim off to begin his stint towards the winning of the war. That's how *he* looked at it! Not much for the young ones, having to go and face maybe death or maiming, when they should be having the best time of their lives now. – They were still only kids some of them.

And there it was, off again! Wailing Winnie. Maybe another false alarm, they'd had a lot of them lately.

Jerry, although he was still sending them over, many never got through the net. A few did and some poor bugger would cop it. Stories of whole shopping streets being wiped out, causing many casualties. But no one was going to sit cringing in a dugout all day wondering. They just got on with their everyday jobs, and took pot luck!

All Mums had to go shopping for food, or whatever there was going. – It wouldn't come to them.

Maureen called out, –

"Down the cellar everyone!"

"Damn and blast it," moaned Joe, still sucking at his pipe. "I swear I'm gonna fall darn these bluddy steps one day, and break me neck!"

"Yers," said Wiley.

"But what a way ter go, eh? – You laying there amongst all those luvverly barrels a beer!"

There was a sudden Crump, which followed this screaming Whoosh, and the whole cellar shook! Mag could tell it was very near, and had a vision of what must be happening up there. – Her stomach turned over.

Though they were now 3-years into the war, and so much had happened that was abominable and ugly, it never failed to sicken her. There must be many people up along the street, now suffering horribly! Some may even be dying or already dead. – It was terrible! –

"Why? – Oh why, won't this awful war end?"

The 'All Clear' had started, so this time, everyone ascended the steps quietly, and without much more being said, departed and went off home, to see whether all was as they had left it a few hours before, and in many cases, – Sadly it wasn't!

Mag had been sitting quietly brooding. Reasoning if she could, in a succession of thoughts, – the whys and the wherefores, – and the ifs and the buts.

"Why did there have to be Wars?"

"What was the purpose and what was the gain? Man still continued to make the same mistakes over and over again!"

"It was all due to greed and wanting more than anyone else. – Wanting to be a top dog in a rat race.

"Why couldn't they get it into their thick heads, that for hundreds of years, others like them had been doing exactly the same thing!"

"Was that the letter box rattling?"

Maggie pulled herself up stiffly from the armchair, and went to look. She bent and picked up a buff envelope. It looked official. Her heart missed a beat. –

"Shall she open it?"

Sitting herself down again, and plucking up courage, she ripped open the envelope quickly. It had to be quick or she would never have opened the thing!

The words, as she started to read, didn't seem to make sense at first. – What were they trying to tell her?

Running her eyes through the letter in her badly shaking hands, Maggie managed to make out some sentences, until it finally penetrated her muddled state of mind, what they were telling her. How some survivors had been picked up from the sea and that they had been taken to several hospitals. Some confusion had been caused over identification etc, etc. "But now, we are pleased to inform you that A. B. Seaman Robin Hope had been among the survivors, and more information would be given out when it was available!"

Mag gave a cry, and trying to control her shaking, she stood for a moment, – and then went off like a rocket! Banging at Kate's door, she waited for it to open. This seemed like years instead of just seconds!

Almost falling into Kate's arms, Mag gave her the letter to read herself, as she had no breath left. Then Kate usually so imperturbable, – was now quite over the moon!

"Maggie dear how can I tell you how I feel, I am so pleased! – Sit down and do try and calm yourself!"

There was no denying the condition they were both in, and what did Kate say now? – There was nothing left to say, but Mag's usual remedy, – her own!

"Maggie, nah 'ow abart a nice cuppa tea, eh?"

"Oh Kate, I mus' find Bert first, I've gotta let 'im know our good news!"

But she had to curb her laughter at Kate's little mimicry of her, and it was the first laugh she had had, in a *long* time!

Happy now, Mag was literally 'on top of the moon' as she almost flew round to Percy's shop, and what happened after that remained forever in Mag's memory. She had never before seen Bert cry, – but now he cried tears of joy, and Mag she joined in with him, standing there in Angus Percy's Emporium surrounded by bundles and parcels, gimcracks and ornaments, knick-knacks and Rembrandts, with their arms about each other.

"Ow Mag, darlin'!" and Mr Percy crept quietly away, – this was no time for *him* to be hanging around.

Now, it went without saying, how quickly the good news about Rob managed to travel, and was the talking point in the 'Crown', for quite a few weeks!

"'Eard any more abart Rob yet Mag?" and "When's that Rob a yours comin' 'ome then?"

Mag couldn't say much more than she knew already for quite a while, but the change in both her and Bert's manner plainly showed in the weeks to come, but they tried not to get too impatient waiting for more news, but altogether it was quite a trying time.

Jess, when she had heard the news about Rob, almost boiled over with excitement, and took Gwen off to the 'Wheatsheaf.' Even roping in Nell and Florrie for a few celebration drinks.

That was a turn up for the books if you like! All were the best of friends now, since that fiasco when they'd first met. Miss 'Shortarse' herself, although all mouth and trousers at the time, had turned out to be a real chip off the old block, as Jess was to find out as time went on.

Even Snowy noticed to his great delight, things had improved. He reckoned he'd led a *dog's* life during the past few months, everybody seemed to have been walking about with a hang d*og* look on their faces, and he had been in the *dog* house too, quite a few times. –

"The way these humans carried on!"

Now Young Jim, he had actually got his finger out at last, and written home a letter in *Jim's* own jargon, first of all saying how glad he was to hear of Rob's reappearance after so long, and what had happened.

"Can't wait to see him Mum! When's he coming home?

Nice down here in Wiltshire, though I can't tell you where abouts! Lots of hills. We have to slog up and down 'em. Not so good. Grub's not so nice as yours is Mum!"

"'Ope yer all OK! Lots of luv, Jim."

"That's it then," said Mag, "But at least 'e did write!"

"That boy's in the wrong mob!" was Bert's reaction to Jim's letter. "'E's always got 'is 'ead in the clouds. 'E'd be better orf as a Fighter Pilot!"

And what about Jim himself? – Jim was hot! – Jim was out of breath and poor Jim wished with all his heart he could be sitting by Wapping old stairs throwing pebbles into the River Thames, right at this very minute, never mind whether he thought how smelly or how mucky it was!

Instead, he was puffing and blowing, running up hill and down dale on Salisbury Plain, in full battledress and kit, complete with rifle, sweating and swearing along with other rookies, all doing the same thing.

"I wants me 'ead tested, that's what I wants!" he muttered as he toiled along ready to drop.

He had been at this camp for almost four weeks. Twenty-eight days of being kitted out, shouted at and bawled at, by a very red-faced, thick-skinned, insensitive sergeant major.

Did he like being in the Army? – If you had asked Jim that, when the platoon arrived at the end of their foot slogging ordeal, he would not have been able to give you a plain or definite answer, – for why? – He lacked the breath!

To be fair though, – that is what he was there for. – To be broken in, and he was most definitely broken, *and done in* one way or the other!

He doubted that he had any feet left! Surely these weren't the boots he had been issued with. They felt more like armour plated clogs!!

Did they say the Army marches on its stomach? – "Not this bunch I 'ope, by the look of me plates a meat!"

Poor Jim, now didn't he know, that all raw recruits thought exactly the same damn thing!

Now Peg Miller, – She'd had enough of seeing every blooming evening, the long faces, the grim miserable looks, all you heard was nothing but war talk.

They couldn't go on like this! Going across to the Bar, she whispered a few words into Maureen's shell-like ear, and after a couple of dubious shakes of her head, Maureen eventually gave Peg a nod.

"Alright," she said, "Yes, we'll have a go. Certainly, we need to do something to liven them all up! I'll leave it to you then, to do your best!"

Les he was pleased with the idea of a Housey-Housey evening, – "Don't know why I didn't think of it meself!" – So it was all cut and dried.

"And yer can make a poster," said Mag to Les. So it all seemed to be going very well, and with many suggestions.

Until Joe he piped up, as if to put the mockers on it all by saying, – "What abart 'Itler?"

"Yer don' fink were askin' that bastard, do yer?" said a voice at the bar. – "'E'll be most unwelcome!"

Maureen hoped this scheme of Peg's wouldn't be marred by any Air Raids, but Mag was all for it and also had a very nice idea, which sounded pretty good too.

"Maybe Kate and Tommy would like to come along?"

"But what do we do about prizes?" Maureen asked.

"No," said Peg, butting in. "It'll be like this," –

"Everyone puts a tanner or a bob maybe, for a card of numbers, and the winner gits the pool. Brilliant, eh?"

"D'yer want yer glass filled Wiley, or are yer gonna stand there all evenin' lookin' like a cod wiv it's marf wide open?" called Mag from the other end of the bar.

She was feeling a bit surprised no one had asked her if she had heard anything about Mavis, though to tell the truth, she had been doing a bit of wondering herself.

Talk about telegraphy, – or was it telepathy! – One or the other she thought, for just as Mavis's name had flitted across her mind, she heard a voice say quite loudly, and it sounded like Joe's inquisitive tones.

"See they caught that bloke then! The one who tried ter do that woman in. – Yer must know 'er! – She used ter come from somewhere around this way!" Mag, she pricked up her ears at this, but said nothing. It would be in the newspapers or on the radio for sure! So all the rest of that evening she was itching to get home to find out.

She was met by Bert at the front door, who was dying to talk about what he had heard. He couldn't wait to say, –

"Your Mavis was a sly old one, eh luv?" –

"There wasn't any flies on 'er!" –

"She could keep a secret well couldn't she?"

This was his summing up!

After Mag had read the papers. Bert said to her, –

"Yer couldn't 'ave known then, abart that Eddy bein' 'er *real* 'usband? – Jus' goes ter show yer, – don' it?"

Well, poor Mag had been really shocked to say the least and was deep down dismayed and quite hurt at Mavis's deceit, and how the subsequent disclosure of her dark secret had come to light. – "What a Stupid Cow!"

Everything now had been revealed, of how Mavis had cleared off with Sid Lewis, after he'd given her a taste of a bit of luxury. She'd left Eddy with numerous debts and evidence of other illicit affairs she'd had! –

"No wonder the poor bugger had lost his temper and tried to do her in! – Still, he shouldn't have done that to poor old Mav."

Maggie was shaken, she felt she had been hit by a sledgehammer, and wasn't so sure *now*, who she felt sorry for, – Mavis or Eddy. Though there wasn't much to choose between the two of them!

So that episode was over, – now she would put it out of her mind. She wasn't going to lose any sleep over it, Mag had other worries, *closer* to home.

"'Ere Bert, – Wonders will never cease!"

"We've just 'ad anuvver letter from young Jim! 'Ere, read it. 'E's bin shifted! 'E's stationed somewhere up in Suffolk. It's in a village near Bury St. Edmunds. But listen ter this! 'E says there's a load of American soljers up there! – G.I.'s they're called!"

Mag seemed to be in quite a good humour, having received this exceptionally long letter from her usually concise, – keep it short and to the point, Son.

Bert listened patiently to Maggie's spasmodic narration on all Jim had been up to at his new camp, with one eye on a newspaper, filled with the progress of the War overseas, and also one ear cocked taking in all Mag had to report.

"I fort yer arst me ter read Jim's letter?" he said after a few minutes, – "But alright, – git on wiv it," he added with a big grin. Mag smiled, and carried on, –

"Seems those Yanks up there are snappin' up all the gels and our lads don't git a look in! Jim, 'E says too, – They are always chewing lots a Gum! And the way they talk! – They carn' even speak proper, – they seem pretty barmy!"

"Poor Jim! 'E soun's really cheesed orf. 'E's arst abart Rob 'an says. When's 'e comin' 'ome." She then gave over the letter to Bert, saying, –

"Well Bert luv, yer carn't say young Jim's been missin' art seein' a bit of England! That's more than me, or you ever did!"

"Blimey!" – Mag thought then, –

"Why don' I keep me bluddy marf shut!" She had quite forgotten. Bert never had much chance to see a lot of anything, not even during his brief training, and his service had been cut short, owing to his horrific wounds. Luckily, her Faux Pas went over Bert's head, and Mag knew however, the best way to make amends, and that was, –

"Cuppa, – Bert luv?" –

"Ow abart a nice pot a Rosie Lee?"

Chapter: Twenty-eight

The next couple of weeks went by as usual with apprehension anxiety and fear for the future. Battles were raging everywhere, whenever you turned a page of a newspaper, – one newsreader on the wireless telling you how the Jerries were now at the gates almost of Stalingrad hoping to get to Moscow, and that Sweets *were* going to be rationed! Bad and Sad, as everyone listened to Vera Lynn singing, – 'That Lovely Weekend.'

More tears than cheers, it seemed!

But the one good thing on the minds of the eager customers of the old 'Crown and Anchor' was the twice-weekly sessions of 'Housey-Housey'.

"That was the most brilliant idea of yours Peg love!" said Maureen. "Seems to have caught the imagination of quite a few people around!" The old Pub was full this evening, and they were running out of seats and tables. Most of the crowd now had their cards on their laps.

As she'd been getting ready, Mag had a good look in the mirror and noticed the tired lines around her eyes, *and* a few grey hairs. Blimey! Poor Maggie. Was she getting old? No wonder, it was no picnic, – daily life now was just one long slog. Never mind, she took a little longer than usual tarting herself up before she went along to the Pub.

Mag patted her hair down, and put a little more rouge on the tip of her finger and rubbed it into her cheeks, she'd looked a bit pale of late. She opened a drawer and got out the little bottle of 'Californian Poppy' perfume, Bert had bought for her birthday. She liked that, and the 'Phul-nana' scent. They were Mag's favourites.

It was 'Housey-Housey' night again and although it had done wonders for the clientele and had swelled the ranks of new customers, – the poor band of devotees, the eager beavers, the 'Bar-Stewards,' were always crashing into each other, with more liquid refreshment for thirsty throats, especially the lucky ones to call 'HOUSE!'

There was 'Beer, Beer, – Glorious Beer,' all over the shop! Ah, but these were grand evenings, they all agreed. 'Just what the Doctor ordered,' and took the thought of war right away for a couple of hours. As Mag had hoped, she'd managed to coax Kate and Tommy along a few times and they took to it like ducks to water!

Bert was pleased, he'd cheered up, with Tommy to talk to, but they always had an ear cocked for that blasted Siren!

It was forever touch and go, venturing out anywhere, but no one was giving in to fear and certainly not the Cockney!

"Yer go an 'ave a funny run Adolf!"

This was to be a special evening! It was Maureen's birthday, – and she hadn't really wanted to admit it. For it was her fiftieth.

"Go on wiv yer gal, yer still only a chicken yet. Wait till yer gits as old as me." said Gladys, who had found a new lease of life when the 'Housey-Housey' came to the Pub.

"No one could be as old as you Glad, me old mate," said Joe, pipe in mouth and a twinkle in his one good eye.

"Yer must be knockin on 90! Am I right? Poor Gladys, she nearly choked on her glass of Guinness.

"Yer cheeky bugger!" she said, –

"Nah, yer kin buy me anuvver one, fer yer Sauce!"

"Ready everyone?" Called Les, "Let's have some hush!"

344

"The first number is, – Waaaaitt – for it! ..."

"21, – What do you know? My age! Key of the door."

"22, –Two little ducks. Well ain't that funny?"

"Who shuffled these?"

"51, – That's what you will be next year Maureen love!"

And so it went on. Les, a real expert at this it seemed, added to the enjoyment of the eager, breathless, open-mouthed and expectant gathering of hopefuls there, till someone at the back yells out "HOUSE!"

"Bugger me!" said Gladys, tutting. "I only wanted one more, – Didn' I? – S'always the bluddy same, en' it?"

While all this was going on, there was not a day that went by when Mag didn't wonder when she was going to hear more about Rob, and tried to keep her mind on staying calm and not get too hot under the collar. Bert then decided it was time he took Mag out for an evening, somewhere nice. Bert not beating about the bush, thought it would be a change for him as well! –

"Gor' Blimey, I fink we deserve it! – Eh Maggie luv?"

But Mag tried to put a damper on those fine ideas of his.

"How can we go orf art anywhere? – It's too dicey! – Nah, yer can see that can't yer?"

But Bert he *wasn't* going to let it go at that. He would have a word with Kate.

"Leave it to me Bert." Kate said, "And take that miserable look off your face! It doesn't become you!" She laughed a little at her outspoken remarks.

"Fanks Kate, I knew yer'd help me. No wonder you an' Mag gets on ser well!"

"Oh, go on with you Bert. If it hadn't been for you and Maggie, I'd still be sitting here alone with a face as long as a fiddle, so to speak!"

"Mag, – 'Ow long will it take yer ter git ready termorrer evenin'? – We're orf art luv, an' don' arst me where we're goin', – 'Cos I ain't tellin' yer!"

"Why are yer so determined Bert?"

"Well, yer ain't exactly bin the life an' soul of the party lately, 'ave yer nah luv? So I fort, – be nice fer you an' me, ter go art somewhere nice!" Mag put her arm around his shoulders, saying, –

"Ave I ever told yer Bert, me ol' mate, that it was the best days work I ever done, when yer arst me ter marry yer!"

He frowned and looking at her said, –

"Ain't yer got that roun' the wrong way ducks? There's somefin' not quite right there!"

"No!" she laughed, seeing the look on his face.

"Don' you worry! – I 'ad me eyes on yer, a long while a'fore yer arst me ter go art wiv yer, Bert 'Ope!"

Maureen was the first one to commend Bert for his good idea, and spoke to Maggie saying, –

"Go on! – Off you go Maggie, and have a nice evening, you have both earned it. – I'd say!"

The atmosphere next evening, was charged with the usual excitement and anticipation in the old 'Variety Music Hall,' up along there in the Whitechapel Road. It was beginning to fill up with a boisterous crowd, surging down the gangways to the stalls, and up there in the Gods, the eager, more energetic and cheeky ones, clutching bags of monkey nuts, pushing up the front to get a better view.

It *was* a pleasing scene, as Mag took a look around the old Music Hall, at the long draped red-velvet curtains, and at the lights in rows along the walls, each lamp set in plaster, with effigies of nymphs and cherubs.

346

The lights dimmed, the curtains parted, and then the voice of the bright and breezy comedian, 'Tommy Trinder' came resounding out, –

"Champagne Charlie is me name, Champagne drinkin' is me game!" This act put everyone in a pulsating mood, with breath-taking deeds of the Acrobats and clever jugglers to follow. Then came the pathos, with the plaintive eye watering success of the 'Little Match Girl', – sung by a budding young lassie with movie star capabilities, who had the whole theatre in floods of tears.

Next came the rollicking and overwhelmingly funny 'Suzette Tarry', who almost brought the house down with her capers. How everyone laughed. This finished off the proceedings.

Well, Maggie was struck dumb at the colour and atmosphere and the whole new world, she had entered.

It was so nice Bert, I did enjoy it! – Did you?"

"Nah, why d'yer arst me a soppy question like that Maggie luv? It's a toss up who was most over the moon abart it all. Don't git ter see very offen, nuffin' as nice as what we just sin, eh lass? – C'mon let's git on 'ome, eh?"

But it flashed through Mag's mind for a few seconds, as she remembered with a pang, – The kids would not be there to greet them, saying eagerly, –

"What yer brought 'ome fer our suppers, Mum?"

Maggie blinked a bit and tucked her arm through Bert's and snuggled up closer to him. "Nice moon ternight luv, lets go fer a walk darn by the river," she said.

Although the muck and remains of the damage done to the wharves and twisted ugly piles of smashed cranes, still lay about there, looking grotesque in the moonlight, they both tried not to look at them and just strolled. That's if you

347

could stroll through the bits of debris, along by the sad looking river. A few craft, a pilot boat, and a sand boat went by, the moonlight picking out the faces of the river men there on the decks. One waved to them, Mag waved back.

They came to the Dock where a long, long time ago, Mag thought sadly, Bill and George had stood at the gates, Summer and Winter alike, calling their usual, "G'night Missus!" as she went by.

"Let's go 'ome Bert, this place gives me the willies," she said, trying not to shiver. She wanted to get away quickly. – Too many ghosts were lurking around these old battered and butchered Docks. Would they ever come into there own again? Something told Mag, –

No never! – at least, not as every living soul around here had once known them!

Wailing Winnie had not been belting out it's stomach churning cacophony quite so much and sounded less urgent of late, and there were times, when Mothers felt confident and brave enough, to venture out into the park to take the kids. Something they'd not been able to do for such a long time. No wonder some of their small faces were now pale and wan, resembling those of little old men.

Seaside trips had become, well a thing of the past. Many people doubted if any of the Amusement Parks with their king size attractions of, 'The Laughing Policeman,' and the 'Bearded Lady', 'Bumper Cars', 'Ghost Train', and all the fun of the fair, were still left standing, after all the bombing on the Kent Coast!

The thought of their day out at 'Sarfend', was just a long ago memory. Jess too, was remembering all those outings from the Pub, and riding along in the Charabanc with Rob and Jim. She was now idling some precious time away, strolling slowly along the lane, – though not now, looking for bird's nests.

It was nearing the end of Autumn and the trees had almost finished shedding their leaves. The big Oak was ridding itself of its many acorns in such a way, that a startled Jess, looking up, wondered what on earth had hit her on the head, and was most surprised when she spotted a squirrel, enjoying his early breakfast, sitting comfortably, high up there on a branch.

He was nibbling away and chucking acorns down, – not specifically at her, even though it seemed like it! This was the first time she had ever seen a squirrel.

"Oh! You lovely little darlin' you!" she exclaimed. But no attempt at flattery was going to induce the squirrel to come down, – he never batted an eyelid and just carried on nibbling! A voice then interrupted her fraternisation with this squirrel.

"Now you know we musn't keep on meeting like this!"

The voice sounded a bit familiar, and Jess was not so surprised to see standing there in the lane, just about where she had seen him the first time, the same Soldier, the know-it-all, bird watching fellow. It was kind of uncanny, and she wondered, – "Where does he come from?"

"Oh, It's you!" Jess said, though not exactly in a cold tone, but like the time before, she didn't want to stand there talking. – Anyway she had to get back to the farm.

"I have ter go, I must be back at work!"

"Oh, Yes! – I will walk along with you. – You're going my way, I take it?"

"How does he know which way I'm going?" she wondered, now becoming a little jittery, Jess started to walk back along the lane, with the Soldier striding beside her. What could she do but keep going. – "Oh, dear!"

She reached the Farm gates and as quick as a light the bloke opened it. "'E's still 'ere!" she thought.

"Fankyou!" Jess said, hurrying into the farmyard.

"Goodbye!" she called and thinking, –

"At last, I've got rid of him!"

But No! She heard his footsteps behind her still, and then a voice suddenly called out. It was the Farmer's wife, Mrs Coles and quite excited she was too!

"Why Mark! What are you doing home? How lovely, come on in. Hello Jess, so you've met then?"

"Blimey! Why didn't I recognise 'im? That face! So 'e's the son of the 'ouse. – That's Mark!"

She felt rather like one of those out there chewing at the grass in the fields, a bit Sheepish.

"What must 'e 'ave bin finkin' of my be'aviour?"

It was an irksome day and Mag had been feeling a little guilty about her Ma, over there in Hackney, but she had the comforting knowledge that Flora had the good company of Stan, her man-friend. It was useless trying to make the journey for them to see each other, as well as careless and stupid, what with the bombing, sporadic as it had been lately, – but they never knew from one day to the next what was in store for them! 'Stay put' was another piece of advice splashed on all the billboards.

But this did not apply to Jim. It would be a few more weeks before he finished his training! And would it be perhaps too indiscreet for us to say, – he was now in sight of the rolling hills of Somerset and if you wanted to know what impression Jim had of Army Life, you might be surprised to learn, he actually liked it! – Jim Hope was now, as he would proudly tell you, a member of His Majesty's Armed Forces," but for the present he was only a Private in the Royal Artillery. But who knows? How long would it take before he became a Field Marshal? That was the question, and what would Bert, his Dad be thinking if he could see young Jim now?

A good guess would be, that he'd feel quite proud of his once too ambitious, impulsive, hair-brained, but loveable son. There were great things in store for him!

What would it be? – Giant field-guns, – Tanks?

Chapter: Twenty-nine

"Why does this blasted bit ov 'air persist in 'angin in me eyes!" Mag moaned

She pushed the self-willed lock of hair in question from her forehead with soap sudded hands, sighed, and catching on to the back of the nearest chair, she slowly and painfully pulled herself up from her kneeling position.

"This scrubbin' the floors every uvver day is doin' me bluddy 'ead in, as well as me blasted back!"

Finally standing up, and practically looking like a letter S, she thought, –

"Blimey, ain' I crotchety this mornin'? I s'pose its 'cos nuffin' seems ter go right, fer any ov us any more!"

Poor Mag, – she did try and all, but it was the thought of Rob, which was forever uppermost in her mind, always niggling away at her, –

"When am I goin' ter 'ear somefin'?"

"Don't they bluddy care?"

"Isn't it time I 'ad some news?"

"A letter, ov some sort, at least!"

Just then Maureen came out from the other bar, wiping her hands on a teacloth and saw the condition Mag was in. She was almost doubled up by the bar.

"Come on now Mag!" she said. "You have done enough for this morning. You are to go home right away, – I insist!

As she listened to Maureen giving her, her marching orders, she knew she was in no mood to argue. So after she had emptied the dirty water out of the bucket and wrung out the wet cloth, and hung up her overall, she picked up her shopping bag with a sigh of relief. Yes, she'd had enough for one morning, in fact, had just about all she could stand.

"'Bye Mag! Have a cup of tea when you get in, *and* get some rest will you? – I'll see you tomorrow love!"

Maureen turned away, so she was slow to see the expression on Mag's face at that unforgettable moment, missing the look of sheer and utter disbelief, which was clearly visible. Mag was standing motionless, looking across at the doorway, where she could see the tall figure of Rob, who at that moment had appeared. But Maureen did hear his voice, – when he, all smiles said, –

"'Ello Mum. – It's me, Rob. – I'm 'Ome!"

Luckily, Maureen was just able to stop Mag from collapsing flat out on the floor. The shock and surprise had been a little too much for her, quite unprepared was she on seeing her big boy, after all this time.

Those long wearying fearful months, when her unswerving faith and constancy, was at times hard put, to stop it slowly dwindling and eventually disappearing altogether. – As it was, Maggie let out a high pitched shriek and ran straight into Rob's outstretched arms.

Only then did Maureen feel it was time to leave them both together, and crept away with the sound of Mag's sobbing, as she clutched her boy tight against her.

"Rob, its true ain' it?" –

"Don't let it be a dream lad, – Please!" –

"Let's look at yer?"

She leaned back and took an appraisal of her son, as he stood there looking slightly self-conscious. He too at the same time, noticed how care-worn was his mother's face. She was showing signs of the stress and strain of this blasted War, and why, what was it all for? It was not only the men who were fighting these bloody battles. The women who were left behind were in the front line too! Maybe some of them suffering even more so. Always trying to cope with food rationing, bombing, and losing their loved ones and the constant worry of all kinds of unforeseen and unexpected catastrophes.

"Come on Mum. Let's go 'ome. Yer look all but done in!" He took her arm and her bag, –

"Blimey Ma! What yer got in it? It weighs a bluddy ton! Yer sure yer ain't got the Pub's takin's in 'ere?"

Mag just laughed. Laughed, with complete joy and happiness. She tucked his arm in hers, as they walked along the road home. No longer was Maggie tired!

"That's me rations lad, – I done a bit a shoppin' 'fore I went ter the Pub, she explained. Yer must a got a lot ter tell us nah Rob luv, eh? But what's we gonna 'ave first is a Cuppa! – Nah! Not a cuppa, but a pot! – full a Tea! – An' then yer kin talk to yer 'eart's content!"

Mag was trying to make light of it all, but there was no escaping the fear that Rob would have to go away again. But No! She wouldn't think of that now! – "Wasn't she feeling just too blessed 'appy? Fer Gawd's sake! But Bert, he had ter be told a'course!"

"First fing we'll do Rob, is ter go an' find yer Farver. I bet 'e'll do 'is nut when 'e sees yer!" She then took a quick glance at Rob. Mag hadn't been long in noticing the ugly scar on Rob's temple and withheld asking any questions, but her tummy had turned over imagining what an ordeal he must have been through, – And, he was so thin!

"My Gawd! – 'Ere, look who's turned up!" Bert had said to Angus Percy, who was all smiles and with a look, which matched Bert's expression of sheer disbelief, when Mag with Rob beside her, walked into the Pawnshop.

Angus did no more then, but to give Bert his marching orders, saying, – "You get off home! – There's a much better place for you to be right now, and that's not here dusting bronze effigies and busts of long gone Venus de Milos, or spoof imitation Constables!"

He chuckled at Bert's obvious discomfort, but couldn't guess how much Bert really wanted to get back and hear Rob's description of all that appeared to have happened. That was going to take some time, by the sudden pallor that came over Rob's face. He had evidently been overcome by all the excitement and he truly wasn't fully recovered from his long stay in Hospital, it seemed.

They were to learn all about it, but only after, when Mag had got him back home and she'd made him go straight to bed. Though Rob did manage to reveal the drastic news that no more would he be sailing the Seven Seas, but now he had been assigned to shore duties at Devonport.

"That's enough nah! No more talkin' me lad. Yor goin' ter rest. Tomorrer's anuvver day!" and she tucked him up in his bed. "G'night boy. Sleep tight!" and then left, closing the door quietly behind her.

Kate continued to be Maggie's tower of strength during the coming weeks. She seemed to be always there, just when Maggie needed a shoulder to lean on, not overlooking the fact that she was only too pleased, to call on Kate's expertise as a nurse to Rob on his bad days, and realised it would be a long while before he could erase from his memory, those traumatic days and nights when he lay close to death's door. That is if he ever could forget them! But, he felt a pang whenever he thought of poor Nobby, who had not had *his* good fortune in surviving that Hell! Nobby, he had become one of those ship's that had passed in the night.

Now Maggie's neighbour had ideas up her sleeve. Christmas was only weeks away and things that happened were changing, and for the better, it appeared.

There was one big event which impressed and stimulated everyone. – The Radio stations were agog with the startling news that Japan had bombed Pearl Harbour and this had ultimately jolted the U.S.A. into joining the conflict, that we alone had suffered for so long! Now we not only had their Lease Lend, but also we had their fighting men and machines, *and* the whole of their might as well.

"Yer'd better watch art nah, d'yer 'ear Adolf? – And you too, Musso', bowf a yer. – Your days are numbered!"

All this set Kate thinking. It was time to stop Mag having to worry for once, about Christmas dinner this year. She would have them all in, to spend it with her and Tommy. Although it would be their very first Xmas together as man and wife, it could be a very good way of celebrating two great events, – their marriage and Rob's homecoming. – Yes, it sounded good!

For Kate, it was her happiest time, and considered herself to be the most fortunate of women to be married to Tommy, and in the weeks that followed her marriage, had been just simply sublime.

Just to be near him and see him sitting opposite her at the meal table, or lying back in the armchair taking a well earned nap, which was his want to do.

This was all *she* needed from life. Kate would watch him as he slept, and never ceased to feel great compassion, for the way life had treated him. She was so fortunate to have him and his love, and only knew she would do all she possibly could, to give him all the things he had missed for so many years.

Her heart went out to Tommy and the magnitude of the great love she felt for this man, must have in some way reached over to him as he sat dozing, – for quite suddenly his eyes opened and he caught sight of her looking at him. A broad smile crossed his face, one which for Kate was as sweet as a caress and she vowed, that no matter what happened in their future, be it fair or foul, – these idyllic moments would stay firmly locked in her memory.

What more could she do then, but cross the room and sit herself down on the arm of his chair, where she slowly bent her head and kissed him.

Putting on an air of surprise, he said, –

"What was that in aid of darling?" whereby Kate pouted and pulling a face, she made a pretence of being dashed, and pulling herself up said, –

"Alright then, – I won't make you any tea!"

But she was too late to escape the bear-like clasp of Tommy's arms, as he grabbed her, –

"Oh no Mrs Holt! To hell with it! I can think of much nicer things to do than sitting here drinking tea!"

"Besides," he said, –

"Too much tea is bad for you, did you know that? – But this isn't Kate!" He then kissed her, so hard and for so long, that he nigh on suffocated her!

What was to happen after that preliminary performance, was nobody's business and all thoughts of Christmas, Maggie and just about everything, – 'Went for a Burton!'

Well and why shouldn't it? . . . . .

*   *   *

Mr Angus Percy was not so much his usual smiling congenial character of late. For trade was not good. Not good at all! His shop, which had always been Chock a block with Whatnots, Knick-knacks and shelf loads of unredeemed clobber everywhere, was looking the worse for wear. – It had the appearance of a 'No-man's-land!'

But what else could you expect? There *were* no clothes to be pawned. For half the citizens of the Square mile around Rupert Street and the surrounding localities had, in some cases only the clothes they stood up in. Except for the help of the 'Womens' Voluntary Service', (W.V.S.) and some- times Parcels from abroad, and 'Make do and Mend'. It certainly would have been a sorry state of affairs! –

And then, Bert's Bombshell!

"Here we are back ter square one again, Mag luv!" –

"Do yer know, – Percy's 'ad ter cut me 'ours nah?" –

"I've got ter find anuvver way of makin' a few coppers!" So Bert was now again a bit like Barney's Bull. Would he be getting the push from his job? The past few months had seen him just kicking his heels, looking for things to do in Percy's shop. It was only a matter of time now, he knew. Poor Bert, he'd be no use in the Forces. He couldn't even hold a knife properly, let alone a rifle!

Sitting slumped in his chair when Maggie came in the back door, – he was certainly no welcome sight for her!

"Ow, Gor blimey Bert! What der yer fink yer look like?" she said, – "Come on git yerself art a that chair an' make me a cuppa tea, an' fer Gawd's sake liven yerself up! Nuffin's as bad as yer fink it is! Summat's gonna turn up, yer'll be surprised!"

She had said all this, but Mag had been coming back from the Pub, bypassing the worst bombed-out streets and dodging gangs of labourers trying to make a decent path through the immense amount of debris. Great cement blocks, amidst fallen lamp-posts, intertwined with twisted steel from window frames and what once had been the main stays of a house, now just heaps on the ground.

There were no ways of escaping any of it. She felt sad, but she was not going to let Bert sit there looking like a heap of rubble himself.

Maggie's voice acted like a dose of 'Kruschen Salts' to Bert. He smiled, got up, and shook himself just like Snowy.

"Yers" Mag said, "And if yer not careful yer'll be lookin' like 'im too, wiv that 'ang-dog look on yer face!"

Good old Mag, she had that way about her. She soon shook him out of his doldrums, –

"Anyway! 'Ere ol' bean, I've got some good news fer yer! Tommy's gotta pack up bein' pot man darn at the pub. Les, 'e says ter me. 'Ow would your Bert like ter do it nah Tommy's got a new job? 'E can't do bowf, – well!"

Bert almost suffocated Mag with the biggest kiss she'd had in a long, long time.

"What are yer me ol' darlin'? – What would I do wiv'art yer eh?" and he was off to the old 'Crown', like a light to see Les, and would strike while the iron was hot.

Well Mag not only had to make her own tea, but drank it on her own. But she had a smile on her face about as big as the proverbial Cheshire Cat and to add to her delight, Bert returned looking like a dog with two tails!

And so another anxious Christmas of despair and despondency had come and gone with the usual round of going through the motions. It was a nice surprise though for Maggie and Bert to be invited to Kate and Tommy's, along with Rob, also Jess and Jim who had been allowed home on leave. And what a real special Christmas it had turned out to be, after they all tried to put the thoughts of war out of their minds, though Mag had her own thoughts about Rob, but attempted not to let it show.

It was good to see the three of them together again and as 'Jerry' had seen fit to keep a bit quiet for a while, they had a couple of nights, 'Wailing Winnie' free! Which was accepted gladly by everybody and it meant much more than any Christmas present, ever did!

Now Bert was enjoying his part-time job as, 'Man of Most Needs' at the pub. It had helped to put back, "Some dignity into his life!" he'd say, being in the midst of people who knew him and spoke to him on their own level, and not look upon him as a half-wit because of his deformity.

Percy's kept going, with Bert's help, for a few hours a week. So it was 'All's quiet on the Home front!' 'Praises be!' everyone said. – At least for a short while! – Jess loved it, being at home for a little time, to find and visit some of her old friends. – But liked most of all, being with Rob.

She frowned and felt sad at all the terrible bomb damage done and listened with a grieving heart of the news when someone who had been part of her life, had been blown to pieces, along with other poor souls.

Jess had been glad to get back to her exacting job, though she was used to it all now, even with the mucking out and the long hours. Yet it was not just for the cows Daisy and Belle but also other animals on the farm. But, –

She had this quickening of the heartbeat, when she thought of Mark. Mark? Yes! – Boy, how she had missed him. Would it be too much of a surprise to know that's what was clearly marked on the cards for them? It was as plain as the nose on your face! How had it happened? – Well, it all began like this, with the bird's nests, – we all knew that!

Then it was on this one special morning, when, ...

"Jess! – Are you there?"

A voice was calling her from the farmhouse. It was Mrs Coles. "Would you take the bike and hurry down to the Vet in the village? It's really urgent. One of the cows is having difficulty calving. Hurry! Ask him to come quickly, please Jess! Leave what you're doing, I'll get Gwen, when I can manage to locate her!"

Now this was nice! It was as if someone had given Jess a half-day holiday, as she peddled rapidly along the lane, striving hard to dodge the ruts and avoid plunging into the ditches at the side of the cart tracks. Talk about, 'On the 'Rocky Road to Dublin'. Why was it called that? She went flying along, really enjoying this unexpected break.

The cold wind did not deter or spoil her elation, except for when it blew her hat off. –

"Blaaast it!"

She grumbled and jumped quickly from the bike, but she hadn't noticed the damned great root of a big Elm tree jutting out just as she did so. She tripped and twisted her ankle, and the bike, not a light-weight-one, fell on top of her, and there she lay stunned for a minute. But then, – who should come along, was the Good Samaritan himself, – in the form of Mark.

Now wasn't that just ducky? It couldn't have happened in a better place, and luckily just at the right time!

"Are you alright?" Mark said, looking worried.

Now this was just what Jess thought then, –

"Why is it most people, always the first thing they say when someone hurts themselves is, Are you alright?"

"Of course they're bluddy well not alright! That's why they're in this damned mess and say, 'Blimey it don' half hurt!' Ain't people funny?" – But back to basics though.

She looked up at Mark with a screwed up look of pain on her face and winced, trying not to let the tears well up in her eyes too much.

He bent down and gently lifted her into a more comfortable position, and tried to examine her foot.

"Oouch!" she cried, "I think I've sprained me ankle!" "Oh dear!" she said, "I was just on me way darn ter the Vet's fer yer mother. One of the cows is in labour an' havin' a tough time. – What shall I do nah?"

"Hold on, don't panic, we'll think of something!"

He stood up. "Wait!" he said, "I know! I've only just been talking to a mate of mine some little way back there. Now you just keep still and don't move!"

She half smiled, – "That's somefing I can't do!"

He was off, – grabbing up the byke, Mark rode back down the lane, leaving Jess helpless and hoping he wouldn't be gone too long.

She shivered, – it was very cold and scary. The old gnarled trees, stood stark and bare, ominous and threatening against the leaden sky. She shivered again, this time with fear. "Please hurry!" she prayed. She felt afraid and her foot was paining her like hell. "Why did this 'ave ter 'appen?"

But Mark, true to his word was back in just under ten minutes and was pleased she hadn't tried to do anything stupid and move her foot.

"Its OK!" he said, "I caught him up and he is bringing the Vet back directly."

"Fank Gawd!" said Jess. That calf, when it does git born, won't know 'ow much trouble it's caused!"

It was great to lay in bed after she'd had her foot seen to. Mark with a bit of kerfuffle had got her back to her digs, and by no other way than letting him carry her, after her failing to hop and skip some part of the way.

Sympathetic Mrs Allen, turned out to be a real Florence Nightingale, after she espied Mark struggling up the front path with Jess in his arms.

Although the stalwart sturdy soldier looked capable enough of carrying heavy kitbags of bulky proportions, plus rifle, etc, etc. But poor Jess, she was no lightweight. How she'd ever had aspirations of becoming a Ballet dancer, was mind boggling. Neither fat nor thin, she was none the less rather a challenge to Mark's strength, as well as to the limit of his chivalry.

But eventually they arrived on Mrs Allen's front doorstep, causing a bit of a stir for a moment or two, especially when Benny saw them.

"Mummy, Mummy, Jessie here." he called, puzzled why she was being carried.

"What happened? Oh! My goodness! We'd better get her up to bed." said Mrs Allen, clucking about like a Mother hen. Jess was soon put to bed with orders to rest her foot.

"That's torn it!" the rueful Jess looked down her nose, "What's Daisy an' 'er mates goin' ter do nah?" But she had no need to worry. Mrs Deakin had one of the other Land Girls temporarily take her place for a bit, and who did it turn out to be? –

None other than Nell, – Miss Shortarse herself!

And so, – that's how it all began.

*   *   *

What was that bright orange ball up there in that unusually blue sky? It was something they had not been seen for quite a while. – Could it be the Sun? – Glory be!

Now she would be able to have a good wash up today. There was a nice wind blowing, – not cold, and maybe Spring was not so far off.

She could get the net curtains down, – what was left of them! If Jerry had had his way, there wouldn't be anything at all! Mag sat looking around at the sad state of her kitchen and scullery, – at the walls where shrapnel had pitted it with holes. It was not a bit of use though, wasting your energy renewing or patching anything really, – that evil maniac had not finished yet. – Not by a long chalk!

Mag sighed and tried to turn her mind back to the days, when she could get up and look out of her window and not see muck, mess and rubble up to her eyeballs, or watch the faces of weary men who were trying hard to clean it all up.

"Well Snowy, me ol' mate, this won't do! It's abart time I got me finger out, eh? – I can't sit 'ere mopin' all day!" she realised. – "An' I kin 'ear Rob gettin' up. – Better get the kettle on!"

As Rob made his entrance through the doorway, Snowy stirred. He pulled himself up from his warm corner. Yawned, stretched and scratched himself and waddled slowly over to Rob. He was no longer a fluffy little puppy, but had grown into a handsome terrier. But at the sight of Rob standing there also yawning and scratching, Snowy regained some of his high spiritedness. With his tail wagging he came across to the yet only half-awake Rob, put a spurt on, and almost knocked him over.

"'Old on there Matey!" Rob cried, "Give us a chance, I ain't got me eyes open yet!" but anyhow made a grand job of fussing over Snowy, who lapped up all this attention. Yet Rob, though he appeared to be relaxed, was far from it. He had been home now for some weeks on compassionate leave, but that could not last!

What was going to happen to him, to all his dreams, his hopes of sailing the high Seas, discovering new territories and countries he had never ever heard of? – All that had gone for a Burton. – Kaput, – finished!

Oh yes! – He would still be with his beloved ships. But confined to a shore base in Devonport or somewhere else like that. But at least he *was* alive. Rob thought, "That's more than some poor souls were!" remembering them struggling for their survival in that icy Atlantic Ocean. Hearing the screams and dying prayers of so many, as they slowly sank beneath the hungry waves. – Rob shuddered!

"Where's me tea Ma?" he said, "Come on then dog, let's go and take yer fer a walk. – He couldn't keep on like this!

Off they went together down the garden path. Snowy yapping excitedly, dashing in and out between Rob's legs. Mag watched them till they disappeared from sight, and yanking down her nets, she filled the sink up with water. Her day had started, – "Who'd be an 'ousewife?"

Rob, with Snowy made their ways down to the river, stopping at intervals, waiting while Snowy investigated each lamppost as they went. On reaching Wapping old Stairs, they halted. Suddenly, when like a flash he thought he saw Pete his old mate walking towards him! He swore he heard his voice, quite plain too,

"Hi'yer Rob, where shall we go terday? – Let's go over the brickfields. Might find a dead body over there, – eh?"

He started to walk quicker, passing the pathetic sight of the mutilated Docks. There would have to be a colossal overhaul if they were to be brought back to their original condition. – If ever?

Meanwhile, what was our Jim up to at this moment? Maybe out on the Barracks Square in an Army Camp, somewhere on the East coast of England being yelled at by a red-faced, jaundiced Sergeant-Major, who'd had, during his Army career as a drill Sergeant, classed all rookies as unadulterated idiots!

As far as Mag knew Jim was stationed near a village which was now seeing an influx of servicemen from the U.S.A. These newcomers, as Jim described in his letters to home, were likened to people from outer space, with their snazzy uniforms. They all looked like officers and already wore medal ribbons? – Yet they had seen no action as yet!

"What bluddy chance did any of our boys stand with the local girls?" Jim moaned in these letters. "It was enough ter make yer spit! – And, Got any Gum Chum? – The kids call out ter the G.I.'s. – But how they like 'em!"

"Like 'em or not, – They're 'ere ter stay, – They are our Allies and we will be fightin' alongside 'em!" and what a grand job they made of it too, as it all turned out! Jim would tell his Ma later in his letters home.

Chapter: Thirty

Come rain, Come sunshine or cloud, the people of Brody Street and beyond plodded their ways during the months ahead with the same doggedness and stiff upper lip attitude that had seen them through these trying years, and which never failed to surprise any outsider who happened to stray through their confines.

But it was only fair to say, that this could be said of anywhere now on this little island, who alone had stood the brunt of Hitler's murderous attacks, hoping to bring it to it's knees. As old Joe Grimley so many times had pointed out *very* positively, –

"Just let that bastard come within an inch a me or mine. I'll take 'is gun and stuff it right up where it 'urts most, *and* where he wouldn't show 'is Muvver!"

Harsh words! – But Mag and Bert continued to go about their daily business. Maggie at the Pub, always with a smile which belied her deep down concern for her three one time saplings, now seasoned adults who were scattered around the country, all doing their bit, and poor Bert, bent on keeping up with the pressures, was worried just as much as Mag about the kids, but doing his best not to let it show.

The air raids had long since been a topic of conversation. But now it was part of everyday life, no matter whether you gave yourself palpitations shaking your fists at the skies, screaming, – "Yer Bastards, don't yer ever git tired?" when the now familiar drone of the 'Heinkels' and 'Dorniers' came within earshot.

And so the days dragged on, the same queues for food seemed to get longer, the lines of the weary-eyed waiting to be issued with blankets to replace those which had become damp and mildewed by use in the Dugouts and Shelters.

But things had begun to brighten up with Spring now going onto Summer which brought out the more daring ones who chanced their arm on paying a visit out into the countryside. But sadly not the coast, unless you wished to get entangled with the barbed wire netting and land mines set on the beaches. No, the seaside was most definitely *out*!

It was a Sunday, and a very hot one too! The Pub was very near to its full capacity, with the ever-faithful regulars and perhaps a new face here and there, bringing it a curious look or two. Mag leaned across the bar counter with a glass brimming with Ale.

"Oi, you gonna cop 'old a this Barney, or 'ave I gotta neglect all me 'uvver customers, while yer stand there gassin'?" She brushed away the perspiration from her brow.

"Blimey, ain't it 'ot Glad? The sweat's runnin' right orf a me. – I swear I've lawst a few poun's this past week!"

"Shame, the kids these days don' git a chance ter git ter no Seaside, poor little buggers!

"D'ya remember the outin ter Sarfend Glad? Wonder what it looks like darn there nah? Pretty bashed up far's we kin 'ear ov it!" The only bit a seaside the nippers' git ter see is that bit a shingle near ter Tower Bridge. Poor little blighters! – Same again Joe? – Okay mate, comin' up!"

Meanwhile, not so many miles away in the sweltering heat of the countryside, but wisely out of the burning rays of the Sun, – two people were lying together under the leafy canopy of a spreading Oak tree, watching the patterns of light made by the Sun, as it shone through the leaves above.

It was so quiet, not a murmur, except for the occasional calls from the wood pigeons or the faraway whistle of a steam engine.

"It's so lovely here Mark. I would never have believed that anywhere could be so peaceful!"

Mark leaned over resting his head on his hands and looked down at Jess. He pulled at a piece of grass and tickled her nose with it. Jess reached up and pulled his face down to hers and kissed him.

They had been there for some time, finding it very inviting, this spot out of the hot Sun. Jess in the quietness there, as they lay among the leaves, was going over the events of the past months, since that unfortunate accident with her bike. Or could it really be said, – wasn't it a fortunate one, when Mark couldn't have been more concerned and distressed over her sprained ankle.

Jess as expected, lapped up all the attention and the fuss she had caused, as it succeeded in bringing matters to a head much speedier than anticipated. She had captured her man! So came the day when Mark opened up his heart to her and in no other way than with a short and sharp, –

"Will you be my girl, Jess?" Jack Blunt, that was Mark!

Of course she would become his girl. Wasn't that what she intended? In the end that is what came to pass. Jess was as happy as a Sand boy! – or should it be Sand girl?

Maggie puffed as she mounted the steps up into the yard with her heavy washing basket, and letting down the line that still squeaked, she started pegging up the assortment of well worn socks, shirts and pants. –

"Blimey! – Bert will certainly have to have some new ones, or he will soon be riding bare arsed to York!!!"

"These will soon dry!" she said to herself. The Sun was really boiling down! She then heard the sound of her name and on looking up saw Kate leaning over the wall, looking slightly flushed, –

"Mag, have you a minute to spare? Can I come over? I have something I am simply dying to tell you!" Could it be Mag's imagination, or was Kate acting unusually chirpy?

"Come on in then, I'll put the kettle on!"

No sooner had she lit the gas under the kettle, and Kate was in. She didn't wait to sit down, but blurted out the news, she'd been bursting to tell Mag.

"I couldn't tell you before now Maggie, – not until I was entirely sure, but can you guess?" – I'm going to have a baby! – Can you believe it dear Mag?"

Poor Mag gasped, she just stared at Kate. It took her some time to grasp what she was saying.

"Are yer sure Kate? – Ow, when did yer find that art?"

This *was* a turn up for the books.

"I'm so pleased!" she said, eventually throwing her arms around her friend. She was aware of tears forming in her eyes. – A Baby! – Dear Kate she would have her dearest wish fulfilled.

"Come on luv! Nah we do 'ave somfin' ter celebrate. An' what uvver way better'n this? – I'll git art the cups!"

As she set to, to make the tea, she thought, –

"What a great day, Gawd knows how Kate must feel! – I'm behavin' as if it was me!" This was news right out of the blue, something she had never expected. Kate must have dreamed, but would never have believed she would be blessed at her age. – After all she was over forty!

For a few days, Kate's news would take Maggie's mind off many other things. A baby! It conjured up a train of thought. It would be lovely fussing over a new little mite. It took her mind back to her own feelings of joy at holding soft cuddly helpless little beings, to her breast.

"'Ere, ol' gal, – Wotch it! – Yer'll start gittin' all broody agin yerself, if yer ain' careful! – I ain' got no time ter wipe me own nose na-ah!"

Bert came in the back door, just then. Throwing his cap playfully over at Snowy, and flopped down in his chair. The terrier ambled over to Bert with his cap, expecting to be made a fuss of, but he was not rewarded. No such luck. – Mag sensed Bert had something on his mind. –

"What's wrong?" she asked.

Bert came out with it bluntly, –

"Angus had a stroke last night. He's dead gal. Poor ol' devil, nice bloke really, but 'e was gittin' on a bit!"

"That's sad mate!" said Mag. "'E was *good* ter you! Wonder what'll 'appen ter the shop?"

"'E's got a son somewhere, but 'e's a bit toffee nosed though! 'E won't want ter take it on. So it's anyone's guess!" Bert replied and continued, –

"Well, that's that then! Where's me tea gal?"

Bert shook off this bad news, but it seemed now that part of his past had gone. It was time he changed the subject.

Abruptly Mag blurted out, –

"Kate's avin' a baby! – Ow abart that then?"

"Gor' Blimey! – She ain't is she? – Well!"

Bert was flabbergasted, but quite pleased, as Mag sensed a twinkle appearing in his eyes.

"So Tommy's gonna be a Dad. 'E'll 'ave 'is work cut art. I'll say! – Still if it turns art ter be like any of our lot, 'e won't 'ave much ter moan abart! – 'Ave yer 'eard from Rob or Jim, by the way?"

"Nah yer know what they're like fer writin' Bert. D'yer expect ter git a letter every day? Not from Jim yer won't!"

But they'd had a long letter from Rob a few days back. He was doing alright at Devonport, but he thought he may be getting sent to Portsmouth. He didn't mind that! Perhaps he might look up some of the old faces? He'd made friends with quite a few people there, while doing his training.

Rob, sadly continued to suffer lapses of memory and severe headaches due to his head wounds. But Mag was happy to know he was no longer stuck out there God knows where, and in peril from U-boats.

Jim never ever did say much about his whereabouts, –

"We can't Mum, we ain't allowed!"

But he was somewhere on the South Coast, maybe doing his darnedest to compete with the G.I.s from the Camp a mile or so away, having to watch them filch from under the British Tommy's noses, all the eager local girls at the Palace Ballroom dances. "Tain't fair!" he used to say, when a kid. "Why couldn't I have been six feet tall, like most of these foreigners?"

As the War dragged on, food got shorter, but Bert now, with more time on his hands, had taken heed of the 'Dig for Victory' campaign, so Mag always knew where to find Bert, – Up to his eyes in fertiliser. – In other words horse manure for his Rhubarb, and so on.

Though the back garden was about the size of a couple of postage stamps, he appeared to act like a dog with two tails, when he brought into Mag his first bunch of carrots, and, – "Look luv, 'ave yer ever seen such a lovely turnip?"

Understandably she was pleased for Bert, it gave him something to do.

Of course there was still the threat that Jerry would put paid to all his efforts, but that was the risk they all had to take. The raids had not ceased by a long chalk.

Every now and then the Siren would sound out its monotonous but spine chilling Caterwauling! But everyone had long ago, got used to this ugly row! People though, could somehow tell if it was going to be a bad night, or maybe that 'Silly-Sod' sitting on the other side of the Channel, was just taking them all for a lot of blasted idiots!

Bert found it was time to do his bit in the 'Home Guard' now, and it was 'All hands to the pumps!' even if he did only have one of them fit to do what was needed. But he was as good as the next man, he said.

Life jogged along as usual and then, Jess had some good news. – There was a wedding in the pipeline. She had been home for a long weekend and it was then, she broke the news to Mag and Bert, who could see the rapturous look on their Jess's face. It would have taken a blind man not to notice how their girl had changed.

She had grown into a more self-assured woman with more than just a positive outlook. For Jess knew what she wanted and was now going to get it. That was to be married to Mark! They knew he would not be at his present camp for much longer and would be transferred, and she wanted to be his wife, no two ways about it. Who knew, the way things were going be? He would most likely be whipped away at any time, and perish the thought, they might not be with each other, for a very long while.

Their wedding date was fixed, and on one very warm September morning, Jess and Mark took their vows, with just a few of her pals, – Gwen with their one time arch enemies, Nell (Miss Shortarse) and Florrie, plus a couple of

Mark's army mates. They finally tied the knot in the Bethnal Green Registry Office. But it could have been done in front of his holiness the Bishop of London for all they cared, having eyes only for each other! Maggie cried, Bert gulped, Kate wiped away a few little tears, and with just a smattering of onlookers outside the building throwing a few handfuls of confetti, the proceedings were over.

"'Bye Mum, 'Bye Dad," when the time finally came to disappear to a well-chosen quiet village inn, for a brief honeymoon.

So another wartime wedding had taken place and there appeared to be many of these! No time for the conventional white weddings of old with all the fripperies in these uncertain times. Jess and Mark as man and wife with eyes for no one else, disappeared off into the unknown, for the beginning of their life together.

"So your Jess has got herself married then?" Mabel's enquiring voice echoed across to the bar. Maggie looked over to where Mabel was sitting. Bet your life she would have soon learned of the news. You couldn't keep anything quiet, not where Mabel was concerned!

"Yeh, and if yer finkin', Mabel what I know yer finkin'. Its No! She's *not* in the family way!" This was met with, –

"I never fawt such a fing, Mag gal! Good luck to 'er. That's wot I says. Not much fer the young-uns, these days."

She seemed so sincere that Maggie wished she had not been so bitchy. But you could never tell with Mabel. She was a right funny bundle.

But Mag *was* feeling humpity, she had to admit it. Would there ever be a day when she didn't have something to worry about?

Now it was about Jim this time. Apart from a couple of days leave a fortnight ago, she had not heard a dickybird from him, and Bert's behaviour, had also been a source of wonder to her! He could never be called a noisy bloke, but he had been exceptionally quiet for some days! Mag had put it down to him missing Jess his girl, who was now a married woman, and as it was well known, all fathers never liked their daughters being taken away from them, by another man. She was no longer his watery headed, up in the clouds little girl, – She belonged to someone else now.

Mag was waiting for Bert to come back from the Pub, she had prepared a midday snack and had his Cuppa ready.

"'Ello luv! I've got a nice pie 'n Mash 'ere fer yer and anuvver treat too. I've knocked yer up a nice Rice puddin'. Dunno wot it'll taste like though!"

He mumbled something but continued sitting looking down at his plate, not bothering to even pick up his fork and try it, but suddenly he spoke, –

"Bin busy 'ave yer luv?" he asked her, but when she answered, he went off again into a brown study.

Mag had had enough! –

"Nah look 'ere you, Bert 'Ope! – What's wrong wiv yer? Yer've 'ardly spoken since yer came in that bluddy door. – What's the matter? – Come on, art wiv it!"

Looking up at her then, Bert took the bull by the horns.

"Maggie luv," he said, leaning over and taking her hands in his. Mag sensed he was having a struggle to begin, then he spoke and dropped his bombshell.

"Yer know when Jim came 'ome last. – Well, 'e told me somefin' but made me promise not ter tell yer yet, because yer not ter worry! But it's this, – Our Jim, 'e's been drafted overseas. – Where? – I don' know!"

Mag sat open-mouthed listening to all this. She couldn't quite grasp it at first, but suddenly she came to life and said with such vehemence, that even Bert couldn't believe it!

"D'yer know what yer sayin'? Yer mean ter tell me yer wasn't goin' ter let me know! Why fer Gawd's Sake? What d'yer fink I am? Saying I wasn't ter be worried! Well what d'yer fink I'm doin' nah?" she shouted.

"But Mag luv. Jim specially said, don't tell Ma, not till I've gawn, as I can't bear ter say goodbye. I may be gawn fer a long time!"

"He said ter me, – Dad, don't let Mum feel too bad, I kin take care a' meself. You just take care a Ma, that's what 'e said gal. Yer can't blame 'im, put yerself in 'is place! –'E's not a boy nah lass, 'e's a grown man!"

Mag had slumped into a chair and sat staring into space. She looked as if she had been hit over the head with an axe handle! And there she stayed for a good ten minutes. Then with a sudden burst of anger, she banged her fist on the meal table, causing Snowy to jump up from his quiet reverie there in his usual spot on the hearthrug, and quickly scarpered out of the open back door.

"When is this bluddy lot goin' ter end?" she shouted, –

"All frew some cold bludded evil bastard. Why ain't someone done that sod in before nah? – I know I'd crucify 'im if I got 'old a 'im! – Then she burst into tears.

"Come on me ol' gal. Nah yer kin see why I didn' want ter tell yer! Dry yer eyes come on, I'll make yer a good strong cuppa tea!"

Bert continued to hold her tight against his chest, till she stopped crying. "'Ere's me 'ankerchief, such as it is!"

She blew her nose. Her eyes were red as she looked up at Bert's face and thought, –

376

"Poor luv, 'E mus' be feelin' every bit as bad as me!"
and dried her eyes.

"Nah where did that soppy Snowy slope orf ter? Go an'
git 'im in! An' 'ow abart that cuppa tea yer promised me!"

She forced a smile, –

"Cum over 'ere an' sit a minute wiv me, ol' mate!"

For the next few days it was impossible to get a word out
of Maggie. She went about her daily routine with a most
dejected expression, quite unlike her usual cheerful self.

Even Kate, when she invited her in to show off some of
the preparations made for her forthcoming happy event,
failed to penetrate the wall of apathy surrounding Mag.

Her thoughts were forever miles away wondering, how
was Jim? Where would he be now, and was he safe?

But the object of her thoughts at that precise moment,
was squatting on the crowded deck of a jam-packed
troopship out in the Atlantic Ocean heading for the Middle
East, and he wasn't feeling very much with it! In fact, he
wondered why the hell Rob had gone on so much about
joining the Royal Navy, and wanted to travel the world.

Jim knew where he would rather be at this minute, and
that was not sitting here feeling as if he had fetched his
innards up, back there in the Bay of Biscay.

His face was a pale shade of green, which matched his
mate's. The decks were awash with slime and seawater. A
sorry state of affairs! This wasn't going to be no Franchot
Tone or Clark Gable film epic. This was the real McCoy!

Back in Portsmouth, Rob had been given a post in a
tactical establishment. Not bad! But it was no longer his
dream come true. Poor Rob seemed to have been one of the
unlucky ones. – But at least he was still alive!

And Jess? She was back with her mates at the Farm Daisy and Belle, who didn't appear to have missed her. They still carried on chewing the cud, and practically ignored her. But it was touch and go now, when Mark was going to get transferred.

Jess was on tenterhooks. How was she going to face the days ahead without him near? It had been complete heaven, the short time they had spent together. She had never believed she could be so happy!

Mark was an absolute darling. What more could she have wished for in life, and how she loved him!

Chapter: Thirty-one

It was so quiet now at home! Mag didn't like it. How she would give anything to hear the voices of Jim or Rob arguing over the meal table, or even Jess in one of her weepy tantrums. She'd never realised at the time, how much she would miss it all.

She sat mooning by the fire, now the nights were drawing in, with the first fogs of November, smogs, – they were called. A mixture of smoke and fog, when you couldn't see a hand in front of your nose, as well as making you want to cough your lungs up.

She put the wireless on, it was Alvar Liddell with the latest news. She pricked up her ears. Was there some good tidings at last? He was saying how the bloody battle of El Alamein had ended in victory for the Allies, and the Church bells would be rung for the first time since the start of war, in celebration of our victory.

Now Mag knew from the heavily censored Airgraphs she had received from Jim, he was out there in the desert somewhere, and her mind had long been filled with fear at having one day to receive that dreaded buff envelope from the War Office.

But it was time she was on her way to the Pub. It proved to be a much livelier evening in the Bars, when the good news had taken hold, and there was almost a pre-war atmosphere prevailing. It needed something like this to boost the war-weary, in other words, "Somefin' ter cheer us poor buggers up!" As old Joe rattled off, with much feeling.

Some of the pubs once regular customers returned to down a few drinks, and toast the 'Desert Rats' those brave boys who had sent Rommel's Army packing in disarray. Even Kate and Tommy appeared in the bar.

"Why Kate luv. It's grand ter see yer bowf in 'ere!"

She looked blooming, did Kate, the prospect of motherhood certainly became her! Tommy evidently showed his deep concern for her. He fussed around Kate like a Mother Hen!

They were all there, – Mabel putting her two pennorth in. It was like old times. Mag for a while found she felt like her former self! Someone started thumping out 'Tipperary' on the Joanna, and this soon started the ball rolling, and when 'Bless 'Em All." came to the fore, followed by 'Run Rabbit Run" – You could have heard the row, streets away!

January had come in icy cold with a vengeance, but none took a lot of heed. They were more taken up with the gradual turn of events. 1943 saw the tide turning. Jerry wasn't getting it all his own way!

Our planes started bashing up Berlin by daylight and soon the Nazis were in retreat in North Africa, and Italy was not too happy either? – Mussolini does a bunk and goes into hiding it seemed, as Churchill said proudly, –

"We British are showing that we still have a sting in our tail!" It gave everyone heart, even though the Air Raids started to get more severe and you couldn't be off taking notice of 'Wailing Winnie' as they became more frequent.

But the effort of getting in and out of the Air Raid shelters was beginning to take it's toll on the older ones, –

"We're not gittin' any younger, we ain't!"

"Bugger this fer a lark!"

Their creaking joints, arthritic knees and things, caused many a moan, –

"Sod it! I'd rather stay in me bed. If I'm gonna die, at least I'll die in comfort!"

There was a horrific accident in March when during an air raid, 178 people were killed by falling headlong down an escalator in a Bethnal Green Underground shelter. Someone tripped, causing a pile-up, and there was no way to stop them from falling. There were many such tragedies, and sadly there were many more to come!

But the month of March saw a happy event, one which had been eagerly awaited, with ever increasing bouts of impatience. Kate was getting fidgety, as well as finding it difficult to sit still and let Tommy do all the fiddling, keeping the house tidy. Kate being Kate, very house proud!

"Yer'll just 'ave ter git used ter the clutter luv! You wait till yer little 'un starts ter walk, then yer'll find art! Still it isn't 'ere yet! – Yer'd better git a move on gal!" said Mag.

Secretly she was on thorns too! Waiting for the feverish knocking of Tommy at her back door, begging her to get the midwife! That happened before many more days had elapsed, after Kate had become aware of things beginning to happen.

It was then that the buxom comely form of Nurse Brown with sleeves rolled up to the elbows gave out her orders with Sergeant Major efficiency.

"I need lots of hot water, and make sure the child's clothes are ready and aired!"

It was all hands to the pumps, with Mag in her element. Didn't she know all about these matters? The fluster, agitation, the impatience and then the gratification when it was all over and the wonderful sound of the baby's first cries as it entered the world, and sadly what a world it was just now! But nothing would ever surpass the look of joy on Kate's face, as she gazed down upon the tiny bundle of her now sleeping baby son, snuggled so tightly against her breast. The smile on Mag's face too almost matched Kate's.

But it was Tommy's countenance, the shyness and modesty he showed as he approached Kate's bed. He was overcome with unspoken words of all the things he so much wanted to say, of his great happiness. But his desire to cry then became too much in the end, and kneeling at her bedside, he buried his head gently against the slumbering babe, and taking Kate's hand in his, he let go all his emotions. – Tommy sobbed, unashamedly.

Maggie, had quietly minutes before made her departure. What a truly blessed event for these two happy people, who had waited so long to be rewarded.

So another milestone had been reached and dealt with.

It had been a glorious Summer, the Harvest had been plentiful, the hay gathered and stacked. It was now Hop-picking time again. Jess was forever filled with wonder, at the ever-changing sequence of events, there in the countryside. The seasons as they came and went, never failed to fascinate her. It was hard work, but she was glad about that. It took her mind away from worrying too much about Mark, who now had been finally transferred to the Sussex coast, where there appeared to be quite a lot of activity going on, one way or another!

Even the main roads to the Kent Coast were becoming more busier. It seemed that wherever you turned your eyes, there were army vehicles heading some place or another. A cheery wolf-whistle would accompany a wise crack or two from the boys in uniform. You never saw a miserable look on the face of any of these lads, but Jess would ignore any of their near the knuckle suggestions.

Gwen, she had made a conquest one evening while out on a binge to the 'Wheatsheaf' with some of the Land girls. The pub was being besieged by a party of Canadian soldiers from a camp nearby, and the newcomers who had arrived only a week or two earlier, soon became well-known for over indulgence in their discovery of the local Cider! As was to be expected, a few arguments with the British Soldiers from the Barracks erupted. But it turned out O.K. in the end. –Well – 'Boys will be Boys!'

Gwen wound up getting chatted to by a nice Canadian lad from Quebec, who soon regaled her with the delights of his hometown.

"You be careful!" advised Jess "Or yer might wind up bein' carted orf back there! Some of 'em, I heard, 'ave the gift of the gab, tellin' yer they own a mansion, and then yer find art, all they got is a garden shed!" she chuckled.

"'E's only after yer money!" she added, "What money?" laughed Gwen, – "I ain't got no money. I ain't even got two ruddy 'apennies ter rub tergether!"

But Jess herself had no interest in advances that were made to her. Her thoughts were only of Mark, and of the next time she would see him.

"Please God don't let it be too long!"

It was an exceptionally warm Sunday afternoon in late September, when a small gathering of well wishers attended the Christening of young Edwin Thomas Holt. He by nature of all babes at times like this, let out a resentful yell as the tepid water was splashed all over his forehead.

"That's a good sign! It's supposed ter be lucky!" said a voice, nudging Gladys, who hadn't wanted to miss any of this, not forgetting Mabel who was right up the front.

Maggie, as his Godmother, took the baby from the smiling vicar and placed him back in his Mother's waiting arms. The party then walked off towards Brody Street for a bit of a do. As for Kate and Tommy, it had been a proud day indeed. – "A day an' a 'alf ter remember!"

So another winter loomed, and as the nights had begun to grow longer and colder, the war weary folk of Brody Street and all the local confines, looked forward with apprehension to maybe more food shortages and renewed bombing. Jerry thought he had left them alone, far too long this time, and tried again to shake 'em up a bit, with a bomb or two, here and there.

But these hardened East-Enders, only stuck their two fingers up at them and went about their business as usual. Side stepping new heaps of bricks, broken window frames, glass and a few more holes made in the roads. But all this was now part of their life.

Christmas came and went once again, and Jess brought her Mark home for a chance to see the New Year of 1944, in with her Mum and Dad, and wondered what this coming year had in store for them? It seemed this bloody war would go on forever! Though there were some bits of good news, that got through. Old Joe Grimley was having an argument, (a friendly one mind you), with Wiley Fox at the bar, –

"What's the bettin' this lot'll be over in a few months! We got 'em on the run nah!" It was the housey-housey evening, and the Pub was full. There had been a mad rush for the tables, with the odd bit of advice at times. Not very polite, at the irresponsible act of halfinching someone's table, who from the time since the housey-housey had been introduced, had put their moniker on it!

"Oi! That's our table, me an' Mabel's, – 'Op it! We've 'ad it ever since it started!" Gladys was having a moan.

Les called across to them with a little chuckle, –

"Here watch it both of you. Sounding like a couple of kids! – We don't want to start another war now, – do we?"

Maggie was polishing glasses. An endless job, with her thoughts miles away, first with Jim then with Rob. But it was Rob she felt sympathy for. Since his last visit home at Christmas she'd had him in her thoughts and knew he wasn't happy working at his desk job.

That was not for Rob! She had seen a far away and lost look in his eyes. He had not deserved such rotten luck! It was a devilish twist of fate that Jim should be the one who was now doing the travelling. She'd had an Air Letter, – 'Censored' of course, – from somewhere in Egypt, it could only have been Cairo! Jim, he'd been on a bit of leave from his base in the desert prior to being shifted somewhere nearer the theatre of war.

It appeared that in a Bazaar there, he'd bumped into one of his old pals from school and he couldn't believe in such a coincidence! – But miracles like this *do* happen! – This bloke Sammy, he was something in the R.A.F. and was serving out there too.

"Yer could 'ave 'nocked me darn wiv a fevver, I couldn't get over it!" He wrote.

Now Maggie admitted she'd been concerned about her Ma Flora. She'd received no news of her for a while, and felt some guilt. "I'll 'ave ter go and see the old girl Bert! Not that I'm relishing the bus ride much. It's been quiet lately, though I reckon I'll see a lot a changes on the way, – and what kind a damage 'as bin done, by the bombin'?"

As she'd feared, Mag saw sights that could only be described as horrific. Streets of houses obliterated beyond recognition, places she had known since childhood. Warehouses markets and churches were just heaps of rubble, pushed to one side to make a clear way for traffic and pedestrians. She wondered where they would begin to put it all, as she journeyed along on the Bus.

Mag arrived eventually in the familiar surroundings, where she had spent her young life, and the same house she had been born in. Luckily these were still standing! But directly the door had been opened to her knock, she wondered why she had bothered to come!

She was met with, – "Blimey, wonders will never cease! Yer don't mean ter say, that after all this time, yer've put yerself art ter come an' see me!"

Time it seemed had not mellowed Mag's Ma, in fact it had cultivated a hardness and acidity in the tone of her voice, and before the day was half over, – Mag was ready to get her hat and coat back on.

But there was one thing that had puzzled her. Where was Stan the boy friend? There seemed to be no evidence of a man's presence anywhere. And as if Flora had read Mag's mind in some uncanny way, she volunteered an answer in her curt abrupt fashion, –

"Stan, – If yer wondering' where 'e is? 'E's, gawn orf, – 'E packed 'is bags, an' went, – We 'ad a row!"

Mag had no need to ask why, – She knew.

"It's a wonder 'e'd stayed as long as 'e did, poor bugger!" – Stan, had he more sense than she'd given him credit for?

Maggie had always considered in the past, Sunday dinnertimes at the 'Crown' to be the best. When the men gathered around the bar to discuss the goings on during the past week, and of the bustle and activity in the although now much depleted Docks, and of the many different happenings, some comical and some not so funny. Such as an occasional accident, tragically leaving an entire family without a breadwinner. It was a hard life, even for the most able of workmen.

All these and other events were talked of, over the Sunday pint, before tottering back home for their dinner, prepared as usual by poor Mum, face flushed and perspiring, and with a ruddy backache to boot, catering for all their inner wants. Then with the washing up out of the way, having to sit and watch their now satisfied spouses, lay opposite them in an armchair, with mouths wide open, 'Snorin' their bluddy 'eads orf!'

Such were the glories of a Sunday. But none went by without the ever-faithful regulars to the Pub, – Joe, Wiley, and Barney Bull, propping up the bar. Among the subjects of their conversation was chiefly the progress of the War, with many comments on what they would do if they were in charge! Some listeners nearby would mutter to whoever was within earshot, – "Gawd 'elp us!" –

Old Joe, sucking at an empty pipe, told how he was totally convinced, – "Somefin' was in the air!" and that there were too many Army tanks and personnel to be seen, making their way along the roads towards the South Coast and along by rail.

"You mark my words, Somefin's up!" He'd vow.

So the weeks went by, while the people went about their business, with always the hope of some good news to help

387

them through the days, but the threat of Jerry being only, just across that strip of water, awaiting his chance to invade, was ever prevalent. But Mag, she was anticipating an invasion of another kind.

Letting her heart rule her head, she felt it her solemn duty, to invite her Ma for Easter. Bert, he had hit the roof, but gave in after Mag touched his soft spot. After all she was her Mother, and the kids were not available for her to have a go at now. – That was one good thing!

There was no telling though, what kind of answers they would have given to her tiresome moans and groans.

"Poor ol' Flora!"

Mark was home on leave, It was a welcome and unexpected visit right out of the blue, on a clear late April morning with a slight breeze, after days of intermittent showers of rain, which soon turned the farmyard into a sea of slippery mud.

Not something acceptable to the land girls trying to trudge through it, even with their sturdy gumboots on, to get to the barn where the cows were waiting patiently to be milked. – It was a quagmire!

Naturally, it was a pleasant sight, to see the Sun after so much rain, which Jess with Gwen soon took advantage of, with a walk along the lane, during a break. Gwen giving Jess an ear bashing about Greg, her Canadian boy friend, – absolutely besotted she was with him! Jess listening, but mostly thinking only about Mark. Time hung heavily for her waiting for the day she would welcome him back.

They'd reached almost to the end of the lane, Gwen still gabbling away, when Jess came suddenly to an abrupt halt, then let out an almighty shriek, and shot off down the lane like a rocket, towards the figure of a soldier seen walking quickly towards them.

"It's Mark! It's Mark!" Her joy evidently knowing no bounds, she simply threw herself at him. He was almost bowled over, and could be in no doubt as to her absolute delight in seeing him.

"Why?" she was saying, "What? How?" Jess, she was overjoyed, asking him so many questions!

"It's only a short leave Jess. We may be moving soon. Don't ask me where. – Can't say!"

Mark was tight-lipped, and was now more interested in quenching an almighty thirst.

Jess, dancing attendance on him then, almost forgot the poor ruddy cows. They were still stuck somewhere out there in the meadow. Daisy and Belle and all their cousins, would *really* feel, put out to grass!

Maggie took a look around the back garden. She'd noticed, with a little lift to her spirits, the signs of some of Bert's efforts to bring a touch of colour to their pathetic postage stamp back yard.

There were a few wallflowers out, – she loved their scent, some stocks and a few late tulips. Fortunately for Bert, there was now no 'bluddy Ginger Tom from next door,' to rake up the soft earth.

He'd been called to a higher place a year ago. Kate had been upset for a bit, but she had her babe now, who lay out in his pram in the warm sunshine, sleeping away to his hearts content.

Young Eddy Holt seemed to be growing in leaps and bounds! Mag looked up, hearing the sound of Bert's voice, he had just come from the Pub.

Since the demise of Angus Percy, there'd been the eventual appearance of a Saviour in disguise. According to Bert, a relation of Percy's had taken over the business. Hence, – "I still got me job Mag lass!

"Good bloke this cousin of Angus's, I gits on like 'n 'ouse on fire, wiv 'im."

No marks for guessing Mag's obvious relief at this news.

"What's fer dinner gal? – I could eat 'n 'orse!"

Mag's thoughts then flew to Jim. That was *his* favourite and unvarnished statement, every time he opened that back door. – Blimey, – how she missed those kids of theirs!

"I brought a paper in Mag, it's full a talk abart this so called 'Second Front'. Puts the wind up yer it does! What's gonna 'appen I wonder?"

"Stop that talkin' abart the perishin' war Bert!"

"Sit an' git this darn yer!"

She put a plate of bubble and squeak and rissoles in front of him. A most appetising smell arose! It was a treat for him. The remains of Sunday dinner and a bit of rolled brisket of beef.

Yes, they were managing, and they hadn't starved yet, although there was an indication of them looking a bit on the lean side, like most people around. It was certain, there were no obese ones either! Everyone seemed to be healthier in some strange way!

Chapter: Thirty-two

TO HELL AND BACK

They journeyed from factory, fields and farms,
When the call came, the call to arms.
Resolute and bold, they showed no fear,
Ready to fight, for all they held dear.
Leaving sickle and lathe, scythe and sheave,
Embracing loved ones, they prepared to leave.
To face the foe in dyke, ditch and trench,
With the smell of death, blood and stench.
The Battle of Britain saw mastery in the air,
El Alamein, Tobruk in desert warfare.
Our heroic fleets battles for valour renowned,
And the courage shown in the Blitz on the ground.
Should their supreme sacrifice, suffering and pain,
Battling for our existence, have been in vain.
We owe a debt, that can never be repaid,
To our fighting forces, in the parts they played.

'Oh to be in England now that Summer's here!' Flaming June started off with dull and dreary weather. Rain clouds filled the sky and doubt filled the hearts and minds of the thousands of troops, who lined the Channel Coast, with anticipation of what might be in store for them.

For the hour had come. The waiting was almost over.

Mag had very little on her mind as she bent over the washtub, scrubbing away at Bert's shirts and other bits and bobs. For today the Sun had broken through the thinning clouds and there was a light wind. It was a darned sight brighter than it had been for many a week. With a bit of luck she'd get her washing dry. She listened to someone, as she worked, rattling away on the wireless. Nothing really very interesting.

Then the programme was abruptly interrupted, and the animated voice of an announcer butted in, and with a kind of relief it seemed, he gave out the message which as Mag listened, – still with her scrubbing brush in her hand, it sent a cold shiver down her spine.

What was it the announcer was saying? –

"This morning our combined Forces began landing on the beaches of Normandy."

"Today is 'D-Day' the day for which our services have been preparing for months, and in every one of their minds, they know it will be no easy walkover, but are ready for anything the enemy throws at them!"

The announcer carried on talking, but Mag wasn't listening, it was all too distressing to contemplate.

"Ow my Gawd, – those poor lads, – what must they nah be goin' frew?" Some a them were only kids!

So, as was to be expected, this latest uplifting news was the main talking point, and the most noisiest, in the old 'Crown' that evening.

"Good luck to our lads, all of 'em out there!"

"Now they'll need as much of it as they can bloody well get!" were the unanimous words of approval, from the groups around the bars. –

"Not Run Rabbit Run. – *Nah* we say, – Run Adolf Run!"

Mag was never the one to show her true feelings, – one reason being, – she never had the time! –

"Besides it didn't do no bloomin' good anyway."
"Cryin', only gives yer more lines on yer face!"

All hell was being let loose from Artillery fire from the German guns situated behind the dunes. Shell bursts filled the sky as wave after wave of landing craft spilled their cargoes of tight-lipped intrepid yet resolute troops of the British Expeditionary Forces onto the vast beaches of Normandy. Sounds of machine gun fire spitting from a Messerschmitt or a Stuka as it screamed down mercilessly on to the hundreds of troops as they scrambled off the landing craft.

These were the bloody scenes that met Mark and his counterparts as they speedily and perilously criss-crossed the beaches, haphazardly dodging the enemy fire, and perhaps with hope and good fortune, to reach a place of safety. Having to stumble many times over inert bodies of fallen comrades, sadly there would be countless instances such as this, and this was only the beginning of the long awaited invasion of Europe, – 'D. Day.'

Mark and his band of brothers were that fearful day the forerunners, who would take part in liberating Europe and in the eradication of tyranny, hopefully once and for all.

It was so quiet here this Wednesday afternoon, just sitting for once doing absolutely nothing, except thinking of the past, when she *would* have enjoyed some peace and quiet! She looked around the kitchen, it was so tidy, too tidy in fact. No evidence of Jim's comics laying about. No Rob's coat slung over the back of a chair, or Jess's toiletries, – a hairbrush or a Picturegoer magazine, –

"That's this week's Mum, don't chuck it art!"

Mag looked towards the dresser, and her eyes settled on a picture, – a snap taken of the kids at "Sarfend," romping on the pebbled beach. She took it down and sat with it in her hands, staring at each of their faces, smiling up at her. And then that bloody orchestra on the wireless, started playing 'Dannyboy' didn't it? – That done it!

Mag burst into tears and for a time, there was no stopping her. In the quiet solitude of her kitchen, she cried until she could cry no more.

Then exploding as she did, more often than not, she called all warmongers, – those callous, senseless fanatics, – these candidates for the loony bin, all the names under the Sun, and this was just smooth talk for Mag! After drying her eyes, she arose from her chair, filled the kettle, and that meant just one thing, – You guessed it!

Rob, he had been kept busy with all the activity in Portsmouth there, with the entire goings on just now. He found much satisfaction in a new post and was no longer confined to a desk. Mag hadn't heard from Jim for some time, but she'd learned not to expect too much from her youngest son, and one of them was writing letters home.

Meanwhile all Jess had on her mind was the whereabouts of Mark. She knew he had been on the move, and now with the long awaited news of the Allied landings in Normandy, she didn't dare think that he might be in one of the first waves of landing craft.

Gwen too was down in the mouth, her Greg had been among the first of the Canadian troops told to be ready. So things were beginning to happen, and it was with apprehension as well as much admiration for the troops involved, in what must for them, be a complete Hell on Earth, as one listened in to the news on the wireless.

Down at the farm in the comparative peace of the countryside, on a day such as today, Gwen was busy mucking out the herd. While Jess was crossing the farmyard, still like a mud pond after the rains of the weeks before, she happened to look across the fertile green fields, now abundant with corn, slowly turning golden yellow.

She had heard a strange droning sound, it was hard to decipher. What could it be? It sounded rather like a clapped out motorbike. She placed her hand up to shade her eyes from the Sun, and stared. What was this she was seeing, fleeting across the sky, some way away. It was shaped like a sword. A black ominous looking object, with a flaming tail.

"Gwen, 'ere! Come quick! Look at this!" she shouted at her. Gwen at the sound of Jess's excited voice, came running, but then stopped stock still, as suddenly without any warning, the droning noise ceased and the machine or whatever it was, nose dived towards the ground. Within seconds there was a terrific explosion and palls of smoke filled the sky. For a moment or two, Gwen and Jess thought an aeroplane had crashed, yet it seemed this was something quite different! But as the day wore on, they'd put this happening at the back of their minds, until Mrs Coles appeared at the door of the barn, – calling to them, –

"Come and listen to the news. They are talking about this new thing the Germans have got. Must be what you thought you saw Jess!"

Meanwhile, back home in Brody Street, Mag was feeling at a loose end, then thought, –

"I'll chance a walk up the Commercial Road!" having found the weather too nice, to stand ironing a daffy of clothes and things. Though feeling a little guilty, she said, –

"Blow it they can wait, – it'll git done, some time!"

"Beautiful day!" Mabel remarked, when Mag bumped into her as she turned the corner of Brody Street.

"Orf art luv, – 'Ow's everyone?"

"Bit too nice ter stay in. En it?"

Spending a few minutes chatting to her neighbour, who was always very keen to keep people wasting time, standing there nattering. Mag made her get away.

She noticed as she walked along, how the streets in some miraculous way had been cleared of the worst of the blitz bomb damage, but it was a sorry sight to see how many houses and the very shops, whose windows she had often gazed into, but had to be content in doing only that, had simply disappeared! Mag came at last to a small street market, where many like her, were milling around the stalls, picking over pieces of merchandise.

She never ceased to admire these stall-holders who, whatever the weather, stood there be it hail rain or snow, bawling at the tops of their voices, hoping at least to take home a bob or two at the end of the day.

"'Ere lady, 'ave a butcher's 'ook at these, – 'Ave yer ever sin such beauties?" One hopeful bloke was yelling out, holding up a scalepan, full of ripe rosy red apples.

"Go-on, – 'Ere, – Yer can't moan at this, nah!"

"'Two bob the lot!"

And so it went on, as Mag wended her way along through the crowds, glad to be out in the sunshine. It was a cheerful atmosphere, and Mag was very pleased she'd made the effort. But the time was knocking on, and children were coming out of the school at the end of the road. She had better get back home now, as Mag had bought some nice Bloaters for Bert's tea. It was then as she started to make her way across the street, that she became aware of a peculiar sound coming from over the river. No, it wasn't a plane, yet she couldn't fathom out what the hell it was! Others had heard it too, and were gazing up at the sky.

"Bugger me! What is it Missis?" one fellow cried, standing near to Mag. "It looks like a flyin' dagger! An' that row its makin'! It's got flames comin' art the back?"

Then without warning this strange object suddenly went silent and the sound of a whoosh was heard as it plummeted and nose-dived into a row of defenceless houses.

It seemed only a couple of streets away. There was heard a tremendous explosion which rocked the ground. As all these terrified onlookers gazed, some were suddenly knocked off their feet, most were screaming. It was Bedlam! Children were crying, dust and smoke billowed everywhere! Some, unlucky ones at even this distance away, had been hit by flying glass from the huge blast. But what must it have been like in the actual street where this thing had fallen? – Mag dreaded to think.

The truth was, when the news reached everyone, in no time at all, was that a whole row of houses had been reduced to rubble. The sights that met the eyes of the ARP men and the many willing helpers, was of people scrabbling frantically at mounds of debris, trying to find the poor unfortunates, who had no foreseeable warning, of what was going to happen, in no way at all!

The sights were pitiful to see. A child only a toddler, who would never again play with the dolly she was still clutching when they dug her out. An old lady, luckily she was still breathing had survived. She was found under her stairs, and was rushed off to Hospital. But the death toll though not high, could have been much worse, if it had not happened when most people were away at work.

Mag was sick at heart, and the whole area for streets around was paralysed with fear and apprehension, of what the next days or weeks ahead, held for them.

So had started a new reign of terror, by the VI Rocket. A deadly sinister weapon unmanned and fired from somewhere across the Channel, maybe from Belgium, hoping to terrorise London as intended. The engine would cut out several minutes before reaching its target, and then crash down without any warning! – This was an even more frightening missile, a new type, *flying* bomb.

The Air Raid siren was useless now, as one never knew when to expect a sudden appearance from one of those 'Doodlebugs' as they came to be known, and as time went by, more explicit terms were used. A bit harsher on the eardrums! Now this was to be the start of a new topic of conversation in the 'Crown', after what had been a long period of only talking about the Second Front. Barney's voice would boom out over the top of all the din, –

"The Buggers, they ain't gonna give up are they?"

There seemed to be nothing they could do about this new threat! People just had to grin and bear it. Ultimately it was a dodgy situation. Never knowing whether you could venture out, in case one of these sinister objects would suddenly drop out of the sky and blow you to kingdom come! But as people had done for almost five years now, they thumbed their noses and branded Adolf Hitler even more of a lily-livered coward than before.

Maggie was studying Kate's face, as they sat together one afternoon having tea. Kate with her small son Eddy on her lap, proudly gazing down at him with such an intense look of devotion. Eddy, almost eighteen months old, had grown into a fine toddler. 'The apple of his mothers eye.'

but more so, the boy was ever a source of wonder and gratification to his father.

Tommy was a happy man, he had everything he wanted. A good wife that he loved, and a healthy son. What more did a man need! Maybe only one thing now, and that was for this war to stop. To put an end to all the fear and terror! To live in a world where people were content with their lot and not covet what someone else owned and had toiled for.

One day, he vowed, when this war was finished, he would make a good home for his two loved-ones. There would be a lot of work to be done to rebuild this country, and to oppose any other tyrant who might try and impose his greedy unprincipled will onto this peace-loving nation.

There was the sound of the back door opening. Tommy appeared in the doorway. Mag got up to go, as she felt she'd been there long enough. "Don't go Maggie!" he insisted and turned and picked up Eddy, and spent a few playful moments with him, the baby enjoying all the fun! But then Tommy's face hardened, saying how he had helped to clear up some of the mess at a terrible scene of carnage, caused by another bomb a couple of days before.

He had experienced sights he'd never imagined! But he couldn't bring himself to burden Kate and Mag, by telling them the harrowing description which he had seen, so he changed the subject, wanting to know all about Mag's boys, and what of Jess? – Poor Mag. She must miss them a lot.

It was evident that the 'buzz-bombs' weren't going to put paid to the residents going about their usual everyday activities. Mabel and Gladys among other neighbours in the street, still persisted in bringing out their chairs and would continue to sit in the Sun, –

"I ain' affrighted a those daft buggers sendin' over their toy planes. If I wanna sit artside me front door, I will!" said Mabel. Besides she wanted to get out of the way of her old man Will. He'd got out of the wrong side of the bed that morning. The truth was he was bored bloody stiff! What could a bloke do when half his day was taken up with doing the housework. Nothing would ever get done if it were left to Mabel, the lazy cow!

Why hadn't he taken the bull by the horns and cleared off with Dolly ages ago? Given half a chance, he'd be off now. But he'd come from a God-fearing family and his old Ma, would never forgive him if he did.

Mag came out of her front door and locked it, pushing the key back through the knocker hole.

"Wotcher Mag," Mabel shouted across at her, –

"Don'cher ever git fed up wiv that job a your'n?"

"No Mabel, –I don't! – I enjoy workin' 'ard!" –

"Not like some!" She muttered under her breath, and went on down the road, bumping into Kate, out pushing the baby in his pram and spent a few moments indulging in some baby talk to Eddy, who instantly recognised her and rewarded her with a big smile and gave her the benefit of some new words he had picked up from his proud Mum.

"I can see who he is going to take after," Mag said, and continued on to the Pub.

There was quite a hubbub of conversation going on as she went in the pub front door. It sounded as if they were all having a private war of their very own. Maggie took up her usual place behind the counter, and listened as she washed some of the dirty glasses.

"They ought ter 'ave their bleedin' 'ands cut orf, like they do in these 'ere, uvver forin' countries!"

"Reckon their the lowest a the low! Goin' in pinchin' fings art a 'ousis, that's bin bombed!"

"Yeh! There was too much a that goin' on last time. – I'd like ter cop the buggers!" said Wiley.

"I bet no one would git the chance ter pinch anyfink orf you Wiley!" said Joe. "They wouldn't 'ave time, yer got eyes in the back a yer 'ead, you 'ave!"

"That's enough!" Les said, as he came into the bar. We don't want no arguments now, – do we?"

It was sadly noticeable how the number of dockers who frequented the Pub had decreased. Though the amount of Docks able to function had dwindled a lot, a few of them managed to carry on. There was no let up on the wharves, unloading the huge cargoes urgently needed. 'Old Father Thames' was timeless, and he was determined to keep busy. Nothing would ever change.

Meanwhile at Portsmouth, a now satisfied Rob had settled down in his new job in the dockyard, as he told Mag in his last letter home. His experience in repairs and maintenance of some of the many types of ships in the London Docks, had come in handy. This was far better for him than sitting at a desk pushing a pen. He was still with his beloved ships. And to make things even more satisfactory, there was Ellie. – A nice young thing, who had taken a shine to Rob. He'd met her in a pub on the foreshore with Mick his new mate. This had made Mag feel a lot happier about him. "For yer know what sailors are!"

But now as usual it was Jim, that lad with a head like a sieve, slaphappy, but so loveable a son! She hadn't heard for some weeks now, where his regiment had been shifted. But no news is good news. So Mag she just had to hang on.

*   *   *

What's a Doodlebug Mum?

The clouds were lifting, war almost won,
Was it too much to hope?
Discovering to our bitter cost,
We were on a slippery slope.
In the month of June in '44
We faced a deadlier threat.
To violate a war weary land,
Our nightmare – not over yet.
From lucid sky, a fearful drone,
It was like no sound I'd known.
Striking fear in the hearts of men,
Spellbound – I stood as stone.
For to my eye, a fiery cross,
Discharging Hellish flame.
It ploughed a path, with insolence,
Its duty, to kill or maim.
A sinister unmanned terror,
It fell with awesome hush.
But no cowardly act, such as this,
Could our dogged spirits crush.
Innocents perished as they slept,
Or on their way to work.
Yet no tyrant, whoever they may be,
Could cause our duty to shirk.
Let them despatch their pilotless plane,
Doodlebug rocket or bomb,
Had they not heard of our bulldog breed,
Who'd survive this maelstrom?

Chapter: Thirty-three

The news that came over the air the next few weeks was not good listening, although it was followed keenly by everyone hoping upon hope that the 'Jerries' soon would be thrown out of the Low Countries and Hitler was on the run. But there was much fighting and loss of life before that would happen!

One morning Jess found Gwen in a right state, the poor girl was almost devastated and hung on to Jess in a flood of tears until she was able to speak. She poured out her fears, still sobbing, –

"I'm sure something has happened to my Greg! They say there's been a lot of Canadians killed and taken prisoner, in fighting at Dieppe! Oh Jess, I hope he is not, one of them!" and that sparked off thoughts of Mark then. She hoped and prayed that if he was among those first to land in Europe that he was safe! It was frightening, listening to the account of the battles going on over there! Jess was not the only one, she knew!

Although Mrs Coles put on a brave face. It belied her true feelings. She was scared to death about her only son, but talking to Jess and Gwen relieved some of the anxiety she felt about Mark's safety.

But as if everyone now, had not enough to worry about, there appeared a new threat! The 'V.2 Rocket!' This Buzz Bomb proved to be even more deadly than the V.1!

These new rockets weren't given a name. People were just running out of ridiculous quips about these devices contrived by a madman. It was no joke this new rocket! It was an outrage! Nobody could hear it coming. Travelling faster than sound, it would be seconds after the bomb had hit the target, there came this screaming Whoosh! – It was frightening!

How much more did they have to bear? These were the feelings of the war weary people of this Island!

In a flurry of excitement, Mag opened the letter, tearing at the envelope, she called to Bert who was out in the yard.

"Come in Bert quick! We got a letter from Jim at last!"

It had a foreign postmark on it, but Mag hadn't a clue where it was from.

Bert came in, wiping his muddy boots on the back door mat. He had been tidying up before the winter really set in. Already it was pretty nippy out there, with the first smogs and now frost. He'd sighed, – "Anuvver year nearly over!" It was a right succession of events, one damn thing after another, the same, year after year!

"Nah gal, what's all the noise abart?"

"We've 'erd from Jim. 'Ere read it!" said Mag. 'E's in a place called Burma. Not much of a country! 'E says 'e's always wet frew, an' mentions the name Rangoon an' all!"

"Alright 'en, let me read it!" Taking it from her. He was as anxious as she, to find out at last about Jim.

"We ain't bin 'ere long!" The letter read –

"It's the Monsoon season. They calls it that, I calls it somefin' else! It don't just rain, it comes darn in buckets! And the mud, – We are up to our ruddy necks in it! It ain't a bit like Egypt! There, it was all flies and sand!" Jim went on to finish with, "I'll let yer know more next time, that's if I don't sink in the mud, and they can't find me!"

404

"Yeh!" chuckled Bert, "and 'im bein' such a short arse, I doubt if they'll ever miss 'im!" Bert, he didn't have any room for the Japs, – "I just 'ope that boy keeps 'is eyes open all the while 'e's there."

Maggie now felt better, hearing from her erstwhile Son out there in Burma. All she wanted was to get this coming Christmas over and done with, and quick. It didn't mean anything at all now. The way things were happening here nearer home. It might not be so long before the boys would be back. Paris had long been liberated and the Jerries now chucked out of Russia, and the Allies and the Red Army were advancing into Germany. There was good reason for believing the worst was almost over.

All this was being discussed this evening over the Bars at the 'Crown'. The Pub was packed to capacity, everyone was in good spirits. Barney Bull, taking a huge swig at his beer, slapped his knee, saying, –

"Well I says ter meself when I 'eard it. Nah, ain' that the best bit a news fer a long while, me old Cock Sparrer."

"Terday will be a day long remembered!"

"But, I can't believe that evil Bastard 'Itler would ever 'ave the guts ter do 'imself in."

"Good riddance ter bad rubbish. I say!"

Everyone there in that Pub that evening was jubilant, as they discussed the news of the discovery of Hitler's dead body in his bunker, him having committed suicide. Not before time, they all agreed, as if in once voice.

Maureen and Maggie were having a hard job, trying to cope with the orders which seemed to come from everyone at the bars, all begging service at the same time.

If this is what it was like now, what of when the war did come to an end? Because it seemed jolly well certain by now that it *was* going to happen. – But when? And what a day that would be! The mood of everyone was changing, not just in Brody Street and neighbouring streets, but in the whole country, in fact world-wide.

Would it be too much to begin to plan? Too early for rejoicing, with all the news splashed over all the front pages of the papers, and by the tone in the voices of announcers on the Radio?

Mrs Coles put her head round the door and called loudly to Jess, who with a pitchfork in her hand was crossing the farmyard from the barn, where she had just finished cleaning out the pigsty.

"Jess! Come quick! I've had a letter from Mark. Let's hear what he has to say!" She was very excited and her face flushed from cooking over her hot stove.

Jess wiped her hand across her forehead, she was sweating hot from her task, which was not exactly a job that she enjoyed, – quite the opposite. It was very unsavoury and far from aromatic. – But somebody had to do it!

"Poor things, the pigs!" Jess felt very sorry for them.

Mark's letter was over two weeks old and in it, he admitted to being mentally and physically exhausted with all the heavy fighting, throughout France and Belgium. But luckily he had come through it unharmed so far, and was optimistic with the progress the forces had made.

"Now mum, we have hopes, this lot will soon be over with, though there's still lots of mopping up to be done. You keep that kettle boiling, as the first thing I want when I walk into that kitchen is a nice cup of tea, and not like the ditch water *we* have to call tea! I hope Jess gets her letter, I sent hers and yours together."

But Mark had no wish to say anything of the horrific scenes, the triumphant forces had witnessed as they proceeded into Germany! They had come across the most shocking sights! The Death Camps filled him with such horror and disgust, that he would never forget the hundreds of starving, only half-alive, gaunt skeleton-like prisoners, peering through the barbed wire fences. Sad and hollow-cheeked with vacant staring eyes and blank void, expressionless faces.

What human? – That is if you could call anyone who would do this to a fellow being, a human! This was something that had been going on for maybe ages, but no one had heard about, or if so, they had never believed it, or ever bothered to do anything.

But here was the true evidence. Bodies, – hundreds of them laying about rotting, in shallow graves in heaps feet deep, just thrown in haphazardly. It was an awesome, unforgettable sight!

Mark could not bring himself to mention any of this in his letter. But he concluded with the hopes that he would be seeing them soon, and to, –

"Keep the home fires Burning, Mum."

There was the sound of voices, everyone talking at once. It was like a swarm of bees, a continuous hum, rising to a crescendo, as the customers in the old 'Crown' downed more and more pints of 'Wallop'. They were certainly getting some practice in, for the real thing!

So far the news was coming through in dribs and drabs, that the war was all over bar the shouting. Mag was wishing she had brought her roller skates with her, she'd never moved so fast, but not speedily enough for the clamouring customers. Maureen and Les were well on the way to collapse. Chucking-out time couldn't come soon enough!

"Gawd 'elp us when we do get definite word that the War has ended and its really and truly over!"

But a few more hours must pass before Churchill would tell the waiting people of Britain that 'Today, May 8th was V.E. Day.' It was all over, well and truly, positively, – Over. – Nobody could believe it!

Now everyone could celebrate and that was exactly what they did! What greater occasion was there ever, than the day when Germany surrendered. Crowds danced in the streets, sang, cried, cheered, lit bonfires and climbed lamp posts. There were fireworks and rockets, but these were not enemy rockets. These were red, white and blue flares. People rejoiced and sang until the early hours, in all the towns, all over Britain.

But none were going to enjoy themselves and celebrate, quite like the people of Brody Street later that week!

Mrs Miles from number ten was watching with a worried look, – "Nah mind 'ow yer go wiv me pianer! I've 'ad it a long time! But it don' mean ter say, I want the daylights knocked art ov it!"

This was just one of the many preparations on this special day, chosen for the Brody Street Party. Everyone who was able, had a job to do. Flags and bunting were being hung on lines stretching across from one side of the street to the other. Trestles and tables were set up. Stools and forms to sit on, came from all quarters.

Some of the ladies of the hurriedly contrived committee were busy slapping margarine on mounds of bread, all donated along with utility cakes and biscuits, made out of

Gawd knows what? But whatever it was they soon disappeared down the hungry throats of the kids and adults at the tables. That was when they weren't drinking or dancing, and as the evening wore on, Tommy acquired an accordion from somewhere and knocked out all the old favourite songs like, – 'Nellie Dean,' 'Lily of Laguna,' and then the piano joined in with good old 'knees up Mother Brown.' And Mother Brown really did come into her own that evening!

The sounds of laughter and jollification joined up with other streets, who too, were having their parties. All were making one hell of a din!

Even if you were deaf like old Florrie Webb. She just did what everyone else did, even the Okey-Kokey! All joining hands, and with Bob the Policeman turning a blind eye to many a misdemeanour.

Following my leader, it was a laugh doing the Conga as dozens joined in, even those from other streets. This went on until the early hours, no one seemed one little bit tired, not even the kids.

They'd been let of the hook and were enjoying it, racing about until they dropped, – Would they ever forget that evening you ask? There would be one answer, in one voice, – an emphatic, – NO!

Yet with V.E. day over, it wasn't to be the end of all hostilities. The war in the Far East was still raging but although Maggie was celebrating V.E. Day, knowing Rob and Jess at least were safe, she was worried!

For there was that young Jim stuck out there in Burma! What news that still filtered through was not altogether good. She could not settle or be happy until that boy was back home here in Brody Street.

So with the war in Europe at last over, everyone tried their best to rebuild their lives, with the worst behind them. Little by little they picked up the pieces, but it would be a long while before everything returned to normal.

Their minds were scarred with the terrible bombings, the lives lost and, – All for what?

Their streets were still bombsites, homes ruined, the pitiful sight of the battered docks.

Maggie, on this warm brilliant sunny afternoon, strolled with Kate, and her little son Eddy walking beside her. Now over two years old, he was a replica of Tommy, and how he must have looked at that same young age.

They had taken it into their heads to amble along by the river, and here they stopped to look across the now quiet lazy looking river Thames sparkling in the sunshine. This old river still just rolled along unperturbed and resigned, 'Down to the mighty sea."

What sights if had seen, and what tales could it tell? Maggie loved the 'Old River' and wouldn't want to live anywhere else. – She was born here and would die here! Then shaking her head, as if to bring her mind back to the present. – "Come on Kate let's go 'ome, and I'll make us a nice cuppa tea, eh? – This place is givin' me the willies!"

"Until me Kids are back wiv me 'ere, where they belong. It won't be the same fer me."

Picking up Eddy, Maggie carried him home, holding him close. He felt warm and cuddly. Just like her young babes!

So Mag carried on with her life, and watched the days come and go, popping along to the old 'Crown and Anchor'. Listening to the moans and groans, first Joe, (he was knocking on a bit now!) then Mabel, – a bit long in the tooth too, – nothing there would ever change!

Bert? – He was a good old stick! – As long as she had him, she would always be content.

There was only one thing left now. Everyone was awaiting the last peg to be put in the hole. For they must surely get word soon, that the war with Japan was over.

It had to be!

The Yanks had the Japs by the throats, and when news came through, of the dropping of Atom Bombs on Hiroshima and Nagasaki, however horrific and abominable. This was to be the final death blow!

Once more the flags and bunting were brought out and put up for V.J. Day, with Mrs Miles's piano dragged out in the street for yet another street party.

There was one question in peoples' minds though. Whether this good lady had ever played the damned piano herself? – As no one had yet ever heard her!

So there was more fireworks, bonfires lit, and dancing in the street. Nearly six years of a bloody barbaric and unnecessary war had come to an end. – Was it worth it?

Of course it was!

The world had been liberated from tyranny, it was free of oppression and man's inhumanity to man.

But for how long? Only until others of the same identity came out of the woodwork, as History had shown for centuries before.

The worst was over. Now must come the rebuilding of the Peace and the damage done to millions of minds and bodies, and it would take a very, very long time!

But for now, all that the residents of Brody Street had in mind, was having a bloody good knees-up, and letting their hair down, – 'Maybe its because we're all Londoners, an' live in London Tarn!' – Me ol' Cock Sparrers !!!

It was a chilly day, no Sun, just a few breaks in the cloud every now and then.

A few dry, sere leaves fluttered along the pavements, some coming to rest in a pile alongside her doorstep, soon to be swept away by Maggie, out early on this Autumn morning. Although she had now not much of a doorstep left, thanks to the Jerries, she kept a bit of pride in her little bit of Brody Street. – Her's and Bert's!

She shivered, – she wasn't going to hang about, out there too long. – And that's a fact!

"Its time I went in an' put that kettle on, an' got Bert up," but she really could do with a nice cuppa herself.

"I wonder!" thought Mag, "Wevver the Postman's got any letters fer me terday?" as it was now round about his delivery time. She bent down to put the front door mat straight, ready to go back inside.

"Fank Gawd that's done!"

But then, she thought she heard a familiar voice. –

"No, – it can't be, she must be mistaken!"

But as she turned around, she saw, – not five yards away, – a figure in Khaki uniform, with a heavy Kitbag slung across his shoulder, wearing a huge smile!

Poor Mag gasped, and almost keeled over, –

"Ow Gawd Almighty!" she shrieked.

"No Mum, it ain't!" said the soldier, –

"It's me, – Jim! – I'm 'Ome!"

A Reminder!

There'll always be a welcome,
Down in Brody Street,
For the kind of folks who live there,
Are the best you'd wish to meet.

Whatchyer me ol' Cock Sparrers!
That greeting, you'll be bound,
To hear on all street corners,
'Bet yer a penny, to a pound!'

For there's none to beat a Cockney,
Even cheerful, when he's down,
You'll discover his kind of humour,
From Hackney to Canning Town.

If you chance to be around this way,
Ask anyone you meet,
Where to find humanity and warmth,
Yeh, – here 'In Brody Street!'